HUNK HOUSE

Books by Ben Tyler

TRICKS OF THE TRADE

HUNK HOUSE

Published by Kensington Publishing Corporation

BEN TYLER

HUNK HOUSE

KENSINGTON BOOKS

http://www.kensingtonbooks.com

For R. T. J.
(With you, all things are possible.)

ACKNOWLEDGMENTS

I am grateful for my patient and gifted editor John Scognamiglio. Also, for my ally and literary agent Robin.

William Relling Jr. discerns the errors of my ways and astutely offers his invaluable insight and guidance without judgment.

Mr. Brian Dawson generously arranged for a tour of his dungeon, and patiently addressed a gazillion naive questions. Gail J. Angel, proprietor of Pasadena's first Queen Anne Victorian, was a gracious and generous docent for her beautiful, historic home. Brenda Thomson-Knox provided my introduction to Ms. Angel.

I am indebted in immeasurable and innumerable ways to Kevin Howell, J. Randy Taraborrelli, Mark, Peter Christensen, Allen Kramer, Michael Archer, Kevin Fabian, Julia Oliver, Steve Sanders, Steve Trombetti, John Fricke, Rick Lorentz and Mark Reinhart, Chris O'Brien, Muriel Pollia, and Mr. Billy Barnes.

Also, of course, Jerry Bruckheimer, Lolita Davidovich, Pauly Shore, Dave Sheridan, Maurice Ravel, Cher, Prince William, Peter Jennings, Ralph Nader, Archduke Ferdinand, and Romania.

WANTED
SEXY GAY MEN FOR NEW TV PROGRAM. NO ACT-
ING EXPERIENCE *PREFERRED*. SEND AUDITION
TAPE AND RÉSUMÉ IMMEDIATELY TO KRUQ-TV, BOX
69, DULCIT.

Chapter One

"Cocksuckers!?!" thundered an incredulous Gallo Ratner, owner and CEO of KRUQ. The call letters described Ratner's dinky, family-owned cable television station in Dulcit, Iowa, which broadcasted over an anemic fifteen thousand watts. He was reading aloud the ad in the *Rainbow Rag*.

"This is Iowa, son, not your sodomite Hollywood!" Ratner snapped at Hamilton Ipswich Peabody III, the Harvard Business School–trained senior programming director at KRUQ. Hamilton had wound up in pitiful Dulcit after enduring a public debacle in L.A. over his sexploits with the ABC affiliate's morning news anchor and then ditching his job as a segment producer for Bob Goen at *Entertainment Tonight*.

"Where would you be fixin' to scare one up 'round here for this 'reality' TV show of yours anyway?" Ratner demanded.

Murmurs of agreement issued from the four other station employees in the room. Today was their weekly programming strategy meeting, held as always in the dark, dingy, faux wood–paneled conference room at the station. Decorated once in the early 1960s, the room looked like Darrin Stevens's office (the first one) on *Bewitched*, but had long since turned shabby with time and lack of care. The furniture—fashionable for its day—was scratched, gouged, broken-down, and depressing. Even the once-beige shag carpet was now baby-barf-yellow. A dark foot-traffic trail was worn from the door to the conference table, and a moth-eaten elk's head had been stuffed and mounted to give the place an aura of masculinity.

"One?" said Hamilton to his boss, arching an eyebrow. "We need six, Mr. Ratner. I've already signed up four."

"Four queers? In Iowa?" Ratner scoffed at the notion. It was as preposterous as any network casting Tom Arnold as the lead in another sit-com. "You must've had to go as far on up as Chicago to fetch 'em. Ain't no Nancy boys in these parts. Just hard-workin', hard-bodied, beer-swillin' all-American farm boys and their daddies workin' up a good sweat when they're plowin' the south forty or actin' up the devil with their cars and girlies come Friday night."

Hamilton looked away for a moment and rolled his eyes. "It wasn't too difficult—even in Iowa, sir," he said. "Statistics indicate that homo-sexuals are ten percent of our population, and even—"

"I'm telling you, mister," Ratner cut him off, "I've lived here all my life, and the only queers I ever seen was when I served in the U-nited States Marine Corps." Ratner's rheumy eyes took on the glaze of one whose memory had just jumped the tracks of time. He was seeing him-self from the point of view of yesteryear, when he was a young stud, a hundred pounds lighter, in a Quonset hut with his butt-naked buddies, their dog tags jangling a metallic noise against the velvet-smooth skin of their muscled chests. His voice took on a softer tone. "You would've thought that the command for Lights-out was an order for a free-for-all in them barracks. We, er, *those* lads would start in jumpin' 'round and switchin' bunks like rabbits in a warren."

Easing back into the present, Ratner faked a dry cough. "I like you, Hammy, but this idea is a waste of your time and ours. Creating a pro-gram like "Survival" meets "Big Buddies," or whatever they're called—but with gay people? Ridiculous. That ain't gonna fly in Dulcit. No siree, Bob!"

"I've already lined up a sponsor, sir," said Hamilton.

Ratner did a double take, then smiled as though he'd heard the *ker-ching* of a Vegas slot machine paying off his quarters. "Why aren't you other boobs as resourceful as my Hammy here?" he said, looking around the table. "But who in these parts would be darned loco enough to fork over the bucks for this type of program?" he asked.

Hamilton withdrew a check from his briefcase and waved it under Ratner's bulbous nose. "A consortium, actually. One is a partner in one of Hollywood's biggest studios, the other runs a whole cable network. They were pals of a pal when I was in L.A. They know a good gamble when they see one. Notice the number of zeros? It won't pay for the whole program, but it's enough to get more than a good start."

"A 'reality' program?" sneered VP of station management Stacia

Ratner, the boss's thirtysomething daughter whose face was not entirely unlike that of the moose head on the wall. Rather than look directly at Hamilton, she examined her Medea-red press-on fingernails as though they were retractable.

Desperate to please her daddy, her dismissive tone echoed that of her father's first response. "Sponsors or not, a television program 'bout men who sleep with other men? Come, come, Ham. It's absurd!" Stacia adjusted her eyeglass frames and brushed strands of Miss Clairol "Believe You Me It's Almost Natural Blonde" hair from her face. "In the first place, who'd ever volunteer to be 'outed' on the TV, let alone tune in to see 'em bakin' pies, or puttin' on a talent show or sponge-painting the living room walls for a full hour every week?" She made a less-than-feminine snort.

"Or discussing art history," Hamilton countered. "Or reading the latest Edmund White. Or debating social issues, such as George W's reserved bleachers seat in the lowest of the seven circles of Hell. You'd be surprised at what makes a hit show. Who could have predicted that the Olsen twins would have had a career? Plus, the planet is a little more enlightened now. There are some who find no shame in publicly being who they are."

Hamilton continued. "But stereotypes are hardly what this program is all about. This is not 'Marvin Stewart Living.' I'll explain again. It's comparable to all those network hits—*Survivor* and *Big Brother* and *The Mole* and *Temptation Island*, only with a gay motif."

"Motif?" Stacia snorted again.

Hamilton addressed the rest of the staff. "You were all hooked on those programs, weren't you?"

Grunts of general agreement issued from some at the table, their respective eyes turning to the senior Ratner for guidance on how they should respond.

Ella Randolph, the station's receptionist and tape librarian, tentatively piped in. "They had homosexuals on *Survivor* and *The Mole*," she said in a voice that trilled like a very old Snow White.

The world suddenly stopped as everyone turned toward Ella, who hardly ever uttered a syllable at a programming meeting. She usually just took her seat at the table and continued knitting booties for her grandbabies.

"There was more than one of 'em on that island and in the Outback, if you ask me, praise the Lord," she continued. "The cute blond who shaved his chest? All of the gay men I've ever seen are very attractive. They floss regularly. They trim their nose hairs. And they're very polite. They never abandon their divas—except maybe Diana Ross," she added.

"It's true," said forty-two-year-old Rex Ratner, a corpulent, red-cheeked younger facsimile of his father. Rex served as the CEO's assistant/whipping boy. If you closed your eyes when he spoke you'd swear it was Truman Capote's whiny voice. "F'r instance, take that nice weatherman over in Des Moines? 'Member how he looked without his shirt all last summer when he reported the forecasts from over at Beaver Lake? That big blue vein that ran from his right bicep clear up to his shoulder and across his chest?" Rex made an involuntary fanning gesture with his right hand. "He sure made my ratings soar!"

"Denny Flowers is *not* gay," Stacia bellowed.

"What cornfield did you crawl out from, honey," Ella countered. She stared at Stacia as if she were a moron who believed wrinkle-faced Dr. Laura got a bum rap when audiences kissed her ferret-faced, skinny-assed, queer-bashing hiney into audiovisual oblivion. "He's as queer as Mr. Brady Bunch!"

"Denny can't be gay! He's my favorite weatherman!"

"Then close your ears to this news flash," advised Ella. "He dates my sister's grandson, the Delta flight attendant? You know? The one who joined the mile high club with his copilot that night when Greg Louganis was aboard a red-eye."

Ella turned to Hamilton. "Back to your idea for the new show, Ham. I'd tune in. You know for sure they'll at least take off their shirts. And they have to shower!" She paused. "With cameras recording their every move, I'd wager that a lot of people would watch. Think you could get 'em to do the full Monty?"

Hamilton smiled, picturing the possibilities. Real-life stories with six gay men, all strangers to each other, forced to share a house. *If only I could get this narrow-minded Ratner clan of interbreeding halfwits to share my vision,* he thought. *Men and boys dropping their pants for a big payoff was what gay sex in general, and this program in particular, is all about.*

"Think of the potential ratings," Hamilton said to his boss, encouraged by Ella's enthusiasm. "It's a win-win situation! It would be relatively inexpensive to produce, we already have a sponsor, and it's guaranteed to draw audiences, just as Ella predicts. You want an Emmy don't you? Here's your best shot!"

"I for one don't want to see a bunch of queers taking their clothes off—especially on my TV," raged Bull Smith, slamming a meaty fist on the table. Bull was a twenty-four-year-old part-time truck driver, part-time maintenance man at the station and a full-time troublemaker. Although he was a dead-ringer for seductive Lorenzo Lamas (during his motorcycle-riding *Renegade* series period), his miserable personality canceled out his considerable natural physical endowments: sculpted face, wide shoulders, powerful physique, and long sexy hair.

"Again, folks," Hamilton reminded, "may I reiterate? That's not what this program is about. And by the way, it's not PC to call gays 'fags,'" he addressed Bull.

"Kiss my PC ass," muttered Bull, loud enough for Mr. Ratner to overhear and give him a stern look.

"Try 'queer' if you can't say 'gay' or 'homo-sex-u-al.'" Hamilton was not the least bit intimidated by Bull. "You don't have to watch the program! Try *Touched by an Angel* or reruns of *Highway to Heaven*."

"That Michael Landon was too darned pretty to be straight, if you ask me," Bull muttered.

Hamilton countered impatiently. "Perhaps you'd prefer *The Lawrence Welk Show*? I'm sure he's still blowing champagne bubbles somewhere in syndication."

"Boys," cautioned Mr. Ratner.

"Here's the long and short of it," Hamilton continued in his most authoritative tone. "The program I'm proposing may appear to be similar to the other 'reality' shows. But the big variation is that we'd have six gay men sequestered in a house, monitored in every way, shape, and form twenty-four hours a day, for six weeks. We get to know the contestants as real people."

"Why not *sixty* men instead of six?" Stacia interrupted. "With sixty you could stage a full-blown Egyptian orgy!"

Hamilton looked at her for a long moment. Finally, he said, "Roman."

"Beg pardon?" Stacia said.

"Romans had orgies. Not Egyptians. Different cultures, different continents."

"Excuse me, Tom Bergeron!" she scoffed.

Hamilton proceeded to pass around copies of a proposal bound in red leatherette report covers with clear acetate windows through which they could all read:

HUNK HOUSE
Fall Season

"Six is all we can afford," he said, answering Stacia's question. "There's food and utilities and the cost of running the house to think about, not to mention the expense of renting the cameras and sound equipment we'll need. And the winner gets an all-expense-paid trip to West Hollywood, California, and a walk-on role on a soap opera, like *Days of Our Lives*. I've kept the cost of everything down to the bare minimum. It's all there in black and white for you to review."

"Hunk House?" Old man Ratner read the title aloud, in a tone that spoke volumes about his reservations. "Wait a goldarned minute, son. You wouldn't be one of 'em, would you? A homo, I mean. You know they have an agenda to recruit straights. That Ellen DeGenerate got a toaster oven for her efforts. You could be bringing 'em in to take over Dulcit, and win you a microwave."

"Mr. Ratner, sir," Hamilton said. "Ellen was a fictional character. I mean she's a real person, but she played a fictional Ellen on television, like Roseanne playing someone named Roseanne. Or Cybill Shepherd playing an actress named Cybill. Or Bette Midler playing—well, she played Bette Midler—but you get my drift?"

He didn't.

Hamilton tried a different tack. "Would I still be suffering a broken heart because my sweetheart and I split up a year ago if I were gay? Would I have moved here, all the way from Los Angeles, just to alleviate my pain? Do I wear an earring? Do I play Pet Shop Boys tapes in my car or own a pair of ruby slippers? Do I have a Ricky Martin calendar in my office? If I were gay, I probably wouldn't even bring up the subject of gay because then you might *think* that I was gay."

"Makes sense, I suppose," Ratner harrumphed. "But what's a pet shop got to do with being queer? And who's this Ricky Martin fella? Is he Dino's son? By the way, where is Dino these days?"

"Living with Michael Landon," Hamilton deadpanned.

"So he is queer!"

"No, sir. Dead, sir."

Ratner frowned, his thick eyebrows knitting together to form one huge gray caterpillar across the bridge of his red-veined nose. "You still seem to know a lot about *them* and what *they* like."

"He's just a well-read, sophisticated big-city boy," Ella said, coming to Hamilton's defense.

"You do dress awfully good, if you ask me," Bull said suspiciously.

"I'm from L.A.," Hamilton offered. "Give me just a little time here in Dull City . . .

"That's Dulcit!" Bull cried, pledging allegiance to his hometown.

". . . and soon enough I too will be wearing powder blue socks with brown Rockports and elastic-waist duffer-Dockers tugged up above my beer gut. Just like all the other men in this town."

Hamilton looked around the room, making eye contact with the other five KRUQ staff members. "You gotta think outside the box, people," he pleaded. "You've got to think of pulling this piddling station out of Chapter Eleven! Otherwise, why am I here? Why'd you hire me in the first place? I'm only here to help. But I need your support."

"You'll offend viewers with a program like this one you're proposing," Stacia retorted, snapping a wad of Double Bubble, looking to her father for approval.

"Lots of viewers, probably," Hamilton admitted. "But think of all the bombastic church sermons sentencing us to eternal damnation. Free publicity!"

Ella proclaimed, "With the right contestants—interesting guys, viewers are sure to come back each week to find out what's going on in their lives. We'll have to carefully select and interview hundreds of applicants. I hereby volunteer to help."

"And just think of the ancillary sales," Hamilton appealed. "During our next pledge drive, the home videocassette edition alone will be enough of a hot ticket to keep those phones ringing!"

"But where's there a vacant house in Dulcit that's large enough to accommodate six men and all the crew and equipment?" Stacia countered.

Ella piped in, "What about the old Maynard place over on Elm? It's a Queen Anne Victorian!"

"A hellhole rattrap is more like it," Stacia blasted back. "I wouldn't have anyone set foot in there even for a dozen Emmys."

Old man Ratner mused. "I always did fancy winning an Emmy. Preferably two, one for each end of the mantel."

"That house is where I found old lady Maynard after she'd been up there dead for a week," Stacia said. "It still reeks of cat piss. Those damned things started eating her alive when she couldn't get out of bed to fetch their Fancy Feast!"

"Those sexy young men on your favorite soap are mostly gay, I hear," Ella interjected, still thinking about well-toned, bare-chested men.

Hamilton resumed his pitch. "I just think this is an idea whose time has definitely come. Nobody else has done it. But they will, eventually, given the proliferation of reality shows. They already have gay sitcoms on television now. You probably all watch *Will & Grace* each week. And there's that Showtime series *Queer as Folk* that got huge ratings. The world's getting progressive. And how about *Tales of the City* and its sequels? I'm only suggesting that we beat the networks and our rival stations to the punch. Somebody's damned well going to do a program like this. We could and *should* be the first!"

"An Emmy, eh?" Ratner said again.

"Who knows? Maybe even an Oscar. If we're so successful that we can turn the extra footage, the outtakes, into a documentary feature film." Hamilton pushed all of Ratner's vulnerable ego buttons.

Ratner turned to the final page of the proposal with the budget breakdown. He studied the figures for a long, silent stretch of time. Hamilton held his breath. The room remained hushed.

"You're the Harvard man, Hammy," Ratner finally said. "If you can get more sponsors and keep from going over budget . . ." he wavered for a moment.

"Does this mean yes?" Hamilton asked eagerly.

"No!" Stacia protested. "This is ratings suicide!" She looked at Bull for support and received a noncommittal shrug.

Ratner took another look at Hamilton. Then he looked at Stacia and Bull, Ella and Rex, then back to Hamilton. "I just better not get any complaints from the damned FCC!" the old man said.

Chapter Two

The ad was microscopic, buried between *GWM, Midwest leather slave looking for open-minded masculine nonsmoker,* and *Man's man searching for slim, smooth-chested take-charge guy for wrestling and other fun games and stuff.*

Everything in the freebee newspaper, the *Des Moines Rainbow Rag,* was printed on pulp paper. The ink too easily rubbed off and smeared its readers' hands. The hands, in turn, smudged the readers' dicks (the *Rag*'s circulation being 99 percent male), who were teased by the grainy but sensual photos of hot studs with no shirts that revealed hard bodies. Captions offered escort services, massages, and practically anything else a man could imagine for fun and sexual satisfaction.

The paper also provided ads of twenty-five words or less at no charge. However, *gratis* meant there was no guarantee of where one's message would be placed in the classifieds.

Hence, squeezed among all the begging and bravado from Iowa's sex-starved hayseeds proclaiming Herculean genital endowments was the most important ad in the history of KRUQ. The ad that could potentially save the station from looming bankruptcy and send miserably unhappy programming director Hamilton Ipswich Peabody III back to the Emerald City of L.A. where gay men were as ripe for seducing as picking oranges off a backyard tree.

It was sheer serendipity that eighteen-year-old Luke Ryan saw the ad. He seldom ventured as far away as the big city of Des Moines from his parent's farm in Orion. But on this Friday night, after an unusually barren day of only one blow job—from his sulfur-smelly science teacher, Mr. Hartnett—Luke was crazed with lust. He desperately needed to get fucked or at least have his dick sucked. He decided to drive the fifty-plus miles to Tes Tease, the only gay bar he knew about in Des Moines.

However, once there, he quickly became bored with being leered at by the crowd of factory workers and truckers, who were mostly his daddy's age. Their bloated guts hung over brass belt buckles holding up faded blue jeans that had been run through a couple of dozen rinse cycles too many. Luke decided to leave the smoky, beer-smelling dive and take matters into his own hand, literally, in the comfort of his bed—if he could wait that long.

It was only because of the picture of half-naked British pop star Robbie Williams featured on the cover of the *Rag* that Luke even bothered to grab the paper from a Take One rack on his way out the door. While driving home, still stiff and practically exploding from lack of action, and glancing to the passenger seat on which lay the picture of hairy-chested Robbie, he decided that waiting until he could lock himself in his room with the *Rag* would give him the most satisfaction.

Parking his Dodge Dart in the yard beside the barn of his parents' farmhouse, Luke rolled up the *Rainbow Rag* and stuffed it into the waist of his jeans, under his flannel shirt.

Sneaking into the house was nearly impossible. The rusted spring on the screen door that led into the mudroom and then into the kitchen practically screamed in agony in the quiet Iowa night. Every inch of wooden floor from the porch to the stairway cried a protest under Luke's weight. The stairs to the second-floor bedrooms, covered with thin, worn carpet, failed to muffle the sound of his footsteps on ancient boards.

Still, on the second-floor landing, Luke was almost to his room when he halted at the sight of the glow of a cigarette in the blackness. Then came his father's imperious voice.

"D'ja get any t'night?"

"Scared me," Luke said, his heart leaping.

"Playin' with the girlies?"

"Just playin'."

"Boy as pretty as you gets to play a lot, don'tcha? With the boys too, I 'spect." Pop sighed with disgust. "Get yourself fucked tonight?"

Luke blanched and felt his face turning red with guilt and rage. He never knew how to respond when his father denigrated him with condescending remarks about his sexuality. But he had learned not to cry the way he did when he was twelve years old, and his old man had caught him in the barn, sucking off a high school boy behind the bales of hay. His father had come upon the scene and went wild with shock and hatred. He grabbed Luke by the collar of his flannel shirt and shoved him against the wooden wall of the barn. He concurrently thrashed his son's face back and forth, and pummeled his body with his fists, while screaming, "You're not my son if you're a fucking faggot! You're a fucking bastard, and I won't have you in my house if this is the way you're gonna turn out!"

The other boy, who Luke didn't even know because they were in different grades, pulled up his jeans and fled in terror.

It was only after Luke had lost consciousness that his father had stopped the blistering brutality and let his son's body slip to the cold dirt floor. He stepped back and looked at his son with loathing. When Luke finally opened his eyes, his father ordered him to tell his mother he'd been in a fight at school. "You're to blame for the messed up face, boy, not me," his father said before lumbering out of the barn.

For weeks thereafter, Luke wandered around in a daze, disinterested in sex, and feeling like a freak. As much as he hated his father for the beating, he hated himself equally for giving in to his lust for other boys. Although he'd always been told it was wrong, Luke couldn't believe anything that felt so good, and didn't hurt anyone, could be bad. The healing of his remorse took months.

Finally, on a Friday afternoon, his science teacher stood beside him in the classroom. While reading aloud from the textbook, the teacher slipped his hand into his pocket and began working himself up. Luke knew what the guy was doing, and when the bell rang, Luke stayed behind. Not only did he need to slake his own hunger to taste another man's meat again, he knew he'd pass the class with an A, if he let his teacher go down on him. He left the school building determined to get back to sex, but never again let his father find him doing what just came naturally to him.

Now, standing in the darkness facing his nemesis, Luke wanted to tell his old man to go fuck himself. But he knew better. Pop would sure as hell beat Luke black and blue again if he ever sassed back. Instead Luke simply said, "It's Friday night, ain't it?"

"It's mornin', queer boy," his father said, coming up a few paces to stand face-to-face before his son.

Queer Boy had become Luke's father's nickname for him. He used it often.

"Hey, Queer Boy," get your ass out to the tractor and start your chores!"

"God damn you, Queer Boy, can't you see I'm busy watching the television. Don't be makin' so much noise with your records!"

"Jesus Christ, Queer Boy, I've had it with your lazy ass sleepin' in on Saturdays!"

Although his mother didn't like to hear her son called Queer Boy, she never spoke up against her husband. Luke had become used to it. The words no longer stung.

"Can I go to bed, then?" Luke asked.

"Go to hell, for all I care." Pop exhaled a lungful of tobacco smoke directly into Luke's face.

Luke coughed and sidled past his father and continued on to his room. *I'll be so rich and famous someday, you'll have a heart attack and die*, Luke said to himself as he closed the bedroom door against his father's heavy sigh. He quickly stripped naked and slipped under the bedcovers. The light on his bed stand was a dim 45 watts, but it served to reveal Robbie.

Flipping through the paper, Luke discovered that the "cover story" was deceiving. It was merely a quick Q&A with the hot rocker, probably lifted from some major magazine. But the one photo of Robbie was enough to keep Luke hard. He imagined himself playing with such a superstud.

Wanting to savor the nearly unbearable need to climax, Luke began reading what were usually, at least for Des Moines, fairly lascivious personal ads:

Masculine, muscular, bi athlete 42. VGL *smart, no bull. U B hard hunk, top, late teens, into sports.*

Let's massage together. 6' brn/brn, smooth, passive, likes rough play. Needs spanking, please.

Luke continued to scan the tiny type, processing the abbreviations he'd learned to decipher: SWM, GWM, VGL, S/M, B&D.

Then he spotted a new one: KRUQ.

Luke couldn't connect the initials with any particular sex scenes he'd ever heard about. He read the ad and couldn't believe what it said.

He read it again, then carefully tore it from the page. He brought the torn sheet to his small desk and re-examined it under the brighter illumination of a halogen lamp. "Yes!" he said in a low growl of excitement.

He'd been prepared to end the night jacking off with a fantasy about Robbie Williams or imagining one of the studs in another ad. Instead he opened the top drawer of his desk and took out a spiral notebook and a blue Bic pen that was just starting to leak. On lined paper he wrote out what he thought a résumé might be. Then he composed a quick cover letter and hid the material under a couple of *Green Lantern* comics. He closed the drawer.

The rest of the night was long and nearly sleepless. Luke only jacked off twice, trying to take his mind off the exciting possibility of actually being on a TV show. In the fantasy that produced his biggest load, he was a television star making a guest appearance on a morning talk show.

His TV segment is over. He's back in the Green Room taking a shower before changing into his street clothes. Before he has time to dry off, the door opens. It's the show's heartthrob host. He enters and locks the door behind him. The two face each other. Their respective erections broadcast their thoughts as clearly as James Earl Jones's voice enunciating, "This is CNN."

The host walks over to Luke, who holds a white bath towel by his side. The host pins Luke's naked body against the wall and plants his lips on Luke's eager mouth. The two suck each other's faces as if there's only as much time as between station identification breaks. Luke unbuttons the host's shirt and feels his smooth, hard-muscled chest and tight abs. The host pulls Luke away from the wall and pushes him onto the sofa. Luke groans in anticipation as he watches the early-morning stud tear off his tie and unbutton the rest of his shirt. He rips open his pants. On his back, looking up at the ravenous host, Luke gasps with pleasure as his legs are pushed back against his shoulders and he feels his hole filling with the dick of the man who wakes up America each morning.

"Matt," he groaned as he climaxed.

Saturday morning finally arrived. Ordinarily, Luke would be embracing his pillow until noon—or until his father revved up the tractor outside his window trying to make his son feel guilty about sleeping instead of doing chores. Today, Luke rose before dawn. Slipping his bare ass into jeans, he didn't bother buttoning the top of his 501s or his shirt. He picked up his scuffed cowboy boots with the worn-down wooden heels and crept out of his room and down the stairs.

Once downstairs, he quickly searched the hall closet and found his father's Sony VHS videocassette recorder. With his boots in one hand and the VCR in the other, he went out the back screen door. Sitting on the porch steps he pushed his bare feet into the old but comfortable leather boots and strutted across the dew-covered yard to the barn. Amidst the squawking of the chickens and lowing of the cows, he set the camera on a sawhorse and adjusted the lens to film his audition tape. He framed a bale of hay on which he would sit and pose.

During the night he had rehearsed what he might say. His monologue consisted of a trumped up biography—impossibly high SAT scores, bogus sports activities, and college clubs. He gave a rundown of these (false) accomplishments and his age (he lied that he was 21).

He pushed PLAY on the recorder.

"If it's someone with star quality you're lookin' f'r, I'm y'r guy. Shucks, I've been told I could make a man cry just from lettin' him touch me in certain places, if you know what I mean. They say I've got what you call charisma."

While nervously speaking to the VHS recorder, he unconsciously pinched his nipples. Slowly and seductively, he ran his fingers up and down his sternum. He then slipped off his shirt, tossing it onto a bale of hay. He adjusted his tumescent cock a few times through his jeans, not for any intentional effect, but just because it was in the way. He spoke extemporaneously about plans to move to Hollywood to become an actor.

"If you pick me to be on your show," Luke concluded, "I'll be very grateful. I've got to get out of Iowa!" He stared at the lens for a long while. Someone had once told him, "When you look a hot guy in the eye, just think 'cock, cock, cock.' You'll be sending out powerful vibrations, and they'll pick up on it." He silently prayed that his unspoken enticement would get through to whoever eventually watched the reel.

After concluding his "performance," Luke rewound the tape and played it back. He saw himself on the small screen that was attached to the camera. He looked hot—even to himself—like Narcissus peering at his own reflection in a pool of water. In fact, he liked what he saw on the tiny silent screen so much that he had to jerk off.

Milking the last of his juice into the bale of hay, he looked over at a cow that seemed transfixed by what she was watching. "Here's a treat for you, Bessie," he said, feeding her a meal varnished with his load, thus eliminating the evidence in case his mother or father should come in. Bessie chewed dispassionately.

"Not exactly Thirty-one Flavors," he said apologetically. "But maybe this'll give an extra kick to Dad's milk!" He laughed at the notion of his fool of a father unintentionally consuming his own son's semen.

As Luke put his shirt back on, he was startled—and so was his mother, Audrey, who clutched her chest as if unexpectedly finding a stranger in the barn. "Just makin' a video for a class science project," Luke said holding up the camera, bearing witness to the fact that he was being enterprising on an early Saturday morning.

"I should've known better than to think you'd be up early, out here doin' my chores for me," his mother said playfully. She adored Luke and, unlike Luke's father, she wouldn't expect her son to do anything he didn't feel like doing.

"Coffee's on," she said as Luke left the barn with a guilty expression on his face.

"Thanks," he called over his shoulder.

He returned to his room. Soon after, with his résumé, letter, and videocassette sealed in an envelope, he addressed it as instructed in the ad, got into his Dodge Dart, and drove to the post office where he mailed off his fate.

After school on Tuesday, Luke came home to find a message under a Pillsbury Doughboy magnet on the refrigerator. "Call Ella at KRUQ. 515/282-2828. Urgent! Hugs, Mum."

Except for Luke, the house was empty. His father was in the cornfield, his mother at a choir rehearsal at their church. Luke's heart raced as he picked up the telephone on the wall next to the refrigerator and punched the number on the message.

One ring. Two rings. Three rings. Four rings.

Luke looked at his watch to see if it was past business hours. It was only 3:15. Finally, the ringing stopped and a shaky voice on the other end announced, "KRUQ, Channel Three. How may I direct your call?"

"Ella, please."

"Speaking," said the Katharine Hepburn imitator on the other end of the line.

"Er, this is Luke Ryan. You called me?"

"The stud!" Ella said. "What a tape. Wanna be on TV?"

Luke said, "Don't everybody?"

"Not me. At least not the kinda shows they do here. Now if it was a soap . . ." she trailed off, thinking about the men on *The Bold and the Beautiful* and *Days of Our Lives*. "When can you come in and meet with our senior programming director and the producers? Tomorrow morning would be best 'cause we're in a hurry."

"What time?"

"Nine o'clock. Sharp," Ella said.

"What should I wear?" Luke asked. He immediately wondered if it was a naive question. To a job interview, you usually wore a suit.

"Casual. Very, *very* casual, if you get my drift. No need to get gussied up. A tight-fitting T-shirt'll do. And wear those hot-looking jeans you wore on the tape."

"You liked my tape?"

"Honey, it's the talk of the station! But remember this is just an interview. Can't promise you'll be selected for the show. But, darlin', I have a hunch . . ."

"Great. Tomorrow, at nine."

Luke hung up the telephone. He walked up to his bedroom exhilarated. Although he knew that bookwise, he wasn't an Einstein, he also knew that for some inexplicable reason, people, especially men, were always extra nice to him. He'd once overheard Mr. Pudwell, his phys ed teacher, talking about him to Mr. Hartnett, his science teacher. He described Luke as "A stud with sexy, drive-up-over-the-curb, crash-into-brick-walls good looks."

The fact had been validated many times. More than a few of the school football players had wrestled with him in the woods behind the football field. He sucked them off. They sucked him off. Teachers were the same. Some of them kept him in detention hall until the coast was clear and then gave him a blow job. Mr. Hartnett was especially curious about Luke's banana-sized rod and his sack of low-hanging balls that bounced on Hartnett's chin like a beanbag. That was why Luke seldom thought about prowling for sex. It just naturally came to him—and often.

When the alarm finally buzzed at 6:30 the next morning, Luke didn't have to be called as usual to breakfast by his mother, who had already been up for an hour feeding the chickens and frying bacon.

"Well, aren't you bright-eyed and bushy-tailed this mornin'," she said when Luke came into the kitchen and reached for the glass of orange juice she had set on the table for him.

"No time for breakfast, Ma," Luke said. "Gotta big geography exam, and Pamela Bay promised to go over possible questions with me. I'm late."

"Pamela, eh?" his mother said with a smile. "I thought you and she were over. You spend more time with her brother Jeb, hangin' out together till all hours, even on school nights."

"Ma," Luke complained. "Jeb's just a friend," he lied. "So's Pam. Gotta go."

"What about your schoolbooks?" Mrs. Ryan asked as Luke pushed open the screen door, empty-handed.

"In my locker," he answered on his way to his car.

"What're they doin' there, when you could've been studying for the test last night?" Mrs. Ryan called after her son. "Oh, and by the way, who was phoning you long distance from Dulcit?"

But Mrs. Ryan's questions were drowned out by the Dart's revving engine as Luke's beat-up sedan rumbled out of the dirt driveway.

Back in the kitchen she rolled her eyes, thinking her son, stunning though he was in the looks department, would most likely turn out a dunderhead like his father, whom she married only because she couldn't get enough of his dick. "Like father, like son," she sighed and returned to frying bacon.

Chapter Three

It was a little before nine when Luke pulled into the KRUQ parking lot. He was disappointed at the small size of the building and the fact that there wasn't even a gate or a guard with a special pass for him, like he'd heard happened at movie studios in Hollywood. From the outside, painted yellow with white trim, KRUQ looked more like a tract house than a television station. The only evidence that he was at the right location was a transmission tower in the backyard and a rusting tin sign over the front door that announced in block letters: THE GREAT TASTE OF GRANDPA'S HEAD. IT FOAMS! MORE SPUME THAN THE LEADING BRAND. GRANDPA'S ORIGINAL ROOT BEER/KRUQ-TV 3.

Luke shrugged. He parked his car and walked to the two wooden steps that were also painted yellow, except where footsteps had worn away the color. The stairs looked temporary, as though two strong men could easily carry them away. The door was no different than what would be found at an ordinary house. It even had a brass mail slot and door knocker. The only exception was a small plastic sign thumbtacked at eye level that announced that business hours were from 8:00 A.M. to 5:00 P.M.

Luke looked at his watch. Ignoring the door knocker, he entered the building and found himself in what looked as though it must once have been someone's living room but now served as a sort of lobby. There was an old, unoccupied desk. On the desk, a sign next to a black rotary telephone said: RECEPTION. RING BELL. Beside the sign was a small, rusting, dome-shaped bell like the type a motel registration desk might have. Luke looked around for signs of human activity; then still finding himself alone, he gingerly tapped the bell. Except for the echo of the ring, the room remained silent.

"Hello?" he called out. "Anybody here?" Luke wondered whether he should tap the bell again. He didn't want anyone to think he was impatient.

After another minute of silence, however, he rang a second time. Immediately he heard the sound of water flushing behind a door with a rectangular metal plaque with gold-colored lettering that announced: RESTROOM.

The door opened and a woman of maybe sixty emerged, tucking a frilly pastel pink blouse into the top of her black slacks. She turned off the bathroom light and exhaust fan, closed the door with one hand and fanned her nose with the other. "I heard you the first time," she said pulling at the top of her pants and snapping the elastic waist. "Some things you can't hurry. Are you Luke?"

"Yes, ma'am," Luke said. "I'm sorry, was I interrupting?"

"I was nearly done. Got the breakfast out. 'One meal in. One meal out.' That's what keeps your colon clean. I'll finish that *Reader's Digest* piece about penile enlargements later. D'ja ever think the day would come when medical science could pump that thing up longer an' fatter than your average *who-ha* can handle?"

"No, I never . . ."

"You only need a good six inches to get the job done right in the first place." Ella studied Luke's wide shoulders, his large strong hands, and size eleven shoes. "But I don't reckon that's anything you'll ever need to worry about, bless your heart." She cackled at her own observation. "Okay. You're here for *Hunk House*."

"What's *Hunk House?*"

"The TV game program you wanna be a contestant on."

"Is that what I'm here for? To be a contestant on some game show?" Luke was disappointed. He expected at least a movie-of-the-week. Or even something cheesy from Aaron Spelling.

"Trust me, you're gonna have a blast. It's not like any other game shows you've ever seen. That's not exactly true, but we like to think we're a little original 'round here. You could be famous. Like Richard Hatch! By the way, we were very impressed with your videotape."

"I made it myself."

"I could tell. Now first I'm going to have you meet Hamilton, the fella who thought up this whole thing. You have to be interviewed by him and Stacia Ratner. I'd join in, but they want me to be the greeter. They must think this is Wal-Mart or something."

"What about the other contestants?" Luke asked.

Ella shook her head. "Why don't we just get you situated with Hamilton. He can answer all your questions."

She led Luke through another door into a short corridor, along which were four similar doors—former bedrooms, Luke guessed, two on either side. At the end of the hall was yet another door with a nameplate: HAMILTON I. PEABODY.

Pausing outside the doors, Luke asked, "Is he nice?"

Ella reached up to knock. "A total doll," she whispered. "But if you ask me, he really needs a boyfriend. You two'd be cute together."

She rapped on the door, then turned the knob and entered the dreary office. "Hamilton," she announced, "this is Luke Ryan."

Hamilton came out from behind his desk to shake Luke's hand. "Great to meet you, Luke. Here, take a seat." He motioned for the young man to sit in the chair facing his desk. "Loved your video. Great touch with the hay. And your shirt, or lack thereof."

"I'll just leave you to have some private talk," Ella said, closing the door behind her.

"I didn't know what you wanted on the tape, so I just thought I'd give you a sample of what some guys have said they liked from me," Luke said.

"You've got great instincts," Hamilton said, cocking his head to examine Luke's peaches-and-cream complexion, blond hair, and green eyes. Luke's shirt was open at the neck and down three buttons, hinting at the smooth physique Hamilton had already watched so many times on the video.

"Some very nice fellas have said I've got pretty amazing *instincts*, if that's what you're callin' it," Luke agreed.

"We all thought your body was like, oh, I don't know, Michelangelo's *David*, or something." Hamilton chuckled.

Luke frowned, puzzled. "I don't watch foreign movies. Sorry."

"*David?*"

"Name's Luke."

"No, Michelangelo's . . ."

"It's Luke. Like the Skywalker dude."

Hamilton started to explain the most famous statue in the world but decided it wouldn't be worth the effort. "Of course we couldn't see *everything* you have stored away, like a squirrel in winter," Hamilton winked. "But I suppose we will eventually, eh?"

"Everything?" Luke asked. "What kind of show are you making anyway? Is there a nude scene or something? I'm really kinda shy. I don't think I'd know what to do."

Hamilton laughed. "It can be anything you and the other guys want it to be."

Luke nodded. "About the other guys? What exactly is this program all about, and how many other guys are in it?"

"There are supposed to be a total of six men sharing a house. But we're in a fix. We go into production day after tomorrow and so far we can only round up five, you being the fifth. We need six! Know anybody who might be interested in playing?"

"And be competition for me? I don't think so! But what exactly is this all for?" Luke asked. "I mean, what do I—we, have to do to play and win?"

"Here's the pitch," Hamilton explained. He laid out the scenario: six gay men, one house, six weeks of games in which one player a week is dumped, the winner receiving a trip to L.A. and a walk-on role on *Days of Our Lives*. He asked if Luke was still interested.

Luke was quiet for a moment. "Hell, yes! I'm gonna win me a trip to California!"

"And with a face and body like yours," Hamilton said admiringly, "I'm sure you'll end up being a movie star. Just like Matt Damon. Only don't ever forget the people who gave you your first break." Hamilton paused. "I'm as desperate to get back to Hollywood as you are. Okay. Now, we've gotta go see Stacia."

"Who?"

Hamilton sniggered. "The dragon lady."

Hamilton picked up the headset off the cradle of the old rotary telephone on his desk and dialed Stacia's extension number. "Luke Ryan's here. I'm bringing him in." He hung up without saying good-bye.

As they walked down the hall, Hamilton warned Luke. "Don't be intimidated by her. She's a bully, but it's only because she's under the thumb of her daddy who's the station owner. She's desperate for his approval. She compensates by trying to make everyone else feel inferior. I'll be with you the whole time, so just be relaxed and answer all her questions truthfully."

"Is this some kind of a test?"

"We just need to know as much about you as possible so we can make sure you're a good match for the other contestants."

"It's not like that smart *Jeopardy* show, is it?"

Hamilton chuckled. "Good one. Answer everything she asks in the form of a question. It'll drive her nuts! No, this is simply a sort of personality evaluation. But there are some pretty personal questions on the list. You up for it?"

Luke shrugged. "I've come this far."

Hamilton opened Stacia's door without knocking. "This is Luke," Hamilton said, making the introduction.

Stacia didn't bother to get up from behind her desk, nor did she look up from a yellow legal pad on which she was drafting a memo. "Stacia," Hamilton said again, "I'd like you to meet Luke Ryan."

"In a minute," Stacia complained, tucking strands of hair behind her ear.

Hamilton didn't wait for an invitation. He reached for a chair, pulling it up to one already in front of Stacia's desk. He motioned for Luke to sit beside him. For a long moment, there was nothing but the sound of Stacia's pen gliding across her tablet.

"Is it just me, have I done something wrong?" Luke whispered to Hamilton. "Or is she this rude to everyone?"

Hamilton laughed. "Touché!"

Stacia stopped writing and looked up at Luke. "I don't want this one on the show. Get him out!" She pushed more hair behind her ear and immediately went back to writing.

Hamilton was about to say something in Luke's defense, when Luke stood up. He said, "Sorry, ma'am. I hear you won't even have a show unless another moron shows up by tomorrow." He turned toward the door.

"Sit down," Stacia snapped, calling him back.

"Stacia's daddy owns the station, so she doesn't think she has to be civil to anyone," Hamilton said to Luke. "Missy, let's just get on with the interview, shall we?"

Stacia sighed. "I'm making this brief. I've got a luncheon."

"It's only nine-thirty, isn't it?" Luke said.

She stared at him with antagonism. "Are you gay?"

Luke was taken aback by the question. "Isn't that what you advertised for?"

"Are you sure? You don't look gay to me."

"Stacia," Hamilton interrupted, "what exactly does 'gay' look like to you? Charles Nelson Reilly or Kevin Spacey?"

"How long?" Stacia addressed Luke.

"How long what?" Luke asked.

"How long have you been gay?"

Luke laughed. "Are you serious?" He looked at Hamilton. "Ya mean how many years? Let's see, I'll be eighteen, er, twenty-two, in November. You do the math."

"Claiming 'no choice,' eh? Any social diseases?"

"Like gonorrhea or syphilis?" Luke asked.

"Ah, you know your social diseases," she smirked.

"I'm very healthy," Luke said.

"How often do you have sex?"

"How often do you pee? Excuse my language."

"Don't get sarcastic," Stacia ordered.

"I have sex about as often as most people say they pee. I can't help it. Men are just nice to me all the time. It just feels good, so I get into it with 'em. Nothing unusual about that, is there? I can't help if I like sex so much. It's the best thing in the world. So how often you pee is probably how often I have sex."

"I drink a lot of water," she deadpanned.

"I suck a lot of dick," he said looking her straight in the eye.

Stacia stopped their verbal parry for a moment. "How long could you go without sex?" she continued.

"Go without sex?" He was incredulous. "I never tried *not* to have sex. Has anybody? Except for nuns and priests—and I hear they don't have such a high rate of success.

"Intentionally *not* had sex? Can't say that I actually intentionally *have* sex, but it happens all the time just the same."

Stacia said, "This program is going to have you locked in a house with five other men for six weeks. Could you go six weeks without sex?"

"Depends, I guess, on how nice they are to me. Heck, I know straight guys who've been in jail who get buggered a hundred times more than they want. Why are you even asking, since this is going to be a house with all gay men? Of course, there'll be sex. It's always been impossible for me to avoid. Unless they're all trolls, in which case I don't know if I can take six weeks of that. When can I see pictures of the others?"

"You'll meet them day after tomorrow. *If* you're accepted. But you have to avoid sex 'cause you can't have intercourse on TV. FCC rules."

"What's wrong with sex?"

Hamilton jumped in. "Luke, this doesn't mean you won't have sex. If there's someone in the group you're interested in, I'm sure you'll find a way to get off." He was trying his best not to scare away this badly needed potential contestant, who, from what he'd seen so far, could become the star of the program.

Stacia interrupted. "No sex! There'll be cameras in every room—including the bathroom and shower—plus microphones hidden in even the most out-of-the-way places."

"But what if I don't like the other guys?" Luke asked.

"Tough titty," Stacia snarled. "Once you sign on, we're locking you up in a house for six weeks and throwing away the key. You won't have television. Or newspapers. One phone for emergency use only. No Bernadette Peters CDs."

"Is she the Spice Girl that left the group?"

"And you say you're gay?" Stacia huffed. "You'll just have each other's company. I hope you're good at making friends, because if you're selected you may be with some of these guys for a long time. That is if you make it to the end. One of you gets sent packing each week."

"What if I want out on my own?" Luke asked.

"You'll never see California on KRUQ's dime, that's for sure," Stacia said.

"I know how much you want that *Days of Our Lives* gig," Hamilton reminded him. "The trick is to get along with everybody as much as possible, so they don't kick you out when everybody meets weekly to vote and decide who goes and who stays."

"Hamilton," Stacia said, "You're the so-called brains behind this program. Why don't you take over with a few pertinent questions?"

Silence filled the room for a moment. "Luke, what about another man turns you on?" Hamilton finally asked.

"Turns me on?" Luke considered. "I know if I were smart, I'd probably realize I'm supposed to say something like brains and a sense of humor. Like that would win me a Mr. Congeniality contest."

"I just want to know what *really* gives you a woody for another guy?"

"Different things," Luke said. "Full lips and a full load of dick in a guy's pants, I guess. The usual. Muscles. Tattoos. Big tools. Although I'm big myself—or so I've been told—in case anyone's interested. I just like what guys do to me. I don't really have any preference. They're all just nice."

Hamilton shifted in his seat, trying hard not to look down toward Luke's crotch. "On the other hand, what's a total turnoff for you?"

"That's easy. Brains and a sense of humor." Luke laughed at his own joke. "Heck," he amended, "everybody seems to want to fool around with me. When they come on to me, everything gets kinda fast and furious. I've learned to just like the action. So it's cool that they don't want talkin' and wastin' time. Just fuck me or suck me and I'm cool."

"Well, that's succinct," Stacia said, throwing down her pen and folding her arms.

Hamilton asked, "And what would you do if it were just down to you and one other guy in the house and he happened to want . . ."

"Little ol' me?"

Stacia rolled her eyes and said, "Holy Christ! There really *is* a turnip truck."

Luke pondered. "This is like, 'if I was the last man on earth' kinda deal, right? Heck, if I'm there for six weeks, ain't nobody gonna be that much of a turnoff! I've done it with some butt-ugly teachers who wanted to flunk me out of their classes, until I changed their mind for 'em. I can get it up when I have to. And sometimes I don't have to even get it hard. Guys just want to touch it. I'm not choosy. All I know is, if there's a hole, you've got to plug it up, right?"

"Like a dike," Hamilton, smiled, agreeing.

"Holy smokes! There ain't no lesbians on this show, are there?" Luke recoiled in horror.

Hamilton quickly explained, "No, no. A dike. Like what the Dutch build in the Netherlands to keep the sea from flooding the country."

Luke blinked, uncertain.

"What else, Stacia?" Hamilton asked.

Luke looked at her, shrugged, then smiled.

"How 'bout you, Luke? Any questions for us?" Hamilton said.

Luke nodded. "Yeah. How much money do I get paid? And what happens if I don't win? Are there 'lovely parting gifts' like a bedroom suite or washer and dryer? What can I bring to the house and when do I start?"

"Zip. Nothing. No. A toothbrush. Nine A.M., day after tomorrow," Stacia answered his questions rapidly with a satisfying smirk. "Here's the contract." She pushed a sheaf of papers and pen toward Luke. "And since you're really only eighteen—you lied about your age on the tape, but you put your correct birth date on your résumé, you boob—you need parental approval."

Luke's face turned red.

"Just bring the contract back with you day after tomorrow," Hamilton reiterated. "And make sure your parents fill out all the stuff about who to call in case of emergency and such."

"Your father'll have a *fit* when he comes in."

Luke's mother had a worried expression on her face. Luke had just announced that he'd been suspended from school. "Oh, Lord, he's going to be so mad. *Why*, Luke? Why did you let this happen again?"

"It's that old Principal Stouffer, Ma! My car broke down yesterday on the way to school, and he thinks I cut classes on purpose again."

"Don't lie to me," his mother said. "I know he's right. You were in Dulcit yesterday. Don't deny it. I spoke with someone at TV station KRUQ. Stacia Someone. She called to make sure we signed some kind of contract they gave you to be in a show."

Luke dissolved. "I'm sorry, I lied to you, Ma. Really, really sorry."

Mrs. Ryan pursed her lips. "Bring me the contract. And hurry, before your father comes in."

Luke ran up to his room and returned with the papers Stacia and Hamilton had given him the day before. He handed them to his mother.

"What kind of show is this?" Mrs. Ryan asked.

"It's like that *Survivor* show you liked so much."

"Are you going away?" she asked, alarmed.

"Just for six weeks—or less if I don't win."

She signed the parental agreement where a small x had been marked next to a line that said "signature" below it.

"What about Pop?" Luke asked.

"You just leave him a note saying you were suspended and you're embarrassed, and you couldn't face him, so you left home until the suspension is over. I don't like lyin', to your father, or anybody else. It's not the Christian way. But it's better than havin' him hurt you."

Luke was used to his father's temper. He was accustomed to the quick unexpected outbursts and tried to always be on guard against sudden tirades. No one ever knew when the irrational monster would appear from behind his father's deep-set eyes. Luke stopped trying to anticipate what would make his father angry. Everything about Luke seemed to irritate him. The understanding between them was that Luke was a disappointment to the family. Despite his handsome face and masculine bearing, Luke was not the son his father had expected. Luke could play as much football as anyone else, or join the Marines, and still, his father would only think of finding his boy in the barn, with another boy. One mistake and it had cost Luke the keys to his father's heart.

Luke's perpetual mantra was, *I'm leaving home ASAP, and I'll only return when I'm rich and famous. That'll show the old bastard. I'll be a success and make him see how wrong he was about me. If he doesn't love me, the world will!*

"Ma . . ." Luke continued.

"Don't talk. It's hard enough that I have to stay here without you. Just eat your dinner tonight as though nothin' unusual has happened. Then go to your room and leave durin' the night."

Luke hugged his mother, and her eyes were filled with tears. "I might be back in just a couple of weeks," he said. "It's possible that they won't want me there."

"I've got cookin' to do," Mrs. Ryan stated, drawing from her son's embrace. Then she took three potatoes out of a sack and placed them in the sink and turned on the tap.

Luke left the kitchen without another word. All the excitement he'd felt about getting a break and being on television was gone. In its place was an emptiness that couldn't be filled by thinking about the sexual possibilities of being with five other gay men all at one time in some TV show house.

Still, lying on his bed with his hand tucked down the waist of his jeans, unconsciously rubbing his cock did take his mind off his problems for a while. Luke was still Luke. And sex didn't have an on/off switch in his mind.

Chapter Four

At 3:00 A.M. Luke shifted his car's transmission into neutral and slowly pushed his Dodge Dart, headlights off, backward down the dirt driveway to the rural lane that ran along the Ryans' property. Once on the blacktop road, with more muscle required than he thought possible, he planted his feet on the pavement to stop his car from continuing its backward motion.

Turning the steering wheel through the open window with one hand, he maneuvered the car until it was on the shoulder of the road. Then he put his full weight into pushing the car forward until he was a good hundred yards away from the house. As the vehicle continued to move, he jumped into the driver's seat and turned the key to start the engine. Checking his rearview mirror for any sign that his father had witnessed his departure or was following him, he saw the red glow of a cigarette in the background of the front porch.

Within twenty minutes, Luke was alone, driving the otherwise deserted highway. He struggled to convince himself that all that had transpired over the past few days was a gift. No more school. No more Pop. All his dreams were poised to come true: fame, fortune, and stardom. Everything he wanted was coming his way. The only thing he'd miss was his mother. He uttered a prayer that his father wouldn't take his anger out on her, demanding to know where Luke had run off to.

By the time Luke arrived at KRUQ, it was an hour before dawn. He drove into the deserted parking area with the crunch of gravel amplified in the otherwise quiet night. He parked, turned off his headlights, which had illuminated the dark eyes of KRUQ's building windows, and shut off the engine. Then he crawled into the backseat, put his leather jacket over his shoulders, curled into a fetal position, and tried not to feel homesick or worry about the coming weeks. Soon, he was fast asleep.

The sound of car doors slamming and voices outside his vehicle roused Luke from a near wet dream about Mr. Pudwell, his phys ed instructor. It was daylight. He peeked out the window and shrugged off his jacket.

What he saw was a group of four men. Each one he looked at seemed sexier than the next. They were milling about, shaking hands, and introducing themselves to one another.

Luke climbed into the front seat and checked himself in the rearview mirror. "Shoot! I'm a mess," he muttered. His hair was a thicket of tangles, and he had crust in the corners of his eyes. He was sure his morning breath was probably as bad as a cow's stall. He dug around between the seats searching, to no avail, for a stick of chewing gum or a Tic Tac.

Luke looked at his watch. Eight fifty-five. "Dang, I'm almost late," he said, shocked that he'd slept so soundly.

He opened the door and stepped outside the car into the chilly April morning, carrying the manila envelope with his signed contract. No suitcase. No toothbrush. No shaving razor. Just the clothes he was wearing: jeans and his flannel shirt, which was untucked and wrinkled.

The other guys immediately noticed Luke. They stood in silence for a moment, taking him in with covetous eyes, evaluating his potential as a contestant and simultaneously plotting variations on how to seduce him. "Hey," Luke greeted them cautiously, as he ambled up to the group of men.

"Hey, back at ya," said a guy with a smile that revealed oversized teeth. He wore a small silver earring and held out his hand to shake Luke's. "Cameron," the man announced, locking eyes with the newcomer and looking Luke up and down, sizing him up.

"Cameron. Nice to meet you. I'm Luke Ryan." Luke faced the others. One by one, each took his hand and offered greetings and their names. The next guy, Marco, was of obvious Latin descent. He had a warm smile that showed off two deep dimples. He wore his sideburns long and sported a black goatee.

Richard was serious and couldn't bring himself to smile. His deep-set eyes were almost hypnotic to Luke. His greeting was perfunctory and Luke immediately picked up vibrations of anxiety or insecurity.

Then there was Zeth, for whom Luke immediately got a woody.

"Cool name," Luke said as he smiled and took in the whole package: Zeth was about five feet nine inches tall and built like a swimmer. He had a whisper of facial fuzz, nothing that needed to be shaved, and creamy skin showing at the V-neck of his collar, which was opened down several buttons. It was hard for Luke—and Zeth—to take their eyes from each other's. They exchanged a warm handshake.

"Shall we go in and see that Stacia bitch again," said Cameron, who already seemed to be the leader. All the men chuckled in conspiratorial agreement.

"'Course that Hamilton dude makes up for her," Marco added. "I bet he's smokin' under his pinstripes! Wouldn't mind being in a house with him for six weeks."

"With Hamilton, I think six's your luck number," Cameron joked.

The group filed up the steps, opened the door, and entered the KRUQ lobby. "My boys!" Ella squealed, hugging each one as they formed a semicircle around her. "Welcome! Looks like we're all here." She called off, "Luke, Cameron, Marco, Richard, Zeth. All present and accounted for."

"Someone's missin'," Luke observed. "There's s'posed to be six of us, ain't there?"

"There'll be a full house," Ella promised. "Hamilton and Stacia are hammering out the final details."

Ella guided the men to a folding table on which she had arranged Krispy Kreme doughnuts, an institutional-size pot of coffee, and cans of soda submerged in a tub of melting ice. "Help yourselves, guys," she instructed. "Yap it up while I go see what's going on with the bosses."

As Ella left the room, the men started to pair off like kids at their first day of summer camp. They played at being congenial and sociable, though each knew full well that if they were planning to win this game the others were essentially mortal enemies. No one said as much, but each man knew he had to be more duplicitous than anyone else in the group in order to survive the six weeks.

Finally, Hamilton came bouncing into the lobby from behind the hallway door. His necktie was, as always, neatly knotted and his hair perfectly combed. "Guys! Guys! I'm so happy you're all here. It's the big day, isn't it! And you all look great." He shook each man's hand, remembering their names. "So, are we ready for orientation?"

Expressions of approval issued from the five men.

"Okay," Hamilton said, "follow me and we'll get started. We'll go to the conference room and spend an hour talking about the whole adventure you're embarking on. Anybody need to use the toidy before we start? No? Then, off we go."

The five hunky men, accompanied by Hamilton, pouring into the hallway, took up most of the space in the small corridor. Ella had reappeared and commenced snapping pictures with a disposable camera, capturing for posterity the start of Day One. In the small conference room, all the chairs were on one side of the table facing a white board on which a list was numbered in red marker under the headline: RULES.

As the group settled down, Stacia, who didn't bother saying hello, joined them. She scanned the men, looking down her nose, and then sidled up to Hamilton. She sat on top of the credenza at the front of the room, her legs, under a pink skirt, crossed at the ankles. Repositioning her eyeglasses, she took over the orientation like a drill instructor.

"Starting this moment," she began, "you've signed your lives over to KRUQ. You'll do exactly as you're instructed and follow all the rules I've written on the board."

"Sounds as though we're slaves to her master scenario," Cameron whispered to Luke. "I might get more of a charge out of this than I thought."

Stacia continued. "For the sake of spontaneity, we don't want you getting to know one another just yet; not until we go over to the house, which'll be fairly soon. So no talking to each other and no making dates to meet in the men's room."

"I'll take it from here, Stacia," Hamilton interrupted. "Guys, this is going to be a learning experience for all of us, especially for you and for our audiences. What we'd like is for you all to get to know each other *on camera*. This is just for the sake of our television viewers. They should feel as though they're invisible ghosts in the house, and you're the new tenants who've just moved in. You're going to be exploring not only the residence, but also each other.

"The audience is just coming along for the ride. Your job is to be completely natural, and our job is to let the viewer visit but not second-guess what they'll be seeing from moment to moment. You're probably a little scared. I want them to be a little scared, too. After all, none of you—including the audience—knows what to expect."

"Sex!" Cameron called out, eliciting a burst of laughter from the other contestants.

Hamilton smiled. "A program like this has never been done before. Everything must be impulsive and impromptu. We'd just rather you guys not interact until you're in the house and the tapes start rolling. Okay?"

"The rules, people," Stacia said, reclaiming their attention. "Pay attention here because any infraction and you'll be clipping coupons in whatever shabby farm town you're from rather than living the high life in L.A.

"Rule number one: No sex! I know it's hard—pun intended—when you're a queer, but you're here to work not to play with your dicks. There are cameras in every room. No fucking. And no sucking.

"Rule number two: Same for masturbating. Don't even think about it. Even whacking off under the sheets will be picked up by the cameras and the mikes, especially if you're the type who makes noise. And the cameras in the bathrooms are real!"

"We can always steam up the bathroom, can't we?" Zeth said. The others laughed.

She ignored him. "Rule number three: Language. This is Iowa. We don't want to have to bleep half your bleeping conversations because you have potty mouths. The F word is unacceptable. It will definitely cost you points. Did we mention the point system?"

Hamilton explained, "They're like the demerits you got in school."

Stacia rolled her eyes. "Now we know what you learn at a fancy prep school. At the end of each week, any points—plus or minus—that you've racked up go toward the grade that helps determine who stays and who is dismissed. This is just a portion of the credit. Actually, fifty percent of the vote is subjective."

"In other words, fifty percent is a popularity contest?" Marco asked.

"How you make yourselves the Belle of the Ball is entirely up to you," Stacia said.

"For what other infractions could we lose points?" Richard pouted.

Stacia looked to Hamilton, who answered, "As Stacia said, swearing, being caught having sex or masturbating, er . . ." he stalled for a moment. "Smoking inside the house, stealing, those sorts of things."

"We didn't sign up for charm school," Richard countered petulantly.

"Of course not," Hamilton said. "But you also score positive points for winning games we've devised. More about that later. Just play fair and square and treat your housemates with the same kind of respect that you would ordinarily treat anyone, and things'll be fine. You guys are all decent, otherwise we wouldn't have chosen you from the hundreds of applicants we had. I don't for a minute think there'll be any discipline problems."

"Sometimes I *need* discipline," Cameron said. Several of the other chuckled.

"Every bad boy will be punished, I assure you," Hamilton chimed in. "But maybe not in the manner you'd prefer." He winked.

The hour raced by. Hamilton and Stacia covered as much information as possible without giving away too much of what they hoped would be a great opening episode of the men exploring the house and discovering each other's eccentricities.

"One last thing about the house," Hamilton said. "It's old. It's the only house we could find large enough to accommodate everyone plus the crew and equipment. It may actually be haunted. I don't want to paint a negative picture, but it doesn't have all the modern amenities of, say, the Palmer House in Chicago, so you'll be roughing it a little. Fortunately—or unfortunately, depending on the way you view things— there are six bedrooms so you don't have to share with anyone."

"Separate bathrooms, too?" Zeth asked, his eyes shifting from Hamilton to Luke.

"Sorry, only three. And they're small. They were added long after the house was built, so they were probably closets. Afraid you'll have to share. However, as contestants are eliminated over the weeks, you'll have more privacy. But remember, the cameras and microphones are everywhere. Even with the lights out, the infrared cameras will be taping you.

"Ready for action, guys?" he concluded. "Let's go out to the van and take off for Hunk House! By the way, you're going to be blindfolded en route. In case you're asked to leave at some point, you won't be able to find your way back."

"If I'd known that, I would have brought my own cowl," Cameron said.

Hamilton smiled. "Also, Stacia and I have to stay behind for a bit to clear up a situation. Your driver, Carl, will take good care of you. And, even though we aren't officially going into production until the sixth man arrives, the tapes and microphones will be on from the instant you arrive. From this moment forward, Big Brother will be watching." Hamilton smiled again. "Oh, and right after our business, we'll come over and officially throw away the key! Good luck everybody!"

The men followed Hamilton and Stacia out of the conference room and back into the lobby, where Ella was waiting with long strips of black felt. One by one she stood on her tiptoes and tied the blindfolds as tightly as possible. Then Hamilton and Stacia led each man out the front door and down the steps to the waiting van. When the men were all settled, looking more like victims being led to a firing squad than potential TV stars, the van pulled out of the graveled yard and headed to the Maynard mansion.

Chapter Five

Once the van had pulled away and was out of sight, the entire production had passed its point of no return—but *without* the sixth contestant. The *joie de vivre* that Hamilton had faked so well during the past hour disappeared, along with the color in his face. He became as pale as a Styrofoam coffee cup. His worst fear had been realized. There hadn't been hundreds of applicants for the show, as he had claimed. Luke Ryan was the last to apply for the program.

"You've seriously messed up, Hammy," Stacia said with satisfaction, as they re-entered the building. "A screwup like this and my old man is gonna have your ass on a skewer. Mr. Hamilton I. Peabody will be running back to L.A., minus his dick. It's good riddance, as far as I'm concerned."

"Three cheers for your good fortune," Hamilton said.

"I just believe in being honest. Unlike others who work at this station."

"Thanks so much for your vote of confidence, Stacia," Hamilton scowled. "I'm only here trying to save your stupid station, and I've never received one bit of help from you."

"Why should I help the handsome Ivy League smart-ass Daddy hired. He should have given me the job," she retorted. "Unless you think of some way to save yourself in the next five minutes, he'll see that I was the right one all along. There's not much time. Daddy's due here any moment, and you'll have to tell him you've completely blown all the sponsor's money, as well as what he personally invested into the program. He'll be broke. No station—and no house for those Emmys you promised him."

"I never *promised* any Emmys. I just said it was possible that if the program was a hit he might get an Emmy."

"Yeah, like it's possible he'll pat you on the back and say, 'Good college try. Better luck next time, son.'"

Stacia turned away, opened the door leading to the hallway and her office, and hummed as she walked down the corridor. "By the by, Hammy," she called over her shoulder, "I want your stuff outta my new office right after Daddy fires you."

"I feel sick," Hamilton said to Ella, who was seated at the reception desk and had witnessed the entire scene between him and Stacia.

"I'll bet you feel like diarrhea, don't you?" she said, sounding compassionate. "I had a boss like her once. After I gave twenty-five years to that company, she called me into her office one afternoon and said my services were no longer needed. I was shocked. I thought I was going to get a promotion. I expected to retire from that place with a pension and full benefits. But the hardest part wasn't wondering how I would feed my lazy unemployed husband or our three young'ns. The hardest thing was holding my darned sphincter!"

Hamilton moaned. He dropped into a chair and held his head between his hands. "Ella! Ella! What am I going to do? This is my career! It's L.A. all over again; only the scandal has changed!"

Ella stood, walked over to him, and put a hand on his shoulder. Then, to Hamilton's surprise, she bellowed, "Listen up, Mister I-Don't-Know-What-I'm-Going-To-Do Crybaby! You went to Harvard! You worked in L.A.! You can come up with a solution! Didn't you learn anything useful in those places?"

"Nothing that'll get me out of this mess," he said, crestfallen.

"Let me tell you about your mess, Mister. You can't fool me. I've been around twice as long as you have. Here's how I see it. That sweetie who broke your heart was your boyfriend. Maybe some handsome blond actor, or some fella you met in West Hollywood on a hot summer afternoon. It was very romantic. You went to the fancy hillside house your rich mommy and daddy probably kept you in. He had strong, wide shoulders and smooth skin that made you ache when you touched him."

"Ella!" Hamilton erupted, embarrassed.

"So, you thought you were in love. Nothing wrong with that. But after a time, you found him in your bed with another actor. And it broke your heart. That's why you're here. I'm right, or am I right?"

A long moment of silence followed. Then Hamilton said, "The ABC commissary. Morning news anchor. It was spring. *He* had the Hollywood Hills place. Great shoulders. Great pecs. Chest, arms, thighs, you name it. A perfect package. But he had a weakness for hunky cameramen. I was wiped out when he dumped me. I wanted to get as far away from him, and Los Angeles, as I could. I left my job at *Entertainment Tonight*. Then this one opened up."

"Well, it's time to snap out of it, Hammy. But first, you have to think about *Hunk House*. You have to volunteer to be the sixth contestant. You're going to come out of the closet to Old Man Ratner, tell him you've been lying about being straight, which nobody believed anyway—and volunteer to be sent up there yourself."

"Me? In *Hunk House?*" Hamilton blinked. "I couldn't."

"You haven't got any choice. Besides, you're just as sexy as any of those other men. You might even win."

Hamilton smiled in self-conscious appreciation. "There's a problem," he said.

"Give me one good reason you can't be the sixth contestant at *Hunk House.*"

"Conflict of interest. First of all, as the guy who came up with this idea, I'm not eligible. Plus, I'm the one who devised all the rules. The games. The whole thing. I'm even the host."

Ella looked defeated. "Hadn't thought about that." She was silent. "How about getting one of your gay friends? You must have someone you could call to do the show."

"In Dulcit? Who?" Imitating Mr. Ratner, he puffed out his stomach and said, "'Cocksuckers? Son, there ain't no Nancy boys in these parts. The only queers I ever seen was my Marine Corps buddies.'"

Ella howled at the spot-on impersonation.

"And you called *me* a 'closet case,'" Hamilton said. "To paraphrase your remark about there being more than one queer on the *Survivor* island and the Outback, I think there's more than one poof on our staff. But to answer your real question, No, I don't have any gay friends here. Or at least no one who can come out. Getting fucked in Dulcit is an oxymoron."

"Pity. You're just wastin' your youth. When you get to be my age and look back at the age you're at now, you'll kick yourself for not being somebody's bitch. God knows I do—church marriage vows or not."

Hamilton protested. "I've been too busy trying to establish a reputation and get this show ready. I haven't even thought much about sex—until our applicants started sending their tapes."

"You work so you can avoid any emotional attachments!"

"Probably. And for what? My life crashed and burned in L.A.; and now, practically before I've gotten my career off the ground in this dump, I'm through! I thought I'd build up this station's ratings and get discovered by a network big shot, or at the very least, take over Ratner's job. What a fool I've been!"

Ella suddenly wasn't paying attention to Hamilton's lament. Her mind was focused on something more important. She then said in a very serious tone, "You made an interesting point about someone else at the station. Who else do we know here who's gay?"

Hamilton shrugged.

"Rex, of course. But not only would he *not* fit through the door of Hunk House, he wouldn't fit in as a contestant. He has a lot of the right attributes: he's a weasel and a liar and a cheat. But Mr. Ratner would *never* let his son be part of this program. I'm sure he suspects his boy's a fairy, but as long as Rex doesn't officially come out, Ratner won't say a word. Being a queer on TV would give the old man an aneurysm."

Ella once again fell into silence. Then with a snap of her fingers, the sound of which ricocheted off the walls and echoed in the room: "Why didn't I think of this first?" she mused. "There *is* someone!"

"Who? The water delivery guy? I admit, he's one of the few guys in Dulcit I have the hots for. He looks exactly like Oscar de la Hoya, for Christ sake!"

"No. This is serious. Think for a moment."

"Ella, we don't have time to play Twenty Questions."

"Shush. Who works here who's not a Ratner—aside from you and me?"

"Ummm?"

"He's buff, and he's hot as a pistol. He's got a certain dangerous sex appeal."

"Ummm?"

"He only works here part-time, and he hasn't been in on any of the meetings where you discussed the specifics of the show."

"Ummm?"

"Give up?" She smiled. "Hint. His IQ is about the same as roadkill out on Route Twenty-nine."

"Bull?"

"Bingo!"

Hamilton sputtered, "For crying out loud! He's the most homophobic, sullen, surly, hostile slug in Iowa! He'd turn mass murderer if he were locked in that house! The man's certifiable! Besides, he'd be so hated by the other men that he'd be killed or outed from the house the first week, if not sooner!"

"That'd solve everyone's problems, wouldn't it?" Ella beamed. "He'd only have to be in the house for a week. And he wouldn't have to interact with the other men if he didn't want to."

"Sure he would. I've got a bunch of games and activities they all have to participate in to score points for determining the ultimate winner."

"More demerits if Bull refuses to participate! They'd *have* to kick him out!"

Hamilton scratched his head. "How on earth would you even get him to consider doing something like this?"

"It's not altogether up to him. First of all, if Mr. Ratner goes along with the idea, as an employee Bull would have to do what the old man demanded."

"He'll quit."

"Doubt it. There's that loan on his truck he's got to pay back to Ratner."

"He could get another job."

"In Dulcit? Ha! There's nothing between here and Iowa City. No Wal-Mart. No McDonald's. Maybe a filling station. Already he can't survive on what he takes home from his other jobs. Plus any employer would do a background check, which Ratner never bothered to do. But *I* sure did."

"You didn't have the facts of my past exactly correct."

"I did, but I wanted to see how honest you'd be with me."

Hamilton regarded Ella with admiration. "What'd you get on Bull?" he asked.

"Let's just say he's ambivalent. And, he's a lot more into those fashion magazines than you'd ever guess in a zillion years."

"Aren't they his girlfriend's magazines?"

"What kind of idiot pills have you been takin', Hammy?" Ella said. "When d'ja ever see him with a girl, except Stacia?"

Hamilton thought for a moment and realized that Ella was right. Each time he'd been to a bar and saw Bull there, he was always alone or talking shop with Stacia, draining a couple of mugs of suds.

"It's true that all the girls want him, ever since he was a tyke," Ella said.

"Who wouldn't? He's got a majestic body."

"And that long curly hair is a real turn-on for some. I personally know a few of them girls who've tried to get 'im. More than one has talked to me about their frustration. You know how it is. Everyone comes to me because they think I'm such a clam."

"This is all circumstantial evidence, I'm afraid," Hamilton said, hardly believing he was defending Bull. "Besides, how could we ever approach him to do the show?"

"That's a very delicate proposition. I didn't know if we should go straight to Mr. Ratner and tell him our problem and convince him that Bull's our last and only hope, or go straight to Bull and blackmail him into agreeing to be on *Hunk House* on his own. But we'd better decide fast."

"Maybe we could tell Bull there's an urgent problem that requires his maintenance expertise?" Hamilton schemed.

"Then throw away the key without Ratner knowing?"

"He'd know soon enough when the daily tapes started coming in."

"And we could be accused of kidnapping, since he hasn't signed a contract," Ella suggested.

Hamilton pondered for a moment. "I think we should tell Bull that Ratner made the decision, but that all he has to do is stay locked in his room."

Ella nodded. "Good. But I'm glad I won't be there when you tell him. All heck's gonna break loose."

Just as she was speaking, Old Man Ratner came through the front door, all smiles. "The big day!" he thundered. "I trust all is in order?"

Hamilton stammered, "Ah. Er. Couldn't be better, sir. I'm going over to Hunk House immediately. If you see Stacia, tell her everything's settled and she doesn't need to stop by."

"That'a boy, Hammy," Ratner said, slapping him on the shoulder.

"Never did want my daughter messin' 'round with all those men anyway; queer or not, they're still men, and my Buttercup's a sexy woman."

"Yes, sir," Hamilton said, slipping into his suit jacket, thinking only a father could conceive of his old maid daughter as sexy. He winked at Ella, who smiled back conspiratorially at Hamilton as he picked up his car keys and left the building.

Bull, shirtless, with his jeans hugging his hips, tinkered under the hood of his pickup truck beside the old Streamair house trailer that he called home. "You're a total space case," Bull laughed at Hamilton, who leaned against the trunk of a tree. He looked up at the programming director and wiped his grease-stained hands on an old, frayed towel. "If I didn't think you were joking, I'd bust open that melon head of yours," he added.

"Yeah, I'm a caution, I am," Hamilton said without a smile. "You, a contestant on *Hunk House*? Where do I come up with such rich and equally ridiculous material? Eh? I should'a been a comic on television. I'm hysterically funny, even to myself. Ray Romano doesn't have anything over me."

"Thing is, everybody loves Raymond, but not everybody, especially me, loves you," Bull parried.

"Touché," Hamilton said, still not smiling. "Guess I kill—even when I'm not trying to."

"You almost crack me up, man," Bull said, gazing at Hamilton. Then, in a serious tone he added, "If I were you, I'd get my pin-striped, candy ass back to the station before somebody permanently changes the channel you're on. Get my drift?"

Hamilton felt his face turn red from trepidation. He knew that Bull was like a diamondback rattler, coiled and ready to strike. "What if I made the small suggestion that maybe you don't have a choice, that you *have* to spend one week at the old Maynard mansion?"

"Then I'd have to shove your suggestion up where the sun don't shine," Bull said, folding his arms over his bronzed, muscled chest.

Hamilton, maintaining a distance from the volatile Bull, continued. "For one thing, it's an order from Old Man Ratner," he lied.

"Na ah."

"For another, Stacia agrees it's the only way to save her father from bankruptcy and their house from being foreclosed on," he lied again. "You know the old man's put all he'd saved, and then some, into this show."

Mentioning the potential dire straits that Stacia was in, caught Bull's attention. "Na ah," Bull snorted again. He looked at Hamilton's poker face for a clue that might give away his hand.

"Ya, ha," Hamilton said. "That's not all. For spending just one week at Hunk House—you can stay in your room the whole time, if you want, 'cause you'll be voted out right away—Ratner's going to forgive the loan on your truck."

"How do you know about the loan?" Bull asked with a look of deep suspicion.

"I know because Ratner told me that he'd forgive your loan if you played along for just one week. He needs to recoup his investment." Hamilton was lying about Ratner, but had promised himself that if he somehow convinced Bull to stay over at Hunk House, he would find a way to take over the loan as an expression of his appreciation.

"Ain't enough money in all of Dulcit to get me to be locked up with those gay people you got over there," Bull charged.

"Either you go along with Ratner and get your truck free and clear," Hamilton said, "or you get your greaseball ass kicked out of KRUQ, plus the loan still stands, plus Stacia might not have a place to live, plus . . ."

"You're a liar!" Bull yelled. "I don't believe anything you say. Show me some proof. I think you just want some real eye candy on your stupid show. I know how I look. I know that girls—and guys, like you and Rex—think I'm hot stuff. No way am I being outed on television!"

Hamilton instantly caught Bull's self-indictment. He pretended not to notice that Bull caught himself when he bellowed, "I'm not being outed on television." For the first time since his conversation with Ella, he thought perhaps the old woman wasn't completely off her rocker regarding Bull's closeted sexuality.

"My proof?" Hamilton continued. "For one thing, I know about the loan because the old man told me. Isn't that proof enough?"

Bull looked skeptical.

"Well, he also told me that you need other part-time jobs to make ends meet, and that you'd be a fool to pass up this opportunity, especially since you don't have to do anything other than show up at Hunk House."

"I musta been crazy to confide in that old man," Bull said with a flash of anger. "Never tell anybody your secrets, 'cause man, then they're no longer secret, and people'll use your personal information against you."

Later, as Bull sat in the passenger seat of Hamilton's car, he began to perspire and simultaneously shiver, as if the temperature had been knocked down to morgue refrigeration levels. *How could I let this happen?* he asked himself. *How could I be going to join the* Hunk House *program?* Bull knew the fear he was experiencing. It wasn't the first time he had unintentionally let down his guard and found himself face-to-face with some unpleasant realities in life. His body vibrated as he thought about being locked up with five gay men.

"You're going to be fine," Hamilton insisted as he saw anxiety on Bull's face.

"I ain't responsible if somebody gets hurt in there," Bull snapped. "I'm only doin' this 'cause I ain't got a choice. And for Stacia, and her kiss 'n' tell old man. Do you hear me?"

"That means you'll keep your promise and not let on to anyone that you're not a real contestant."

"What, and have people think I'm queer? I don't think so," Bull said. Then the realization came to him. "Oh, Christ, people will think it anyway 'cause I'm gonna be exposed on the TV. I'm never coming out of my room for a solid week. Hear me? Never! And you can't make me."

"I won't try to make you do anything, Bull, I promise," Hamilton tried to sound reassuring. He remembered what it was like to be thrown into summer camp with a bunch of tough kids he didn't know. With this memory from his youth he suddenly felt a little sorry for Bull who would soon be facing his worst fears, or perhaps, his greatest fantasy.

Chapter Six

One by one, each man, still blindfolded, was slowly led up three steps on the wraparound porch and ushered through the open French doors of Hunk House. Each could hear his footsteps echoing on the hardwood floors of the foyer and could smell a combination of mildew and disinfectant as he was escorted into what felt like a large open space.

When the five men were finally together, they were instructed by an unfamiliar voice—a camera operator—to remove their blindfolds. Adjusting their eyes to the light took a moment, but when all was in clear focus, they found four Stedicams practically in their faces. They were in what was probably once a grand main parlor. The house was an old Victorian with lots of dark wood furniture and lampshades the color of old newspaper. Half-dead creeping Charlie's and philodendrons lined the windowsills. Porcelain figurines of coquettish girls courted by fifeplaying young admirers decorated doilied coffee tables. The room also boasted a grand piano, an ancient rolltop desk, and furniture that had been well used over many decades.

"Looks like my grandmother's attic," Cameron said, the first to acknowledge the old-fashioned ambiance of the place. "Must be part of the test to see who can keep their depression at bay the longest."

Marco echoed Cameron. "This place is like Norma Desmond's house. Where's the dead monkey? I suppose Hamilton is our Max! It gives me the willies."

"Well," Luke said in a cheery manner, "at least it's home. For a week, maybe six, anyway, depending on who gets the boot first."

Zeth oohed and ahhed at the interior design. "Look at this old wallpaper!" he exclaimed. "Wait, they didn't have wallpaper when this place was built. The plaster's hand-stenciled!"

"Big deal," said Cameron.

"Man," Zeth continued, "look at the hand-carved mahogany fireplaces! *Definitely* brought over from Europe!" Walking into the dining room, which adjoined the parlor, Zeth pointed to the ceiling. "Check this out, Luke! Pressed tin, pressed leather and paper! You can see they were drifting into the Craftsman era 'cause these are Craftsman-like ceilings. But you can feel Nouveau, too." He pointed to another fireplace. "Look at this incredible carving!"

The Stedicam operator swirled around, capturing their sound bites, as Zeth continued to tour the house and the others began to follow him like a docent. "This would have been the men's parlor," he said looking into a room opposite the dining room. "After dinner, the women would have gone upstairs to their own parlor for sewing and gossip. The men would be down here smoking pipes or cigars."

"Where'd you ever learn so much?" Luke asked, impressed.

"Just interested in old stuff," Zeth said.

"So where's the last dude who's supposed to be with us," Richard finally said, looking around.

"I don't know who he is, but I already don't trust him," Cameron said. "He could be working for KRUQ. Be careful guys. He may be a saboteur, like on *The Mole.*"

"So much for hidden cameras," Luke said, pointing to a Sony VHS recorder positioned inside the glass cabinet of a fake Chippendale hutch.

"And look at this microphone dangling from the dining room chandelier," Cameron quipped. "It's like something out of *Singin' in the Rain,* trying to hide the sound equipment in Lena Lamont's tits. Maybe we should count how many of these devices are scattered through the house."

The men followed Cameron around the living room and discovered three more videocameras and an equal number of microphones. Then they set out to explore the rest of the house, climbing an enormous *Gone With the Wind* stairway that led from the front hallway entrance up to the second level. A camera was taped to the banister on the landing, focused on the stairway. Three of the bedrooms were located on the second level of the house. Names printed in ink on strips of masking tape and adhered to each door indicated the assigned rooms.

Cameron stepped forward and opened a door. "I'm taking this room," he declared, ripping off the masking tape stenciled with Luke's name.

"What's the matter?" Luke complained. "You need to be next to the bathroom in case of an emergency?"

"I don't want anyone telling me where I'll sleep," Cameron said handing the balled-up tape to Luke.

"You're not taking my room." Luke put his fists on his hips. "If Hamilton wanted us in specific rooms, he must have a reason." Luke did his best to unravel the gob of tape and haphazardly re-adhered it to the bedroom door.

"You gonna be a troublemaker for me?" Cameron asked.

"I just want things fair," Luke said, standing his ground.

"Why should you get the best room?" Cameron barked. "And why are Richard and Zeth up here, too?" Cameron turned to the camera. "I'm not spending six weeks in some servant's room, let me tell you!" he bellowed. "My space had better be as decent as Luke's."

Marco, not seeing his name on the door of one of the prime rooms, agreed. "Yeah."

"I'll have it out with Hamilton, when he gets here, I will!" Cameron said.

As the men investigated their new home, they kept a mental count of the cameras and microphones set up around the place. It seemed odd, at least to Richard, who'd had experience as a salesman at Radio Shack, that the equipment was so antiquated. With all the high-tech surveillance devices that could be rented at a relatively nominal cost, the cameras were no more than VHS units with tapes that had to be changed every two hours. "We're going to have guys in here all the time changing these cassettes. This is really amateurish. It's going to be a crappy six weeks," Richard declared.

"Maybe you won't have to stay, Richard." Hamilton had just arrived with the sixth member of the team. "Guys," Hamilton said, standing at the foot of the stairs, "this is Bull Smith."

Bull's discomfort was obvious. He was quaking in his shoes, even though the others perked up when they got a look at the six foot four inch stud whose broad-shouldered frame and fantasy-inducing good looks temporarily took their minds off any problems with the living accommodations.

"He's very shy, so do your best to make him feel like one of the boys," Hamilton suggested.

"One of the boys?" Bull said, offended.

"Not boys," Cameron said, walking down the steps and sidling up to Bull. "Just men here. Men who like being with men. Isn't it great, Bull? Nothing but sexy men!" He attempted to wrap an arm around Bull's shoulder but was pushed away.

"Shy or not, you'd best watch yourself with me," Cameron said, glaring at Bull. "I'll give you a break this time, but don't you ever push me again. Unless it's onto a bed."

As the words left Cameron's mouth, Bull leaped at him but was held back by Hamilton. Cameron grinned ravenously. "I think our rooms are probably close to each other," Cameron added. "If you need anything, feel free to make your inhospitable attitude up to me. Seems there aren't any locks on the doors, so just come on in. I'll be expecting you."

"I'm going to my room," Bull growled to Hamilton. "Where is it? And don't call me for dinner."

"Behind the kitchen," Hamilton replied. "Sorry. It's one of the maid's quarters."

"La-de-dah," Cameron said as Bull left the foyer in search of his bedroom. "He's bound to be as much fun as Dick Button dragging some poor skater's ass across the ice just because the kid missed a quad jump."

"Give him a chance," Hamilton said. "He hasn't been out as long as you guys have, so he's skeptical."

"What's his background?" Richard asked.

"You'll find out soon enough, I'm sure," Hamilton said. "Remember, you guys are here to explore each other and make this the greatest show since the original *Survivor!* Let's get started. Everybody find their rooms, wash up, and be back in the main parlor in half an hour. The games begin!"

Thirty minutes later, the group, minus Bull, had reassembled in the depressing parlor/dining room, which could be divided by a sliding pocket door. By now, the guys were used to the cameras and the crew moving about the house, replacing tapes in the various machines.

"It's almost dinnertime," Hamilton announced to simultaneous cheers from the hungry men. "However, this is more than dinner. It's the first of our games. Let's get those blindfolds on and off we go."

"Where to?" Luke asked.

"A restaurant," Hamilton said. "Not too fancy, but no diner either. Outside of Dulcit, of course."

The promise of food succeeded in coaxing Bull out of his room. He was starving but had decided a hunger strike was no way to get out of *Hunk House*. He was stuck for at least a week.

Each man donned his blindfold and was again taken to the van. The ride wasn't long; soon enough the van stopped and the doors opened. Leading each man out, Hamilton allowed him to remove his blindfold.

The restaurant was expecting them. A camera operator was already inside to capture their entrance. The maître d' smiled and ushered the men into an elegantly decorated side room. The table was set as though a party coordinator had made the arrangements for a state dinner. There were place cards indicating where each man was to be seated.

"Okay, gentlemen," Hamilton said after each had taken his assigned place at the table. "There are three parts to this game. First, the wine. You have a choice of two bottles. Study the labels carefully; although they appear identical, one is a fine French wine and the other is spiked with Ex-Lax. Choose the right one and you'll have a lovely meal. Select the other and you'll be up all night fighting to sit on the toilet. You may ask two questions before making your selection, but you'll only have ten minutes after your questions have been answered.

"Second, the menu. There's a 'secret special,' though it's not identified as such on the menu. But, the man who orders the 'secret special' will get a sumptuous grapefruit pistachio torte for dessert. If no one orders the 'secret special,' all of you will be served the same entrée: sweetbreads."

"What's that?" Luke asked.

Hamilton smiled. "In case you think it's a sticky bun or something glazed with honey, here's the scoop. It's the thymus gland of a calf."

Cameron blanched. "Say what?"

"It's lymphatic tissue," Hamilton continued. "It produces T-cells for the calf's immune system. Yum! Very tasty," Hamilton spoke with the kind of glee that made Vincent Price a star of horror films.

"And what's the third part of the game?" Cameron asked.

"When you get past the wine, and the dinner, it's simply a matter of table manners. Whoever is judged the most civilized at the table will score an extra ten points. Ah, here's our waiter Charles. I'll return soon."

Most of the men had never been in such a refined restaurant. They were used to waitresses—old ladies with blue paper mantillas—scratching out their lunch or dinner orders on a small pad and pouring coffee without being asked for a cup.

"I'll take some of *him*," Cameron quipped to Luke when Charles, dressed in traditional black pants and white shirt with black bow tie and vest, approached the table.

"Gentlemen, may I start you off with a bottle of wine?" Charles asked, placing two bottles on the table. "I'll leave you to decide which bottle you'd prefer I open."

The six men stared at the two bottles; they looked precisely the same. Cameron reached across the table and took one of the bottles. He examined the label. Then he picked up the other bottle and held it beside the first one looking for anything that distinguished it.

Both bottles appeared to contain red wine. The labels were black with a gold printing: *Chateau Fruiterie*. There was an etching of a vineyard on each, with a stone house in the background. On the back of the bottles, there was another label with an outline of France and several gold dots. The dots apparently indicated the area where the grapes for the wine were grown. Cameron read a warning about the content being 13 percent alcohol and that it should not be consumed if one was pregnant. "I can't see anything different," he said, passing the bottles to Marco.

Marco, the others learned, was a Coors man. He didn't know why some wine bottles had twist-off tops and some came in a handy box for $7.99, while others cost more than a week's paycheck. He, too, read the labels and didn't see anything unusual.

And so it went, each man taking his turn with the bottles and declaring that they were absolutely identical. Zeth said he thought there was something different about the concave bottoms and both had what felt like serial numbers imprinted in the glass. But the group decided that these were probably lot symbols to identify the vintage or some such thing.

When Bull reluctantly accepted the bottles from Richard, he immediately said, "You dolts. There is something different. Look at the outline of France and the number of gold dots on this bottle and the number on this one." He held up each bottle separately. The one in his left hand had three gold dots; the bottle in his right hand had six. "This is the only difference. Six dots. Six men," Bull said, placing the bottles back on the table. "You jerks decide what it means."

The men began discussing what questions they should ask Charles.

Zeth suggested, "How about asking him which one he'd prefer to drink?"

"Even if he told us, how do we know he'd be telling us the truth," Cameron complained.

Luke piped in. "Maybe we should ask him if he speaks French. There could be something else on the label, besides the number of dots on the map of France, that would give us more clues."

Charles returned to the table. "Are you ready, gentlemen, or do you have any questions?"

"Do you speak French?" Cameron asked.

"Oui, Monsieur."

"Translate this label for us." Cameron said with a trace of irritation in his voice.

"*Oui*. Er, yes. Chateau Fruiterie means, House of Fruits. Rather apropos," he said, rolling his eyes. "Bordeaux is the region in which the wine was produced. And the year is obviously in Arabic numerals, as is the alcoholic content, and the surgeon general's warning is in English. I presume none of you are nursing."

"Your tip is decreasing by the second," Cameron snarled.

"Well, that was dumb," Marco complained. "Except for the name of the wine, we didn't learn anything new."

"So why does one bottle have three gold dots on the map and the other has six?" Luke asked the waiter.

"Very good question, sir. I believe one label is meant to confuse."

"So which bottle would you choose?" Richard asked Charles.

"I apologize, gentlemen, I'm only permitted to answer two questions."

"How would you like your rectal temperature taken with one of these bottles, Charles," Cameron threatened. "Would wine spoil at ninety-eight point six degrees?"

The waiter smiled. "I'm sure that would be excellent, sir. Now, I'm told you only have a few moments to make a decision. Shall I take my leave or do you wish to place your order?"

"Give us until the deadline," Cameron snapped.

"Very good, sir," Charles said, placing the forbidding bottles back on the white tablecloth.

"What the fuck are we going to do?" Marco said, looking at the uncertain faces around him. "I say we take a vote. We have a fifty/fifty chance of being right."

"And of being wrong," Luke said.

Cameron and the others glared at the two bottles as if they were hot wires to a bomb, and they had to select which one to cut to prevent detonation. Of sorts.

Finally, Cameron picked up one bottle, then the other. He held them up to the group and asked, "Who votes for the one in my right hand that has three gold dots?" The others all looked at each other, but no one offered a pick. "Who votes for the one in my left hand that has six gold dots?" Cameron asked. Still no one stirred.

Bull spoke up. "For what it's worth, and I don't give a fuck if you're wrong or right, it seems logical that the six gold dots are significant. Six dots. Six men. Of course I don't really know what it means."

"Then mind your own business," Cameron snapped. "Besides, you wouldn't know a Merlot from a Cabernet."

Charles returned to the table. "I'm ready to open your bottle, gentlemen," he said in an officious tone.

There was a long moment of silence. Then Cameron said, "Out goes Y-O-U," and handed a bottle to Charles.

"Very wise choice," the waiter said, complimenting Cameron as he began removing the foil covering the top of the bottle. But before he plunged his corkscrew into the stopper, Luke called out, "Wait! How many gold dots are on the map of France?"

Charles turned the bottle around. "Three, sir."

Luke looked to the others. "The rest of us didn't get any say about which bottle you open. Cameron just took over."

"Someone has to be a leader," Cameron said. "I don't see any of you exhibiting survival instincts."

"Are you changing your mind, sir?" Charles asked.

Luke was silent. Then, slowly, he raised his hand. "I vote for the other bottle."

Zeth tentatively said, "I vote for the one with six dots on the map."

Marco was silent for a long moment.

"And you, sir?" Charles asked him.

"Six dots," Marco said.

Richard looked hard at Bull, then to Cameron who was fuming. "The most dots wins," he said.

"One more vote?" Charles asked, looking at Bull.

"Abstain."

Charles tallied the score. "One vote for the bottle with three gold dots. Four votes for the bottle with six gold dots. One abstention. I will open the other bottle."

He then removed the foil from the second bottle and withdrew the cork. He took a white napkin and cleaned the area round the top. He poured a small amount into Luke's glass.

"Is that all I get?" Luke asked.

Charles seemed amused. He gave a wan patronizing smile and instructed that this was simply for him to taste. "You may let me know if this is acceptable to you, Jethro."

It dawned on Luke that he'd seen a movie where some waiter offered a small sample of wine for Sean Connery to taste. With this in mind, Luke swished the red liquid around the glass, held it up to his nose, and inhaled the aroma, just as Sean had done.

"So far, so good?" Zeth asked.

Luke brought the rim of the glass to his lips and tilted it back ever so slightly, allowing the tiniest amount to pass his lips. He then made a face that sent the entire table into a panic.

"Sorry," Luke said, "I've never had any wine before." He took a larger sip and made a smacking sound with his lips and tongue the way he'd seen Niles Crane do on television. Luke's poker face gave nothing away. He paused for a moment to consider what he'd just ingested and took another, larger sip. "I don't know nothin' 'bout wine, but this tastes good to me."

Sighs of relief bounced around the table. As Charles poured six glasses, Luke received pats on the back from everyone but Cameron and Bull, both of whom sat stone-faced regarding the others with contempt.

"I think we just passed the first test," Luke said. When all the men had been served he said, "I'd like to propose a toast. To Bull! His noticing the different number of dots saved our asses."

"Literally," said Richard.

The other men, with the exception of Cameron, raised their glasses and ad-libbed "Hear! Hear!"

At that moment, Hamilton reentered the room and presented himself at the table. "Bravo, guys!" he enthused. "You did it. You noticed there was a difference in the bottles and you used your powers of analysis to determine there were six dots and six men and six glasses of wine in the bottle. Enjoy the wine. Charles'll bring you another bottle—no tricks this time, I promise. Now it's time to open your menus. But remember there's that secret special. Someone has to order it, or you'll all be served sweetbreads. You have ten minutes to review the menu before Charles returns. Good luck."

Hamilton disappeared, while the cameraman changed a videocassette tape.

The menu wasn't extensive. After the listing of appetizers, salads, and soups, there were no more than four selections under each entrée of fish, chicken, and beef. The descriptions, written in italics under the name of the item, made each entrée sound like the most delicious food imaginable.

The men took their time making their decisions, asking others—except Cameron—if they'd ever had sole fillets with onions, mushrooms, and white wine; chilled watercress soup with leeks and crème fraîche; or spring lambe dabue with champagne and fava beans; or black pepper blini with smoked salmon and dill cream.

Presently, Charles returned to the table. "Are we all set, gentlemen?" he asked. "Who would like to begin?" he looked at Cameron with a slight smile that said, *I double-dare you to choose the secret special.*

"Okay," Cameron said with a sneer, "I'll start with green lentil and bacon salad. Then the Chicken Tagine with Olives and Lemon."

"*Tajine de poulet aux lives et au citron,*" Charles said.

"I told you to speakee de Ingee," Cameron challenged.

"Very well, sir."

"Aren't you going to write down what I ordered?" Cameron asked.

"I'm fully prepared to take your orders without need for writing them down, sir," Charles said. "I have an excellent memory. Now, how would you like that cooked?"

Charles went around the table accepting each man's order and repeating, "Very good choice, sir," and taking his menu before progressing to the next man. When he got to Bull, who had been brooding with his arms folded across his chest ever since arriving at the restaurant, the waiter asked, "And our hero?"

Bull was silent.

"I would be delighted to take your order, sir," Charles said.

"Beef. Just scare it with the fire."

"Very good, sir," Charles said. "Rare." He walked away.

"And another bottle of wine," Cameron called as Charles left for the kitchen. "Hell, it's free, we may as well indulge ourselves. And save room for lots of dessert. The show's buying. Let's take advantage.

"What's your problem, Bull?" Cameron demanded. "Shall we play Twenty Questions?"

"Hamilton advised us to make friends if we don't want to get booted off the show," Luke said.

"Take his advice or don't," Cameron said. "The sooner they start eliminating people, the better the chances for me and one or two others who may have a chance."

"At this point, we're all equal," Zeth added, "so don't go projecting who's capable of staying the full six weeks. You can't count anybody out yet."

Luke and Zeth had begun trading eye contact the moment they were seated opposite each other. Luke opened their conversation. "So, Zeth, why'd you apply to do this program?"

"I'm from a real small town," Zeth said apologetically. "Clement Flats, over by Statlerville. I want to get to California and make myself a star, just like Dolly Parton did. I'm going to write songs like her and be in movies. How 'bout you?"

"Orion," Luke said. "I'm goin' to L.A., too. I'm hopin' to be an actor, and I need to win the grand prize to make it to stardom. I wish you luck, but I wish myself better luck."

"Fair enough," Zeth said, still staring into Luke's eyes and silently transmitting how much he'd like to be naked next to him.

Eventually, the others all gave similar testimony for being on *Hunk House*. All except Bull who refused to answer any questions.

"Speaking of making friends, guys," Cameron said, looking from one to the other, "I want you to know I'm here for you. Most of you are younger than I am, so I'll leave my door open twenty-four hours a day, in case you need me—for anything."

Bull said, "I'm not here to be your friend. That goes for all of you!"

"The invitation still stands," Cameron continued. "That house might get awfully scary at night. You might need to take your minds off the ghosts."

"We're not supposed to be caught in bed with anyone," Luke said.

"You really are naive, aren't you," Cameron retorted. "Of course they want us to sleep together. I'll bet those so-called rules were made specifically so we'd break 'em! Nobody'll watch some boring program about guys just sitting around and talking and doing a few stupid human tricks. They want to see how long you can hold off getting fucked, and how it fucks you up to try to abstain. They want our dicks on camera whenever possible. I guarantee it. All that stuff that Stacia said about the FCC is baloney. Look at that *Queer as Folk* show. The FCC didn't do squat to interfere with all the stuff that went on there. Our show's hardly any different."

Richard added, "Plus, anything that's too explicit they can edit. But they've gotta have a hook for the show. And it's not just to see how many gay guys it takes to change a lightbulb or who can recite all the lyrics to 'YMCA'!"

"You queers better do exactly as Stacia said," Bull spoke up. "Otherwise she and Hamilton'll haul your fairy asses outta here before the end of the first week."

Luke settled his eyes on Cameron. "Maybe Bull's right. Maybe you and Richard are just tryin' to get us sacked so you'll end up the winners."

As Cameron began to defend himself, a team of five waiters, including Charles, arrived at the table with trays piled with plates that were covered with silver domes.

Cameron said, "Great! I'm starving!" Charles personally placed a covered plate in front of him.

"Ready?" Charles asked the other waiters. "One, two, three!"

With a synchronized flourish each waiter lifted the lids high over the heads of the diners. The wide smiles that greeted the arrival of their food faded when they saw that each plate held identical meals. Sweetbreads.

"*Bon appétit!*" Charles called, looking directly at Cameron, then leading his wait staff back to the kitchen.

"Mmmmm. Looks tasty. Like chicken," Hamilton said, appearing in the doorway. "No secret special was ordered. So here's your reward. I had bites in the kitchen. Just don't think about what it is you're eating, and it'll go down without much nausea. Also, I guarantee it's better than what those island and Outback survivors had to eat. No maggots or rats on these plates, I assure you. This is *haute cuisine.*"

"It'll be fun to watch these sissies eatin' a *thymus* gland!" Bull chuckled.

The men pushed the breaded, fried meat around on their plates and tentatively sliced small portions with their steak knives. They took tiny bites. Luke declared his food was actually edible. "Like squirrel meat," he said. The others followed and were soon swallowing chunks whole, chased with large gulps of wine.

A half hour later, the men finally sat back and waited for Hamilton to reappear with a tally of who employed the best table manners. "I've been watching you all very carefully, from a hidden spot," Hamilton said. "First of all, I commend you all—especially Bull and Luke—for choosing the correct wine. That's twenty-five points for all of you. As for the sweetbreads, I'm glad you liked them. But if one of you had ordered the vegetarian cassoulet, you would have had whatever you fancied from the menu, and an additional fifty points."

"The menu wasn't clear," Cameron protested. "I didn't know what a Cass Elliott or whatever you called it was. That's not fair."

"Be a sport," Hamilton said in a cheery voice. "But I have to subtract fifty points from each of you. So you're all in the hole, so to speak. Still, you can make up for it during the etiquette phase."

Hamilton took out a clipboard and began to go down the list of names. "Starting with Bull, because you used your sleeve instead of your napkin, I'm withdrawing twenty-five points."

Bull grunted.

"Cameron, you pushed your peas onto your fork with your fingers! Ugh! That'll cost you five points for each time. I'm only putting you down for two because that's all I actually saw. Although when I see the tape, you may lose more. For now your score is negative thirty-five.

"Luke. Never, ever gargle with wine or anything else at the dinner table. I don't care how much it tickles your tonsils. Ten points off your score. And, another five points off for holding your fork in your fist. Watch how Zeth holds his utensils. You're now thirty-five in the hole, too.

"Marco, except for sculpting your mashed potatoes into the shape of a penis and arranging your peas to spell C-h-a-r-l-e-s, I don't think you made any faux pas. Still, that's unacceptable behavior in a restaurant. Ten points off.

"Richard. I don't think you made a single mistake. But I'm not adding any points either, because it was inappropriate to give Charles that note suggesting you meet in the men's room stall. As Stacia said, 'We're not here to play with our dicks.'"

"I didn't want to play with my dick," Richard countered. "I wanted to play with *his* dick."

Hamilton pursed his lips. "Zeth, you too were pretty spot on. But, my friend, dropping your food accidentally on purpose to avoid eating it is no way to behave. That waiter who slipped on your sweetbread may be in traction now for all I know. Twenty-five points taken away. You're minus fifty. Now, do you dare risk coffee and dessert? Could earn you more points . . . or subtract some?"

Chapter Seven

Lights out was ten o'clock each night. It was nearly that time when the men returned from their restaurant outing and the first small game in the larger contest. Individual toiletry kits had been provided by Kmart in return for product placement, such as store-brand bottles of mouth-wash and toothpaste, all of which would be caught on tape when the men performed their ablutions. They took turns in their assigned cramped bathrooms, then went to their respective rooms.

Luke stripped naked and pulled down the covers of the large sleigh bed that occupied his room. The house was hot. The windows were old, and he couldn't open them. He flopped on top of the sheets.

With the ubiquitous red light of the videocamera shining above the bedroom door, Luke lay awake in the otherwise pitch-blackness with the sensation that the entire house had settled into some eerie state of sedation. It had been an exhausting, exciting day, but Luke wasn't tired. At least he didn't feel as though he could fall asleep anytime soon. Too many thoughts ran through his head, including pangs of homesickness. He'd never been away from home for as much as a sleepover with friends. He tried to comfort himself with thoughts of Zeth, the man he found most attractive among the group. As he felt himself grow hard, he fantasized that Zeth was outside in the hallway with his hand on the doorknob, ready to enter the room, and climb into bed with him.

Luke was deeply engrossed in his fantasy when he heard a sound, a sort of click. At least he thought he heard something. *But these old houses are always making odd noises*, he told himself, so he stayed alert for a moment then got back to his fantasy. He imagined Zeth's warm strong body next to his, until his sexy scenario was interrupted again by another sound in the room. He opened his eyes to the darkness and immediately noticed that the red light of the camera had gone out. Luke relaxed, thinking the tape must have run out and that someone would come soon to replace the cassette.

For a moment, he thought about getting up to rewind the tape, when suddenly, from out of the abyss of blackness, he felt a hand gingerly take him by the cock. He made an involuntary gasp and the hand suddenly disappeared.

Luke wasn't afraid. Lying on his back, he waited. The hand returned. This time Luke welcomed the visitor, who climbed up on the bed and pressed his naked body on top of Luke's. The stranger placed his mouth over Luke's, and the two began kissing passionately but quietly, neither wanting to wake the others in the house or have their sounds picked up by microphones.

"We can't be doing this," Luke whispered breathlessly.

The stranger's lips left Luke's and made their way down his chest and hard stomach, finding his stiff shaft pulsating to the double-time beat of his heart. A tongue glazed Luke's long penis then swathed its head. Lips parted and swallowed as much of his eight-and-a-half inches as possible. With a slow assured rhythm, the phantom's lips and tongue continued to slither up and down Luke's rod until he moaned. The lips continued their deft movement until suddenly Luke's cock assumed its own thrusting rhythm, forcing itself deep into the hot moist chamber. Finally, with gritted teeth and uncontrollable heavy breathing, Luke discharged his hot load. There came a choking sound followed by a lustful suckling, until Luke was completely emptied of his semen.

Then a voice that Luke didn't recognize whispered, "Can I get off on you?"

"Yeah," was all that Luke could say as he lay spent of energy. As long as he didn't have to do any work, he didn't care what this unknown man did to please himself.

Straddled by muscular legs, he felt the man begin to masturbate.

Luke raised his hands to the man's chest, which was hairy and obviously pumped through years of lifting weights. He found the man's large nipples, and squeezed them hard between his thumb and index finger, then roughly flicked at them.

"Oh, yeah," the man groaned and within a short while his breathing came in short bursts. Then Luke felt the splash of the guy's semen on his chest. It was a big load. Luke decided it could only have come from someone around his own age.

The man relaxed a bit, then massaged his discharge into Luke's chest. He scooped a bit of jizz onto two fingers and brought them to Luke's lips. Luke opened his mouth and tasted the warm cream, which smelled faintly of ammonia. He moaned with satisfaction, and the man spooned another two fingers' worth onto Luke's outstretched tongue.

"Who are you?" Luke asked.

"Shh," the man commanded. Once more he put Luke's cock into his mouth. "You tasted so good," he whispered.

"So did you," Luke said as quietly as possible.

"Go to sleep."

"But . . ."

And with that, the man got up from the bed. Suddenly the red light of the camera came on an instant before Luke heard the door creak open and closed. Although he was still hot and sweating, he pulled the top sheet to his waist to avoid the camera's all-seeing eye. Soon he drifted to sleep.

Morning arrived, not with an alarm ringing but with a knock on Luke's door. A voice insisted it was time to "rise and shine," and that breakfast would not wait.

Luke, still groggy, remembered the episode from last night. But was it real, or a dream? He touched his chest and found the remains of dried semen and realized it hadn't been a dream after all. Soon he'd face the other five men and find out with whom he'd broken the number one rule about no sex.

Luke put on his only change of clothes: jeans and boots and carried his shirt to the bathroom. He looked admiringly at himself in the mirror before spotting another camera. He turned on the water tap at the sink and splashed cold water on his face, and then finger-combed his hair. He took a pee, disregarding the camera's little red light. After washing his hands and using a small wet towel to clean off what remained of the petrified sperm on his chest and sternum, he put on his flannel shirt but didn't bother buttoning it before walking down the stairs to the kitchen.

He arrived in the kitchen to find the other men assembled at the large, round oak table. "Richard's made coffee," Cameron said, welcoming Luke, "and Marco's toasted bagels."

Luke looked at Cameron, wondering if he was the spectral lover from the night before. Cameron seemed a logical choice, since he'd made no bones about taking advantage of available sex regardless of the rules. Luke looked to Zeth and said, "Morning. How'd you sleep?"

"Probably 'bout as well as you," Zeth responded ambiguously. "And the others. We were all pretty worn out from the first day."

Marco came by with a bagel. He put his hand on Luke's shoulder as he set the plate down in front of him, then walked away. Luke wondered if it was some kind of acknowledgment of their having been lovers just a few hours before.

"Coffee?" Richard asked, pouring a cup before Luke had an opportunity to respond. "Butter and cream cheese?" he added, pushing two tubs toward Luke. This behavior didn't seem at all like the sullen Richard from the day before.

Luke had been suspicious of everyone before he came to the kitchen and now each man gave off signals that he could easily misconstrue. They all appeared to be extra nice to him this morning. If it had only been one man who went out of his way to make Luke feel good, he might have a better grasp of who his visitor had been. But they were all nice, as men often were to him. But no one gave himself away.

After accepting a second cup of coffee from Cameron, Luke asked, "Anyone seen Bull?"

"Probably still in the sack, afraid to come out. I heard him moving furniture against his door last night." Cameron laughed. "That stud's got major problems, if you ask me." Then, in a whisper, he added, "If I didn't know better, I'd say he was either a walk-in closet case or, *gasp*, straight!"

"He's too good-looking to be straight," Richard said.

"Can't make generalizations about straights," Luke advised. "There's a few who are good-lookin' enough to be queer."

Marco agreed. "My gaydar's on the fritz. I've had my eye on him from the beginning. He's checking us out, too, and I'm not sure he's totally queer. But I'll wager he's not completely hetero either. Let's just say I know his type. Under the right circumstances, he can be had. Anyone here interested?"

"I wouldn't say especially so," Cameron acknowledged, "but his type is hard not to want to get fucked by. He could be dangerous. Which is part of the fun."

"Speaking of dangerous," Luke interrupted, "did anyone hear anything during the night?"

"What do you mean?" Cameron asked. "Creaking doors? Disembodied voices? Chains rattling in the basement?"

Luke noticed that except for Zeth, the others laughed at Cameron's joke. "I tend to talk in my sleep," Luke said. "I had a dream. Could have maybe woke someone up."

The door opened, and Hamilton came strutting in. "Morning, men!" he exclaimed. "Everyone sleep like babes?"

"The pillows were too soft," Cameron complained.

"The pillows were too hard," Richard added.

"The temperature in the room was way too warm and the windows wouldn't open," Luke said.

"Ten o'clock's way too early to go to bed," Cameron complained.

"We'll see about those pillows and the stuffy rooms," Hamilton promised. "Are you ready for another fun day of games? Where's Bull?"

"Games, yes," Cameron said. "Bull, who knows or cares. He's the most aloof queer boy I've ever known."

At that moment, Bull walked into the kitchen.

"I heard that, you pissant. I'm proud I'm not like you perverts!"

"That's the spirit," Hamilton interjected before Bull or anyone else had an opportunity to say something that could blow his cover. "We should all be celebrated for our individuality. Our diversity. I feel exactly the same way, Bull. Here, have some coffee."

Bull reluctantly accepted the coffee as he leaned against the molding of the door frame. His body language made it clear he didn't want to sit at the table with the others.

"Have a bagel," Marco said, offering him a plate. It was only Bull's hunger that made him accept the toasted breakfast, although he ate both slices without so much as a dollop of cream cheese. Hamilton refilled Bull's coffee mug, then began to outline the day's activities.

"Today is 'Find the Lost Puppy Day,'" Hamilton announced. "It's a contest that will show audiences your humanitarian side. Two teams of three men each will hit the Animal Rescue League shelter looking through a maze of cages for a specific dog. If the canine is found within two hours there's one hundred points for each member of the team."

"What if the dog's not found?" Bull asked.

"Then you won't win any points," said Hamilton.

*   *   *

It was raining when the men arrived at the outdoor shelter. The teams were quickly assembled. Bull, Luke, and Zeth were on one, and Cameron, Marco, and Richard were on the other.

They began their search with only a color photocopy of a cute German shepherd dog with a red collar. The dog's name, according to Hamilton, was Schultz.

"Here, poochy, poochy," Bull called, searching among the packs of dogs.

The smell of wet dog was pervasive, but all were determined to find the right canine. There were dozens of German shepherds, but none matched the description. Finally, their time was up.

The woman in charge of the shelter was especially distraught and chased them away as if they had all peed on her wall-to-wall carpet.

"Jeeze, you'd think we killed the dog!" Zeth said of the woman's behavior as they began their ride home.

"Maybe we did," Hamilton admitted. "I promised her we'd find this dog. The deal was that we could film two hours at the shelter. If we didn't find him, he would be euthanized along with all the other unclaimed dogs. To make matters worse, it was a Seeing Eye dog in training that belonged to a little boy who was heartsick at the loss of his friend."

"Oh, Christ," Bull moaned. "How could you not tell us ahead of time. We would have made a better effort."

"Maybe he was already found and returned to the kid," Hamilton said.

"Maybe he was already dead and we were searching for a dog that was in a heap of ashes," Richard added.

The men were dejected by their failure. No one spoke for the rest of the ride back to the house. After only one day, the place was already beginning to feel like one of the cages they'd just left.

"So far nobody has any positive points," Cameron said as he took off his jacket and threw it on the sofa in the living room. "What the hell kind of game is this?"

Groans of agreement came from everyone, except for Bull who had immediately gone to his room and closed the door. He was remarkably upset by the events of the day.

"What's tomorrow's game going to be?" Cameron continued. "Stick your dick in an outlet and see how many volts you can conduct before your balls explode?"

However, the next day was more fun. Each man was given a dose of Viagra that Ella had procured from Old Man Ratner's medicine cabinet. One at a time, they were taken into the basement, instructed to strip down to an extra-long, white T-shirt, and then doused with water. Hamilton took Polaroids of each man from below the waist up to the neck. All that could be seen in the photos was each man's obvious endowments through his diaphanous wet T-shirt.

When the men dried off, each overwhelmingly horny, they assembled for a game of "Tom or Harry Dick?" Individually, the men were taken to the parlor, which had been turned into a study, and allowed to examine the six color photographs. The object was to connect the cock with the man. For each correct answer, the prize was sixteen points. Any man who matched all the others would get a bonus of four points, for a total of one hundred.

It was no effort for each man to quickly identify himself. But no one figured all the others correctly. Although Bull, who had been coerced into the game with the promise of a beer if he won, came the closest, matching four men, including himself, Cameron, Marco, and Luke.

Bull didn't fare so well during the next day's game: "Old Movie Stars." The object was to guess the name of a celebrity based on a famous line of dialogue, or a clue connecting the person to whom they were once married, or which studio they were under contract to, or how they died, or what famous scandal was associated with them.

For this game, Hamilton chose to play music on a boom box that sounded as frenetic as that used on *Who Wants to Be a Millionaire*, or *The Weakest Link*. Hamilton acted as facilitator. It was basically a game of twenty questions. There were four rounds, and each correct answer garnered twenty-five points for the player.

Marco was the first in the hot seat.

"She starred as Gilda," Hamilton said.

"Pul-eeze! Rita Hayward! Jeeze!"

"Wrong!"

"It was Rita Hay*worth*, you dumb ass," Cameron said.

Marco fumed. "Fuck! I meant Hayworth. I love Rita Hayworth! You gotta give that to me because I knew it! *Cover Girl! Gilda!*"

"Sorry," Hamilton said. "Wrong first answer." Richard was next. "She's Joan Fontaine's sister," Hamilton said.

"Ah, I know this one! She was in *Gone With the Wind*. She was one of the sisters. Scarlett hated her because she married Ashley. Ooo! Ooo! Um. Melanie . . . no I mean, Olive. Ah, Olivia. Olivia De Haviland! Yea! Yea! Olivia De Haviland!"

"Yes," Hamilton cried. "Twenty-five points. Okay, Doris Day's first movie." The question was posed to Zeth.

"I happen to be Doris's biggest fan," Zeth said.

"Que Sera Sera," Cameron deadpanned.

"It was *Romance on the High Seas!* Warner Bros. Nineteen forty-eight. Directed by Michael Curtiz."

"Twenty-five points!" Hamilton enthused.

"Smart-ass!" Cameron said. "How can you younger queers know anything about Doris Day?"

Zeth batted his eyelashes. "Want me to sing a chorus of 'On Moonlight Bay,' or 'Love Me or Leave Me,' or 'Sentimental Journey'?"

"Not unless Stevie Wonder accompanies you. She's into dark meat, you know," Cameron teased.

Hamilton continued. "Rumor had it that when this actress died they'd discover she was really a man."

"That'd be Bea Arthur," Cameron said joking. "Or maybe Elaine Stritch."

"Wrong!"

"I'm kidding. Everybody knows the correct answer is Mae West," Cameron said.

Hamilton paused for dramatic effect. "You gave an incorrect answer. Two incorrect answers as a matter of fact."

"But you didn't ask if it was my final answer!"

"No points," ruled Hamilton.

Bull felt like a complete idiot. He couldn't have correctly answered any of those questions, yet the other men seemed to know the drill as easily as reciting their ABCs. He didn't want to score any points, but he didn't want to make a fool of himself either. From what he'd observed so far none of the answers were Reggie Jackson or Pete Sampras, so there was every probability that he really wouldn't know any of the answers.

Looking around and regarding each of the other men, including

Hamilton, Bull reluctantly acknowledged a small amount of admiration for them. *These guys may be queer, but they're kinda smart*, he said to himself. *Come to think of it, most of the gay guys I've ever run across seem smarter than most other guys. They know things about the world and what goes on outside of Dulcit. I've actually learned some good stuff during the past few days. And now I know some movie trivia. But they must think I'm as thick as a brick.*

Bull was the last contestant. "Who won the *first* Best Actress Academy Award?"

"May as well say Marilyn Monroe, 'cause you know I ain't got a clue! She's the only dead old star I know."

"Wrong!" announced Hamilton.

Round two of the game began. When the other contestants had had their turns, it was back to Bull. "This star's real name was Lucille LeSuer," Hamilton said.

"The Green Giant. Who the fuck knows?"

"Joan Crawford," Hamilton said.

The rounds continued. When it was again Bull's turn, Hamilton asked, "Randolph Scott and Cary Grant were more than just room-mates. They were . . ."

Cameron interrupted, "Here's a hint. They were switch-hitters."

Bull looked puzzled. "Yankees? Dodgers?"

Cameron snorted. "They didn't play baseball, you twit!"

"No hints," Hamilton instructed.

"I formally petition to take away Bull's pink card," Marco added.

Hamilton made the sound of a buzzer to indicate that Bull had failed again.

"Fuck buddies, you imbecile," Cameron sneered.

Finally, when it came to his fourth and final round of questions, Hamilton asked Bull, "Name the star who had eight husbands, is always sick, and sells perfume."

Bull thought hard. The other men made impatient, heavy sighs.

"Ya *gotta* know this one!" Cameron erupted.

"Okay. I'm gonna make a guess."

"No clues," Hamilton reminded.

"Did she used to be fat and now she's fat again?"

"Can't help you."

"Okay. This is just a guess, but I think . . . I think it was Elizabeth

Mont . . . No. Wait. I think it was Elizabeth . . . Ard . . . No. Wait. It was, she was married to one of her husbands twice . . ."

"Yes!" Marco said enthusiastically.

"Hush!" Hamilton warned. "He's got to get this on his own."

"Jeez, Louise," Bull muttered. "I'm just gonna come out and say, Elizabeth Tay . . . No. Wait. Yeah, okay, I'm gonna say, Tay, um Liz, um, Liz Taylor?"

The room erupted into a standing ovation. Bull smiled with genuine satisfaction.

Bull had actually answered a movie star question that didn't have Sylvester Stallone, Arnold Schwarzenegger, or Jean-Claude Van Damme in the answer! Mostly, he felt more confidence with the men and with himself. Except for his antagonistic relationship with Cameron, he felt camaraderie with the other men.

Three more days of inane games came and went, until Hamilton called for a contest in which each of the men had to write and present a commercial—specifically a public service announcement about practicing safe sex. As an act of generosity, Hamilton gave each man one hundred points, partly because he was sure the program would air the makeshift spots and perhaps win a Humanitas Award for its contribution to education about safe sex. The men were especially pleased with Bull's naive but sensitive public service announcement.

"Sex is fun. Sex is great. But if you're smart, you'll masturbate." Bull announced in a singsong voice, as if he were making a guest appearance on *Sesame Street*.

Finally, on Friday, the men were seated in the main parlor and told to write down something personal about themselves that they'd never told another human being. It could be something of which they were proud or ashamed. They could reveal any skeleton in their closet, but it had to be the truth.

The papers were then collected, and one by one after Hamilton read the revelations, the others had to guess to whom the secret belonged. Whoever correctly matched the man with the secret received twenty-five points.

Hamilton reached into the bowl and withdrew the first piece of paper. He slowly read the scrawled confession. "'I once seduced my English

teacher in order to pass his class.' Good one. Now whose sworn statement is this?"

After each man made a guess, Marco correctly identified Luke.

"He was after my ass anyway. I didn't have to do anything but let
him have a mouthful," Luke said matter-of-factly.

Hamilton read the next revelation. "'I once sucked off Anthony
Quinn.'"

Within seconds Cameron guessed it was Marco. "How'd you come
up with Marco?" Hamilton asked.

Cameron shrugged. "He let it slip the other day that he'd never met a
man who didn't like to get his dick sucked. Plus Quinn was in Iowa
doing a made-for-TV movie just before he croaked. Marco sucks a lot of
dick, although I can't imagine ever touching Anthony Quinn's!"

"It was more effort than it was worth," Marco agreed.

Hamilton read another slip of paper. "'My doctor says I have the
largest balls he's ever seen.'"

"I know!" Richard called. "It's me!"

"Judging by the Polaroids I took the other day, I'd say that was wish-
ful thinking, Richard," Hamilton chuckled.

"It's Bull," Luke, Zeth, Marco, and Cameron said simultaneously.

"Sure. Why else would he have that nickname," Richard agreed.

"What's your answer, Bull?" Hamilton asked. By now, after nearly a
week in the presence of the other men, Bull was beginning to interact in
the games and, still a sullen and reclusive guy, he at least would speak
when addressed directly.

Bull turned red. But as the other men made him the center of their attention and started joking about his testicles, he fessed up. "They're way
too big," he said simply.

"Never *too* big, Bull," Richard said.

"I think we deserve some proof," Cameron said.

Bull shook his head. "You'll just have to trust me."

Luke desperately tried to remember if his phantom lover had extra
large balls. He was certain the guy was well hung, but he hadn't explored the adjoining parts of the man's anatomy. He'd have to study on
it, he decided.

Chapter Eight

On Saturday night, the end of the first week arrived. It was time to tally the scores and have each of the men vote on who would stay and who would leave *Hunk House*.

Hamilton spent the day scoring the contestants, while the men pondered who would stay and who would leave.

Dinner was brought in from the Eat 'n' Run Diner and the men were allowed one beer apiece. By the time they completed their blue-plate specials and downed their Pabst Blue Ribbon, it was time for what Hamilton called the Out House segment of the program.

With cameras rolling, Hamilton gathered the men into the main parlor. He had a CD of the soundtrack from *The Mission* playing on his boom box. He called for a "group hug."

"Okay, men," Hamilton said in a solemn tone, after everyone had taken a seat. "You've all been through quite a lot this week. You've made some new friends, and maybe some enemies. Now's the time to take the black marker and white cardboard beside each of your seats and write the name of one man. I trust you've thought about this carefully. Write the name on the cardboard and place it facedown in your lap until I call on you. Ready? Go."

The men were seated far enough apart, so no one could see what the others were writing. Cameron crouched behind a potted ficus. Marco was in a corner, sitting on the piano bench. Richard sat on a wing-back chair near the fireplace. Zeth sat on the floor near the mahogany fireplace. Luke sat on the first step of the hall stairway. Bull hunkered behind the sofa.

As soon as the men finished, they gathered around Hamilton who stood before the large stained-glass window. He read off each man's compulsory game score. He explained that the man who was voted out would lose another 50 percent, and that man would be the first casualty of *Hunk House*. However, he added, even if the other men cast a majority vote, if the unlucky contestant's total game score, including the 50 percent subjective vote, made his score higher than someone else's, the next lowest score would be the man who was out.

"Okay, gentlemen," Hamilton said, "as I call your name, please hold up your card to the camera and to your fellow players and speak his name clearly. Cameron, you start."

Cameron held up his card and said, "Bull."

An audible sigh of relief could be heard from Bull.

"Marco?"

Marco's card said "Cameron," and he announced the name aloud.

"Richard?"

Richard raised his card. It read "Bull."

"Yes!" Bull ejaculated.

"Zeth?" Hamilton said.

Once again, Cameron's name was displayed on a card. Zeth announced it with glee.

"Luke?" Hamilton called.

The card that Luke held up read "Cameron."

"And Bull," Hamilton said gravely.

Bull's card read, "Bull."

Cameron cried, "You can't vote for yourself!"

Bull yelled back, "It don't say anywhere that you can't vote for yourself. There's no rule against it. Politicians vote for themselves all the time."

"They're voting to get themselves *in* to an office, not *out*, you idiot," Cameron berated.

"He's right, Bull," Hamilton said. "You've got to vote for someone other than yourself. I'll give you thirty seconds to write down another name."

"Fine!" Bull said, scratching out his name and making a great show of being insanely upset. He immediately wrote down a new name, put down his marker, and insolently picked up the card holding it out at arm's length. "Cameron!" he shouted. "You wanted another name. Here it is: yours!"

"I'm out?" Cameron roared in disbelief. "You assholes outed me? I hate you! I've hated all of you from the start! You're nothing but a bunch of loser faggots!"

"Hold on guys," Hamilton said, raising a hand. "This is like the 2000 presidential election. Cameron's got the popular vote to be outed, but he's racked up enough points from the other games. He's not out. I'm afraid it's Richard who has the least amount of points. Even Bull has one positive point more."

"How can this be?" Bull raged.

Hamilton shrugged. "Must have been your success at the restaurant, or the Tom or Harry Dick game."

Bull said to Richard, "It should have been me. I even *wanted* to go. I'd trade places with you if I could."

Richard put his arms around Bull and hugged him. Bull froze, not knowing what to do with his hands. However, at the last moment before Richard pulled away, Bull patted him on the back.

"All right men," Hamilton said, "blindfold Richard." He handed a black cloth to Cameron who, together with the others, made a ceremony out of placing the band around Richard's head, covering his eyes.

On his way out, Richard said, "I just want to say that at least I got a good fuck out of this. Whichever of you guys came into my bed last night, please get in touch when this is all over. We were awesome together and I'd like to know who you are."

Luke blanched. Someone else had been visited by the phantom?

Hamilton was equally taken aback.

"Take Richard to the front door," he said. "The driver will return you to KRUQ. Thank you for being with us, Richard. We wish you well in all your future endeavors."

"I loved your dick, whoever you are," Richard said as he left.

The camera continued to tape as the remaining members of *Hunk House* gathered for what Hamilton referred to as "their weekly closure." This was to be a time when the contestants discussed the man they "outed" and gave candid reasons for dismissing him.

"Richard was a threat to the rest of us," Cameron said with a self-satisfied smile. "He even had sex with one of you."

"How do we know it wasn't you?" Luke asked.

"Because it wasn't. I follow the rules. And don't forget his behavior with the dog search. He had no sense of the importance of the mission."

"None of us did," Bull defended.

"He was making friends with all the dogs," Cameron continued. "It was as if he knew they were all going to be put to sleep."

"Which they were, unless someone rescued them," Luke said.

"Well, he never really caught on," Cameron added. "He seemed to have his own agenda. Remember how he behaved during the old movie star quiz? He was a poor loser there, too. He didn't even bother to say good-bye or wish the rest of us good luck. He just wanted some fucker to call him!"

"I'll miss him," Luke said. "I think you're treating him bad. He never bothered anyone. And nobody actually voted him out in the first place." He gave a withering look to Cameron.

Bull spoke up. "Richard was okay. When all the rest of you queers were tearing my clothes off with your eyes—don't think I don't notice, or hear you talkin' 'bout how I'd look in bed—Richard never said a word. Not that he wasn't thinkin' what you guys are thinkin'. But at least he had the decency to keep his thoughts to himself."

"But aren't you mad that he voted *you* out?" Luke asked.

"Hell, no. I don't want to spend another night with you guys! I would have traded with Richard in a second. You can all butt-fuck each other to kingdom come. I don't want any part of you."

Hamilton quickly stepped in. "It's early, Bull. Maybe next week at this time you'll be the one we're discussing."

"So have we gotten Richard out of our systems?" Zeth asked the group. "Personally, I thought he handled himself with dignity. He didn't throw a hissy fit. He accepted the verdict and walked away. I think he knows he's better off. But who had sex with him? That's what *this* inquiring mind wants to know."

"Dang right," Luke added.

It was still early, but there wasn't much else to do, so the other men, following Bull's lead, went to their respective rooms.

Cameron, lying on his bed, thought about the close call he'd had this evening. *It could easily have been me wearing that blindfold,* he thought. *Why the hell did I get so many votes? What am I doing to alienate myself from these assholes?*

He finally stripped off his clothes, slipped under the sheets, and turned off the light on the bed stand. He could hear others moving about the house, along with the sound of the smooth whir of the video-camera in his room. "Tomorrow begins a new week of games. I'll *make* myself more likeable," he said aloud.

At the same time, Luke was naked under his sheets, thinking about Richard and also about his phantom lover from the night before. *So it wasn't Richard*, he thought. *Too bad. He was cute.*

Luke had prepared himself in case he received another visit. He left his door slightly ajar before turning out the lights, stripping, and crawling into bed. Luke got hard just thinking about sheets. To lie naked on sheets made his preseminal fluid coat the head of his cock without so much as touching himself, the way some guys get hard whenever they enter a motel room.

He was sleepy and struggled to stay awake, listening to every sound that emanated from the old house. Creaking floorboards, voices filtering up through air ducts, the wind lashing branches against the window. All of these sounds merely served to make Luke drowsy, and soon he was fast asleep.

He dreamed. It was his favorite recurring dream. He lived in an ancient civilization. He was naked and lashed to an altar made from a cold slab of granite. At daylight he would be sacrificed to the gods in exchange for another year of healthy crops.

The high priest, dressed in a golden robe and bearing a candle to light his passage, appears from a stone corridor leading to the place where Luke is being held captive until the religious ceremony at dawn.

The priest is young. The left side of his face has been scarred, and his eyes are set deeply in their sockets. He has long hair and broad shoulders and a goatee. He displays an air of complete authority. He stands over Luke, who has been drugged and is only semiconscious. The priest takes his candle and holds it over Luke's chest. He tips the candle until the melted wax falls onto Luke's chest. Luke moans in pain as the hot wax sears his tender flesh.

With his other hand, the priest begins to caress Luke's face and body, slowly working his way down to his cock, which is twelve inches long and as big around as a prize-winning cucumber. The high priest strokes him until he's nearly ready to explode.

Then he disrobes.

By now, the priest has also raised Luke's legs and lashed his hands to wooden eye hooks, which secure Luke's wrists at the top of the granite slab. His ass is completely exposed. The priest withdraws from the dungeon-like chamber for a moment. When he returns he is holding a cruet of hot oil, which he methodically drips into the crack of Luke's ass. He then coats his own cock and utters a strange incantation.

Then, slowly, he inserts himself into Luke, who, half-drugged, can only moan from the pain and pleasure. He whimpers as the priest continues his incantation and his slow rhythmic thrusting and retracting, thrusting and retracting.

"The Gods," Luke whispers, thinking that they'll reject the sacrifice now that he is no longer a virgin. "Oh, God . . ."

The priest ignores his human sacrifice and continues to drive himself into Luke's young body.

"Worship my cock," the priest demands. "Pray for my holy cum to wash through your body! Beg!"

Now, suddenly, Luke is fully conscious. Someone is actually straddling him, fucking him. Luke reaches up to hold the man's shoulders, to feel his muscled chest and arms.

The man grinds away, his mouth serving as a gag to keep Luke from crying in ecstasy to the rest of the house. The phantom suddenly bolts upright and thrusts harder and deeper into Luke. With one last thrust, and a few halfhearted ones, the man withdraws.

"You made me come without touching myself," Luke whispered in amazement, as the man reached up to Luke's chest and ran his hand through the thick fluid and licked his fingers. He fed Luke a dollop, then got off the bed.

"I know you're not Richard," Luke whispered. "Are you the one who fucked him? You're the best I've ever had. Can't you tell me who you are? Is this another game?"

"You'll have to guess," the man whispered back. "Keep giving your ass to me, and you'll score all the points."

"Stay with me," Luke begged. "Are you doing this to the others, too?"

"Only the chosen ones."

The next sound was that of the camera being turned on again, then the door creaking open and closed behind the phantom.

Luke lay in bed, uncovered and exhausted. He didn't care that the camera was taking in his nudity. He couldn't move. He had just experienced a dream fantasy, but this time while he was conscious. He realized that again he hadn't fondled the man's testicles.

Finally, Luke fell into a deep sleep, until the dream returned, and he awoke with a start. His expectations were immediately dashed when he turned on the light to discover he was alone.

Chapter Nine

For an entire week, almost no one at the station had seen Hamilton. Ella covered for him, telling an irate Stacia that she'd just missed him every time Stacia screamed to know his whereabouts.

"Why isn't he gone for good?" Stacia bellowed. "Daddy was supposed to fire his ass a week ago, after I told him what Ham had done."

"Calm yourself. Hamilton fixed everything. He got the sixth contestant, and I hear mother and child are doing well," Ella said.

"Yeah, well I haven't seen one goddamned frame of video and neither has Daddy!" she ranted as if she were a Hollywood studio executive whose overly hyped made-for-television movie starring Cybill Shepherd as a lesbian nun had been demolished in the ratings when it aired opposite a musical variety special—"The Titanics"—starring Sharon Gless and Tyne Daly. "Tell him I want an update report ASAP!" Stacia stormed down the hall and slammed her office door.

During what was supposed to be Ella's lunch break, she got into her car and drove to the Dulcit Car Wash. There the *Hunk House* contestants were involved in another game. This one had them stripped to the waist, hand-washing cars. The object was to see who collected the most tips and phone numbers from horny customers. And with their gym buff bods, word of mouth was bringing in more business than a blue light special at Kmart.

"No Nancy boys in these parts, eh?" Hamilton said aloud as he watched the satisfied customers come and go.

The guys put on quite a show. They went through the waterworks, then sprayed another contestant with a hose of Turtle Wax, and pretended to polish the guy's ass. Playing "Car Wash" was one of the more fun games Hamilton had devised. And they were getting one point for every dollar and one point for each phone number they collected. By the time Ella arrived, Bull was ahead of the pack by twenty-five dollars and twenty-five phone numbers—from both men and women.

"Where's Hamilton?" Ella said, rushing up to Luke who was signaling to a customer that his car—and washer—was ready for a pickup. Ella saw the man hand Luke a dollar wrapped around a business card. "I've got a sort of emergency," she said.

"He's in the cashier's booth making out with the owner, I think," Luke said, pointing to a small kiosk.

As Ella walked into the shed-like hut where greeting cards, air fresheners, and bootlegged cassettes from has-been recording stars like The Cowsills were also sold, she noticed that Hamilton was smiling a lot and nodding his head in conversation. She saw that he was making time with a man who should have been a *Hunk House* contestant. Ella prided herself on never making judgments based on appearance, but this guy obviously didn't live in Dulcit, or else he was new to the town. He must have been, dressed as he was with an earring and muscle man tank top, because no straight man in Dulcit could wear a tank without it showing off a beer belly.

"Hamilton," Ella called in an agitated voice. She waved for him to come to the door.

"'Scuse me, Brad," Hamilton said to his new friend.

"Hell's breaking loose at the station," Ella said.

"The proverbial fan?"

"A real stinker. Stacia's livid."

"'Cause I wasn't fired?"

"And you haven't been in the office."

"She knows where I am, for Christ sake!"

"She's insisting you come in with the videotapes from last week. She wants to start editing right away."

"No problem," Hamilton said calmly. "Tell her I'll be in around six tonight. She and Ratner and I can watch the footage together. You should stick around, too. I want you to see the expression on her face when she sees who the sixth contestant is. She hasn't a clue yet, has she?"

Ella shook her head. "She thinks Bull's out driving one of his truck routes or something."

"Go back to the station, tell her you spoke with me, and to order a pizza or Chinese because we're going to have a "Wonderful World of Dulcit" film festival."

"I knew you'd pull it off Hammy," Ella said with a smile. "She's gonna need a box of Depends!"

By the time the car wash closed, Bull was by far the winner of the game. He'd washed fifty cars and collected nearly one hundred dollars and forty-seven business cards or telephone numbers. He was proud. The others were proud of themselves as well, because each had cash *and* dates. Although they couldn't keep the dates, Hamilton allowed them to hold on to the cash. He kept score, then made the guys give him all the phone numbers. They could spend their money on anything they wanted and take it back to Hunk House.

Bull bought a case of Pabst Blue Ribbon. Cameron bought a *Playgirl* magazine. Zeth purchased a couple of bottles of red wine. Luke selected a new toothbrush and other toiletry articles including condoms, and Marco bought a cheap audiocassette player and some tapes from the car wash. They were all happy housemates when they arrived home and dispersed to their separate quarters.

After their dinner of KFC, which had been sent over by Ella, the men gathered in the living room. Since there was no television or radio, they had to make their own diversions. They had slipped into the habit of one man each night revealing a little bit about his past. No one wanted to give too much away, but it was therapeutic for them to talk about their lives, almost like a support group in therapy or a twelve-step program. On most nights, Hamilton served as facilitator. But tonight they were on their own.

Cameron droned, "When I was a kid, my favorite program was *The Wild, Wild West*. Every week Robert Conrad got his shirt torn off and got tied up. And I got a huge boner. So big I couldn't hide it."

Hamilton was in the conference room with Stacia, Mr. Ratner, Ella, and Mike, the tape editor. From the first moment the television monitor began revealing what was going on in the house, Ratner's jaw had dropped. His mouth remained open for an hour. Not even the distraction of one tape ending and another being replaced in the machine reduced his shock. Stacia, on the other hand, keeping a close eye on her father, was delighted by his shock. Now she had Hamilton right where she wanted him.

It was after eight o'clock when Ratner shouted, "Enough! What in tarnnation are you doing over there at Hunk House? I've never," he stammered, "n-n-never seen anything so goldarned dirty in all my days!"

"This is a rough cut, Mr. Ratner," Hamilton tried to calm the old man. "When Mike starts editing, it'll be so different, it won't have any resemblance to this, I assure you!"

"A rough cut!" Ratner continued. "Hamilton, I had more confidence in you, boy! I thought you were going to give us a look into what makes a homo tick! You said we'd find out that men who like men aren't the devil's work after all. But with this—nothing but a bunch of paddycake games and nudity—"

"And sex!" Stacia exclaimed.

"This is nothing more than pornography!" Ratner shouted.

"I never said it was going to be the queer version of *Ozzie and Harriet*, Mr. Ratner," Hamilton continued. "This is just the footage from the first few days, sir. Wait'll you see how the show progresses."

Ratner blustered, "If this is any indication of what's to come, we're in big trouble!"

"Aren't you going to give Hammy any credit for finding the sixth contestant and getting the program started in the first place?" Ella spoke up. "He knows what he's doing. You should trust him."

"Trust?" Stacia snapped. "Who is the sixth contestant?"

"Bull Smith!" Ella announced.

"He volunteered," Hamilton said.

"He propositioned Hamilton to let him join the house," Ella lied. Hamilton gave her a look that said, *Don't go overboard.*

"What can I say? He's as queer as your favorite weatherman," Ella said. "You certainly know how to pick 'em."

Stacia folded her arms over her breasts and looked at Ella. "What are you trying to pull?" she asked. "For your information, Bull and I have been fucking since we were both twelve. He's straight."

"I'm closing my ears!" Mr. Ratner yelled, standing up so quickly that his chair collapsed with a thunderous crash. "You're a big girl, Stacia, but you'll always be my little Buttercup and I don't want to have to imagine you having sex—with *anyone!*" He stormed out of the room.

Hamilton and Ella regarded Stacia dubiously.

"Bull's going to marry me . . . someday . . . when he feels mature enough. And let me tell you, his . . . *privates* are as mature as a giant redwood. So what are you two really up to?"

Hamilton shrugged. "What can I say? Bull's joined the other team?"

"He *hates* queers," Stacia said.

"That's what all closet cases say," Hamilton explained.

"How often do you do *it?*" Ella asked.

"Not that it's any of your damned business," Stacia said, "but often enough to keep me satisfied."

"For me, when I was married, it was three or four times a night seven days a week," Ella lied, remembering her early days as a wife.

Stacia looked confused. "Is that normal?"

"Don't know," Ella shrugged. "It was normal for us. And when I got together with the girls for coffee every Monday morning, that seemed to be within the range of what they were up to."

"I have a *friend* who does it on all the national holidays. Isn't that normal?" Stacia asked.

Hamilton laughed. "Normal? It might be normal for a mailman who has those days off, but not for lovers, or people who claim they're in love."

Stacia's face turned white. Hamilton and Ella knew she was talking about the regularity of her sex life with Bull. They could see the wheels turning in her head; she was wondering if there was a chance he might like men more than women.

"Maybe Bull's just experimenting," Ella chimed in.

"I didn't see him in any of the footage." Stacia reclaimed her composure.

"He was shy the first few days," Hamilton explained. "You'll see more of him on the next few tapes. And much more as the latest ones roll in."

"You've corrupted him! That's what's happened!" Stacia exploded. "I knew you were a sissy, Hamilton! You're just here to recruit new members! If you've brainwashed Bull into being a homosexual, I'll rip off your *cojones* and feed 'em down a garbage disposal! And as soon as you let Bull out of your filthy hands, I'll take him to that place that turns gays into straights!"

"What, that Exodus commune? Don't you remember the founder of that place who was on *60 Minutes?* He got caught in a gay bar a while ago. Back to The Promised Land of fairies and fruits. Guess his ex-lesbian *wife* wasn't man enough!"

Stacia stood up and she, too, knocked over her chair before storming out of the conference room. Only Hamilton, Ella, and Mike remained.

"Mike," Hamilton began, "we need to work really fast editing all this stuff. Can we begin right away? I've got to spend the day with the guys, and I need you to edit while I'm at Hunk House. Then at night ... I know this is going to be a killer schedule, but I'll view your edits and suggest changes, if that's cool with you."

"I'm at your disposal, Ham. This is the most fun project I can imagine. By the way, is it true that Bull's queer?"

"We haven't figured that out yet." Hamilton smiled. "However, even if he was straight when he went into Hunk House, I have a feeling he's going to be a changed man when he comes out."

Chapter Ten

"Jesus Christ Almighty! And I mean that with all due respect. Save my heathen ass!" Hamilton sobbed as he knelt at the altar in the St. Ethel Mertz the Divine church in Dulcit. Towering before him was a life-size, plastic faded statue of the Blessed Virgin Mary.

Genuflecting under a dirty stained glass window, in the small, quiet sanctuary, his head bowed in supplication, Hamilton softly cried, "Please! You've led me to the Valley of the Shadow of Death. Now let me out! Take me back to Hollywood, before I do whatever the agricultural equivalent is of going postal! Point me to the path that leads away from dull, dull Dulcit. At the same time, could you please do something about my lust? It's driving me nuts being around beautiful young men and not being able to touch!"

Hamilton wasn't Catholic. He didn't even attend church. He did brunch. But he figured it couldn't hurt to beseech the Virgin for a favor now and then. He hadn't asked for anything important in a long time. He'd learned to store away all his relatively insignificant prayers ever since working in L.A. as a segment producer for *Entertainment Tonight*.

Every day, in that glamorous studio where stars clogged the hallways and rest rooms, Hamilton tried to keep himself from wasting his prayers. He may have silently wished, "Dear God, please let the world know that screen stud Val Miller has the smallest dick in Hollywood, just to balance his colossal ego." Or, "Christ, don't let that shrew Kate Beckinsale call me a faggot again in public." And, "Lord, prevent Christine Lopez from smelling of boiled hot dog water and stinking up the room the way she did the last time I had to do a preshow interview with her at her recording studio. Let her see the light—and a bottle of Bean-O."

Hamilton had come to carefully choose the favors he asked of God. Those daily pleas for wrath against Miller, Beckinsale, and Lopez were never uttered aloud. He saved his invocations as if they were redeemable with specific point's values, like the Weight Watchers ads with Fergie.

He hoped there was still something of value left in his celestial account, although he knew he'd spent a sizable wad of those prayer points last year when he begged to leave Los Angeles. He'd prayed to get out of Tinseltown, and voilà, the same night after visiting a church, he was fired from his job as a segment producer for Bob Goen.

It felt like an instant miracle, although it wasn't exactly what he'd prayed for. He'd asked the priest to bless him with a new life, one in which he wouldn't have to face his news anchor ex-paramour. He wanted out of Hollywood—at least for a year to cool off and reexamine his life.

From then on, Hamilton believed that sucking off a man of the cloth was all that he needed to bypass the hierarchy of saints and angels and J.C. himself in order to get his prayers to the Big Head, pronto. Recently he'd discovered that preachers were generally happy to toss up special appeals on his behalf. Hamilton knew it wasn't his devotion to the church. It was because he was cute and willing to tithe in a way that didn't require money to be tossed into a collection plate.

Hollywood had mostly been glamorous. At least Hamilton had had a cell phone and a BMW (leased). And entering through the famous gates of Paramount Pictures on Melrose Avenue each morning, where *ET* was taped, was a blast and gave him a daily charge. Mary Hart had been nice to him, and Bob too. But it was a nightmare working with the acting/singing/ hip-hop talent that the show profiled nightly.

After several years of putting up with the arrogance of Eddie Murphy, Adam Sandler, Mike Myers, Whitney Houston, Jerry Bruckheimer, and Michael Bay, and flash-in-the-pans who would never be heard from again after the humiliation of their latest flick or video release, as well as his domestic disaster with the ABC news anchor, Hamilton had a meltdown. The church became his momentary refuge. And Dulcit quickly became his destination.

However, after a year in Iowa, and with his reality show not going well, he was sorry he ever appealed to leave Hollywood in the first place. He wasn't sorry about the priest, even if his penis had the rings of a dead tree stump to identify its sixty-odd years of age, he was more sorry he'd lit a candle and put an entire dollar in the Lucite offering box, because now, not only was he stuck in Iowa, he was practically broke and couldn't afford a one-way ticket back to Sunny Cal. Working as a programming director for a piddling cable television station didn't pay squat.

"I wanna go home!" Hamilton wept to the Virgin. "I'll suck up to that Miranda Richardson creature again. I'll take the hits from flying videocassette tapes thrown in a Mare Winningham rage! I'll do anything, even suck off Detective Sipowicz! My show's in deep trouble and I just can't spend my life here in Bible Belt oblivion.

"Hell, I can't even get laid anywhere within fifty miles from this *Little House on the Prairie* patch of nowhere land. And you keep tempting me with those to-die-for men on my program! Jesus, Joseph, and Mary. Anybody. Please," he implored in a whiney voice, "send me a sign. This is a nine-one-one! I don't want the impossible. Just a little help with my show so I can get my ass out of Mayberry! And maybe a one-nighter with a hard-bodied top. Please?"

"Return to Hollywood," a voice whispered. Hamilton opened his eyes, then decided it was only his inner thoughts echoing through his consciousness. He continued his prayer.

"At least send Kevin Spacey or Matthew Broderick here to do location work on a film. That would make it seem as though I were back in the industry. And I could be their workout buddy. I'd give 'em massages. I'd role-play shower scenes from *Oz* and be their bitch/ho. I'll do anything to get that Hollywood excitement back again!"

He paused. "Is anybody listening? Am I making myself clear? Maybe I should be doing incantations in Wiccan! Anybody up there—I'll even take *down* there—interested in exchanging one used soul for a job that pays a ton and lands me in the top ten of *Premiere* magazine's Hollywood Titans?"

"My son," the voice whispered again. This time Hamilton realized it wasn't his imagination or a spirit voice from the plastic Virgin. Hamilton looked up at Mary's beatific smile, on which someone had applied red lipstick. Then he looked at a hand-carved Christ bolted to his cross. He started to get a hard-on because the Son of God was sculpted with a lean sexy body that advertised shapely brown nipples and too much muscle definition for someone whose last supper had been quite awhile back and was supposed to be starved and hanging by a couple of thorns at death's door.

"My son," he heard again and turned around. A priest sat in the front pew, his white collar in his hands, and his black shirt opened down three buttons revealing a V zone of cream-colored skin. He was probably Hamilton's age of twenty-seven. "Satan had you in Hollywood," he said. "Now you're here in peaceful, God-loving, righteous Dulcit. Which place is preferable?"

"Hollywood!" Hamilton raved without a moment's hesitation. "Real showbiz! Not the type of crap I'm wallowing in over at KRUQ!"

The priest smiled. "Do you remember why you left L.A. in the first place? Have you forgotten your misery?"

"Father, I was a fool to run away from personal and professional problems and give up all the daily excitement!" Hamilton felt silly paying that kind of respect to a guy his own age. "I'm lost. I need guidance. My life is supposed to be producing TV shows. I'd even do *Hollywood Squares* and put up with the Black Plague in the center square. The station owner where I work hates my new show. He's hated all my programming ideas. I couldn't even get Candice Bergen, who doesn't even have much of a career anymore, to come to these parts. I failed persuading a has-been like Molly Ringwald to be a guest on a cooking show at the station. I *have* to get back to Hollywood! My creative ideas weren't any better there, but every one else's were so much worse!"

"Have you tried clicking your heels? Metaphorically speaking, of course. Ask and you shall receive and all that jazz."

"What's it look like I'm doing here? I'm not polishing your chalice."

"Would you like to?" the priest asked with a grin.

"I'll do anything to get out of this Mayberry."

"Have you tried asking Don Knotts to do one of your shows?"

Hamilton thought for a moment with a blank look of incredulity. He didn't fully understand the question or the reference.

"You said something about Mayberry. He was on . . . Never mind. You also complained that you couldn't get laid. That's a fallacy. Dulcit's teaming with herds of sex-starved holes—and boys and men, too." The priest stared at Hamilton telegraphing his precise thoughts.

Hamilton wasn't stupid. "Would you get God to make my show a hit and get me out of Dulcit?"

"I guarantee I'll take you from Dulcit to kingdom come, or at least an inferno of carnality. Perhaps I'll even open your mind to the possibilities of why the Lord sent you here in the first place," the priest suggested. "Although why in Christ's name *I'm* here myself is a totally perverted mystery!" He rolled his eyes then caught himself. "I think you need to take your pants, er, your *mind* off of your troubles, so you can be an open conduit through which God can plant His seed for miracles. Do you follow me?"

"You sound like dialogue from a bad porn movie."

"I do, don't I," the priest said with a lascivious grin.

"Or from *Mr. Rogers' Neighborhood*. Which I guess is practically the same thing." Scooting on his knees to where the priest was seated, Hamilton placed his head on the lap of the clergyman whose pants were filled with a holy erection as solid as the wooden Jesus.

The priest petted Hamilton's head to comfort him. "Shall we pray together?"

Hamilton nodded.

"Upstairs in the rectory?"

Hamilton nodded his head again and he could feel against his cheek the fire stick that had grown inside the priest's trousers. The priest was hunky. More important to Hamilton was his personal connection to God. Hamilton figured if the sex was good, the priest, like the others, would say a secret prayer for him. Then all his problems would be solved. In no time he'd be heading back to Los Angeles or on to a network job in New York. Hamilton didn't think playing with a priest's pud was any worse than sleeping one's way into a vice president's position in a corporate environment.

The St. Ethel Mertz the Divine church was small and only required a short flight of stairs from a secret room behind the altar to reach the second floor living quarters. In just a few moments, Hamilton and Father James, as he finally introduced himself, were butt naked and wrestling with each other on the priest's waterbed. To Hamilton's great surprise and delight, Father James had the gym-pumped body of a West Hollywood hustler. A tattoo of an upside-down crucifix was dyed on his ripped stomach. Hamilton was so fascinated by this, that he almost went into autoejaculation.

They were both ravenous for each other. Hamilton had gone more than a year without feeling another man's body and it seemed that sexy

Father James had also been abstinent for a long time. The two men cannibalized each other in a heightened state of animalistic sexual zeal. Father James, as the dominant master, was wreaking beautiful havoc on Hamilton's grateful ass.

Hamilton was so unconsciously deep into this powerful sex that at times he thought there was a storm raging inside the church. He would swear he heard thunder and the darkened room frequently seemed illuminated by flashes of lightning. At times, in Hamilton's delirium, Father James seemed to glow in the dark, like a phosphorus apparition.

Suddenly, after their third steam-filled climax of the afternoon, the tape-recorded church bells automatically began to toll from speakers in the steeple, calling all of Dulcit to evening worship service. Hardly anybody ever showed up.

"Christ," Father James said, exhausted and catching his breath and still smothering Hamilton with kisses. "I've got to do the sacrament."

Hamilton, lying on his back, his chest heaving from all the physical exertion, said, "How many rosaries?"

"What?"

"How many decades of the rosary to get God to answer my prayer?"

"He's already answered one of them," Father James grinned and leaned over Hamilton's naked body. He dragged his extra long, Gene Simmons tongue from Hamilton's navel to his lips and snaked it down his throat, tickling his tonsils. "You got laid didn't you? Let me have a word with Him and I know He'll take good care of you and *all* your needs," Father James said with a fiendish smile. "Gotta go. There's always that fucking Mrs. Watson waiting for absolution for one trumped up sin or another. I think she wants me. God I want out of this dump! If I get Him to show you the light, you'll have to promise to take me back with you to Hollywood. I have a pad there on Gardner near Fountain. We could share."

"You're from L.A?" Hamilton asked, incredulous.

"I'm just here on temporary assignment. You don't think a guy who looks as good as me would be a full-time priest, do you?" Father James blanched. "I'm an actor. I only do this when there's no work. My last gig was three years ago on *ER*. Maybe you saw me. I was Scrub Nurse Number Three. No freakin' lines, but I stood behind Anthony Edwards while he was getting bawled out by the parents of a wiseacre kid who jumped on the subway tracks and got dismembered under the wheels of a train. What was left of his mushy body parts were heaped on a bloody steel tray in the morgue."

"What do I really have to do to make my show work and get the hell back to Hollywood?" Hamilton asked.

"I have two words for you: Ben Dover."

"Oh, I'm too exhausted. And you've got Mrs. Watson waiting downstairs."

"No. Ben *Dover*. That's my stage name. Introduce me into your program and it'll be a hit."

Ben Dover, Hamilton said to himself, trying not to laugh. "Stage name? Is *everybody* in show business?!"

"Hey, some actors get their realtor's license for the lean times. I decided to go to divinity school. It worked for Karol Wojtyla."

Hamilton gave him a quizzical look. "And she is?"

"The Pope, you boob. "The big cheese at the Vatican. The Pontiff! Pope John Paul II!"

"Right. He was an actor and a playwright. What a show he's putting on now!"

"So we're partners? Tit for tat and I go back to L.A.?"

"Deal," Hamilton said, still catching his breath after a decathlon of sex. "Just tell him to make it quick."

As Father James continued dressing, he said, "Didn't they teach you in Sunday school that 'God works in mysterious ways, his wonders to perform?' He has his own time frame for creating miracles."

"The only thing I learned in Sunday school was that sex with his representative here on earth was supposed to make Him work harder on his miracles," Hamilton countered. "You've got clout with the Man. You're like God in the flesh, letting him have a taste of what it's like to be in a human body. And what a body!"

"Don't you think we've sinned?"

"It was heaven!"

"What if it was the devil who made our cocks ignite and explode?" Father James added.

"Then bravo for Beelzebub because my dick's never been so on fire. And, I could go through eternity with your hot poker!"

"Guess even in a priest there's more than a little devil."

"You're sexy with or without that bit of Lucifer in you!" Hamilton said. "He better not stall just so He can enjoy the pleasures of the flesh with *my* flesh. I'll do anything that he wants just make my show a hit and get me out of this purgatory called Dulcit!"

"Come back tomorrow for another . . . service. Maybe by then you'll have found the answers to your prayers."

"By the way," Hamilton said, "I've never seen you before in this hick town. Wasn't there a different priest for this church? Some old geezer with chapped lips and veins popping on his nose who did the midweek radio sermon? Father Winthrop?"

"Oh, he retired."

"I heard him this past week."

Father James stalled. "Reruns. That's what you heard. Reruns. The best of the best. He went back to Ireland. Now I'm 'the best of the best'," he grinned.

Hamilton looked askance at Father James. There was something peculiar about this priest. He wasn't the pasty-faced, Ichabod Crane incarnation like the other churches had on staff in this Pettycoat Junction of Iowa. Father James had the body of a marble statue from Greece and the genitals of a porn star. Also, in the rectory, there didn't appear to be any religious paraphernalia. No crucifixes. No wells of holy water. Not even a Bible on the bed stand, although a copy of *My Best Man* was on the floor beside the bed.

"But your being on the show is not going to solve my problems with the program," Hamilton said. "The whole format has turned to shit. It's not the fun-but-edgy *Queer as Folk* kind of program I imagined. Most of the contestants are wimps."

"I'm getting a message from God," Father James said, closing his eyes and placing his fingertips to his temples.

Hamilton rolled his eyes. "Go do your sacrament."

"No wait. God said to make some drastic changes."

"Duh!"

"Really. I just heard him say, 'Duplicitous cocksuckers.'"

"God said, '*duplicitous*'?" Hamilton joked.

"The whole message was, 'Duplicitous cocksuckers doing deceitful, dishonest, treacherous, cheating, lying, corrupt, unthinkable atrocities to each other.'"

"I'm impressed," Hamilton deadpanned. "God watches *Big Brother* and has an elevated vocabulary. All those adjectives for 'asshole.' "

"Wait. There's more. Add Ben Dover to your show, and the serpents in Hollywood will court Hamilton the way they do David E. Kelley. He'll be bigger than Regis."

"Bigger in what way?" Hamilton asked. "Could be a trick, like the last wish in Genie jokes."

Father James stood before Hamilton and put his full Brendan Fraser lips to his. Hamilton opened his mouth to receive the reptilian tongue and moaned in ecstasy as it slithered passed his teeth and engaged in battle with his own tongue. Hamilton sucked on the appendage until it was withdrawn and flicked about his face and nose and eyes. "You could fuck me with that thing, it's so long and stiff," Hamilton said.

Father James said, "I know how lousy most people's scruples are when there's a buck to be made, and perhaps a slice of the fame pie. It's abominable. It's human nature. Your contestants would sell their immortal souls to be interviewed by Barbara Walters. I know you're doing a reality show . . ."

"How'd you . . . ?"

"What you need is to amp up the jeopardy for these Judas wannabes. Give them *and* the audience something completely unexpected. This isn't PBS, and it isn't the Loud Family you're chronicling. It's a bunch of beautiful gay men."

"Yeah? And where do you come in?"

"How about the church in medieval times. I know plenty of stuff that'll turn on your contestants and your audiences."

"Church stuff? That's a ratings killer," Hamilton dismissed Father James. "Unless it's the latest scandal, fun stuff like that."

"No, not the freakin' routine. I'm talking about all that shit the Holy Roman Church used to do to heretics. Lots of fun!"

"Maybe for the s/m crowd."

"For the whole family!"

"Yeah, the Manson family! Not The Disney Channel family of right-wing Stepford clones."

Hamilton shook his head and pushed back the sheets of the still-warm bed. He slid out of bed and picked up his clothes off the floor. But before he put on his bikini briefs, Father James knelt before him and said, "I'll help us both get back to Hollywood." Then, one last time for the day, he sampled Hamilton's cock.

Hamilton clenched his teeth and quickly released another load of semen into Father James's salivating mouth.

"I'll let Mrs. Watson smell my breath," Father James said breathing into the palm of his hand as he left the room.

As Hamilton walked from the rectory and church, his mind wasn't focused on the most mind-blowing sex he'd ever experienced, although he kept getting flashes of the priest's muscled torso and the upside-down crucifix adorning his abs. Rather, he was concentrating on Father James's theory about changing *Hunk House* midway through the program.

Maybe Ratner was right. The games thus far weren't edgy, except for the Seeing Eye dog incident. And the despicable personalities of the contestants weren't coming through as they did on *Big Brother 2*. The original idea had been to gather six sexy gay men, all of whom wanted to be Rich Hatch clones, get them in a house for six weeks, then stand back and watch the fireworks. So far, there was only the pathetic pop of pistol caps. The more Hamilton contemplated the idea, the more he felt the show might be saved by Father James, or Ben Dover, or whatever his real name was.

Filled with newfound eagerness for *Hunk House,* Hamilton immediately went to his house to try and get a good hold on where the show would go from here.

For days, every time the church bells tolled, Hamilton thought of Father James. The men of *Hunk House* could see his conditioned response, as though he were one of Pavlov's dogs drooling at the sound of a meal bell. Although they didn't know why the bells visibly agitated Hamilton, they could tell something was on his mind.

Chapter Eleven

At the end of the second week of *Hunk House*, it was Marco who was "outed." Tears formed in his brown eyes as he tried to be as gracious as Richard had been the first week. Marco's parting words were almost identical to Richard's. He begged for whoever had fucked him to not forget him and to please get in touch.

"I knew Marco couldn't have made it," Cameron began when the remaining men gathered with Hamilton to discuss why he had been ousted. "He was the weakest link. He made us toasted bagels every morning, for Christ sake."

"While you just sat around on your ass, complaining about everything, and everyone," Bull said.

Grunts of agreement followed from Luke and Zeth. Presently each of them sulked off to their respective rooms, building the tension just the way Hamilton had hoped it would for the program.

Luke was in his room, naked under the sheets, looking at the *Playgirl* magazine that Cameron had purchased and was now circulating for the pleasure of the other men. As he fondled his penis, he heard a soft knock at the door. He quickly took his hand away and pulled the bedcovers up to this waist. "Come on in," he said.

The door opened and it was Cameron, bare-chested and barefoot, wearing only his faded blue jeans. "Mind if I come in for a couple of minutes?"

"Want your magazine back?" Luke asked.

"I just wanted to say hi and ask who this guy is that Marco and Richard had?" He moved into the room and leaned against the wall opposite the foot of Luke's bed. He folded his arms, which bunched his pecs together and made his biceps look larger.

Luke was already hard from looking through the magazine, but he was practically steaming at the sight of Cameron's masculine torso. "I dunno who he is."

"Doesn't matter, I guess. I also wanted to get to know you better." Cameron smiled. "I'm a little camera shy, and it's hard to talk openly when you've got those guys with their lenses in your face all day."

"There're cameras in here, too," Luke reminded.

Cameron laughed a little. "There's no tape in 'em. They just keep the red light on to make it appear that we're being watched twenty-four hours a day. They can't afford better equipment, and they certainly can't afford all the videotape." Cameron moved over to the camera attached to the wall by the door. He pushed the EJECT button and opened the compartment. "See. Nothing inside."

Luke started to get out of bed to take a closer look and realized he was naked.

As Luke was quickly settling back in bed and propping up pillows behind his back, Cameron, with a sleight-of-hand that would have made David Copperfield envious, surreptitiously removed a videocassette from his back pocket and exchanged the cassette that was actually inside the machine.

"Goldarnit," Luke complained. "Here I've been Mr. Goody-goody, afraid of even jerkin' off and all along it was a trick!"

Cameron *tut-tutted*. "It is pretty awful what they're doing, isn't it?" He sat down on the edge of Luke's bed.

"Here we could'a been playin' around and having some fun, if we knew there was actually some privacy," Luke said.

Cameron placed the palm of his hand on Luke's chest. "You know, I've wanted to touch you ever since you got out of your car over at the KRUQ station. You feel real nice. Wanna feel me?"

Cameron stood up and unbuttoned his jeans, then slipped out of them. His penis was as big as Luke's. Cameron climbed onto the bed and under the covers where he found his housemate's horse-size dick throbbing. With Cameron in charge, the two men began pleasuring each other.

"You're just a kid and I'm thirty-two," Cameron said in between deep kisses and tasting Luke's nipples and underarms. "Bet you've been around though. Been fucked a lot. So I'm no big deal to you."

"I don't want your kind of fucking," Luke said, letting Cameron know the boundaries as well as the fact that he'd had more than his share of action during his relatively young age.

"If Hamilton finds out . . ." Luke breathed heavily, enjoying being ravaged with the light on, looking at a real man, not an invisible lover.

"Whose gonna tell 'im? Certainly not me. Not gonna risk getting thrown out of this hellhole when we've only got three weeks left."

"Better not fuck my hole," Luke warned.

"I'm gonna nail that ass of yours until you come without touching yourself."

"Just 'cause you're sexy, you think you can do . . ."

"I don't think. I *know.*"

Cameron raised Luke's legs and pushed them back above his head. He didn't have any lube, so he used the only thing available—saliva. As he made his way into Luke, Luke cried out. It was loud enough for anyone in the house to hear, and Cameron immediately stopped his penetration to listen for any sign that someone was aware of their activities. "Shut the fuck up, kid!" Cameron commanded, which enraged Luke.

"Just get the job over and get the fuck out," Luke spat back.

Cameron plunged ahead, not giving a damn whether Luke was enjoying the sex.

In his fervor, clearly feeling the rise in the level of his own sperm getting ready to explode, Luke suddenly cried out again and pumped—one, two, three forced loads of semen.

Cameron pushed a pillow over Luke's face, smothering his involuntary cries of ecstasy and preventing him from breathing. Cameron had slathered Luke's semen all over his chest and stomach and was on the verge of ejaculation, when Bull threw open the door and stormed into the room.

Cameron, sweating like he'd run a marathon, quickly pulled out of Luke. He positioned himself on the far side of the bed for safety with Luke between him and Bull. Frightened as he was of Bull, the combination of being so close to ejaculating inside Luke and seeing Bull, Cameron suddenly shot his load, spraying like a cat. "Oh, God! Oh, shit!" he moaned, holding his cock.

"You nearly smothered me, you son of a bitch!" Luke cried, catching his breath, then seeing Bull standing in the room, dressed in his jeans and lumberjack shirt.

Bull was raging mad. He looked from Cameron to Luke. "What are the fucking rules in this house?" Bull demanded. "And what'd you do to this kid?"

"It was completely consensual," Cameron defended, almost hyperventilating. "Luke's ass has been hot for my cock—and yours, too—ever since we began this friggin' *Hunk House* game."

"He raped me," Luke complained.

"We had a way of dealing with your type in prison," Bull said to Cameron.

"Prison?" Cameron asked suspiciously. "When were you in prison?"

"All that matters is your ass," Bull said with a vicious snarl. He started to approach Cameron, whose penis had shriveled with fright. "I bet you've never been fucked yourself," Bull said. "You give it, but you can't take it. Am I right?"

Cameron blanched.

"Thought so. Better watch your ass, Cameron, 'cause when I decide to nail you, you won't be able to sit for a month. Now get the fuck outta here!"

Cameron hastily retrieved his jeans and put them on. He sidled past Bull, keeping his eye on the big man. At the door he started to reach up to the videocamera to retrieve his tape when Bull caught his wrist.

"'S okay," Luke said, as he watched Cameron wince in the vice grip of Bull's strong hands, "there ain't any tape in the machines."

Bull pushed the button and out popped a tape.

"You were recording us?" Luke asked Cameron in astonishment. "What'd you plan to do with that? Blackmail me?"

"Nothing, man, I swear," Cameron insisted. "I just wanted a reminder of what it was like to be with you. I swear!"

Bull grabbed Cameron and pressed him against the wall. "When I'm through with you, they'll be dragging videotape out of your asshole. Now get the fuck out of here! I'm keeping the tape!"

The instant Bull released him, Cameron dropped the tape and left the room. He ran down the stairs as if running for his life.

"And what about you?" Bull said, turning to Luke. "Did you like what that S.O.B. was doing to you?"

Luke shrugged, then smiled.

Bull looked confused. "You queers!" he said with disdain.

Luke said, "Don't knock it 'til you've tried it. Guys just know when they want each other. Besides, when was the last time you had sex?"

Bull didn't answer.

"If I didn't think you'd beat me up, I'd tell you something," Luke offered

"What?" Bull asked. "I won't beat you up."

"Promise?"

"Mmm."

"I was thinking about *you* while Cameron was pounding my ass."

Bull was taken aback. "Me?"

"I was fantasizin' about you bein' in Cameron's place. You and Zeth are the two sexiest dudes in this house. I could cream right now just thinking about seeing you naked. I'll bet everyone else, includin' Hamilton, feels the same way. My ma says I've got a sixth sense sometime, and I think you'd like to at least want to know what it's like to get your dick sucked by a man."

Bull swallowed hard.

Luke wiped off his chest with the bedsheet and tentatively got out of bed, his cock still hard. He slowly moved to Bull. They stood facing each other for a long moment. "Mind if I just touch you?" Luke asked.

Again, Bull swallowed hard, but he stood still.

Luke reached out and slowly began to unbutton Bull's flannel shirt. When he reached the last button, he parted the sides of the shirt and gasped. "Jesus Christ! You're more beautiful than I ever imagined. Mind if I touch your skin? Please?"

Bull was frozen in place. He didn't know what to do. A part of him was desperate to retreat back to his room, another part of him was fulfilling a lifelong fantasy. He began to shiver.

Luke caressed his strong chest with its rich dark hair. The sight of his tight abs made Luke's cock jump involuntarily. He removed Bull's shirt and let it drop to the floor, then dragged his hands over Bull's muscled shoulders and arms. "Shit," was all that Luke could say about the god before him.

"Now, I'm just going to unbutton your jeans, so hold still," Luke advised.

Carefully, Luke worked the denim away from Bull's waist and discovered he wasn't wearing underwear. A dark mass of pubic hair erupted like a thicket around the biggest cock that Luke had ever seen. Not only were Bull's balls enormous, his erect cock was like some barn animals'.

Luke dropped to his knees on to the floor and began caressing Bull's shaft with his tongue, bathing it slowly and lovingly, tasting it—the contours of the head and veins of this fantasy man who simply stood transfixed at what was happening to him.

Working in a way that he hoped wouldn't frighten Bull, Luke opened his mouth as wide as possible and inhaled the huge penis. Bull moaned with satisfaction.

Expertly, Luke continued washing Bull with his tongue, working into a rhythm. Bull repositioned himself, planting his feet firmly on the floor. Hesitatingly, he reached for Luke's head and began moving his cock in and out of Luke's mouth, thrusting his wet manhood as far down Luke's throat as possible. His breathing became heavy and Luke prepared for a huge climax.

At last, Bull groaned loudly, and Luke's mouth received a burst of semen so powerful it gushed down his chin. Bull whimpered as he continued his violent thrusting, trying to empty every ounce into Luke's eager mouth.

Slowing down, he removed his cock and allowed it to remain exposed for a long moment. Then he pulled up his pants. "Is that what you queers like?" Bull said in a sarcastic tone that immediately, for Luke, diminished the rapture of the act.

"Didn't I do a good job?" Luke asked as if he'd displeased Bull.

Bull didn't say anything. He was sorry for his tone of voice. On one hand he was a horny guy who had just gotten his rocks off. On the other he was afraid he'd want Luke more and more, like a drug.

"I suppose you've got to get yourself off now," Bull said, derisively.

"I'm fine. I want to make sure you're fine."

"I thought you fags were all selfish pricks."

"I'm not a fag. I'm queer. There's a difference. And I'm thinkn' this is the first time you've let another man suck you off. Am I wrong?"

"So who you gonna tell?" Bull said defiantly.

"Who would I tell? Plus there's no shame. We're gay."

"I'm not gay," Bull insisted.

"Bi?"

"No!"

"Confused? This is just a small part of a gay guy's life. We're the same as everyone else. This action just enhances everything. Don't tell me that pussy's anymore satisfying. It may feel good, but it achieves the same conclusion. Straight guys think there's only one right way to get off, and that's by sinkin' their cocks into a tight little muff. Only you don't have to bring me roses or buy me a new dishwasher!"

Bull smiled for the first time since their encounter. "So there's nothing wrong with what we just did?"

"Only if you think there is. I hear there's some countries that even have laws that let men marry men and women marry women. I learned in world history class that some past civilizations and societies actually put gays, although they didn't call 'em that, on a pedestal. Plus, some of the most famous people in the world are gay. Sports heroes, too!

"Heck, when we're little, we play with other little kids. Boys drop their pants and look at each other. Nobody feels guilty until they're told it's wrong. And there isn't anything wrong, until you're told otherwise and you believe what you're told. Tonight, just like when we were kids, we were just followin' our nature. Okay?"

Bull seemed satisfied.

As he buttoned his pants and his shirt, and Luke went back to bed, Bull made one last comment. "Did *you* like it? Enough to maybe do it again sometime?"

Luke beamed. "Bull, I'll suck your dick any day, any time. And when you're ready to try my ass on for size, I'm as deep as a river."

"You'll keep this a secret?"

"Sure. See you in the morning. You were great. And by the way, what do you say we team up and vote Cameron out next week?"

Chapter Twelve

"For God's sake, what are you two doing?" Stacia screeched when she entered the makeshift-editing bay in Hamilton's office and saw the footage on the video monitor. It was nearly 2:00 A.M. Hamilton and Mike were editing videotape, excising footage of Richard getting a massage from Zeth, deleting the part in which the two men finally stripped naked and caressed each other's bodies.

"Don't get your panties all twisted," Hamilton sighed to Stacia. "We're taking out this footage."

"Have we got a first episode in the can yet?" Stacia asked.

"A pretty good one if you ask me," Mike said, matter-of-factly. "It's so in your face it oughta desensitize viewers to all that follows."

"What do you mean 'in your face'?" Stacia asked.

"It's heavy stuff. You'll get your audience hooked or spooked from the first frame."

"I want to see it," ordered Stacia.

"You can't see a work in progress," Hamilton announced. "It's not something I want you or anybody else around here to view piecemeal. I want you to see the program as a whole; otherwise, you won't get the full effect."

Stacia whined, "If the first segment's so great, I'd like to see what you have. Please?"

Hamilton looked at Mike, who shrugged as if to say, *It's your show, Ham. Do what you want.*

"I don't know that you're ready for this," Hamilton told Stacia.

"If I'm not ready, I can't imagine our audience will be ready. Just show me the first half hour or so. I won't pass judgment on a rough cut. I promise."

"Sit here," Hamilton said to Stacia, indicating a steel folding chair. "I'll be back in a moment."

Hamilton left the room to retrieve a tape from the secure place where he'd hidden all the raw video that came out of *Hunk House*. He returned with a VHS videocassette and turned on the television. He pushed POWER on the remote control for the VCR, then coaxed the tape through the opening and turned off the lights in the room. He and Mike sat back in their own chairs and Hamilton pushed PLAY.

Color bars appeared, accompanied by a high-pitched *eeke* that blasted their eardrums.

Fade to black. Suddenly, as unexpected as a slap on the face, with '80s disco music in the background, the camera caught sight of two men, one with his wrists and ankles lashed to the headboard of his bed, and his bare ass in the air, crying out in what could have been mistaken for agony as another man slapped his face, telling him, "Shut the fuck up, or I'll fuck you so hard you'll be in this bed for a week!"

Cut to another room with two young men, both of them kissing passionately and moaning, "I love you!" They were smothering each other in hot, deep kisses on the lips and their chests and nipples and taking turns sucking their large erect cocks.

Cut to another room—a bathroom, two men. One was seated on the toilet with his head leaned back on the white porcelain lid of the water tank. The other man was spraying shaving cream on the first man's pubic hairs and then held up an old-fashioned straight razor for the first man to see. "Don't move, you little cocksucker, or your dick'll be history," the man with the razor hissed as he lowered the scalpel-like blade and ran the dull edge up and down the man's fully erect shaft before he began shaving around the kid's huge erect cock. The boy moaned in ecstasy as the other man continued to shave first the hair that ran from his navel to the base of his cock's shaft, then started on his scrotum.

"Watch out for my balls," the kid pleaded.

"Just stay still, motherfucker. One false move and I could have you off this show in no time! Why the fuck would you even trust me?"

Cut back to the room in which the men were fucking. They were sweating profusely as they continued their bestial sex. "I want that prostate of yours to give up everything, the dominant man said. "You can do it kid. And you better make it soon, 'cause I can't hold my load much longer."

As if on cue, the boy cried, "Arrragh! Arrragh! Arrragh! Do me! Harder! Don't stop!" Then, he released so much sperm it jetted past his chest and splashed onto his face and into his hair.

"I'm in you, kid! I'm fucking you!" the man cried out as he exploded.

Cut back to the bathroom. The shaving was complete and the man with the razor was now sucking on the freshly cleaned testicles of the boy, sliding his tongue up and down the kid's shaft. The sound of sucking was loud, mingled with moaning.

Slash cut to the room with the younger of the men who moments ago were expressing love for each other. Now the elder was slathering lubrication onto his partner. Slowly, the young man eased his weapon into the other man's body. Gradually he sheathed his entire appendage into the space.

Slash cut to the bedroom in which one man's wrists and ankles had been shackled to the bedpost. He lay on his back, nude, his flaccid cock listing to one side, still oozing.

Cut to: All six men seated around a kitchen table. It appeared to be morning. Each had a cup of coffee and a breakfast plate: toast, bagels, cereal.

Microphones picked up bits and pieces of what each man had to say. It was like eavesdropping on a party and not knowing exactly what was being discussed. As the cameras moved from man to man, their names flashed across the screen. Stacia knew who each man was, but the television audiences wouldn't. With their names bandied about, they immediately took on an identity in the viewer's mind. In quick, single-frame flashes over the names and faces were intercut the hardcore sex of the previous portions of the tape, so that a viewer could tell who had done what to whom.

The one named Marco had been the self-serving top who had ravaged the one known as Richard. The two youngest of the group, Luke and Zeth had been identified with their making love. The two men in the bathroom turned out to be Luke again sitting on the toilet and Cameron wielding the razor.

With jumpy white block letters, the words DAY ONE came on screen for five seconds.

"Good Christ!" Stacia cried. "What have you done? This is not a television program. It's pure pornography! No! No! No! We'll all be in jail. Stop this!"

Stacia went running from the room. In the distance the sound of her office door was heard slamming shut.

Hamilton and Mike looked at each other, then laughed as quietly as possible. "You're a master," Hamilton said to Mike.

"I'm just following your direction, Ham," Mike said, still grinning.

Hamilton nodded thanks. "That'll take care of 'Daddy's Buttercup' for a little while. I swear I'm going to destroy her before she has the chance to get me first."

Mike said, "I'm surprised she didn't fall apart when Cameron first came on screen with that razor against Luke's cock!"

"I think she was in complete shock." Hamilton grinned back. "That's a scene she could never have imagined in a zillion years. Shaving down another man's cock and balls!"

"And then Bull in frame, watching each act! That's precious!"

"Can we work a couple more hours on the real show?" Hamilton asked.

"Yeah. Another cup of coffee and I'll be revved up again."

"Think we can get the third episode finished?"

"We're almost there," Mike said.

Chapter Thirteen

Hamilton entered St. Ethel Mertz the Divine and opened the door to the confessional. "Ben, er, Father James," he whispered to the priest on the other side of the partition. "It's me, Hamilton."

"There is a God! Let's not waste time in this freakin' claustrophobic box. Let's go upstairs and play!"

"I need to talk to you. About your suggestion to come aboard the show."

"Yeah. Yeah. Later. Let's go. I've been listening to these perverted farm wives all morning, comin' in and foisting all of their imagined sins on me. It's all Jimmy Carter's fault. These whores feel that if they even *think* about coveting their neighbor's son's tight ass—or even one of their horse's dicks, for Christ sake, they've *sinned in their hearts.*" Father James sniggered. "I told that cow, Mrs. Watson, that she was skirting the edge of the devil's playground. As penance I instructed that she was to get down on her knees and blow her husband three times a week for a month. Wish I could have seen the look on her puss through the partition!" The priest laughed again at the notion that Mrs. Watson, and the other women, were so devout they'd do whatever the church told them. "This is why parishioners are called a flock. They're all bloody sheep. I'm hanging an 'out of service' sign on your door. Hurry, before Mrs. Watson shows her fat ass in here again!"

Hamilton and Father James simultaneously opened their respective sides of the confessional and met face-to-face. They both immediately were hard for each other. Father James led the way to the room behind the altar and up the stairs to his living space.

After an hour of sex that was as mind-blowing for each as they had remembered from the last time they were together, Father James reached over to the bed stand and withdrew a liquor flask from the drawer. He unscrewed the cap and took a long pull.

Hamilton put his lips on the neck of the flask and leaned his head back to take a small swig. He coughed. "Mmm. Mother's milk," he said of the gin, using an Eliza Doolittle line. He took another pull before handing the canteen back to Father James.

After a few minutes of decompressing from the sex, Father James finally broached the subject of the show. "So, have you figured where I fit in to the program?"

"I have some ideas, but I have the feeling that you've got better instincts about this than I do. I'm afraid I've proved that I'm not very creative when it comes to the format of this program."

"You're right. I've been giving your show a lot of thought. So has God. We have a couple of ideas that I can throw out to you."

Hamilton rolled over and placed his face on the priest's strong chest and embraced his body, caressing the cleric's skin.

Father James began to explain what he'd personally like to see in a reality show with gay men. He began to reel off scenarios that Hamilton could never have imagined. The ideas were dark. They seemed to suit the devil more than a guy who was a part-time priest.

"As I see it," Father James said, "your core audience will, at first, be gay. But I think that if you implement some of these ideas, you'll cross over to the voyeur in everybody. Some of the stuff should be hard for the average Bozo to view. But then so is *Oz* and *The Sopranos* and *Sabrina the Teenage Witch*.

"Now, just for starters, close your eyes and imagine the set. The ambiance is incredibly important. The room is about six hundred square feet. The walls and ceiling are all dark gray. The lighting is very low level, red or amber colors. There's music in the background, kind of New Age or tribal sounds, something guttural and powerful. You don't want the contestants, or the audience, to be comfortable seeing this space. You want them to feel a little edgy, like watching *The X-Files*."

Hamilton rolled over onto his back. Keeping his eyes closed he pictured the room as described by Father James, whose voice had become as mesmerizing as a hypnotist's.

"The temperature in the place I'm seeing is warm. Can't have naked guys being cold. That's not good for keepin' 'em hard. There's a section of the space that's set up like a gym, with weight equipment and even lockers—for everyone's gym teacher fantasy. Another section has mats on the floor for jockstrap wrestling. There's a sling for fucking and other fun stuff, and a rig so you can hoist a guy up and suspend him in the air either by his ankles or wrists. Hanging somebody blindfolded upside-down is a treat for the victim and the viewers alike.

"There's a bondage chair, a bondage table, and a shipping pallet platform with an eye hook in the middle of it. You can tie somebody's balls to the eyehook. The contestant is naked, kneeling with his hands tied behind his back, and there's absolutely no way he can go anywhere or get off the pallet because he's holding the platform down with his own weight. There's a coffin in the corner."

"A coffin?" Hamilton whispered in a drowsy voice.

"Yeah. It's a really cool wooden box—black—like what you might keep workshop tools in, or even toys. But while you may not think it's terribly intense, the person lies down in there naked, their head goes into a separate section, which in a way disconnects them from the rest of their body. Then you tie the person up, close the lid, and lock it."

"Sounds kind of exciting," Hamilton whispered, starting to get hard again.

"The box is an innocent-looking thing. Yet, it's actually very intense. Of course, it's totally dark inside. Totally quiet. Fifteen or twenty minutes is about as much time as anybody could probably stand to be in there."

"It's freaky, but it's turning me on," Hamilton said.

"After an ordeal like that, the guy's gonna need some nurturing because he's gonna be pretty vulnerable when he comes out. He'll be disoriented. You, as the host, will need to hold him. That's very important. On the other hand, perhaps it should be me who gets to hold the naked guys."

"You sound as though you've 'been there, done that,' " Hamilton said, still seeing himself tied up naked and locked in a dark plywood box.

"This is nothing compared to what the Roman Catholic Church did in the thirteenth century to try cases of heresy. I really got off studying this shit, and then practicing what I learned."

Hamilton opened his eyes and took a look at the extremely well-built priest who was now sitting straddling his waist. "Sounds like some heavy head trip or s/m game play."

Father James took Hamilton's wrists and pinned them down above his shoulders. "It's an exchange of power," he said, putting all his strength into keeping Hamilton from being able to move. "How does it feel?" he asked, in a menacing tone. "At this moment you're helpless. I'm in control of you."

Even with haunting thoughts of Jeffrey Dahmer, Hamilton found himself harder still, at the prospect of being manipulated by this sexy man. He admitted he was helpless, but he liked it—a lot.

"That's what we need from your remaining contestants, and, you hope, the viewers," Father James said, releasing Hamilton from the vise of his strong grip. "We need to get them hot and not know if what we're doing is taking sex too far, or not far enough. I think we can do it."

Hamilton admitted that he was apprehensive about such a drastic change in the program. "And here I was planning variations on *The Dating Game, Name That Tune,* and *What's My Line?*"

"Figures. You're too vanilla. Plus that's exactly what would be expected by breeders. You wanna floor 'em with something absolutely out of the blue. I guarantee nobody in Dulcit has ever watched a guy get his cock pierced."

"Ouch!" Hamilton writhed in imagined pain.

"It's just temporary piercing," Father James said, as if it was as common as clipping his toenails. "I've done it before. I've got these really fine needles and I only go through a couple of layers of skin. Most of the time when you pull them out, there's not even any blood. The guy's strapped to the bondage table, and you don't blindfold him."

"Wouldn't it be scarier to be blindfolded and not know what's happening?"

"No way. When they're blindfolded they can't see what actual Hell is like. They can't anticipate what's being done. But, when they're tied down and you make 'em *watch*, it's a real scene!"

"Yikes!" Hamilton said with more than a little apprehension. "Ya think this is going too far for audiences? And for the guys?"

"That's exactly what we want! Push the envelope. Make 'em see things they've never seen before, and maybe never will see again.

"Imagine one of your contestants is bound to a table. He's naked. I pop a needle over his head so he can see it. I warn him not to move because it's a really sensitive procedure. I only want to go through a couple of layers of skin. So there he is, breathing hard and watching with his eyes bugged out. The audience is doing the same. Then I tell him I'm going to pierce his dick. He's like 'Oh, my god, it's my dick! He's gonna stick a needle in my dick!'"

"That's incredibly scary!"

"And some couch potato is yelling into his kitchen, 'Hey Martha! Come quick! Some guy's getting his dick pierced!' *ER* and *Queer as Folk* could never get the ratings this show'll bring!"

"Needles?"

"It's fun. I only go through the top layer of skin, so it's no sweat!"

"This sounds bizarre to say, especially coming from me, but I'm hard just thinking about the head trip of it all."

"It's actually a real rush. It has a cumulative effect and the endorphins kick in as more and more needles are put into a guy. I had to have it done to me so I could write about it in my thesis. There were maybe thirty or forty needles in my body. I was glassy eyed and could hardly talk. But it wasn't from any pain, it was from the endorphins. The part I really got off on was getting my nipples pierced."

"Gotta admit, I've always been fascinated by s/m and that whole pleasure/pain trip that goes on. But I don't know that I could ever follow through."

"I'm not giving you advice, Hamilton, but life's so short, I think you should try a lot of different things and see what really gives you a rush and gets your rocks off."

"We definitely should do this. But my budget's blown. And I can't spend the time creating a brand-new film set."

"Hell, this place, the church, has everything you need! I checked out the basement when I first arrived. Obviously, there were some kinky priests—in addition to me—who were assigned to this place over the years. But we'll have to go on a night schedule, 'cause the sanctuary is open all day. We can't have your men and the crew seen coming and going from St. Ethel Mertz. The games'll have to be filmed at like two in the morning."

"You have to be the Dungeon Master, 'cause nobody would believe me in that role."

"Cool!" Father James said, taking another swig from his flask of gin.

Now I can use my education and all that research I did for my paper. Plus I have a closet of uniforms for every occasion, which I seldom get to use."

"One thing I don't quite understand. While it's a trip for the audience, and maybe for the guys, if they get into it, how is it a game, and how do we assign points?"

"Simple. The man who can go through a series of physical tests without cracking is your winner."

"But they all have to come out of it unscathed."

"We'll have a list of situations they can elect to go through. Each is progressively more difficult, with a higher point value. It's up to them to choose which of the circumstances they'll attempt. So, like flogging would be say twenty-five points. Breath control fifty points. Hot waxing, ten points. The coffin seventy-five points, and so on."

"That'll work. When do we start?"

Father James rolled over on top of Hamilton again but this time, instead of pinning him to the bed, he began kissing his lips and biting on his nipples. "We begin right now," he said as Hamilton responded with equal intensity and passion. In no time, there again appeared to be thunder and lightning in the bedroom. Father James said something in Latin before easing himself into Hamilton.

"For the next week," Hamilton explained to his men, "we'll be doing night games. We're taking a new tack on the situations you're going to find yourselves in, so you'll need plenty of rest during the day."

"What kind of situations?" Luke asked.

"It's a surprise," Hamilton said. "For some of you, this is going to be fantasy time. For others, well, you'll get through it if you want to get to L.A. Let me just say that nothing'll be dangerous as long as you guys follow whatever you're told to do."

"Call me a sissy," Zeth said, "but I don't like the sound of what's going on."

Luke looked to Bull for reassurance. Bull could only shrug as if to reiterate that everything would be swell.

"Stop being such pansies," Cameron said. "So what if it's a little tougher than some of the stuff we've done so far. You had to know this wasn't summer camp."

"Look guys," Hamilton said. "If I were you, I wouldn't worry about anything. I'd just go to bed early and sleep as much as possible tomorrow to get ready for the night games." He was trying as much to reassure himself as he was to help Luke and Zeth.

It was one o'clock in the morning, the start of the third week. Hamilton walked through the house knocking on bedroom doors and rousing the men from sleep. "Wakey, wakey. Let's get crackin'! The fun's about to begin. You're gonna lose points if you don't hustle."

His reveille was answered with three "fuck you's" and a "motherfucking cocksucker."

"Bleep, bleep, and double bleep!" Hamilton said, sprightly.

"You're a freakin' Keebler Elf!" Cameron yelled from his room.

"There's coffee if you need it," Hamilton called from the bottom of the stairs.

Bull was the first to wander out of his bedroom and into the kitchen. He poured a mug of French roast and sat down heavily at the table. He yawned. "After all the years of truck haulin' you'd think I'd be used to waking up in the dark, but I'm not," he said to himself.

Luke came into the kitchen and went straight to the coffeepot. "I now got a lot more respect for my mom. She's up before dawn each day to do chores. I don't know how she does it."

"Guess you can get used to just about anything, after a while," Bull said. "Did you ever think about helping her?"

"She never wanted any. Says I've got the rest of my life to work, that I should enjoy sleepin' in while I can. She liked to think I'd be a father someday and have to get up at all hours to change a diaper or something. She's gotta know now that's never gonna happen."

"Moms can think anything they want," Bull said. "But till you actually tell her you're queer, she'll never believe it. People, parents especially, have blinders on. Old Man Ratner's a prime example. Don't you think he knows that Rex is a big fat sissy? Of course he does. He's not an imbecile."

"You think I should just tell my mom?"

Bull laughed. "You ain't gonna have to say a word. 'Smile, you're on *Spy TV!*'"

"Oh, right," Luke said. "The whole dang world's gonna know pretty soon. But by then I'll be a couple of thousand miles away."

"Ain't no escapin' to L.A. This show's gonna be broadcast nationwide. Probably worldwide. Your ma and pa'll know the same time your cousins and school buds know."

"At least I don't have to go through the whole ordeal of tellin' people."

"May as well have put up a billboard next to the Burger King sign out on Highway Twenty-nine. 'I like whoppers!'"

"But I'll be famous and it won't matter. In fact, it'll make everything all right because if you're on TV you're a star."

"Yeah. We're all probably gonna be stars, even if we don't win. We'll end up in that *People* magazine. And Hamilton'll get us on his old show, *Entertainment Tonight*. He used to be a big shot out in L.A. once, until he got caught screwing a newsman. Nobody big like Dan Rather or Peter Jennings. Some bleached blond twit who probably still hasn't told his parents what he's up to when he's not on camera or covering a story."

Luke looked at Bull.

Bull shrugged then answered as if reading Luke's mind. "He mentioned about his past when he brought me over from the station, after I signed on. Want another cup?" Bull got up to fetch the coffee, then refilled Luke's mug as well as his own.

Cameron was the next to walk in. "Ain't anyone gonna at least toast us some bagels?"

"Toast 'em yourself," Bull said. "Do I look like Marco?"

"Well, how 'bout makin' more coffee? You guys drank practically the whole pot."

"And do *I* look like Richard?" Luke parroted Bull.

"Fuck ya both," Cameron said draining what was left from the glass pot into a mug.

Hamilton considered it his duty to make sure the men were as comfortable as possible, so he prepared a fresh pot and made toast for them. "I'm no cook," he offered. "So if you want anything else like eggs and bacon, you'll have to fend for yourselves. But there'll be muffins in the van. That'll hold you over until we have a break on our new location set."

"Which is?" Luke asked.

"You never tire of trying to get more information out of me than I can give, do you?" Hamilton smiled. "We're just going for another ride."

Hamilton gave the guys a few extra minutes to finish their coffee and butter a couple of slices of toast. Then they were off.

The ride was only a matter of five minutes. When the men arrived, blindfolded, they could feel the hot lights from cameras in front of them as they were led through the quiet chapel. The only sounds were the echoes from their shoes on the wooden aisle between pews. When they were all in the anteroom behind the altar, they heard the creaking sound of a door being opened on old hinges.

Hamilton said, "Okay, guys. Take off your blindfolds 'cause we're going down a flight of stairs, and I don't want any accidents."

The men removed the black felt and shoved them into their jeans pockets. The musty smell of a basement arose from beyond the door and stairs leading to a lower level of the building.

"After you, gentlemen," Hamilton said, as he motioned for them to descend the stairs.

Single file, with Cameron leading the way and Hamilton pulling up the rear, they descended into the bowels of the building. Zeth, who was the second to last in line, could hear Cameron exclaim, "Holy shit," just before he reached the bottom step and discovered where they were.

It was a dungeon, with candles and red lightbulbs. The men stood transfixed, looking around at the furnishings, which seemed to be out of a museum exhibit of the Spanish Inquisition.

"I knew it," Cameron said in a whisper. "Hamilton's been reading too much Edgar Allan Poe. It's like some damn porn flick. God help us."

Then, from behind a black curtain made of tarpaulin, a figure emerged. In the darkness the specter was impossible to see clearly. Then, he lit a flashlight held under his face, and the contestants saw a black leather mask. The Dungeon Master was an obvious body builder who could have been an s/m porn star.

"Take 'em," the master issued a command and suddenly four men who had been camera operators came out from behind the black curtain. They were dressed in a similar fashion, but were far less sexy. Each cameraman was assigned one of the contestants and simultaneously, with the same synchronized choreography employed by Charles and his waiters at the restaurant, slipped handcuffs onto each of the men.

"Hamilton," Cameron said with a nervous quiver. "Hamilton, this ain't no game," he said looking around the room for their facilitator, but Hamilton was not in sight.

"I'm in charge now," the Dungeon Master declared. "And you're not to speak unless spoken to. Is that clear?" He cracked a whip, making each man flinch.

"Now listen to me carefully, because I'm not repeating myself. We're playing a really fun game this time." He chuckled like Caligula. "Over the next four nights, you're going to have four situations to deal with. You get to choose which situation you'll be in, so not to worry, it's not anything that you don't want to do." He chuckled again. "But there are degrees of difficulty with each situation. The easier the exercise, the lower the number of points. The harder the circumstance, the greater the point value. What could be more simple?"

The man took his flashlight and pointed the beam at a white board, similar to the one on which Stacia had written the rules for living at Hunk House. "These are the categories for tonight," he said shining his light on the printed words.

> FLOGGING = Twenty-five points
> COCK-AND-BALL TORTURE = Seventy-five points
> ELECTRICITY = Fifty points
> BREATH CONTROL = One hundred points
> HOT WAXING = Twenty-five points
> PIERCING = Seventy-five points
> COFFIN = One hundred points

"You each get to pick one tonight. But remember the point values. And what's on the board tomorrow night may have a higher or lower point value. It's totally random. There's no use in using your brains to figure out a strategy."

The men studied the disciplines they were required to select. Luke tentatively raised his hand. "Sir. What's breath control?"

"You said 'sir.' I like that." He cracked his whip again. "Breath control. Here's a visual aide." He displayed a large sketch of a naked man with a huge erection; the arm of another man was choking him from behind with one arm acting as a vice around his throat. "If you cut off the circulation from the carotid artery, here, here, and the one at the back, it cuts off the flow of oxygen to the brain and you pass out. Or you could put your head in here," he held up a gas mask. "There's a breathing tube. But all I have to do is put my hand over the tube. It's got a bladder in it so you can breath out, but you can't breath in. Pretty soon you start hyperventilating—and panicking. Don't worry, you're not going to die. Everybody can live without air for a couple of minutes." He laughed.

Luke gulped.

"Here's an analogy for you," the Dungeon Master continued. "Remember when you were a kid and a baby tooth was falling out? But they just didn't fall out, they got looser and looser. And you found yourself playing with the tooth with your tongue. Remember how it hurt, but you couldn't stop doing it? The reason you couldn't stop doing it was that you could control the amount of pain sensation you got. There was a very delicious agony that you were able to manage, wasn't there? You did it a little bit and a little bit more and worked it up in stages. That's what we're going to do. I'm going to be your tongue, and I'm going to wiggle you back and forth in a very controlled way. And by the time we're done, if we've done it right, we're all going to be at the top of the stairs floating. If you do as I say, you'll have a wonderful afterglow. And someone's going to be a star."

Chapter Fourteen

Hamilton was watching from a darkened corner of the basement. At first he could hardly control his repulsion with himself for subjecting these men to such humiliation. He almost wanted to tell the two Stedicam operators to turn off their machines and insist that the Dungeon Master release each man. The four had been stripped naked and tied up on various devices throughout the room. But he was also intrigued. Nobody seemed to be in any danger. In fact, each man had an enormous erection and could be heard moaning with pleasure as the Dungeon Master performed a few minutes of whichever situation they had chosen to engage in. For hours, he went back and forth from man to man. The guys were obviously enjoying themselves. It was only Hamilton who seemed upset by what he was viewing.

Just before dawn, the men were released from their shackles and helped back into their clothes. They were too exhausted to button their shirts or tie their shoes, each of them weak from fatigue. They had to be led to the van, like lobotomized patients at a psychiatric facility.

Back at the house, Luke, Cameron, and Zeth could hardly climb the stairs to their respective rooms. Their feet felt as though they were filled with cement. Bull found his bedroom and dropped himself onto his bed without turning down the sheets or taking off his clothes. The others did the same, falling into deep sleeps.

Hamilton sat in the kitchen for a long while, staring out at the gray morning. He, too, was exhausted, but couldn't quite get the image out of his mind of Luke, his wrists shackled to a steel bar suspended from the ceiling and being flogged with a single tail whip made of soft deerskin. Or Bull strapped to a bondage chair enjoying low volts of electricity from a violet wand, which zapped his testicles and nipples, and then suddenly and involuntarily experiencing a wrenching orgasm that sprayed Cameron, who was kneeling on a padded shipping pallet with his hands tied behind his back and his balls snared to an eye hook in the center of the platform. Zeth was actually smiling as the Dungeon Master stood over him, painting hot melted paraffin on his chest, stomach, cock, balls, and legs.

As he watched birds outside the kitchen window Hamilton thought, *What's Ratner going to think about all of this?*

"Oh, Christ," Hamilton uttered aloud, visualizing being tarred and feathered. He got up from the table. Too tired to go home or to the office, he made his way to Marco's old room. There, he untied his shoes and kicked them off. He unbuttoned his shirt and unbuckled his pants. He folded his slacks and neatly laid them on a chair. He placed his shirt over the back of the chair, peeled off his socks and underwear, and slipped into the bed, which hadn't been made since Marco had last slept there. Although Hamilton could hardly keep his eyes open, he found himself with an unexpected hard-on. It was the idea of lying amid the sheets that Marco had occupied that was enough to turn his thoughts toward sex, rather than the ordeal he was facing with his show. *Your dick really is in your head,* he thought to himself, unable to muster the strength to masturbate. He dropped off into a deep dreamless sleep.

It was nearly dusk when Cameron finally regained consciousness. He lay in bed for a long while, remembering the early morning hours and what he and the others had endured. He couldn't help being aroused by the memory of being doused with Bull's full load of semen. Cameron unconsciously smiled at the memory. *I got seventy-five points for the cock-and-ball torture,* he thought, trying to add the sum of all his previous points. Then he recalled that Bull had earned a full one hundred points for the bondage chair and zaps of electricity. *Didn't look so hard. I'll take that one tonight,* he strategized.

As trippy as the experience had been for him, Luke decided he definitely would not try some of the scenes listed on the board, regardless of their point values. No way would he submit to the coffin or to the piercings. He could end up without enough points to go on to the following week, but he'd take the chance that the others, too, were going for some of the

things that offered a lower return. The stakes were high. The whole outcome of the game could come down to who scored the most during this
phase. But at the moment, Luke was too tired to think about bothering
to go for the gold by ruthlessly playing along just because he was told
to. Sure, he'd go through some other routines and probably have fun.
But he didn't want to risk real pain or doing something that caused his
dick to get soft. Although a room full of naked guys—especially Bull
and the Dungeon Master—made it practically impossible for him *not* to
be constantly hard.

When Zeth regained consciousness, he could feel how sensitive his skin
was after the hot waxing, which had actually been the most relaxing experience of his life. Strapped to a bondage table, his arms and ankles se-
cured to the platform, he'd simply glowed with euphoria as the
leather-clad and masked master dipped a paintbrush into a pot filled
with melted paraffin and slowly stroked Zeth's body from shoulders to
chest, nipples to stomach, and his already burning cock. The challenge
was only worth a measly twenty-five points, but Zeth nonetheless
wished he could select the same situation tonight. *As a matter of fact*, he
thought, *they never said we couldn't choose the same scene twice. I'd go
for it again if they let me.* He tried to remember what else was on the
board that didn't seem too much of an ordeal. *And what if they have
completely different challenges tonight,* he thought. *Then I'm fucked.*

By seven o'clock, the four contestants were seated around the kitchen
table. Hamilton had gone to run the latest footage over to Mike at an
improvised dubbing bay at their new secret location away from the
KRUQ station. Ella had made dinner: fried chicken, sweet potatoes, a
casserole of green beans and onion rings, and hot rolls. The Stedicam
operator circled the table as the men ate and talked about their experi-
ences earlier that morning. Cameron seemed the most optimistic. "I'm
going for a hundred points tonight," he bragged. "I can take whatever
they bring on."

Luke looked to Bull. Although they hadn't had an opportunity to
fully discuss their strategy for outing Cameron, both were pretty sure
that Zeth would vote with them even without them bringing him in on
their scheme. After all, he had written Cameron's name on his cardboard each time the Out House had convened.

"Just out of curiosity," Zeth said to Cameron, "was there anything on the list that you really wouldn't do?"

"This guy in charge is a pro. I've dealt with his type before. Usually these so-called tops, these dominant 'leather masters' have had their techniques handed down to them by other masters. It's a very respected trade."

"What if this guy flunked his training but decided to be a dungeon dude anyway?" Zeth asked. "Like you never know what your doctor's grades were in med school. Just 'cause there's a diploma on his wall doesn't mean he didn't get his share of Fs in gross anatomy."

"Didn't I hear you moaning with pleasure? The guy's obviously good at his job," Cameron said.

"Being bathed in warm wax isn't exactly a scary scene."

Cameron shook his head. "This dungeon shit is probably his whole life. It's his calling. Like you wanting to be an actor out in Hollywood. I can tell he's practiced a lot."

"Still, Zeth's right," Luke said. "We know nothing about this guy, or his helpers—who 'til last night used to be perfectly respectable cameramen. We kinda know them, but the master stays hidden behind his mask."

"We're really at his mercy," Zeth agreed.

"Look, guys," Cameron continued, "you get to choose what your challenge is, so why are you complaining? It's a valid game. You're scoring points aren't you? Look at Bull. He got the most last night."

"And you got the bonus of his jizz jetting onto your face!" Luke laughed.

Cameron smiled. "Lip-smacking good, man."

"That's nothin' compared to the lip smacking you're gonna get if you don't just shut the fuck up!" Bull said.

"Still angry about me fucking Luke?" Cameron taunted.

"I ain't angry about nothin', except seeing your shit-eatin' grin every time you think you've bested one of us in a game."

"I'm a natural winner," Cameron stated. "And I'm gonna do whatever I have to do to win this game. Even if I have to fuck Hamilton. Seems to me he'd be an easy score anyway. The man's practically got a 'Fuck Me' sign on his back. He needs an orgasm soon or he'll literally explode, or his dick'll drop off from lack of action. 'Use it or lose it,' they say."

"I'd say just the opposite," Bull offered in Hamilton's defense. "A guy who doesn't go around constantly leering at other guys—like you—is more likely the guy who gets all he needs."

"Fuck you, Mr. Closet Case."

In an instant, Bull had leaped from his chair and knocked Cameron to the linoleum floor of the kitchen, slapping him. "You asshole!" Bull shouted as Luke and Zeth watched in terror, unable to stop the altercation. "I could kill you right here! But I ain't goin' to jail for a slimy whore like you!"

Bull stood up, hauling Cameron with him, gripping the front of his shirt and tossing him back into his chair.

"Christ, what got into you?" Cameron asked in a shaky voice. "What'd I do wrong? Haven't I been a good sport about everything? Where the fuck do you get off threatening me?" Cameron looked to Luke for sympathy. Luke looked away.

"Figure it out, man," Zeth said as he got up from the table. Luke followed him upstairs. One cameraman trained his Stedicam directly on Cameron's face. Another followed closely behind Luke and Zeth.

"Let's get a little sleep before Hamilton comes back," Luke said before reaching his door.

"Better lock ourselves in. Cameron's liable to come looking for revenge. I can't handle myself the way Bull can."

At that moment, they could hear Cameron lumbering up the stairs. "Fuck all of you!" he bellowed intentionally loud enough to be heard through the thick mahogany bedroom doors. "That's one dude who'll be sorry he ever crossed me!"

At one o'clock, the contestants endured the same routine as the night before, only this time Hamilton wasn't quite the cheery Keebler Elf. In fact, when he knocked on the men's doors and called for them to rise, he said, "Move your asses if you want coffee or something to eat."

Once again they were assembled in the basement of the building that they had discovered the previous morning was a church. The men were greeted by the Dungeon Master and told to strip. This time, on a long bench, the men discovered four plastic dishpans filled with warm water, a travel size can of shaving gel, a towel and a Gillette disposable razor.

"Shave," the Dungeon Master commanded. "And I don't mean your face! I don't want to see a single hair around your pathetic dicks or on that turkey gullet sack that holds your precious nuts."

Luke straddled the bench and did a deep knee bend, lowering his cock and balls into the water. Although he was practically smooth from Cameron's earlier exercise in shaving him, he withdrew his genitals, shook the can of cream, and lathered himself from the navel on down and completely covered his scrotum.

Zeth tentatively drew the razor down to the base of his shaft. He rinsed the razor into the water and took another drag with the blade, carefully avoiding the transparent skin of his cock.

When the men were through with this chore, and had cleaned themselves off with their towels, they all looked at each other's cocks.

"I look huge!" Zeth said proudly only to hear the crack of a whip and the master demanding: "Silence! Who told you that you could speak?!"

"Sorry, sir," Zeth said.

"I didn't ask if you were sorry! I asked who told you that you could speak!"

"Nobody, sir!"

Again the whip cracked. "Am I nobody?" the master demanded.

"No, sir!" Zeth said again.

"Then who told you that you were allowed to speak?"

"You, sir?" Zeth asked, helplessly.

Exasperated, the master once again, in short fragments said, "Who . . . told . . . you . . . that . . . you . . . could . . . speak?"

Zeth worked it out in his head. "My master, sir. I spoke out of turn. I'm sorry, sir." His head lowered in supplication.

"That's my good boy," the man said.

Then came another crack of the whip, which echoed in the basement chamber. "Look up, you cocksuckers. Look at the board and choose what challenge you'll accept tonight."

To each man's delight the list contained the same variety of activities but with the addition of:

> ZIPPER = Twenty-five points
> CATHETERIZATION = One hundred points
> WATERSPORTS = Twenty-five points

Again, Hamilton watched from the shadows behind the stairway as the four contestants selected how they would be controlled for the next four hours. He cringed when Cameron, wanting a full one hundred points, selected to be catheterized. Luke applied for and was granted a hot waxing. Zeth opted for the piercing, and Bull asked for a flogging.

By the time the van arrived at dawn, the men were once again exhausted. With the exception of Cameron, who hadn't a clue what a catheter was used for, and now sat in the van in a state of catatonia, the other men were simply depleted of energy, although floating from an endorphin induced high. Cameron groaned with humiliation and discomfort all the way back to the house.

Rather than drag themselves immediately to their respective beds, Bull, Luke, and Zeth returned to the kitchen and popped cold cans of Coke from the refrigerator. Luke offered one to Cameron who swatted him away as he grabbed a roll of paper towels. He left the room and could be heard whimpering as he climbed the stairs toward his bed.

"He ain't so tough," Bull said. "You could tell from his screaming that he didn't know what the fuck he was getting himself into. Now he'll probably pee in his bed. Should've brought him another roll of towels."

"I felt sorry for him," Zeth said. "He only went for a catheter 'cause he's desperate to win. If he wants to win that badly . . ." Zeth's voice trailed off.

Luke and Bull exchanged worried looks. Zeth couldn't possibly take pity on Cameron. Not after the way he'd been treated by Cameron throughout their entire time in Hunk House.

"He'll do anything, all right," Luke said, looking at Zeth. "He raped me and made a tape of it to use as evidence to get me thrown out of the game."

"Don't be surprised if he's workin' on a way to vote you out," Bull added to Zeth.

"Me?" Zeth said, incredulous. "I've never done anything to him!"

"That's the point," Bull continued. "He thinks you're a wuss. He said it was surprising that you were still in the game."

Zeth scowled. "We'll just see how the votes tally on Saturday," he smiled.

Chapter Fifteen

The next two nights were variations on the same themes as the previous two nights. Into the dungeon, then back to the house, and sound sleep. Hamilton was hardly ever around. He had grown weary of watching the charade and spent the last two nights alone in the editing bay going over Mike's compilation of footage and making cuts and changes. He left the secret location in time to wait in the van for the men and help escort them back to the house.

When finally the week came to an end, Hamilton decreed that they would hold off doing the Out House portion of the show until after their dinner that evening. Each man could spend his day sleeping if he chose, which is what each said he would be doing. For most of the day Hamilton was back at his KRUQ office counting up the points each man had scored before the subjective personal vote from the four remaining men.

To Hamilton's great surprise, the scores were pretty much even. "Who'd have thought?" Hamilton said with a low tone of surprise.

"Who'd've thought what?"

Hamilton jumped. It was Stacia, standing in the doorway. Hamilton had been so engrossed in tabulating the scores he didn't hear her come in. Plus it was Saturday. She never came into the office on the weekends.

"That your *boyfriend* would be poised to win this game. He had a great week. There's no way he'll be voted out tonight."

"Speaking of boyfriends." Stacia smiled. "Wanna hear the latest gossip?"

Hamilton rolled his eyes.

"Just thought you should know that thanks to your perverted television show, and whatever pornographic shit you're making, the police are investigating not only you, but the whole KRUQ station and staff. You'll be prime *boyfriend* material in jail. They'll be bustin' down the door to Hunk House as soon as they've got a warrant. I don't care if *your* ass gets hauled off to the big house, but I do mind seeing me and Daddy and Rex and Ella and Mike locked up for aidin' and abettin' your criminal activities."

Hamilton was floored. There was no doubt in his mind that Stacia was at least partially correct. Nothing stays secret in a town as small as Dulcit for very long, and it was entirely possible that the police were indeed investigating him and KRUQ and *Hunk House*.

"I'm thinkin' you might want to close up shop, Hammy," said Stacia as she smiled and left the room.

Hamilton grabbed his papers, stuffed them into his briefcase, collected his coat, and left the KRUQ building. He got into his Honda Prelude and drove off, heading for the church. Before pulling into the parking lot of the sanctuary however, he noticed a police car conspicuously trying to be inconspicuous. It was parked a short distance from the church driveway. Hamilton decided he'd better not risk being seen going into St. Ethel Mertz's, especially since it was evening. But he had to get word to Father James to be on his guard. He made a left-hand turn down Locust Street toward his own little bungalow on High Street. Once there, he called the rectory.

When Father James answered the telephone, Hamilton explained what Stacia had revealed about an investigation that was apparently underway. He asked what could be done about clearing the dungeon.

"If it's evidence they want, you'd better do something about all the videotape," Father James advised Hamilton. "Wherever you've got it stashed, I'd make sure it was Fort Knox. And," he continued, "if I were you, I'd get over to Hunk House right away and get all those hidden cameras and their tapes, plus the Stedicams and what they got in 'em and either stash the stuff or burn it, pronto!"

"But the show! For crying out loud, we've got our big Out House event tonight, plus two more weeks' worth of shooting. What the fuck are we going to do?"

"You might be able to get this evening's stuff done. It is, after all, Saturday, and it's unlikely the sheriff can get a judge in this county to issue a warrant until Monday, but this is it. Of course, these small town sheriffs don't play by the rules either. Remember that song "The Night the Lights Went Out in Georgia"? Substitute Dulcit for Georgia and be afraid. Be very afraid."

"The fact is, you and I could take all this tape and drive on out to California," Hamilton said. "We've got a killer opening episode and teaser tapes. If we work together we could package this for HBO instead of this fucking KRUQ."

"That's not a half-bad idea," Father James agreed.

For the first time since being sequestered in the old Victorian mansion Bull was looking forward to Out House. By now, he was resigned to playing the game—at least until after Cameron was dumped.

It was nearly eight o'clock by the time Hamilton arrived, visibly shaken. Luke asked about his change of attitude, but he brushed them all off saying he was just exhausted.

"Now, let's get on with Out House," Hamilton ordered. As the four men took their spots in the living room, the Stedicam operators moved about, trying to capture the tension. With the now-familiar music playing on the boom box, Hamilton began the ceremonial act of reading each man's score. Then he asked that each of them write down the name of the man who would be outed.

"When I call your name, please hold up your card and speak the name of the man you've selected to be dismissed from *Hunk House*," he said with all earnestness. "Luke, we'll begin with you."

Luke held up his card. "Cameron," he said, moving the card for everyone in the room to see.

Cameron wasn't smiling.

"Bull?" Hamilton said.

Bull was silent for a moment. Then, he announced, "Cameron."

"And you, Cameron?" Hamilton said.

Cameron said, "Bull," then flung his card at Bull, who tore it into quarters and threw them back at Cameron.

"And now, our final vote. Zeth?"

Zeth looked at Luke, then at Bull, then slowly raised his card. "Cameron."

Cameron crossed his arms and leaned back in his wing chair. "We'll just see about this. Hamilton hasn't decreed that I'm out. In fact, if you all remember, the guy with a lower overall point value is the one who's outed. Have you done your homework, Hamilton?" Cameron asked. "Have you tallied up my points? Surely there's someone else in this room with a lower overall score than me."

"No," Hamilton said, looking at his sheaf of papers. "You lose. You have a lower total score than the others."

"That's impossible!" Cameron cried. "Let me see!"

"Sorry. The decision is final. You get the blindfold."

Cameron stormed over to Hamilton and grabbed his clipboard with all the scores written on a yellow legal pad. "I said, the decision is final, Cameron," Hamilton bellowed as he tussled for his clipboard.

Bull, Luke, and Zeth all came rushing to Hamilton's rescue as Cameron screamed, "Fraud! Fraud! Zeth has fewer points than I do! This is a fuckin' farce! The game's fixed!"

"Can't you just go quietly, the way Richard and Marco did?" Zeth asked.

"I'm not being outed by you faggots! I'm supposed to win this game! I've got more points than all of you!"

"He's right," Bull said looking at the legal pad with the men's scores. Hamilton froze.

"Backstabbing sons of bitches," Cameron huffed. "I'm stayin'. Like it or not!"

Cameron disappeared to his room.

"Jesus Christ," Hamilton said. "I can't believe him."

"I can't believe that we can't believe *you*," Luke said.

"The game *is* fixed, isn't it?" Zeth added.

"It wasn't supposed to be," Hamilton confessed.

"I'm as much to blame as Hamilton," Bull said.

"Bull, what are you doing? Don't! You've come such a long way," Hamilton tried to stop the chain reaction of facts.

"Truth is, the station needed another contestant and I was coerced into playing along," Bull said. "I'm not a real contestant. I shouldn't have gone along with the plan."

The room was silent. The men, including Hamilton, were all stunned.

"All right," Hamilton admitted. "It's true. The show was going into production and we needed one more contestant."

"But you said you had hundreds of applicants," Luke said.

"That was a lie, too. We only had five men apply. I had to have six men in this house; otherwise, I wouldn't have a show. And I've got to have a show! I've got to make good with this so I can get out of Dulcit, just like you guys. I belong in L.A. I could be a great producer for Ed Bradley on *60 Minutes,* or for Meredith Viera on *The View.*"

"So Bull's really not gay?" Luke asked.

"Not exactly," Bull retracted his earlier statement. "I did some things these past three weeks that I've always fantasized doin'. I came in here scared to death because I was afraid of what I might do if one of you touched me. I never had a man touch me before. You all made me feel like nothing but a piece of meat. I resented that. I'm more than just a pretty face."

"I'll say," said Luke.

"I was just afraid to go with my feelings," said Bull. "And I hated the fact that Cameron took advantage of Luke. I don't like to see anyone being used by anybody else for their personal gratification."

Hamilton said, "Guys, I'm really sorry for lying. It was a terrible thing to do to you—especially to Bull, who, I have to say, has totally changed my mind about prejudging people. I've known him for a year and I always thought he was an arrogant, pigheaded, intolerant, queer-hating S.O.B."

"I was," Bull agreed.

"But since getting to know you as a real man, I have to admit you've opened my eyes to how people can change."

Bull smiled. "I don't want to leave," Bull said. "I kinda want to win this game."

"Hamilton?" Luke asked, "it's time you made amends somehow."

"What can I do, other than say I'm sorry?"

"Stop the cameras," Zeth advised. "Let's talk about this privately."

Hamilton agreed.

When the room was once again quiet and it was just the four men, Hamilton explained how he'd originally envisioned the program. "I wanted this program to show gay men in a positive light. I wanted to rid the airwaves of stereotypes. I wanted the heartlanders to have a better understanding of who we are. But it all fell apart almost right away. And I don't think all that s/m stuff helped either. For the record, that wasn't my idea." Hamilton sighed.

"I figured as much," Bull said. "I had you pegged for us playing charades or Pictionary. Your movie star trivia game was pretty pathetic.

And even *that* isn't what being gay is all about! With that stuff you were generating more stereotypical crap. How was I represented? You had it looking like all gay men had to know that Clark Gable wore false teeth and had bad breath. Some of us are into Wayne Gretzky or rooting for the Oakland Raiders! We don't all want to fuck Brian Boitano."

"You're right, guys. I owe you another apology for that," Hamilton said. "We may as well pack it in 'cause Mr. Ratner will fire my butt when the police investigation turns up what we've been doing. Remember Stacia?"

"The ferret-faced bitch?" Zeth said.

"Well, she's wanted my ass in a sling ever since I started working at KRUQ."

"Then she should've been at the dungeon. There's a sling down there," Zeth joked.

"Stacia's not such a bitch," Bull said. "She's just a frustrated woman. I've strung her along ever since we were kids. Not only have I been lyin' to myself, I've been lyin' to her. I can just barely get it up for her. I always knew something was missing whenever we had sex."

"You and Stacia?" Luke said.

Bull defended her. "That's probably why I didn't like you for all this time, Hamilton. It's 'cause Stacia didn't like you. She wanted your job."

"Looks like she'll have it pretty soon," Hamilton acknowledged.

"But she doesn't have to," Bull said. "Look, we've all put a lot of time into this thing. We've gotta find a way to continue. I was at that first pitch meetin' and what we've done so far is nowhere near what you were tryin' to sell us on."

Hamilton sat in his chair, stunned by Bull's courageous remarks. He exclaimed, "Hey, Judy! Hey, Mickey! We've got an empty barn here in the Midwest, so let's put on a real live Broadway show!"

Chapter Sixteen

The men had all retired to their respective bedrooms, so Hamilton began to quietly straighten up the parlor. He replaced the wing chair in its proper location. He picked up the cardboard with Cameron's and Bull's names written in bold black letters. He collected the Sharpie pens and put them in his briefcase, along with the yellow legal pad on which the men's scores were tallied. Then he went around turning off lights.

As Hamilton was collecting his suit coat, he heard the sound of a door creaking open. The sound came from the back of the house, beyond the kitchen. It was followed by the almost inaudible sound of bare feet on the kitchen linoleum.

In the darkness of the living room he was afraid of frightening whoever it must be, so he remained silent and as motionless as possible. A man emerged from the kitchen and made his way through the blackness of the big house. He came within a few inches of Hamilton. But the man's face was always in shadow.

Hamilton watched as the man, bare-chested, tentatively placed a sockless foot on the first step of the stairway. The man began to move slowly up the stairs. He seemed aware of the location of every creaking board as he made his circuitous journey. When he reached the second-floor landing, he didn't turn to look around, so Hamilton couldn't tell who it was, even though a dim night light in the upstairs hall gave off a gray illumination. He thought of Bull, but quickly dismissed the idea.

The man stood for a moment outside Luke's door, then discreetly turned the knob and let himself into the room. Hamilton remained motionless for a long time, perhaps ten minutes. Still, the man did not come out. Hamilton could not hear any sound in the house except that of the refrigerator motor in the kitchen.

The morning sky was clear, the sun streaming in through the windows at Hunk House.

Luke was the first to awaken. He was still reeling from his phantom lover's latest visit, trying to determine which of the men it had been. He ruled out Bull. It wasn't him, although he wished that Bull would make love to him with as much passion as the elusive lover. Was it Cameron? Again, he'd had Cameron, who, like Bull was well endowed and a memorable fuck, but after his denunciation of all the men last night, it didn't seem probable. *Could it have been Zeth?* The thought lasted for only an instant, because he could tell just by looking at Zeth, who was adorable and sexy, that he wasn't the rugged strapping man he'd felt in the darkness of his room.

Who are the alternatives? Luke thought as he heard either Cameron's or Zeth's door open followed by the sound of the bathroom door closing and the water taps being turned on. *Hamilton?* Again, the thought was fleeting because Hamilton simply didn't have the thick shoulders and body frame of the guy who seemed to have made Luke his toy.

"A master," he said aloud. *Could it be that Dungeon Master?*

Luke's thoughts were interrupted by a knock at the door. "S'open," he called, turning toward the doorway.

It was Zeth, dressed only in jeans. He had the body of a swimmer—round shoulders, a lean and well-defined hairless chest. "What's up, man?" Luke asked in a sleepy voice, getting hard and salivating at the sight of Zeth's half-naked body.

"I've been thinking about the show."

"Who hasn't?"

"I spent the night wide-awake thinking about it. I think we—I mean all us guys—ought to take over from Hamilton. He wouldn't even have to know what we were doing. I think we should come up with a plan for making the last two weeks great for television."

"I'm with you, man. I think we got to throw out all the so-called rules and make up our own. Bull will go along with whatever we want."

"We've got to hurry, though," Luke said. "We need to strategize before Hamilton gets here."

"And find a place that isn't bugged with cameras."

"I think we know where all the equipment is. We can always take something apart if we need to. And the Stedicam guys don't follow us into the bathroom. Maybe that's the place to meet."

Forgetting that he was naked, Luke got out of bed, with his morning hard-on. "Christ," Zeth said, staring at Luke. "I thought *I* had a big one. You've got me beat!"

Luke smiled. "Can't help it. Even my daddy's jealous. He once said, 'Holy shit, son, where'd that come from?' I thought my daddy's was big when we used to pee together when I was little. But I musta got a mutant gene or something."

"Maybe your mother fucked a horse."

"You can touch it, if you want to. Lotsa guys want to. I let em."

Zeth shook his head. "I'd just get more horny than I am already and end up depressed. I'd wanna have sex with you."

"Hell, I've wanted to have sex with *you,* ever since we first met. Come on, touch me."

Zeth tentatively reached out his hand and made contact with Luke's cock. "It's hot, man." Zeth slid his hand from the head to the base and groaned. Hesitating a moment he asked, "Can I taste it? Just for a minute?"

"Let's get into bed," Luke suggested. "We'll just do a quick one before everybody else gets up."

Within seconds Zeth was out of his clothes and under the sheets, with Luke on top of him. They were kissing with more eagerness and base indulgence than with anyone they'd ever been with. Luke was used to all types of men, but somehow Zeth was sexier and more comfortable to be around. Zeth's body was almost a revelation to Luke. It was clean and smooth, yet hard in all the right places.

They knew the morning was growing late and at any moment, they could be discovered. Reluctant to do so, but understanding how crucial it was to end their encounter, both were forced to climax far more quickly than they would have liked. Still, the melding of their bodies and the satisfaction each gave the other was fulfilling; the copulation was merely the cherry on top of a banana split.

"I just knew you'd be amazing," Zeth said at last.

"From the first time I laid eyes on you my gut told me you'd be awesome," Luke offered. "I was right."

They smiled at each other—until they heard Hamilton's voice coming from downstairs, instructing everybody to get themselves ready for the beginning of the fourth week of *Hunk House.*

"Fuck," Luke said. "If he catches you here, we'll be in deep shit."

Luke and Zeth quickly dressed, and Zeth slipped out of the room and bee-lined for the bathroom. Luke finger-combed back his hair and made a halfhearted attempt to make his bed.

Presently he appeared at the top of the stairs. He nonchalantly walked down to the front parlor and into the kitchen, where Hamilton was seated at the table with Bull.

"Sleep well?" Hamilton asked.

"As always," Luke said.

"Always?" Hamilton pressed. "Lots of good dreams, I'll bet."

Luke wondered if Hamilton suspected something. Had he seen Zeth leave his room? "Yeah, I always have good dreams. Some nights are just better than others."

"Like last night?"

Just then Zeth came in, looking sheepish. "Hey," he said.

He went to the sink counter and picked up a coffee mug. "What'cha got planned for us today, Hamilton?" he asked.

"How about the camera guys?" Luke asked, looking around and discovering that they weren't being recorded.

"I thought we'd have a free day," Hamilton responded. "It's Sunday. Last night was pretty traumatic. I think we need a breather. Plus I need to refocus on how to get the show back on track. Things aren't exactly turning out the way I hoped. My ass is on the line and I don't have a clue what to do. I thought maybe we could brainstorm."

Cameron eventually arrived. "Guys," Hamilton said. "Since we're all together now, I want to discuss something with you."

The men set their mugs and breakfast aside to listen to Hamilton. "When I originally interviewed each of you, without exception you asked, 'What's the show about?' I distinctly recall saying, 'It can be anything you guys want it to be.' I was being truthful. But I think I've gotten in the way by planning all these games."

"You had to have a plan, didn't you?" Luke said, trying to sound encouraging. "Otherwise, we would've just sat and stared at each other for six weeks."

"Maybe that wouldn't have been such a bad idea. You'd talk eventually, if only out of sheer boredom. Maybe the stuff we got on video would have been more the documentary I hoped this would look like."

"You wanted a reality show," Cameron stated. "All those shows have a bunch of ruthless weasels manipulating each other to keep from getting voted off an island or getting their asses kicked out of a tribe. I don't know what else you could have done."

"I don't know either," Hamilton said. "But I'm hoping we can come up with a way to spark this program and make it really original. I've realized too late that this is simply a rip-off of those other shows. The only gimmick is that everybody is gay."

"That's the problem, right there," Bull said. "*Gimmick*. Being gay isn't a *gimmick*. So far, all this show is about is exploiting a bunch of fucking freaks. If you're a guy who'd rather suck dick than eat pussy, you're a freak. You're some sick-o queer, and it's completely acceptable to laugh and leer. Everybody hates fairies. I read somewhere it's called *heterosexism*. And the way I see it, this show just spotlights that fact."

"That wasn't my intention at all," Hamilton demurred.

"Then why couldn't you have had a house filled with men the world looks up to? It would've been cool to have a movie star or a sports star, a political leader, or a famous writer, a plumber and a single father." Bull frowned. "You'd have had a better representation of the spectrum of gays."

"Any suggestions for righting my wrong?" Hamilton asked.

"Let us just be ourselves on camera," Luke interjected. "Instead of games where we win or lose a bunch of stupid points, let us just be. It'll show the audience that we're normal."

"But we've got to have some way of determining who stays on at *Hunk House* and who gets outed," Cameron said. "We still need some form of activity. A winner has to emerge; otherwise, this will just be some stupid home movie. I say we continue as a game, but maybe add like on-camera interviews or hold like group discussions or something. We need to be seen as men not just as cocksuckers."

"Cocksuckers get big ratings," Zeth said.

"Only if you've got great writers feeding great dialogue to actors," Hamilton countered. "And it seems every new show has to have a gay character on it. Gay on television is not only becoming popular; it's compulsory."

"That's the point," Bull said. "I think some of the things we've done so far might be setting the acceptance of gays back a few steps. I mean that whole s/m contest we went through. It was fun. And although I know it's also a big part of so-called straight sex, most people are just gonna still think of it as kinky gay sex. Tell the truth. How many of you would intentionally watch a guy getting his nipples pierced?"

Everyone simultaneously said, "I would!"

"I think you're wrong about that part," Luke challenged Bull. "I think that's the kind of thing that will make the ratings go up. Reality shows are getting bolder by the week. Ours is the most fearless yet! This is not what's goin' to set the gay movement back. It's the fluff, like playing that movie star game. Straights think that all gays know every song Judy Garland ever sang and we only know trivia about Michelle Kwan or Madonna. They don't believe we know anything about Lance Armstrong or Tiger Woods."

"What's wrong with knowing about the arts?" Zeth added. "One of my personal peeves is that schools cut music and art programs before they ever touch the school's football or intramural sports activities. I think it's important to show that at least one segment of the popula-tion—the gay segment—is attempting to preserve the arts. Even if it just means knowing that Tchaikovsky and Ravel were gay."

"Or Cole Porter, or Leonardo da Vinci, or Hans fucking Christian Andersen, for crying out loud," Hamilton added.

"I have a brother who couldn't watch the ballet in the movie *Oklahoma* because he didn't think real men should be dancing," Zeth continued. "When I told him that Alexander the Great, Michelangelo, Henry David Thoreau, and even a pope, Julius III, was gay, he was like, 'You're nuts! They didn't have gays in those days.' Yeah, we just evolved. Duh!"

"Then what, guys?" Hamilton said looking around the room. "What can we do? How can we keep this show going and still make it a game, as well as a positive reinforcement of how important gays are to soci-ety?"

"Ya really think we're important to society?" Bull asked, hopefully.

"Dang right!" Zeth said. "Hell, if King Richard the Lion-Hearted and Socrates and Plato were gay, then I'm damn proud to be in their company. I sometimes feel like gays are extra special, and that's why we're persecuted. I have this fantasy that someone's going to discover something that proves we're actually *superior* to everyone else on the planet. Then when the masses bow down, we'll be gracious and say, 'You couldn't have known. You were simply arrogant and stupid.'"

"They already know we're superior," Luke said. "That's why they gun us down. They're resentful. Our intelligence and talent intimidate them. They're frightened by our being unique—"

"Guys," Hamilton interrupted, "this isn't getting us anywhere. I've got to go over to KRUQ for some more work. Can you try to come up with a new format for the show while I'm gone? When I bring dinner this evening, I'll include beer and wine and we can have a brainstorming party. How's that sound?"

The men all agreed they'd give the show a lot of thought during the day and suggested that maybe the camera guys should come back to tape them as they talked among themselves and tried to devise a new game plan.

"Great," Hamilton said. "I'll be back at six. We'll eat; then we'll party. We'll save my butt and somehow get us all to California. There's more than enough room on *Days of Our Lives* for four extra-good-looking studs!"

Chapter Seventeen

"**W**ord around town is that something fascinating's happening at KRUQ," Stacia announced entering Hamilton's office. "The Ratner family is importing queers into town, for a TV show."

"Importing? You make it sound as though you're the department of agriculture . . ."

"Yeah, good analogy, and we're importing fruits."

"You're doing a great job. These *fruits* are tasty. You ought to try one. Oh, I forgot, you already have. A big ol' *Bull fruit*. It's caused a sensation at *Hunk House*. Much better than a banana but with some of the same characteristics. Although the Bull fruit has been genetically altered to produce a bigger and more mature seedpod. So appetizing. And healthy for you, too. Tons of protein."

"Christ, you queers are so infuriating!" Stacia bellowed. "We'll see how droll you are when Daddy starts hearing the gossip. You've kept him out of the loop."

"I don't recall *you* giving him a report. He's been welcome to come down to Hunk House any time. Personally, I think your father's afraid of seeing a bunch of cute guys running around in shorts and, God forbid, without their shirts on!"

"You think all men are closet homos, don't you?"

"Remember his little scenario about being in the Marines?"

"It was a time of war. Soldiers aren't in their right minds when they don't have women around."

"He was stationed in Des Moines."

"I've had enough! This is going to hurt you more than it's going to hurt me, Mr. Hamilton Ipswich Peabody the Third," Stacia said as she picked up the telephone and dialed a number on the old rotary telephone. "Daddy? I have some news to report about Hamilton and his *Hunk House* show. Yeah. Urgent. Right away." She replaced the receiver in the cradle and gave a satisfied look at Hamilton. "All your bullshitting has come to an end, Hammy. You're welcome to join me for my tête-à-tête with Daddy. If you dare."

"Whoopi Goldberg on the set of *ET* was never as much of a bitch as you are, Stacia," Hamilton said. "As a matter of fact, I'll accept your generous invitation. As the senior programming director of KRUQ, I should be present at any meeting that has to do with one of our programs or a member of our staff—especially if that person is me."

"It's your funeral, Hammy."

"You're small potatoes, Stacia. I've lived through Whitney Houston, Eddie Murphy, Russell Crowe, James Woods, Barry Sonnenfeld, Michael Bay, and Kate Beckinsale. I can survive you. See you at *Daddy's.*"

The house in which Stacia still lived with her father and brother was as large as the Maynard mansion. The Ratners were well-to-do. Considered among Dulcit's leading citizens, their home was a well-maintained Victorian Queen Anne that occupied a large tract of land.

Driving from the station to the Ratners' house, Hamilton did breathing exercises—deep breaths and slow exhalations—in an attempt to calm himself down. He had to be prepared for whatever curve ball Stacia threw at him in front of the old man.

Hamilton followed Stacia's car as she pulled into the gated circular driveway. Stacia stepped out of her Lexus and slung her purse over her right shoulder. Hamilton collected his briefcase and met Stacia as she reached the front steps of the wraparound porch. She let herself into the house and Hamilton followed.

"Mama taught me to be a good hostess when company was invited or dropped in unexpectedly," Stacia said. "Too bad you're not company. This is not a social call."

"Let's just see your father and get this out of the way."

Hamilton followed Stacia down a long mahogany-paneled hallway, past the front parlor, dining room, bathroom, and kitchen. They arrived in Ratner's study. The old man was in a La-Z-Boy recliner watching

ABC news coverage of the men's figure-skating championships. Todd Browning was scoring the ice with his spread eagle.

"Daddy, sweetheart," Stacia cooed, "you gotta turn the competition off for a few minutes. There's trouble with our *Hunk House* show, and Hamilton needs to tell you what's going on."

Old Man Ratner grumbled about missing Paul Wylie ever since he went pro. "Goldarn it. Philippe Candeloro's coming up next! What's so important that it can't wait?" Ratner demanded.

"I'll let Hamilton explain it all."

"No, Stacia," Hamilton said, "you called this meeting. I'm as anxious as your father to find out what this is all about."

"What in tarnation?" Mr. Ratner said, looking at his daughter, then at Hamilton. "What's going on? And why are you two arguing?"

"We're not arguing sir," Hamilton answered. "But Stacia has something on her mind that she would like you to be aware of. And I'm here to clear up any misunderstandings."

"Daddy, there's a whole lot of things about Hamilton—and the program—that you don't know."

"Has there been gay sex goin' on at Hunk House? I warned you about the FCC!"

"Oh, Daddy, that's just the tip of the iceberg. I think you should have some scotch." Stacia crossed the room to the bar and selected a bottle of Chivas Regal.

Ratner accepted the glass of whiskey and took a large sip. "Get on with it," he demanded. "Start at the beginning."

"The beginning?" Stacia laughed. "That's my point, Daddy. Hamilton here has been lying to you from the very beginning of his employment at KRUQ. You were right. He's a homo, and he's brought more of 'em into Dulcit to invade our God-fearing community."

Hamilton had seated himself on the sofa. He remained quiet.

"He also lied about all the applicants for *Hunk House*. Turns out he could only get five, so he lured Bull Smith into becoming a queer, and now he's a goner. He's become one of them! The topper is, the whole blamed program he promised you is nothing but pornography. I saw some of the footage myself. Hamilton is out to destroy KRUQ, and you, and the reputation our station has for decency and integrity. In just four weeks, he's managed to ruin everything you've created!"

Ratner swallowed the rest of his drink with one long pull, then looked at Hamilton. He kept his eyes on Hamilton for what seemed a very long time. "What's your side of the story, Hammy?"

"Well, sir," Hamilton stalled. "Tell me the truth, did you ever believe I was straight? Ella knew all about my past. Surely you, as the chief, would have as much background on me as she does."

"*I* knew," Stacia answered.

"Hush up, Stacia!" Ratner snapped. He looked at Hamilton again. "And what about the lack of applicants for the program? Did you lie about that?"

"Yes, sir," said Hamilton. "I'm sorry."

Ratner nodded. "I'll save you both a whole lot of trouble. I realized that *Hunk House* has turned into a den of iniquity. There's more sex goin' on in that place than at *The Best Little Whorehouse in Texas*. I didn't get to where I am by bein' blind."

Stacia whined. "Daddy, why haven't you said something before now?"

"I was countin' on one of you to turn things around before I had to step in."

"Surely you couldn't expect me to take over the program," Stacia said with indignation. "This is Hamilton's project."

"Couldn't, or wouldn't? You wanted Hammy to fail from day one."

"I haven't—"

"Stop interrupting. It's the truth. I was right not to promote you. In an executive position, if you see a problem, you have to be able to fix it. You just wanted to see how deep Hamilton's shoes would sink into the shit. And now you come whinin' t'me!"

Ratner turned to Hamilton. "You, sir, are a liar and a fraud. Even though I knew you were queer, I thought you were smart, being from L.A. and Harvard and such. I trusted this program to you, 'cause I thought you were up to the task. I always hate to admit that I was wrong about anything. But it looks like I was wrong about you. Sorry to do this to you, son, but you're fired."

"May I say something, sir?" Hamilton asked.

"Go right ahead."

"I'm not sorry for not telling you that I was gay. My personal life is my own business. So is yours. And in this town, I thought it best to keep my private side private. Don't get me wrong, Dulcit isn't any more homophobic than L.A. But at least in Hollywood there are so many more of us around, hardly anybody pays attention."

"Go on," said Ratner.

"With regard to the program," Hamilton continued, "I didn't keep you apprised of everything that was happening because I was confident, and I still am, that when the show is complete, we'll have an enormous success. I'm sorry that you're letting me go now, because everything is taking a whole new turn. It's very exciting."

"I'm sure you think so," Ratner said. "But this is a family company, and a family town, and families don't have to be exposed to the filth that you've been filming."

"Your little family station can't compete with HBO, PBS, Showtime, The Disney Channel, or the networks." Hamilton said, almost apologetically. "You signed up to broadcast *Donnie & Marie* instead of *Oprah*. And instead of reruns of *Frasier* and *Friends*, you show old episodes of *Ironside* and *Punky Brewster*. By the way, for your edification, Ironside, or Raymond Burr, was queer."

"Perry Mason, a homo?" Stacia sniped. "I suppose next you'll be telling us that Rock Hudson or Liberace were gay, too."

"Will you please be quiet!" Ratner grumbled again. "As a matter of fact, they were," he said looking up at his daughter. "I'm beginning to ask the same question that Ella did, 'What cornfield did you crawl out from?'"

Stacia, now visibly perturbed, said, "Hamilton, I think it's time you left. Daddy's made it quite clear that you're no longer wanted here."

"I'll do my own talkin', Buttercup," Ratner said. "Let Hammy finish his piece."

"It's just that, after being at the station for a year, I know the financial fix you're in. I know all the problems facing your business. I just wanted to turn things around. But I was blocked every step of the way, mostly by Stacia. When I introduced *Broadway on Broadway*, our ratings picked up. And when I replaced *Punky Brewster* in the afternoon with *Mission: Impossible*, people stayed with our station through the news. But because Stacia wouldn't let me add *Larry King Live* after the weather report, people switched to other stations. You insisted that *Lassie* was the appropriate lead in to *The Larry Storch Show*."

"My philosophy has always been, if there's a program *I* want to see, I guarantee others want to see it too!"

"But nobody wanted to see *Temperatures Rising*—even though it starred my friend Joan Van Ark—or *B. J. and the Bear. B. L. Stryker* maybe would have had a chance."

Hamilton paused. "You're absolutely right to fire me, sir. I don't want to be responsible for moving your station into the twenty-first century. Your reasons for programming the way you do are your business. I'm completely confident that you know what you're doing. When *Will & Grace* and *Goodnight Beantown* are offered for syndication, you'll choose *Beantown,* while the rest of Dulcit watches *Law & Order* on the network."

Ratner frowned. "I'll have you know I built KRUQ from the ground up. I must'a been doin' somethin' right."

"Sure, when audiences only had a choice of ABC, CBS, and NBC. Now, with satellite dishes, they've got a gazillion options. And they're not opting to watch KRUQ because, with all due respect, you think *Gunsmoke* should still be running! In case you didn't read the obituary section of the *Des Moines Register,* in 1989, Miss Kitty coughed up her last hairball."

Rather folded his arms across his chest. "Gimme another splash, Buttercup," he said to Stacia. She picked up her father's glass and went back to the bar.

"Here, Daddy," she said, bringing her father his drink. "Now isn't it time to get rid of this city slicker? I wanna start moving my things into his office."

"Thanks, sweetie," Ratner said, acknowledging the drink. "Buttercup, you're more than welcome to Hammy's office." He sipped his whiskey. "But you still can't have his job."

"Someone's got to take over," Stacia demanded. "I'm the most logical candidate."

Ratner snorted. "It ain't fittin' for a purty young thing like my Buttercup to be calling her daddy an 'old fart.' I overheard you, darlin'."

"What I meant was, you shouldn't have to run the day-to-day affairs of KRUQ."

"According to Hamilton, there aren't many day-to-days left. Am I right, Hammy?"

"I can't see the future, sir," said Hamilton. "I can only go by demographics and statistics and the week-by-week, month-by-month, year-by-year drop in the ratings."

The room was silent for a long time. Ratner looked at his drink. He looked at Hamilton. He looked at Stacia. "Didn't your mother teach you manners about when folks drop in?" he said to his daughter. "Offer Hammy a drink."

"He's leaving, isn't he?" Stacia said defiantly. "You fired him. He has to go clear out his office and stop by Hunk House and tell the guys to go home."

Hamilton said calmly, "Thank you, Stacia, I'd be delighted to join your father in a drink. Same thing he's having, please."

"Screw you!" Stacia bellowed. "If you want a drink, get it yourself!" She left the room in a huff.

Hamilton got up from the couch and went to the bar, where he poured himself three fingers of scotch over ice. He returned to his seat.

Presently, Ratner said, "'Screw you?' Where'd she ever learn such language?"

"Not from watching *F-Troop.*"

"You lied to me about being gay, Hammy. And you lied about what your program was going to be."

"I just didn't reveal the truth. And I didn't lie about what the program was going to be about because I genuinely thought it was going to turn out differently. You can plan all you want, but more often than not things don't turn out the way you imagined or hoped they would. The program is a little off track, I admit. But beginning tomorrow, it's going to be different. This morning the guys and I discussed how we could turn the show around. I was going back this evening to brainstorm some more with them."

Ratner nodded. "I think I'll go with you. But after I leave you should stay and try to decide what direction to follow."

"Do you still want to close the show down?"

"That was Stacia who said that. I've invested too much in this show to stop now."

"So have I, sir. I know I'm fired, but if you don't close down *Hunk House*, I'd like to still be involved in some capacity. I don't have to be your employee. But I would like to finish what we've started. I wish you'd consider letting the series continue and not make a final judgment until after all the editing."

Ratner pondered for a moment. "I want the show to continue."

Hamilton smiled.

"But I still don't want you as my programming director."

Hamilton frowned. "Tell ya what," he said. "Let me finish *Hunk House,* and I'll leave Dulcit just the way I found it. A quiet little hamlet in the middle of nowhere."

"This is still somewhere," Ratner said. "It may not be Glitter Gulch or the Universal Studios Tour, but it's home."

"I didn't mean any disrespect, sir."

Ratner held up a hand. "Stacia!" he called. "I wanna talk to you. Stacia?!"

Stacia quickly returned to the den. "What?"

"Just wanted you to know that Hamilton's office is all yours, as soon as he gets his stuff out."

Stacia smiled at Hamilton. "No hard feelings? I'll miss you, Hammy. I'll miss all the fights we used to have. I think I'll talk to Daddy about getting rid of Ella, too, so we can start over completely fresh."

Ratner said, "Sorry, Buttercup, but that's exactly why I could never place you in charge. You don't recognize loyalty. Ella's the best thing that ever happened to KRUQ. And before you go making too many noises about change, Hammy's gonna finish *Hunk House.*"

"You're not serious!" Stacia cried.

"And you're not to get in his way. In fact, I'm ordering you to give him any kind of help he needs. As for Ella and Bull, don't you dare even consider dumping either of them. I'm trying to change with the times, but I won't budge with the basic human values of a reward for a job well done."

Stacia turned bright red. Clearly the afternoon had not turned out as she planned. Hamilton was supposed to be ancient history by dinnertime, but he was still hanging around. The old man was supposed to give Hamilton's old job to Stacia. Instead, he dismissed her.

"Another drink, Daddy?" she asked politely.

"Think I've had enough for now, thanks, Buttercup," Ratner said. "But I think Hammy's ready for another."

"Thanks, but I'd better be leaving," said Hamilton. "But before I go, sir, we haven't decided if I have your permission to go back to Hunk House. The guys are expecting me. We're supposed to brainstorm how to revise the program."

"Go on then," said Ratner.

"Aren't you coming, too?" Hamilton asked.

"Maybe I'll drop by later."

Chapter Eighteen

On the way back to Hunk House, Hamilton stopped at the Eat 'n' Go Diner. He ordered full-course meals for five. Seated on a stool at the linoleum-and-chrome counter, waiting for the short-order cook to package up meatloaf, mashed potatoes, gravy, green beans, and corn bread, he thought he could feel the other customers staring at him. Hamilton wondered if, when the show finally aired, he would be the lead candidate for a community tar and feathering at the very least. He was glad when the five Styrofoam containers were ready and he paid his bill. Even though it was a take-out order, he tipped his chubby waitress 15 percent, and hoped to God the cook hadn't done something disgusting with the food.

"Guys! I'm home!" Hamilton called from the doorway. "Someone want to give me a hand with all this stuff?"

Bull appeared. "There's beer and wine and ice cream in the car. If you could get that, Bull?" Hamilton said.

Bull stepped outside. Hamilton made his way to the kitchen carrying the dinners and carefully setting them down on the sink counter. "Hey, guys," Hamilton called as he loosened his tie, then pulled plates from the cupboard. One by one, Cameron, Luke, and Zeth wandered into the kitchen, followed by Bull with a six pack, a bottle of Merlot, and a gallon of Ben and Jerry's Jelly Bean ice cream.

"Why the wine?" Luke asked. "What's the occasion?"

"This stuff probably needs to be reheated," Hamilton said, turning on the oven, then handing every man a white Styrofoam box. "There's

Pyrex under the counter. You can put a couple of dinners at a time in there. Who wants a drink?"

As Zeth uncorked the wine, the others grabbed a Pabst. When they each had their drinks in hand, Hamilton proposed a toast. "To survivors, one and all! Again, I'm sorry. Especially to Cameron and Bull. You guys are champs. I just want to say, as far as I'm concerned, you're all winners."

"Only the winner is the winner," Cameron huffed. "What are you leading up to?"

Hamilton sighed. "Nothing for you guys to be concerned about. Change is almost always a good thing."

"Which means?" Luke asked.

"That in addition to the changes we're going to brainstorm after dinner, there's been a change of guard at KRUQ." He took a long pull from his wineglass. "I've been fired."

"Why?"

"When?"

"You can't leave us!"

Hamilton smiled at the expressions of support. "That ray of sunshine, Stacia, got her dear ol' daddy to finally give me the boot. However, even though I'm no longer officially the director of programming, he was generous enough to let me finish producing *Hunk House*."

"I don't need this slop warmed up," Bull said. "I'll eat it cold."

After dinner, Luke went to the carriage house beside the garage where the cameramen had their quarters. Presently, the five cameramen were seated among the men of *Hunk House* as they listened to Hamilton, who, after half a bottle of wine, was a little tipsy.

"This is why our show sucks," Hamilton said. "We don't have a strategy. My fault. I never thought about what this program was really about. I figured if I just got a bunch of gay men together, something of value would develop. To a degree, it has. We've got great footage of you guys breaking all the rules and fucking at every opportunity."

"So what's the problem?" asked Cameron.

"The only thing missing is the human interest aspect."

"I'd say there's already been plenty of interest in a lot of humans," Bull countered. "What more do you want?"

"I want you guys to pull out all the stops. You've been before the cameras for four weeks now, you're no longer intimidated. You know each other pretty intimately. There aren't any barriers between you. I want you guys to spill your guts."

"Spill our guts?" Luke asked.

"Yeah, why not," Hamilton replied. "Since I no longer have any reputation to defend at KRUQ, and since you all know that the game wasn't completely fair from the beginning—what with my screwing things up by bringing Bull into all of this—we can go in any direction we want. In exchange, I'm willing to make sure you all get to L.A. and have a part on *Days of Our Lives*. You'll all be winners."

"If we do what?" Bull asked.

"Suck more cock. Tell wild stories about all your sexual conquests. Rat on your family and what it was like after you came out to them. Drag that first lover—they're always shits—through the mud. And flip off Donald Wildmon, Anita Bryant, Phyllis Shafley, George Bush, everyone who's ever openly persecuted gays and lesbians."

"This is how you want to fix the rest of the show?" Luke asked.

"In a word, yes. I want you to go hog wild. Just be who you are, only on videotape. If you had a great childhood with parents who embraced your sexuality, that's fine. Praise 'em to the roof. But if your lives were anything like mine, you should declare war."

"Revenge isn't nice," Bull said.

"Is this to entertain people, or enlighten 'em?" Luke asked.

Hamilton took another sip of wine. "Both," he said. "Just this afternoon, when I was being fired by Mr. Ratner, I was thinking about a documentary I saw in college. It showcased one family for twelve weeks. Viewers saw them on their good days and bad days. During the run of the show, the husband and wife filed for divorce, and one of their kids came out as gay. For me, the program basically showed that all families are alike in the sense that there's always conflict. So far, we don't have any real conflict in this show."

"So, you want us to fight?" Bull asked, tentatively.

"Not necessarily. But we've got to have more drama than just getting our rocks off in a dungeon or having a sex party in our bedrooms when we think no one is looking."

Luke turned red.

"I don't follow," Zeth said. "We've been playing games and interacting with each other just like you told us to. I don't see what the difference is going to be."

"The difference is that we already have tons of footage of all that game crap," Hamilton said. "Now it's time for the audience to get to know you inside out. We'll be able to intercut all the stuff we've done so far with interviews and conversations and debates between each of you."

"So how do we get the points we need to win?" Luke challenged.

Hamilton said. "Arbitrary points. But, I'm promising to make sure you all get to Hollywood. However, the four of you have to agree to throw the game."

"Say what?" Cameron exploded. "What if one of us is really ahead? It's not fair. You know Bull's not giving in now. He wants to be the winner, so already there's no choice. I don't like it."

"I don't like it either," Hamilton said. "But if you look at it the right way, it's a win/win situation for all of you. If we keep going with the games and the points for real, only one of you will get to Hollywood. This way, you all get the trip. Who knows what could happen from that? You're the best-looking men I've ever seen. Hollywood agents will cream to represent you. Teenage girls and little gay boys will probably have all your posters up on their walls."

Zeth said, "Whoever wins, once this is on the air, he'll be a star overnight. *People* magazine'll do a story on him. He'll be famous without even trying."

"Trust me," Hamilton offered. "When we start to do publicity on this series, *People* magazine is going to want to profile all of you. You're all groundbreakers."

"Zeth's right," Bull offered. "I'm not thinkin' of myself here. Hell, I don't want Barbara Walters making me cry on national television. But these guys entered into this house on good faith. Now you're takin' that away. I don't like it."

"Look," said Hamilton. "Mr. Ratner wants to close the show down completely. I convinced him to let me straighten things out. Unless anyone has a better idea—and I'd be thrilled if you did—then I don't see any other choice than to select a winner in advance and just go through the motions of having our weekly Out House meetings until it's down to just two contestants. I don't care who the winner is. That's something for you to decide. But what else can we do?"

"We can keep playing stupid games and find a real winner," Bull retorted. "As long as it's not me."

"But what if it is you, Bull?" Hamilton asked. "Are you ready to be on the cover of *The Advocate*? Wouldn't you rather volunteer to be out, just in case you're the real winner?"

"I could never be the official winner," Bull snorted.

"You didn't think you'd make it past the first week, either. Are you willing to take the risk? Stranger things have happened."

Bull was silent for a long time. Then, he said, "I'll volunteer to be the next one you out. But I'm doing it for my own reasons."

"I'd just as soon know the outcome in advance, too," Zeth said. "I'd volunteer to be out, but only if Luke has a chance to be the real winner."

"Na," Luke said. "I'll be out, too. I wanna get this thing behind us and move on to L.A. with Zeth."

"Hell, I have no problem with that scenario," Cameron stated. "I'd whoop Luke's ass anyway. It was facing off against Bull that I was worried about."

"If we weren't in this predicament, you wouldn't stand a chance against me," Luke countered. "I'm prettier than you are and a whole lot younger, too."

"I'll give you that," Cameron concluded.

"Looks like we have our new path for this program," Hamilton said, happily. "Cameron's going to win, but you'll all go to California. Thank you, guys. We'll start first thing tomorrow. Get some sleep."

Turning to the cameramen, Hamilton said, "Looks like from now on you're all in on this charade, too. I want lots more footage of everything the guys do and say. I don't care how insignificant it may appear. I'll determine in editing whether it's appropriate or not. This also means you're in on our secret. Is there anyone who can't keep a secret?"

He looked at Rocky, the head cameraman. Rocky looked the way a Rocky should: at six-feet-two inches tall, with close-cropped black curly hair, blue eyes complementing a ruddy complexion, black moustache, bright white smile of perfect teeth and two-day-old razor stubble, he was as seductive as any of the *Hunk House* contestants. The one-size-too-small white T-shirts he wore and always tucked into his equally tight black 501 jeans accentuated his rock hard, sturdy, muscular chest and biceps of his steroid built body. *Christ*, Hamilton lamented to himself, *they broke the mold after making this one.*

Rocky had been the only man that Hamilton wanted for the top job of coordinating and shooting *Hunk House*. Hamilton had admired Rocky's work on a few local commercials that he'd shot for KRUQ and the fact that he was gay and out, made it easier to coax him into accepting the assignment. Hamilton left hiring the others completely up to Rocky, who had a network of camera guys, some of whom had gone as far as to graduate from the USC Film School. With little demand for their talents in the Midwest, they jumped at the chance to do the show, regardless of the contestants' sexual identities.

"Rocky, how about you?" Hamilton said.

"I'm the best at keeping secrets," Rocky replied. "Personal and professional ethics. My guys are all cool, too. You won't have a problem trusting us."

Hamilton's smile was warm and genuine, and he tried not to let his eyes linger too long on Rocky. *God, his lips. His chest. His arms,* Hamilton thought to himself with a pang of lust. He was aware that an erection was growing in his pants. He surreptitiously sneaked a look at Rocky's basket. There was definitely something solid in there, and it was pushing against the right leg of his denim fabric. Rocky looked in to Hamilton's eyes, thinking that he, too, was a tempting treat. Their respective gaydar transmitted stronger signals than KRUQ could broadcast.

"I knew you were good for whatever is best for the show," Hamilton smiled. "That's enough for tonight. We'll see you all first thing in the A.M."

Chapter Nineteen

The *Hunk House* contestants had all gone off to bed. Hamilton sat silently in his wing chair. He picked up the empty bottle of wine from the floor beside the chair. "Darn," he said aloud.

"Excuse me. Hamilton."

Hamilton was startled and looked up. Standing in front of him was Bull, wearing only his jeans and looking like the model on the cover of a romance novel. The veins in his arms traveled straight up to his biceps. His torso was dusted with a mat of black hair, like the soft fur on a puppy's belly. Hamilton was instantly turned on.

"What is it, Bull?" he asked.

"I apologize."

"For what?"

Bull put his thumbs in the belt loops of his jeans and stood with his tight stomach only inches away from Hamilton's face. Hamilton swallowed hard as he looked straight into Bull's deep navel and noticed the dark trail of black fur that led down into his pants.

"For makin' you look stupid and like a cheater. I broke my promise to keep my status as a contestant a secret.

"Hamilton," Bull continued, "I'm confused about a lot of stuff."

"Stuff?"

"Feelings."

"Desires?"

"Urges."

"You're shaking," Hamilton said.

" 'Cause I'm following an impulse I might regret."

Bull reached out his hands and pulled Hamilton up from his chair.

Hamilton literally swooned, like Scarlett O'Hara staring up at Rhett Butler for the first time.

"You drunk?" Bull asked.

"You could call it that."

It was useless for Hamilton to even attempt to turn out the lights or pick up the empty glasses and bottles of beer and his bottle of wine. He was working on automatic pilot as Bull guided him to his room.

"Just be gentle with me," Bull asked, in a plaintive voice.

Be gentle with you? Hamilton nearly laughed. *What about me?*

"I just want to try having you hold me," Bull said.

Closing the bedroom door behind them, Bull tentatively took over. He unbuttoned Hamilton's shirt, the way Luke had taught him just a few days before. He gently pulled Hamilton's shirt off his body, then caressed his neck and chest and arms. Remembering the words that Luke had used, Bull said, "Hamilton. You're more beautiful than I imagined."

In slow motion, Bull unhooked Hamilton's belt and worked the button on his trouser's waist. Hamilton was wearing white briefs. Bull eased the briefs down Hamilton's hips and put his face into his crotch. He inhaled the sweet scent from the moist dark hair but did not touch Hamilton's penis with his mouth.

"Let's take off all our clothes," Bull said.

As if modest, Bull turned around and pulled off his jeans. Hamilton saw that he wasn't wearing underwear. When Bull turned around, Hamilton gasped. A dark thicket of hair surrounded the biggest cock that Hamilton had ever seen. Not only were Bull's balls more enormous than they appeared in the Polaroid, his erect cock was more beautifully sculpted than any porn star's Hamilton had viewed.

Hamilton and Bull climbed onto the bed. Facing each other, Bull held Hamilton in a loving, almost protective way. Hamilton caressed Bull's arms, then pushed his face into the cleft between Bull's pecs.

"Bull. Oh God, Bull. You're so beautiful, so fantastic! I've never felt like this with anyone in my entire life!"

Suddenly, without warning, Bull rolled Hamilton over on his back and lay spread-eagle on top of him. Bull placed his lips on Hamilton's and began to kiss him. With reciprocal ardor the kisses were harsh, then soft, then harsh again, as if Bull were discovering the greatest pleasure he'd ever known.

* * *

Bull was the first to awaken. He looked at the clock by his bed stand and saw that it was past nine o'clock.

Hamilton awoke. He looked over at Bull and smiled. "What time's it?"

"The guys are already up. I can hear 'em in the kitchen."

Hamilton reached for Bull's strong shoulders and pulled him back into bed. "Just let me hold you for a few more moments. Please." He inhaled the scent of Bull's body and immediately became aroused. He could feel Bull's dick was already hard, which made it all the more emotionally painful because Hamilton knew he had to let Bull go. The two stayed entwined for a few minutes. "I think it'll be best if you go out there first," Hamilton said at last. "Distract the guys while I dress. I'll pretend to come in through the front door."

"Sounds like a plan," Bull said. "Last night is our secret?"

"Absolutely."

Bull placed a large hand on Hamilton's chest and gently pushed him back against the mattress. He bent over and placed his lips onto Hamilton's. It was a deep loving, passionate kiss that made both men moist and sticky. They wished with all their hearts that they could engage each other again right now. But of course, with the other men practically right outside their door, they didn't dare tempt fate and call attention to their rendezvous.

Presently, Bull extricated himself from Hamilton who had wrapped his arms tightly around Bull's back and shoulders. "Better get dressed. I don't know how I'm gonna get the guys out of the kitchen. But when you hear us move, that's your cue. Race for the front door and pretend you're coming in."

Bull pulled his jeans on, then slipped his arms into his flannel shirt, which he didn't bother to button. He slid his bare feet into his work boots and, without bothering to tie them, left the room without turning back to see Hamilton, who waited until the door closed before quickly dressing in his badly wrinkled suit and shirt.

"Man, you look wasted," Cameron said, when Bull appeared in the kitchen. "You remind me of myself after an all-nighter!"

Zeth offered Bull coffee and a toasted bagel. "That Hamilton hasn't come by yet with no doughnuts," Cameron said in a testy tone.

"Maybe he got hung up," Bull defended.

"Yeah, well it's his job to feed us, isn't it? We can't do it on our own. Just 'cause he doesn't work for the show anymore doesn't mean he can shirk his responsibilities to us."

"Hamilton'll be along. I don't know if he'll be bringin' any food."

"How would you know that?" Luke asked suspiciously.

"Like you said, he ain't workin' for KRUQ anymore. Maybe he'll take us out for breakfast or something since there ain't no more rules."

Zeth said, "Hamilton'll come through. If not, we'll have to mutiny."

"Give him a break," Bull commanded. "The guy's been through a lot."

"Getting fired ain't the end of the world," Cameron said. "How's he takin' it?"

"Hard," Bull said. "He thinks he's a failure."

"He'll find something else," Zeth added. "Plus, he wanted to get back to L.A. anyway. Now he's more or less forced to go back. And, he's taking us with him."

"There's always more to a story than what's reported," Bull said. "Just go easy on the guy, all right? There's stuff going on in his life that you can't imagine."

"Sounds as though you know him intimately," Luke teased.

Bull scowled. "Why don't we all go into the living room and wait for him there?"

"I'm fine where I am," Cameron said.

"I said we're going into the front parlor to wait for Hamilton to come back to Hunk House."

Not wanting to cause a scene, Cameron acquiesced. The men all got up from their chairs with their mugs of coffee. "I'm cool, man. We'll wait wherever you want," Cameron said.

From inside Bull's room, Hamilton could hear the voices of the men fading into the distance. Hamilton gingerly opened the bedroom door and peered out. The kitchen was empty. As stealthily as possible, he maneuvered himself down the hallway and past the closed-off dining room and parlor. He reached the stained-glass front door and put his hand on the knob. The door was locked.

Keys? Keys? What did I do with the keys, he asked himself. Then he remembered leaving them in a bowl on the piano. He thought for a moment. *Okay, so I'll just kick the door so it sounds like I've closed it, then wander back down the hall calling the men as I do each morning.*

Hamilton slammed the heel of his shoe against the thick mahogany door and began calling, "Wakey, wakey! Bull, Luke, Zeth! Rise and shine!"

By the time he'd made his way down the hall to the front parlor, he feigned surprise to find the guys all up and seated together. "You guys are rarin' to go, eh?"

"Who the fuck ran you over," Cameron said, looking at Hamilton's clothes, hair, and beard stubble. "You and Bull get mugged or somethin'?"

"What? No. I didn't sleep much, that's all. Oh, yeah, my car broke down and I had to push it."

"What a crock," Cameron badgered Hamilton. "You've been rolling in the hay with someone." He smiled his self-satisfied, all-knowing smile.

"No. Really. I was thinking about the show until I fell asleep in a chair. I just woke up and figured I'd better get my butt over here. Is there any coffee?"

"You should stick to one story," Cameron smiled.

"I'll get you a cup," Bull offered. He got up and left the room.

"So what were you thinking about the show?" Zeth asked Hamilton. "Did'ja come up with a couple good games for Cameron to win?"

"I thought we agreed that from today on, we'd just be more revealin' about ourselves," Luke said. "No more actual games. Hamilton said he had enough stuff on tape to edit games in where needed."

"Right," Zeth said dubiously. "Well, I think we should get the cameras rolling. We could even wrap this thing up in just a couple of days, if we get sufficient footage."

Bull returned, and Hamilton gratefully accepted the mug of coffee. "Thanks, Bull," he said.

"You're welcome."

"I hadn't thought about that idea," Hamilton continued to Luke. "We really just need maybe two or three days' worth of interaction between you guys and some one-on-one interviews. It could be done. Plus two more mock Out House sessions. Then it's so long Dulcit."

"First, we need breakfast," Cameron demanded. "We're all starved. You didn't even bring an éclair."

"Sorry. Call up the diner. Tell 'em to put it on the KRUQ account and order whatever you guys want. Get me some French toast. Extra syrup, okay?"

Cameron eagerly reached for the telephone and called directory assistance for the number. Each of the men called out his order and Cameron recited it to someone on the other end of the line.

Cameron replaced the telephone onto the cradle. "They're on their way," he announced.

"Bull," Hamilton called. "Run out to the carriage house and get the camera guys in here in a hurry."

Bull hustled outside to where the cameramen were bunking. They arrived quickly, eager to begin shooting.

Within forty minutes, the doorbell rang. "Must be the diner assholes," Cameron said. "I'll get it."

Cameron went to the door. It was locked. The doorbell rang again. "Keep your shirt on! I'm coming," he shouted. He looked at Hamilton. "Why'd you lock the door again? Where are the keys?"

"I found a bunch of keys," Bull announced quickly. "They're probably yours. Let me get 'em. They're on my dresser."

Luke and Zeth looked at each other, puzzled.

The doorbell rang again. "If you don't keep your pants on, I'm gonna take 'em all the way off and whip your ass with my belt!" Cameron called through the door.

When Bull finally returned with Hamilton's keys, Luke nudged Zeth and smiled.

"I'll just get my wallet," Hamilton said, retreating back through the kitchen.

"It's in Bull's room," Luke whispered to Zeth. "How much you wanna bet?"

"Not me," Zeth said as the diner's delivery guy was ushered into the house. He looked as frightened as if he'd entered a cemetery at midnight on Halloween.

"We're hungry, but we aren't gonna eat you," Cameron said.

"This is that house, and you're all fags, right?" the kid asked in a manner that said he was just curious.

Hamilton put his fists on his hips. "We're queers, not fags," he said, signing the bill and handing the boy a twenty. "Be sure to tell all your friends that 'queers' are generous tippers."

"Thank you, sir," the boy said as he backed out the door and ran to his car.

"You guys eat," Hamilton said. "Sorry I look so awful. Maybe I should run home and change."

"Why change—unless you're uncomfortable in two-day-old underwear?" Luke teased.

Hamilton grimaced, then smiled. "I think I will just grab a fresh pair of pants and rush right back. Be here before you've finished your breakfast. Then we can get started. Okay?"

Chapter Twenty

Hamilton said, "Remember *When Harry Met Sally?* Those people whining about their relationships or their lazy husband or wife? 'Ach, you don't know my pain!'" he parodied an old couple who appeared to be the subject of an interview. "'You think it's easy being married to this slob? And the dreck she makes for me to eat! Too salty. Gives me gas. And also the runs. And when was the last time we had sex? Must be ten years ago!'"

Everybody laughed at Hamilton's imitation.

"That's what I need from you guys," Hamilton said. "I want you to reach deep down into your guts and just let it all spill out. I don't care if it's about sex, about your youth, about your first love, about what your plans are for the future. I want your guts. This is where people watching the show are going to really get to know you. They could end up loving you or hating you, but I don't want them not to care about you. You're in their living room. If you want 'em to invite you back, they've gotta find you fascinating."

"Nobody wants to hear any sob stories about how tough it is to be gay," Luke stated. "And nobody wants to hear that it's a really cool life, either."

"C'mon, Luke," Hamilton said. "This doesn't have to be a downer, and it doesn't have to be a pep rally for PFLAG. Just talk about what's important to you. If it really comes from your heart, trust me, it'll be important and interesting to the viewers. I'll give you guys some time to think about what you plan to say. You decide who we'll tape first."

* * *

Within a half hour, Cameron announced that Zeth had volunteered to be the first to take the hot seat.

"Great," Hamilton said. "We've set up a space in the old conservatory. At least it's quiet and the plants aren't all dead or giving off their last whisper of oxygen."

Hamilton, wearing faded blue jeans, a black T-shirt, and white tennis shoes, put an arm around Zeth's shoulder and walked him down the hall to a glass-walled room. A camera was set up on a tripod in front of a wing chair. Within the lens's frame was a bust of Beethoven and a large potted fern. On a cherry wood butler's table next to the chair was a glass of water and a cut-crystal pitcher beaded with condensation.

"Zeth," Hamilton said in an encouraging tone, "please feel free to talk openly and honestly about anything you want to. The camera will be rolling for as long as you like. Take fifteen minutes or an hour. The more you give me to work with, the longer you'll have an opportunity to be on screen. But the really important thing is that you give the audience something that makes them connect with you personally. Give them something memorable, that you're sure no one else could come close to. Try to be totally different from the other guys."

"I'll try. I can talk about anything?"

"Whatever comes to mind. Stream of consciousness. Just be *you.*"

Zeth took a seat on the leather chair. Hamilton clipped a small microphone to his shirt. "Don't think of the camera as an inanimate object. Pretend it's me. I'll be standing right behind Rocky."

For the first time since Day One, Zeth was nervous. Being one-on-one with the camera had thrown him off. He never thought of himself as particularly good at extemporaneous talking anyway and this just amplified the problem.

"We'll give you a couple of minutes, if you need 'em."

"No," Zeth said. "Start rolling. Let's get this over with."

Rocky looked through the viewfinder and focused on Zeth's face. He nodded to indicate that he was ready whenever Zeth was ready.

Zeth nodded back. "Three. Two. One. Hi. I'm Zeth. I'm one of four kids. Three of us are queer, but I'm the only one who ever came out. Either I had more balls than my two brothers—my sister's straight—or I'm the bad seed in the family. Maybe they all tried to spare my folks from pain. Not me. There was something exhilarating about shocking 'em. Although I don't know why they were so surprised when I said I was queer. I was twenty-one. A late bloomer, I suppose. Dad cried. Mom was supportive, at least to my face, although I found out later she went into a six-month depression. Like my sexuality had anything to do with how either of 'em raised me. Jeeze, talk about the ultimate in being self-absorbed. Like the world must revolve around her.

"Actually, now I think they just loved me and were afraid I'd live some horrible life. What'd they know of being gay? They were born and raised in the same small town. All they know are the stereotypes. If they could see some of the butch guys—married guys even, with kids—who've fucked me, they might think different about what being queer means.

"The happiest time of my life was when I was with Pete, who was my first real lover. I'd slept with other guys, lots of guys. But Pete was different. You know how it is when you just connect with someone else? Can't say there were fireworks or whistles, but I knew, I just knew he was the guy I wanted to spend the rest of my life with. He was older, I guess, about fifteen years older. A schoolteacher. Not mine. We met at Tes Tease in Des Moines—that's a gay bar. He was cruising. He didn't even look gay to me. I mean even I had preconceived notions because of stereotypes."

Hamilton kept nodding his head from behind the camera and smiling, as if to convey, "This is great, keep going!"

Zeth continued. "Pete was a professor of cultural anthropology over at Dennis Community College. I loved saying that—professor of cultural anthropology. It made me feel smart just to know him. And the guy was a brain. He should have been at Harvard or Yale instead of dinky Dennis Community. And he was out to his colleagues. I think he was the first man I'd ever met who wasn't afraid of being who he was. Everybody loved him. I don't think they loved him just to his face because it's PC to be nice to queers. I think everybody genuinely thought he was cool. And *I* got to be with him!

"And *built!* This is the fucking truth, I was looking at a travel brochure once while we were dating, 'cause he'd been everywhere and I wanted to kind of brush up on where some of these places were that he talked about. I came across a booklet about Greece. I turned a page and there he was. Only it wasn't really him, it was just a statue carved way in the B.C. times. The statue looked just like Pete!"

Zeth cleared his throat. He picked up the glass of water and took a sip, then returned the glass onto its doily and refocused on Hamilton's smiling face.

"Whatever happened to Pete?" Zeth wondered aloud. "That seems so long ago. We, or at least I, had the best time of my life. He taught me a lot about sex, too. Until I met Pete I didn't know there were so many different things guys could do together.

"I remember one time, he had laid out a plastic mat on his bedroom floor—he was pretty much a neatnick, didn't want to mess the sheets, now that I think of it—and I was on my back and he was fucking me. He had lubed me with some menthol stuff, like what you rub on your chest when you have a cold. I thought nobody else would ever have invented this kind of sex. Then he pulled out a bottle of poppers. He closed one nostril with his thumb and put the bottle under his other nostril and inhaled deeply. Then he brought the bottle down to me. I started to inhale and he lost his balance and accidentally dumped half the bottle down my nose!

"I screamed like the Phantom of the Opera getting acid thrown in his face. I don't even remember him pulling out of me; it all happened so quickly as I raced to the bathroom and cupped my hand under the tap of cold water, scooping water up my nose and screaming."

Hamilton made a sympathetic face.

"I don't know if that was the start of it, but things just cooled between us. Pretty soon we went from five phone calls a day, and me going to his place for sex every night, to four calls and sex three nights, to three to two. And then there were none. It's my fault. I didn't have any self-esteem so I just didn't fight for what I thought was a great relationship."

Zeth paused. "Wanna hear my most embarrassing moment? It was while I was in high school—the first dance. I didn't know anything about *anything* in those days, except that I didn't have or want a girlfriend. I was persuaded by my mother to go. Anyway, I get to the school gym, and there was a live band and most of the girls were standing against the wall at one end, and the guys were at the other end. There were a few faculty chaperones milling about, trying to coax the guys and girls to dance. It was pretty boring. Well, pretty soon, some of the girls started dancing with each other. This kind of broke the ice and guys started to cut in and dance with them. I saw the girls dancing together so I thought it was cool for guys to dance together too. So there was

Thomas Stern. He was a tallish guy, very quiet, like me, and had really pretty blue eyes and peach-colored skin. I asked him if he wanted to dance. And we did. I mean we didn't touch or anything—nobody, not even the girls and guys touched. There was just a lot of twisting of hips and moving our arms up and down and backward and forward.

"Long story short, nobody said anything to either of us. Nobody seemed to care. Maybe they knew we were both queer and it was cool with 'em. I didn't think twice about it, until I got home and got drilled by my parents who were excited that I'd gone to my first dance. "Who'd you dance with," they asked, probably because they must've thought, 'Thank God, now that Zeth's been out with girls he'll take down his Tom Selleck poster from over his bed and put up Madonna.' Since I didn't know any better—I admit I'm not the sharpest crayon in the box—I told them that I danced with Thomas Stern.

"'You danced with a guy?' my father asked. He didn't think he heard right. I said everybody was dancing with everybody else, guys and girls, girls and girls, guys and guys. That's when he told me that only faggots danced together and not to come home crying when I got beat up in the school yard on Monday morning.

"I never got beat up. Nobody ever said a word. I still don't think it mattered to the other kids. But it sure as hell mattered to my parents."

Hamilton smiled, coaxing him on.

"So going back to coming out. I don't know why they—my folks—carried on so when I finally admitted what I thought was obvious. Dad acted like I'd suddenly become a freak on the *Jerry Springer Show*. And then finding out later about my mom. Jeeze. No wonder my brothers never came out. Frankly, I feel sorry for 'em—my brothers. They're still living in the closet and will probably end up having nervous breakdowns. I don't regret coming out. Imagine going through life never being able to touch another man's skin? But I guess I could have handled it better. Although I don't really know how."

Hamilton gave Zeth a thumbs-up to indicate how pleased he was with the way the taping was progressing. He made a gesture with his hands that seemed to say, "Come on, give me more."

Zeth sat silent for a moment, deep in concentration. Presently he offered, "But even though I didn't get the shit beat out of me, as my father predicted, I never did fit in at school. I don't remember really having a best friend. Oh, there were plenty of kids to talk to in the hallway, or in homeroom, or in Chess Club. I was popular enough to be voted a Student Council Home Room Rep. But I didn't have a best friend. This is so interesting 'cause I've never thought of it until just now," Zeth said, staring past Hamilton, seeing himself studying, and reading and listening to music in his room. He didn't remember being on the phone for hours with buddies. But he did remember going alone to see *The Sound of Music* and *Meet Me in St. Louis* at the one revival house in all of Iowa, which was a twenty minute drive from his home to Sternsville.

"I spent a lot of my free time watching old movies and reading. I was always alone. Or at least it felt as if I was alone. Either nobody appreciated the things I did, or they didn't appreciate me, I don't remember. But I do recall my brothers teasing me 'cause I had a fixation on Brian Boitano. For a while I wanted to *be* Brian Boitano!

"In a way, I think I was just ahead of my time. Things that my brothers are just starting to appreciate I loved when they weren't quite 'in.' F'instance, I was ga-ga for Petula Clark. She was famous before I was born, but I bought all her old records—and Ella Fitzerald's records and Doris Day's and Dusty Springfield's. My brothers and sister, and I guess everyone else my age, were into the Spice Girls or Anthrax or whoever was number one at the time.

"Same with books. I discovered Maya Angelou before she became a household name. And Truman Capote. He was my first literary love. Same thing with actors. I still get a woody over David Hyde Pierce. He's sexy because he's smart and super-talented."

Zeth paused. "I'm just rambling here, sorry. But I wanted to tell you all a little bit about me." Zeth smiled. "Ever watch *The Actors Studio?* I like the questions that host always asks the stars at the end. So let's pretend I'm on the stage at the New School, that's what they call the place in New York where they train people to become actors, and in my fantasy I'm a big star, and it's almost the end of the show. The guy always asks a series of questions, the same ones to each guest. They're questions made up by a guy in France, whose name the pretentious host guy attempts to pronounce with a way-over-the-top affected French accent.

"First I get asked, 'What sound or noise do you like?'

"Like Meryl Streep, I'd say, 'rain.'

"'What sound or noise do you hate?'

"'Tractors plowing a field.'

"'What profession other than your own would you like to attempt?'

"Remember, at this point I'm a bigger star than Ben Affleck. I say, 'Competitive figure skating.'

"'What profession would you *not* like to undertake?'

"'Disneyland ride operator.'

"'What's your favorite curse word?'

"This is a question I can't imagine the stars don't already have planned 'cause they're sure to have seen the show before. I mean it's been on for a long time, and all their friends have been on—like Carol Burnett, Paul Newman, Mary Tyler Moore, Sally Field, Matthew Broderick.

"So, on the show, in my fantasy, I laugh and pretend to be embarrassed, like they all do. And with the exception of Mary Tyler Moore, they invariably say their favorite word is 'fuck.' And even though it gets bleeped out, you can still tell they said 'fuck.' Even Mary Tyler Moore eventually said 'fuck.' But my word would be 'cocksucker.' I think that was Meryl's word, too. I suppose that's been used a lot, but I don't remember who else said it. Maybe Billy Crystal. Doubt if it was Tom Hanks. Now there's another sexy dude, but my gay friends don't see it.

"In fact, one of my buds has a fit whenever I say So-and-So is attractive, because the guys I find attractive are sexy for reasons that others don't see right away. I'm attracted to guys who are funny, who have a brain and some talent somewhere. Guess that's just my feminine side. I think I heard someone say, 'Why would Shirley Jones, who's so beautiful, marry a slob like Marty Ingles? The other person said it was because women like to be laughed into bed. I'm the same way. Laugh me into bed. And I hated all the flack that Julia Roberts got when she married Lyle Lovett. Yeah, he may not be everybody's idea of Prince Charming, but I bet he's a heck of a great guy. Who wouldn't want to be with someone really nice like him?

"So that's me, Zeth. If you wanna know more you can click on to my Web site, www dot Zeth at Hunkhousesurvivor-dot-com. I'm kidding. But when I'm famous I'll definitely have my own Web site.

"That's all I can think for now," Zeth said, looking up to Hamilton for approval.

"Perfect!" Hamilton applauded as Rocky turned off the video-recorder and Zeth removed his microphone.

"Was I really okay?" Zeth asked.

"It's exactly what I wanted. You're a natural on camera. I see a bright future for you in Hollywood. You'll have those *Days of Our Lives* hunks eating out of your hands. Or anything else you want eaten."

As the two walked out of the conservatory and into the main part of the house, Zeth continued his cross-examination of how well he had performed. "I didn't know how much sex stuff you wanted. Was there enough? And I didn't want to sound like I was some sad little freak. I didn't come off that way, did I? How about my story about my parents freaking out when I told 'em I was gay? That wasn't too crybaby whiny, was it?"

"You're an actor all right," Hamilton teased. "You gotta be told every moment how wonderful you are. The truth is, you were great! I only hope the others can be half as good as you."

"Are you sure there wasn't one thing I could have done to make it any better?"

Tired of Zeth's ego, which hadn't raised its head even once during the past weeks, Hamilton finally stopped in the hallway. "One thing that could have made it better? Yeah, I suppose."

Zeth was stunned. He expected Hamilton to continue the high praise that had come flooding toward him from the moment the videocamera began to tape him. "What? What'd I do wrong, or could've done better? I thought I did a great job!"

"Just one itsy-bitsy thing. If you'd stripped down and jerked off, we would've had a remarkable show."

Zeth was stunned. "Really?" he asked, as if such a thing would have been possible.

Hamilton rolled his eyes. "How many times do I have to tell you how great you were? It hardly matters. You'll see for yourself soon enough. Now go and have some lunch. And find out who wants to be in the hot seat next."

Entering the kitchen where Cameron and Bull and Luke were making sandwiches while Stedicams circled around them, Zeth said, "What a blast. It's fun to just talk about yourself."

"This kid's got an ego the size of a small European principality," Bull said.

"No," Zeth said, grabbing a Coke from the refrigerator. "It's just that I now know for sure that I belong in front of a camera. It was like being on Leno or a Barbara Walters post-Oscar special, only I didn't cry. Hamilton wants to know who's next."

The other men all looked at each other questioningly. "We can do this the easy way and have a volunteer, or we can draw straws," Luke suggested. "Someone's got to go next if we're gonna get out of here in a couple of days."

"I'll do it," Bull said, sounding to Zeth like a missionary offering himself as a meal to cannibals.

Twenty-One

"There are gonna be some serious changes around here," Stacia said when Ella arrived at the office with a Styrofoam cup of coffee and a dozen doughnuts for the office. It was Sunday, but Stacia had summoned Ella into work.

"Does this have to do with Hammy getting fired?" Ella asked.

"Aren't we *The National Enquirer?* Who gave you the Liz Smith column headline?"

"There's not much that gets past me, Miss Ratner." Ella was in no mood to tolerate Stacia's arrogant attitude. "To prove my point, you could quiz me on just about any subject concerning the lives and loves of the delightful citizens of Dulcit. I could tell you about Rex's *Man Meat* magazine that comes in a plain manila envelope over at the post office each month. Or, if you find it more interesting, I could do a tap dance routine while reciting the pitiful scores from your high school SATs? Or that the nurses in Dr. Downey's office had a good laugh when they talk about why you gotta use that lady's ointment twice a day for six weeks? I could at least give you some advice about that hair color you use. What is it, Miss Thrifty Number Seven? Dear, that's just the tip of the iceberg of my fun facts."

Stacia was horrified.

"By the way," Ella continued. "I don't appreciate you suggesting that I be 'swept out with the old.' "

"You? Swept out?"

"That was your intention, wasn't it?"

"Who said?" Stacia admitted. "Actually, Daddy should'a done it years ago."

"Time's on my side. Makes it pretty hard to find a reasonable excuse that would stand up in court. I don't kid myself. I'm not indispensable. None of us are, including you."

"I practically own this station, you old tart. When Daddy dies, I'll do things *my* way around here!" Then a thought seemed to dawn on her. "Have you been talking to Hamilton?"

"As a matter of fact, I haven't heard from Hammy since yesterday morning. A little rodent—a *rat*, actually—told me all about his termination."

"But no one else knows!"

"The right people always know. Even your thoughts aren't safe in a town as small as Dulcit!"

Stacia frowned, then changed the subject. "We've got work to do. You need to help me dig out Hamilton's office so I can move my stuff in."

"That's Hamilton's job."

"I need to get settled in my rightful place."

"You're in your rightful place. And nothing's settled until Hamilton cleans his own stuff out."

"Don't argue with me," Stacia challenged. "You're just an employee. Get your wrinkled ass in there and start boxing things up."

"Sorry." Ella sat down at the reception desk, removed the lid from her coffee cup, and took a sip. She made a face. "With all our bickerin', my double espresso latte's gotten cold. I'll nuke it for a minute."

She left the room for the tiny kitchen that she was required to keep spotless. She placed her cup in the microwave oven and set the timer for one minute. When the buzzer went off, she retrieved her cup and took a sip. "Ah, that's better." Ella returned to the reception area.

In the time it took Ella's latte to reheat, Stacia left the reception area and entered Hamilton's old office. Hamilton kept his space as immaculate as his suits, so there wasn't all that much to do in the way of cleaning things out in preparation for Stacia to move in.

"Ella!" Stacia bellowed. "Ella! Where're the spare keys to Hamilton's desk?"

Ella made her way down the hall with her cup of coffee, walking slowly to avoid spilling the contents. She arrived at Hamilton's door and saw Stacia attempting to jimmy the lock on the desk drawer with a letter opener.

"Hamilton's far too smart to leave anything of value in his desk," Ella said.

"I need to know where he's keeping all the tape coverage from *Hunk House*. He's stored 'em somewhere."

"Hammy's too smart to put them in his desk. You're just going to destroy . . ."

"There!" Stacia declared with triumph. "I always say, if a burglar wants to get into your place badly enough, he'll find a way."

"So now you're burglarizing Hamilton's private property, eh?"

"It's KRUQ's property. I'm not doing anything illegal."

"How about corrupt and dishonest?"

"Are you accusing me of doing something criminal?" Stacia snarled. "If I were a woman your age, with no means of support other than her job, and not even a pension plan, I think I'd watch what I said around my superiors."

"You got me there," Ella smiled. "Guess I'm just an old relic. Hardly fit for anything but being a gofer and answering the phone."

Stacia looked at her with a satisfying grin.

Ella continued. "But as far as you being my superior—trust me, kiddo, that's a big LOL!" She rolled her eyes, partly in sympathy for Stacia's slowness of mind. "Trust me, the only thing I'd give you credit for being superior to me on would be the size of your *cojones*. You've got a pretty big set of 'em, too. But you don't wear 'em so well! No wonder Bull's turned gay."

Stacia was stunned. "Don't you talk about Bull! He'll be back to normal just as soon as this *Hunk House* debacle is over. I'm all the sex he needs! And, after all these years of you working at this station, you think you can treat me like someone at your level on the food chain? Not for a moment."

"Keep threatening me, Stacia. This is the most fun I've had since the last time I watched Luke's self-made audition tape."

"Don't they ever shut up on your planet," Stacia snapped as she began rifling through Hamilton's desk drawers. "Jeez, the guy's as neat on the inside as he is on the outside. Bet he changes his underwear every day, too."

"And flosses his teeth morning and night. Told you about gay men."

Then, with a wide smile Stacia said, "Bingo! His diary and address book! Oh, nice. Ralph Lauren. Figures."

"Now that's none of your business," Ella insisted. "You leave Hamilton's personal property alone."

"Christ, he's so damned neat. Everything's printed almost as perfectly as if it were written on a typewriter. There's something sick about an orderly desk and a printed diary. What if he makes a mistake? Probably starts the whole page over!" She paused, skimming the pages of text. "I'll be darned. Daddy's all the way through here. And here's your name, too."

"Oh?"

"Where am I?" Stacia complained. "I'm damned important to this studio."

By now, Ella had sidled up to Stacia and was trying to read along. She smiled. "Says I'm one of the few human beings he's ever met. Oh, there you are. He just calls you 'the boss's morose daughter.'"

Stacia blanched. "Morose?"

"Means 'sad' or 'ill-humored.'"

"I've got him," Stacia exclaimed. "He's so anxious to get back to his precious Hollywood. In your words, LOL! He'll never make it back there now. He says some mean things about some famous people. It's dated before he came to Dulcit. Listen.

Stacia began to read aloud:

"This town is a blast, [Hollywood, I guess] if you're rich and famous. However, if you're a bottom-feeding leech like all the agents, producers, and low-level talent, it's a root canal without Novocain! Today, I was required to take Michael Bay's new discovery, Judith Remington, to her gynecologist before her taping of ET. The show's director didn't want to take a chance on losing her if the results of her tests were positive, which they were. Chlamydia! Wonder who transmitted that little love package?

Then there's that beauty, Angela Bassett. Why isn't she a bigger star? She can act rings around Penelope Duncan. If I were in charge of this town, she'd be the queen, along with Meryl and Gwyneth's mother and Jodie Foster.

"He's not being mean," Ella said.

Stacia turned the page. "He'll never work in that town again if I send this on to *Access Hollywood*."

Chris Woodington is definitely gay! He wanted me to blow him in the back of the limo on the way to this afternoon's taping. Of course I did it. He's incredibly sexy. But so fucking arrogant! The asshole intentionally ejaculated all over my suit! No way to get the stain and smell out! He's such a phony. The fact that Rosie O'Donnell has deified him and every teenage girl in the world buys his records and sees his movies and masturbates to his posters (I confess I do the same thing with the one where he's lying in bed with the satin sheet pulled up to just below his naval) is typical spin-city Hollywood.

"He had sex with Chris Woodington?" Stacia gasped.

"Go for it, Hammy," Ella declared.

"Ha! All this stuff about Dustin Hoffman, Tom Cruise, Marlon Brando, Cher, Caroline Rhea, Tom Selleck, and Michael Eisner! This is too precious," she smiled. "I've got his balls in a vice!"

Flipping through the text, Stacia fell upon her father's name.

Mr. Ratner's an honest man with more than his share of problems. He's never been outside of Dulcit, so he doesn't have a clue about what would make his small station grow. And his pathetic daughter can't help. Poor deluded little wannabe. She's been in his shadow for eons. She'll always walk three steps behind the old man 'cause she hasn't got an original idea in her brain. She looks to Daddy for approval. She's defined by what he thinks about her. She should just get married and give up trying to be a muck-a-muck.

Stacia sputtered a nonverbal objection, letting the diary/address book fall from her hands onto Hamilton's desk.

Ella picked it up. She flipped to the back pages. "He really does know Joan Van Ark. And a bunch of other famous people. Bruce Springsteen. Meryl Streep. Kate Hudson. Billy Bob and Angelina. That Matthew Perry from *Friends*. And here's Jennifer Love Hewitt, for cryin' out loud. This is a *Who's Who* of Hollywood! No wonder he kept it locked up. Just out of curiosity, is that cute Campbell Scott in there?" Ella said, momentarily forgetting that she was opposed to spying on Hamilton's personal property.

"This is exactly the thing I need to bust Hammy. Give it to me, you little perv," Stacia said.

Ella turned away, cradling the book. "Ss. Ss. Sanders, Beverly; Sanford, Isabel; SanGiacomo, Laura; Sarandon, Susan; Sargeant, Dick—forgot to take that one out. Sawyer, Diane; Schwarzenegger; yeah, Scott, Campbell, with an asterisk next to his name. Wonder what that means. Where's his e-mail address?"

"It's none of your business. As you pointed out, this is personal information. You're invading his privacy!"

"Yeah, like what you're planning to do is to preserve history."

"Don't question me," Stacia retorted. "You work for me, remember? "You're here to do as I or my daddy or Rex tells you. Got that? Now make me a photocopy of each page," she said. "And make it fast. If Hamilton comes in and finds you copying his personal book, I'll deny any involvement."

"CAMPS at AOL dot COM," Ella stated triumphantly as she left Hamilton's office, squealing as she recited Campbell Scott's AOL address. She went to the ancient photocopy machine down the hall. Its one-page-per-minute performance meant she'd be at the machine for a couple of hours. She lifted the thick mat of a cover and then placed the first page of Hamilton's book facedown on the glass. She pushed the START button to begin printing.

The noise was like grinding gears. A bar of bright white light blasted from within the system and inched from the top of the glass to the bottom, collecting the image in its beam. Four, three, two, one . . . finally, the machine released a copy on shiny paper that gradually passed from its birth canal slot on the side and dropped into a plastic box that protruded like a kangaroo's pouch. "One down," Ella grunted as she lifted the heavy rubber matlike cover, turned the page on the diary, replaced it on the glass, and again pushed the button. Already she was bored.

After only the fourth page, she figured a way out. Stealthily, she made her way back to the front office. Opening a file cabinet drawer, she pulled out the station's complaint letters and slipped back to the copy machine. There, she began copying the handwritten notes scolding KRUQ for interrupting *I Dream of Genie* for a breaking story about a local farmer whose missing wife was found in his grain silo.

She smiled as she went about her duty, then realized that Stacia would probably not give Hamilton's book back to him. She'd claim that someone obviously broke into his desk and had absconded with the diary. Ella sighed. *I'd better make a copy after all—for him!* she said to herself, resigned to staying in the claustrophobia-enducing copy room for several hours.

"I want those tapes!" Stacia hissed to herself. "Where's that temporary editing bay?" She tried to imagine the secret place where Mike was editing the *Hunk House* videotape. No one had ever told her the location.

"Ella!" Stacia screamed again.

Ella opened the door of the suffocatingly hot copy room.

"Where have you been?" Stacia demanded.

"You've obviously never used this machine," Ella said.

"Just get it done! You're so damned slow! Where's the editing room where that Mike guy is working?"

"You're the boss," Ella said. "I don't know nothin' 'bout birthin' babies."

"You're lying," Stacia said. "If you don't tell me where Mike is, I swear I'll go straight to Daddy."

"No one has any authority over me," Ella shot back. "After being a scaredy-cat all my life with people—especially bosses—who thought they could manipulate me with something so little as a threat, I've survived. And I'll survive long after you're gone, or I'm gone, from KRUQ, whichever comes first. As I said, I don't know where the editing bay is. If you hadn't fired Hamilton, perhaps he would have been happy to share all of his secrets with you."

"Gimme back his book," Stacia demanded.

"I haven't finished all the pages," Ella lied.

Stacia fumed. "I'm going over to Hunk House. I may need this for bargaining." Stacia grabbed the leather book from Ella and flounced out the door.

Ella hurried to the reception area and when she saw that Stacia had gotten into her car and driven away, she called Hunk House.

"Yeah, he's doing an on-camera interview," Luke said when he answered the phone.

Ella said, "It's an emergency. I gotta talk to him right this minute. It's a matter of life and death!"

" 'Kay, hold on. Let me see if I can get him."

After a moment Luke was back on the line. "He said he's getting some great material from Bull and can't leave him even for a second. He asked if you could leave a detailed message or let him call you back."

Ella considered carefully. "This is fucking important. Just tell Ham that Stacia's on her way over and not to believe a word of what she says. Got that? Repeat it back for me, will you, honey?"

"Stacia's coming over. Don't believe what she says. Got it."

"Make sure he gets the message," Ella said.

Luke and Ella simultaneously hung up their telephones. Luke returned to the kitchen to grab a Coke, then went into the living room where Cameron and Zeth were in a heated discussion about Lauren Bacall.

"They should'a given it to her just 'cause she's old and she's supposed to be a legend," Cameron said, debating the tired issue about the time Bacall was nominated for an Oscar.

"For once they didn't play sentimental favorite. Did'ja see the look on her face when they called Juliette Binoche?" Zeth said. "No polite smile. Just that old stone face with the veins in her forehead ready to burst from anger. Everybody said she'd get it. And she believed 'em!"

"But she'll never get another chance. They don't make many movies with good parts for old women," Cameron countered. "Instead, you've got Neve Campbell or Cameron Diaz. Even that luminous Ashley Judd's almost too old."

"If they could make a stinker like *The First Wives Club* with older women like Bette Midler and Diane Keaton who've gotta be like over fifty, and that other one—the blonde who still looks damn good, even better than her almost-famous daughter . . ."

"Goldie Hawn?"

"Yeah, Goldie. What's she famous for anyway, except *Private Benjamin?*" Zeth asked. "If those women can get movies, maybe Bacall will again."

"Don't count your Oscars. She's lucky to be doing cat food commercials. I read somewhere that she's called 'The Beast of Broadway,' 'cause she's pretty mean."

"Hey, guys," Luke said, interrupting. "That was Ella on the phone. She was in a pretty nervous mood. She called to warn Hamilton that Stacia's on her way over. She said something about not believing anything that Stacia had to say."

"Did you tell Hamilton?" Zeth asked.

"No, but I've got to warn him. Ella said it was urgent. But I can't interrupt his interview with Bull. He must be getting some good stuff, 'cause he wouldn't take Ella's call, even though she said it was a matter of life and death. By the way, Goldie Hawn may be old, but she's still a knockout."

"Maybe," Cameron said, "but by now I think she's just famous for being famous. Like a Gabor."

"Hope she saved her money," Cameron said. "She lives with that used-to-be hunk Kurt Russell. And if he keeps choosing movie roles like *3000 Miles from Graceland* and *Winter People* and *Captain Ron*, she's gonna have to be the breadwinner."

"But remember him in *Silkwood!*" Luke gushed. "That was the first time I ever saw him—except when he was a kid in an old Disney movie—and I thought I would die, he was so fucking sexy, especially in the scenes where it was a hot night and he was on the front porch of some small shack of a house he lived in—and he wasn't wearing a shirt. Hmm. Spicy!"

"So, now that Hamilton's no longer a KRUQ executive, we've got that bitch Stacia to contend with," Cameron complained.

"You say 'bitch' like that's a bad thing."

The men quickly turned around and found Stacia standing in the arch of the entry to the living room. "Hey, Stacia," Luke said with a smile.

"Hey, yourself. Hello, Zeth. Never expected you to last this long at *Skunk* House. I wagered you'd be the first or second queer outta this place. How can you stand the smell in this old house?"

"Never noticed no smell, until you came in," Luke said.

"Very funny. A bit of an old one, don't you think?"

"Yeah, but you still have a few years left," he added.

Stacia scowled. "It's no wonder you need KRUQ to get you to L.A. You'd never make it on your attempt at levity. Where's Hamilton?"

Luke stepped forward. "He's doing an interview and can't be disturbed."

Stacia looked around. "Bull's missing. I gather he's the subject of Hammy's *Charlie Rose*? Am I right? Where are they?"

"Can't go down there," Luke said. "You'll disturb their session."

"I'll go wherever I damn well please." Stacia tried to push past Luke, but the other men surrounded her like the Secret Service around George W, although perhaps a bit more tightly.

"Let me through, God damn it! I promise not to interrupt. I just want to watch."

Zeth said, "If you're in the room, you'll blow the whole thing. Bull's very nervous as it is."

Stacia changed her tack. "Please, guys," she cooed. "I'll stay out of the way. Won't you at least let me listen to Bull for a minute? He wouldn't mind, I swear."

Luke finally said, "You gotta promise to be very quiet. Stay behind me at all times."

"I'll be a mouse, I promise." Stacia wore a wide, Mary Tyler Moore smile. "I just want an itsy-bitsy little preview. By the way, any of you queers know where the temporary editing bay is?" Her chameleon façade faded for an instant. "Never mind," she continued. "Let's just go listen to Hamilton and Bull, okay?"

Sandwiched between Cameron, Luke, and Zeth, they wended their way down a dark foyer and hallway, past the dining room, the kitchen, and finally toward a room filled with natural light. Before reaching the French doors, which were open, Cameron pulled up short. Stacia bumped into him. He turned around with his index finger placed at his lips and guided Stacia to a place just behind one of the doors. In this location she could see nothing more than an abundance of plants but she could clearly hear Bull's voice.

". . . my ex-girlfriend," was the first fragment of a sentence that Stacia and the other men heard.

Stacia blanched, cocking her head closer to the small space between the door and the door frame where the sound seemed to filter through the air more clearly.

Although Stacia could not see this, in the conservatory, Bull was seated in the wing chair just as Zeth had been a short while earlier. Hamilton stood behind the camera with Rocky and gave Bull large encouraging smiles.

Bull was turning out to be a more intriguing interviewee than Zeth. Perhaps it was his naïveté, but he was completely authentic, and extremely amiable and good-natured.

Stacia and the others continued to listen as Bull exposed more of his identity. ". . . it was a circle jerk out in the cornfield. Just some of us from the football team. It was actually a macho thing for us to do. It had nothing whatsoever to do with being gay.

"If I wasn't so ignorant, I should have picked up on some indicators. But only now do I recognize the hints. What I think was the first one was a show I used to watch called *The Waltons*. There was absolutely no sexuality in that thing. In fact, it was like the most wholesome show ever. But I couldn't wait for Thursday nights to see Richard Thomas, the guy who played John Boy on the show. I thought he was handsome and smart, like the producer of this show, *Hunk House,* Hamilton Peabody. There was this deep emotional feeling I had for John Boy—or for Richard Thomas. I don't know which. I got the character confused with the actor. That was long before I connected the feeling with being gay. And no, I'm not brown-nosing the producer to score more points," Bull chuckled in a self-deprecating manner.

"In retrospect," he continued, "another sign was when I had my first trucking job over near Cedar Rapids. I was working at this company, and there was this really handsome trucker that I did some hauling with. And I sometimes had the urge to kiss him. This was long before I ever connected it to being gay. Looking back, it's laughable because there was absolutely no thought in my mind that this was wrong. I made no association between this unexplainable urge to kiss this man and being gay. I swear.

"Leading up to telling you about my attraction to men, I've got to say I've been practically engaged to a woman now for like ten years, ever since we were in high school. She's real interested in me. But, ya know, I was reading *Newsweek* a couple of years ago and there was an article about genetics and what's bred into us. They used the example of a flower and a rotting dead animal. It said how when we see a flower, we naturally think it's pretty. And when we see a smelly carcass, it makes us want to gag. Oh, I'm not saying my girlfriend's a smelly carcass. Sorry if I gave that impression. The article went on to say that when a man sees a woman and he sees her shape and all of her curves, that turns on the genetic stuff in him that makes him feel an attraction and ultimately a sexual desire. No offense to my girlfriend, but I'm exactly the same way, only it's a hard body that makes my genetic stuff start to run. It's still the shape and the curves, but it's the shape of muscles sticking out, and a hard flat stomach and all that, instead of breasts.

"When I read the article, I realized what was surfacing in me. That's when I started to come out, at least to myself. I think being gay was fighting to surface through me because I was raised as a heterosexual in a heterosexual environment. No one tells you when you're an adolescent that this is 'gay' and this is 'straight' and through time if you just pay attention to your inner feelings you'll figure out which one you are."

Cameron's eyes were filled with tears, and he used a sleeve to wipe his nose, which was beginning to run.

Luke and Zeth both looked at each other and smiled. Although they couldn't empathize with the trauma Bull had gone through, since they had both been out long past any memory of not being gay, they were moved by his truthfulness.

Stacia, too, was on the verge of tears. Her tears, however, were for herself. *This is not getting on the air* she planned. *I will not be the laughingstock of Dulcit!*

"One day, I was doing a haul to Chicago," Bull was saying. "On three different trips I'd passed a newsstand where this hundred-year-old man was sellin' papers and magazines. Each trip I could see a gay magazine there. It took me four trips to Chicago before I had the nerve to buy it! Why was it so hard to buy that magazine in a strange city, where nobody I knew could possibly see me?

"Then I remember driving down State Street or Michigan Avenue, and I saw a guy in what they call drag. He was dressed in pink and turquoise, from head to toe. And I remember this was a setback in my coming out because I thought that's what gay people were. I'm sure somewhere inside of me I knew you could be gay and not dress like that all the time. But it just made me want to go back to my girlfriend. But after I got back, I realized I was still thinking about men. I fantasized about men when I was with her. And I masturbated to pictures of men in that magazine."

Stacia turned red. Zeth and Luke both watched her carefully, afraid that at any moment she might scream or somehow disrupt the interview. She continued to eavesdrop.

"I got so confused and discouraged that I actually called that Gay and Lesbian Center in Des Moines. They set me up with a counselor. I remember we sat on the floor on these big pillows. He answered all the questions that I could think of at the time, and at the end he just kinda patted me on the back. Then he said, 'What you need to do is find out what you like. So go on out to the bars and have sex with everybody you can and you'll find out what you like.'

"That was *horrible*. Remember my story about buyin' that magazine? There was no way I could have walked into a gay bar even in Chicago!

"I drove back to Dulcit for a meeting, just before joining *Hunk House*."

Bull was wise enough not to mention KRUQ or his job at the station.

"Right after the meeting, I called up this trucker the other guys have always said was gay. I introduced myself and said I needed to ask him a personal question. He invited me over for a beer. We sat down, and then another guy came in who turned out to be his lover. A trucker with a lover? That was a new one on me. But then so was a gay trucker. I was a wreck and I said, 'I'm really sorry, but it's takin' every ounce of energy and courage I've got to sit here and talk to you, I don't think I can do it with a third person.' But the partner was real nice and said he didn't mean to interrupt.

"So, we had a long talk and then Frank—that's the trucker—drove me all the way to Davenport to a big disco. When we got inside, my mouth unhinged. I stood there and watched for two hours. I couldn't believe it. Remember my story about the gay guy in pink and turquoise? Here was like all these Northwestern University college boys, like the best-looking straight guys right off the campus. But they were gay! It blew me away. I was ecstatic!"

Hamilton studied Bull and realized why he hadn't had an inordinate amount of protest from Bull when it was determined that he had to join *Hunk House*. And Bull's remarks at that initial meeting where Hamilton had proposed the program were made before he got a different look at gay culture.

Hamilton's heart was suddenly full of love for this man who had struggled for so long and had come so far along a path that he found difficult to walk. There had been a fork in the road and Bull had taken the one less traveled. He adored Bull for his bravery. At this moment, Hamilton knew he had fallen in love. *Was Bull's remark about me and John Boy Walton a sign that he likes me?* Hamilton thought as he stared at the handsome face being videotaped.

"Go on," prompted Hamilton.

"Guess the best way to sum things up is to say that even when I was supposedly 'straight,' I knew I was different 'cause when I'd be driving my routes I'd see, for instance, a billboard for a fancy car. Usually there'd be a picture of a young couple out for a ride and I'd find myself lookin' at the *guy*. I'd always say to myself, *I can't live like they do. I must be gay if I'm cruising a guy on a billboard!*"

Chapter Twenty-Two

Hamilton was beaming, imagining all the places in each episode of *Hunk House* he could splice portions of Bull's interview. What Bull had just revealed was exactly what Hamilton had prayed would be part of this show. Bull had given an intimate look at the struggles that even a gay man who could pass for straight endured. His coming out showed that gays were everywhere and that chances were strong that heterosexuals who claimed not to have ever known a queer would be completely wrong. Bull would redefine *gay* for a lot of the audience.

"You were spectacular!" Hamilton enthused, once Bull had finally run out of things to say on camera.

Bull smiled. "I can probably do more some other time, if you want."

"You could hardly top yourself," Hamilton raved. "Right Rocky?" he smiled at the cameraman.

Suddenly, the euphoria was broken by the cry of a banshee.

"The hell you will, you lying, cheating pervert!" Stacia broke away from Luke and came storming into the conservatory. "What have these faggots done to you?" Stacia demanded of Bull. "We're engaged! Now you say you're a cocksucking fairy! Don't you care how this is going to ruin me in Dulcit? In all of Iowa! Maybe the whole world!"

Bull was unruffled. "It's not nice to call people 'faggots.' "

"If the shoe fits, you traitor to your sex!" Then she sobbed, "Oh, hon. I get it. You're just doing this to win us a vacation to California, aren't you? You decided to play along with this game. Isn't that right? A real man doesn't just change overnight."

Bull looked almost sad. "It wasn't overnight. If you were listening long enough, you heard that it took a really long time to come out. If it wasn't for Hamilton, I don't know where I'd be. He showed me that bein' gay isn't what even *I* thought it was. It's not wrong. It's not a sin. It's just nature."

"Nature, you say? Like Mad Cow disease? Like conjoined twins? Like Pamela Anderson Lee's tits? Nature?"

Hamilton, without Stacia being aware of it, had instructed Rocky to continue recording the outburst. What was being captured on tape was invaluable. It showed opposite sides of the public's perception of sexual orientation. Stacia's ferocious eruption would add even more drama to the show. Hamilton had realized that until now, the program was one-sided, showing how natural the gay men at *Hunk House* felt about their sexuality. Now, audiences would see what gays were subjected to practically every moment of their lives, whether it was in their face as Stacia's diatribe was, or in the silence of the majority of people who hated even the gays with whom they worked or played.

"This is so rich!" Stacia shouted, incredulous. "This town is *filled* with depraved inhabitants. And it all started with you, Hamilton!" She wheeled around and faced her former colleague. "You're the Pied Piper, and now we've got queers coming out of the sewers. Here's a house filled with 'em!"

Bull reached out his hand for Stacia and held it there for a long moment before she finally took a tentative step forward and placed the fingers of her right hand into his palm. He looked into her eyes. "The only difference between the Bull you loved before and this one is that he's finally given up trying to be the Bull *you* loved to be the Bull *I* can love."

Stacia withdrew her hand as though Bull were a leper. "This must be the *Twilight Zone!*" she yelled. "I'm stopping this show, here and now!"

"Your father and I have an understanding," Hamilton said, walking into the focus of the camera lens. With a calm demeanor, meant to convey his patience and authority, he reminded Stacia that *Hunk House* would continue.

"'Fraid not, Mr. Former Programming Director! Your ass has been fired. You're gay and you don't belong in Dulcit or anywhere you have authority over the content of programming that could be considered to corrupt America's youth."

"For crying out loud," Bull grunted, "I used to be pretty homophobic myself, mostly 'cause I was afraid of bein' who I am. But Stacia, you take the cake."

Zeth joined in. "This isn't about gay people in your hometown. And it's probably not even about your boyfriend finding out he likes hard bodies instead of soft ones. I can't believe you actually really feel the way you do about queers. As I see it, you just want Hamilton's job."

"Her daddy already nixed the idea," Hamilton said.

"He probably wants to hire you back," Luke said optimistically.

"I wouldn't go back if he doubled my salary," Hamilton said. "I'm on my way to L.A., just as soon as we wrap this show and get it edited."

"We're wrapping it now!" Stacia cried. "And Hamilton, you and I are going into the editing bay together, and we're going to build a G-rated show that's acceptable to the whole family."

"Hamilton," Luke said. "Remember that call from Ella? She had a message for you. She said not to listen to a word that Stacia had to say."

"Oh?" Hamilton said, looking at Stacia. "Why not?"

"Ella didn't say."

Stacia piped in. "How did she know that you'd been fired, Hammy? She said it was a little rat, but I suspect a little fairy. She says she hasn't spoken to you, but she may have been in contact with one of these others." She looked accusingly at each of the men. "When Hamilton told you he was no longer your boss, which one of you talked to Ella?"

None of the men responded. "This is why I'm closing down *Hunk House*," Stacia asserted. "You're all liars."

"I thought that was one of the aspects of the game," Zeth said. "We were supposed to be as duplicitous as possible in order to screw the others out of points and thus win the game."

"That's not what this was all about." Stacia turned and glared at Hamilton. "Mr. Hamilton Ipswich Peabody Roman numeral three behind your sissy name, I'll make you an offer."

"I'm not bargaining with you."

"You're headed back to La-La Land, right?"

"As soon as the show's in the can."

"Still know a lot of people out there in Hollywood?"

"A few."

"Just for my reference, is there like a special MCI or Sprint or AT&T phone book that only stars can get into, and only stars can get a hold of?"

"Sounds like a winning idea," Hamilton played along, "but no, contacts are made over a grueling and exhausting length of time. Like any other closed society, once a celebrity is 'in,' they only want to associate with their peers. You of all people should understand that concept, Stacia. You never associate with anyone you feel is in any way inferior to you. Count the number of times we had lunch? And I know for sure that in all the years that Ella has dialed your telephone and picked up your Tampax, you've never once had her to dinner."

"She's the help, for Christ sake," Stacia defended herself.

"You never had me to dinner," Bull interrupted. "Did you think 'cause I worked as a maintenance guy at the station and drove a truck for extra money, that I wasn't presentable to your society friends?"

"Of course not," Stacia spat, "I just never thought you'd be interested in the people we have over."

"I might use the wrong fork, right? Or pick creamed spinach from my teeth with a stiff dollar bill?"

"Imagine Dulcit having a 'society'?" Zeth quietly laughed. "D'ya think the wives of the pig farmers are looked down on by the wives of the cattle farmers who are looked down on by the wife of the sheriff? Everybody has to feel superior to somebody else."

Directing the conversation back to Hamilton, Stacia said, "Stars are pretty private people, aren't they? That is unless they want your ass in a movie theater seat or tuned into their television show. Then they're out on talk shows pretending to be ordinary people."

"Not ordinary," Hamilton countered. "Meryl Streep is a genius and could only be 'ordinary' if she were playing the role of 'ordinary.'"

"But still, they're like cockroaches, aren't they? I mean you turn on a kitchen light and they dash for cover. You can't get to 'em 'cause they're like hidden in the floorboards of life. Am I right?"

"I get your drift. Where's this leading?" Hamilton asked.

"I was just thinking how hard it will be for you to be back in Hollywood and not know how to find your old friend Joan Van Ark. Or Teri Hatcher. Or George Clooney. Or Jodie Foster."

"And your point would be?"

"I'm sorry to be the bearer of sad news, but we had a burglary at KRUQ. Your desk was ransacked, and your beautiful forest green leather Ralph Lauren personal diary and phone directory was stolen."

Hamilton blinked. "I see. Did you file a police report?"

"I forgot."

"Any idea who the perpetrator was?"

"No sign of forced entry. Except to your desk drawer."

"Was anything taken from *your* office?"

"Nope."

"From Ella's desk?"

"Nope."

"From your daddy's office?"

"Nope."

Hamilton chuckled sardonically. "How did you know what was taken from my office?"

Stacia stalled. "I did a quick inventory."

"Aside from the desk lamp, calendar, coatrack, and computer, how did you know what to inventory?"

She smiled evilly.

Hamilton turned to the men. "Guys," he said, "you've been very analytical over the past few weeks with some of the games we played. Remember the game with the wine? You figured out which bottle was the good one. Maybe you can help me out with this little quandary I'm having?"

"Sure," said Zeth.

"Luke," Hamilton said, "what did Stacia tell us happened at KRUQ?"

"She said that your office was burglarized."

"Cameron, what did Stacia say was taken from my office?"

"She said it was a forest green leather Ralph Lauren diary and address book."

"Zeth," Hamilton continued, "was there anything taken from Stacia's office or Mr. Ratner's office or from our receptionist Ella?"

"Apparently not."

"Bull, I'm at a loss. How would Miss Ratner have any idea of what was kept in my locked desk drawer?"

"Beats me, Hamilton. I can't even understand how she would know what was missin'."

"I saw you put your diary away and lock the desk yesterday," Stacia said.

"I never had my desk unlocked while you were there. In fact, you stormed out of the room and I followed you, remember?"

"All I know is that your diary's missing. Isn't that enough? And I also know how you can get it back."

"Blackmail?" Hamilton asked.

"Leverage."

"Since when did leverage become a synonym for blackmail?" Hamilton asked.

"Look, you," Stacia announced. "If you ever want to see your diary and directory of all the famous people you know in Hollywood again, this show shuts down now!"

"Forget it. In two days we wrap. Then we edit. And then I leave Dulcit forever—*with* my diary."

"Good idea, Hammy."

Everybody, including the camera, turned toward the French doors. It was Ella. "Miss Ratner's got your book, but she stupidly made me make copies of every page." Ella waved the pages in the air for all to see. "And she wonders why Daddy won't give her your old job. I think the chemicals in her dye job have burned her brain cells."

"You're definitely fired!" Stacia bellowed at Ella.

Ella chuckled. "My dear, you're in over your head. Like the special effects they put into movies these days, things aren't always as they appear. Unless you're ready to have a life-altering experience, I'd go quietly and gracefully back to the station and just do your job. Give Hamilton back his book."

"Excuse me," Luke interrupted, looking at Stacia. "About your threat to pull the plug on *Hunk House?* You may have forgotten that we signed a contract to participate in this program. It's equally binding for KRUQ. I don't recall any language that says, 'the show must go on . . . until we don't feel like playing with you guys any longer.' If *Hunk House* shuts down, you'll have more problems than the U.S. Department of Labor Employee Standards Administration circling you like *Jaws* for terminating Ella based on her age. If you cancel *Hunk House* before we select a winner and Hamilton has had a chance to cut it, I'll get Alan Dershowitz to hang your ass on a meat hook."

"Ella's age has nothing to do with her termination," Stacia retorted.

"Don't worry a hair about me," Ella addressed Luke. "I've been so incompetent for the past twelve years that KRUQ's records are all neatly filed and the office is spotless. I can just as quickly put my hands on a bill from Concept Advertising from seven years ago, as I can a copy of a viewer's letter from yesterday complaining that we show too many re-runs of *Harper Valley P.T.A.* and not enough *Lost in Space* or *Harry O.*"

"You're not the boss of me," Stacia whined. "None of you are. I want *Hunk House* shut down and that's exactly what's going to happen. My daddy's an old fart whose head's buried in yesteryear. He doesn't have a clue about what viewers want. Now start packing your things 'cause I'm calling the old imbecile and for once standing up to him!"

"My, my, calling your daddy an old fart again. I'm disappointed in you, honey."

Stacia wheeled around. The others all looked toward the doorway of the conservatory. Mr. Ratner and Rex were emerging from behind the French doors and entering the room.

"Daddy," Stacia said, breathless from embarrassment. "What are you doing here?"

Ratner moved into the room and plopped his big frame into the wing chair. Rex positioned himself behind his father. Ella moved to his side and put her hand on his shoulder. "Well," the old man began, "I got to thinkin' 'bout what you and Hammy were arguin' 'bout yesterday. I thought maybe I'd been unfair to my Buttercup, and that maybe you should have his old job after all."

Stacia looked confused.

"You practically convinced me that under Hammy's supervision everything to do with *Hunk House* had gone to hell in a handbasket. So I decided to come on down and see just how much of a mess he'd made."

"You have no idea how happy I am that you're here," Stacia said. "Now you can see exactly what's going on in this den of iniquity. You'll be glad to know that I'm closing this place down. No more *Hunk House* to worry about. See, I'm being pro-active, like a good executive!"

"Mr. Ratner," Hamilton interjected, "I accepted your termination of my services. However, we agreed that I could finish this program. Stacia is trying her damndest to usurp my authority and yours, too. The contestants and I have no intention of leaving Hunk House until a winner is selected. Then I'll edit the program and be on my way, just as we agreed."

Ratner waved his hand to indicate he was well aware of their agreement and didn't need to be reminded about the status of the show. "Don't get huffy, Hammy. I know what I said."

"I didn't mean—"

"I may be . . . how'd you put it, Buttercup? 'An old fart whose head is buried in yesteryear?' I don't have the slightest concept of what viewers want. Oh, and I'm an imbecile, too."

"I didn't mean it the way it sounded, Daddy."

"Never mind, Buttercup. You may be right. At my age, I probably should be handing the reigns of the station over to somebody who can be more creative. If I never see another rerun of *Adam 12,* it'll be too soon. Our programming sucks 'cause my head's buried in the sand. That's precisely why *Hunk House* has to go on."

"But . . . but . . ." Stacia stammered.

"You had a lot of interesting things to say about me, Buttercup," Ratner continued. "But I told you yesterday that you were to leave Ella alone. Didn't I make myself clear?"

"But, Daddy," Stacia argued, "Ella's an insubordinate old busybody who broke into Hamilton's desk and stole his very expensive Ralph Lauren diary and phone directory, with all the names and numbers of everybody who's anybody in Hollywood. He'll need it when he goes back there!"

"Ella's not a thief, sweetheart," Ratner said, putting his hand up to hold Ella's hand still resting on his shoulder.

"You're not in the office enough to know what it's like with her," Stacia complained. "After the expense of this show, and the dire ratings we'll get, you're going to have to downsize anyway. May as well start now and with her."

Ella placed her other hand on top of Mr. Ratner's.

Stacia gave them a dubious look. "What's going on here?" she asked.

"What do young people call it nowadays?" Ella asked Ratner.

"Lovers?" asked Hamilton.

Stacia screamed, "You're too old! You're not supposed to be in love at your age!"

Stacia nearly fainted. "How long? How long have you . . . ?"

"Five years," Ella said proudly.

"Didn't think it was anybody's business, so we kept it a secret," Ratner said. "Rex knew. He caught on right away. Now I'd like you to apologize to your future stepmother. She was at the house last night when you suggested that she should be 'swept out with the old.'"

Stacia looked at Hamilton, shock still registering on her face. "Enjoying seeing me humiliated?" she asked.

"Just make your peace with Ella, and leave the *Hunk House* show to me," Hamilton said.

Ella looked at Stacia and said, "I know in your heart you didn't mean all those terrible things you planned to do to me and to Hamilton. You're just upset because you lost your boyfriend, the job you always wanted, the control you thought you had over me, and your love life sucks. That's a lot to take in all at once. You'll feel even worse when you find out that Rex is the new senior programming director."

"Dear Lord!" Rex gushed with happiness. "I feel just like one of the Pink Ladies, and I'm going to Rydell High with Sandy and Danny!"

Chapter Twenty-Three

Hamilton decided that *Hunk House* would wrap production in two days. They would film three outings and simulate the final winner of the game. "We'll start early tomorrow," Hamilton said, as the men finished the dinners ordered from the Eat 'n' Run Diner. "We also need to get Luke and Cameron interviewed on tape, so there's tons to do. Are you guys really cool with Cameron taking the prize?"

"No," Bull said.

"I thought we agreed on the ultimate winner," Hamilton said. "Why the change of heart?"

" 'Cause I realize how really hard we've all worked, and I still think we should go by the point system we first agreed to," Bull said. "But I'm not gonna hold you guys up. If everybody else accepts the way things are, then I will, too."

"Any other objections?" Hamilton asked.

"As a matter of fact," Luke said, "I'm not thrilled with Cameron taking first prize either. Zeth agrees with me. We only went along with the idea because it seemed it would be a good situation for all of us, bein' able to go to Hollywood and all. But now, after everything that's gone on, I'd like to play out the rest of the show for real."

"Guys," Hamilton reminded, "We've only got two days. We'd have to cram three weeks' worth of activities into forty-eight hours. We can't do that."

"What'dya have against me winning anyway?" Cameron asked Bull defensively. "I'm gonna take this game fair and square. You guys'll still get to Hollywood. What's the big deal?"

"The big deal is, what if you don't have the most points?" Luke said. "What if you're not really ahead?"

"I am!" Cameron countered.

"Only Hamilton knows for sure," Zeth said.

"I'm sorry that we couldn't afford an independent accounting firm, like they use at the Oscars," Hamilton said.

"I'm not accusing you, Hamilton," Cameron said. "Mistakes happen. At this point it doesn't seem like there's any way to make sure who has how many points anyway. Plus so much of it was subjective. You added and subtracted points arbitrarily. There's no way to determine a real final winner, so we have to *choose* one of us. It may as well be me."

"Are you saying you'd be willing to put it to a vote?" Hamilton asked.

"Hell, no! I'm the winner. We already came to a decision."

"I think we should vote again," Zeth said. "We don't have three weeks anymore to film more shows, and Cameron is right. There's really no accurate way to tabulate the scores."

"What do you think, Bull?" Hamilton asked.

"A vote? If we do that, we're all just gonna vote for ourselves." Bull thought for a moment. "What if the camera guys did the voting?"

"What?" Cameron blinked. "That's crazy! This is between us! We're the *Hunk House* guys!"

"That's not a bad idea, actually," Hamilton said. "Even I don't know you guys as well as Rocky and the three other Stedicam operators do. They've been here with you day and night. Literally."

"I'm with Bull," Luke said.

"Me, too," Zeth added.

Hamilton looked at Rocky and the three other men. "What do you guys think of placing an anonymous ballot to determine the winner of *Hunk House?*"

"Great!" Rocky said.

"Yeah!"

"Cool"

"Cameron?" Hamilton said. "What about you?"

"This sucks! We had an agreement!"

"But it's really not fair to the others."

"*Hunk House* hasn't been fair since day one! Why change the rules now?"

"I disagree. I think pretty much everything has been fair. And face it, if it came down to a vote to out someone, you'd be the first to go," Hamilton said.

"Then when we vote to out the second guy, it would probably be Bull, 'cause let's face it, Luke and Zeth are in love. They'd never vote each other out," Hamilton continued. "When it's just down to those two, I'd have to tally up whatever scores I could find and make a decision based on whatever their points are. I was talking to the leather guy the other day. He tells me that Luke scored two hundred points at the dungeon that last night for something that occurred in the leather sling, which I don't need any more information about, thank you. So he'd probably be the final winner."

Cameron could no doubt see that what Hamilton was saying was probably true. "But there's gotta be a different way. I was counting on winning, for Christ sake."

"The only other way would be for each of you guys to simply vote for a winner. But of course, as Bull points out, you're all going to vote for yourselves. Or Luke is going to vote for Zeth and Zeth is going to vote for Luke, and Bull is going to vote for one of them. So we're back to nobody voting for you and another stalemate."

"This sucks!" Cameron exploded. "This is not the way it was supposed to be! I even fucked Luke to get him on my side!"

"You really didn't do a very good job of that," Luke said. "It's not that I didn't like you fucking me, but you were so self-absorbed about it. You didn't care if I was satisfied or not."

"Don't lie. You shot your load, didn't you?"

"There's more to sex than just getting off," Bull interrupted. "And, as Hamilton said, and I'm sorry if this hurts, Cameron, but we all think you're a prick."

"The feeling is mutual," Cameron said. "I told you all that when you *illegally* voted me out last week. I feel the same way today. So I'm a goner, right? There's no way even the camera guys are gonna select me as the winner."

"You don't know that," Hamilton said. "I haven't been here every single moment of every day. I don't know if you've made friends with the camera guys or not."

"I didn't know we had to."

"You didn't *have* to," Hamilton said. "But I'd kinda think if you were with the same people almost twenty-four hours a day for nearly a month, that you'd get to know 'em and become friendly."

"I was focused on the guys and playing the games. They won't fault me for that, will they?"

"I'm sure Rocky and the others are completely fair," Hamilton assured Cameron. "So, what's the verdict? Do we vote each other out? Vote for a winner? Or let the people you've been the most intimate with make the final decision? Remember, I'm still taking you all to Hollywood."

Bull raised his hand. "Cameramen," he said.

"Second the vote," Luke said.

"I'm with Luke," Zeth agreed.

"I'm with Luke," Cameron parroted Zeth. "I'll bet you're with Luke. You disgust me. Aren't you even mad at Luke for fucking me?"

"You fucked *him*," Zeth countered.

"But he let me do it."

"And he let me do it, too," Zeth said, with a smile.

"Zeth didn't *fuck* me," Luke corrected.

"The fuck he didn't!" Cameron retorted.

"He made *love* to me," Luke said. "You should try it. Huge difference."

"You ever really been in love before?" Bull asked Cameron.

"Lots of times. I love everybody I fuck. At least while I'm fucking 'em. That's what's so cool about being gay. You can fuck your brains out with a different guy every night, if you want to."

"Yeah, but do you ever think about finding one special guy?" Bull continued.

"Nobody special would stay special for very long."

"How's that?" Zeth asked.

"C'mon, guys," Cameron continued. "You've all been around the track a few times. People never stay the same."

"I dunno," Hamilton interjected. "Look at Old Man Ratner and Ella. Five years they've been a couple. They seem to have grown together."

"They're old," Cameron said. "At their age there aren't any other choices. Being gay is about choices. There's a whole smorgasbord of men out there. And I just want my share!"

"I've *had* my share," Luke said.

"I'll bet you have," Cameron countered.

"I mean it. I've had a good sampling, and I never felt about the others what I feel for Zeth."

"What's so special about Zeth?" Cameron baited Luke.

"If you have to ask, I can't tell you."

"Jesus. Mark my words, in a few months you'll find someone else or Zeth'll find someone else. It happens to everyone I've ever known."

"So, we'll cross that bridge if we ever come to it," Zeth said. He leaned in to give Luke a deep full-on-the-lips kiss.

"Okay, so it's settled," Hamilton said. "Rocky and his crew will pick the winner. He and I will meet after you guys hit the hay, which should be right now, 'cause you're getting up at six. I'll be here with coffee and doughnuts, and the cameras will be rolling. We'll film three Out House scenes, and the finale in which I announce whoever Rocky and his guys determine to be the Hunk of the Year."

The house was now quiet. The men were in their rooms. Hamilton, Rocky, and the three other cameramen sipped beers and talked about their ultimate responsibility. "I don't even want to know who you guys are voting for," Hamilton said. "I think they all deserve to win. But I've seen in the editing bay what you guys have seen through your camera lens. So I have my theories about who should be the ultimate winner, but it's entirely up to you.

"What I need are runners-up for fourth place and third place. When it's down to just two contestants, I'll make a big to-do about the game scores being responsible for determining the winner. We'll get together early tomorrow and I'll make up the signs for the guys to hold up with the name of whomever you select in each placing category. D'ya think we can go through this fairly quickly?"

"Shouldn't be more than a few hours," Rocky said. "Remember, the guys have to tell why they selected the person whose name is on their card. Better tell 'em to ad-lib something that sounds legit."

"Tomorrow we'll film the outings as if they were on subsequent weeks."

"Gotcha, chief," Rocky said to Hamilton.

"Okay, that about does it. I'll see you all real early."

As the men began to collect their beer bottles and to file into the kitchen, Hamilton tapped Rocky on the shoulder. He turned around with a smile and said, "You've done a great job, Hamilton. This has been a really fun assignment; the best I've ever had in Dulcit."

"That's what I need to talk to you about. You may tell me it's none of my business and to go fuck myself, but I thought I would at least ask you what you thought of Luke's feelings for Zeth and if that makes a difference to you."

Rocky's smile faded. "Makes no diff. I'm happy for the dudes. Why do you ask?"

" 'Cause I know you've been seeing Luke."

"I see him every day. I photograph him every day. Just like the others."

"You see him for sex, which is cool with me, but I don't want him or Zeth or you to get hurt."

Rocky blanched. "Like what are you saying man? That I sleep with guys? I'm straight. What are you talkin' about?"

"Hey, if you and Luke are having fun, I'm all for it. But the guy thinks he's in love. Don't confuse him anymore by sneaking into his room at night and fucking him. That's all I'm saying."

"Man, you've got some nerve," Rocky practically shouted. "I had you figured all wrong. I thought you were a smart, decent guy. And now you're accusing me of having sex with a man—a minor no less? You're fucked up!"

"I saw you the other night, Rocky." Hamilton was lying, but he had analyzed the situation and figured Rocky was the only possibility. "I didn't say anything because Luke didn't say anything. I figured he must like you. But I'm just suggesting that you consider his feelings, and Zeth's feelings, too."

Suddenly Rocky backtracked. Defeated. "I had the feeling you knew. But for whatever reason you've been a sport. He really is in love with Zeth, isn't he?" Rocky said in a dejected tone. "But I'm in love with Luke, too, for Christ sake!"

"What's he say about that?"

"He doesn't know I exist. We fuck in the dark, like I've done to the others—except Cameron and Bull. He only knows that a mysterious stranger fulfills his fantasies. And he fulfills mine! He's everything I ever wanted in a guy! The fact that we're so fucking compatible sexually is a turn-on. I swear, we both shoot our loads practically the moment I'm inside of him. All I think about is his ass! You gotta see that I love him just by the way my camera moves solely around him."

"I'm not telling you what to do, Rocky, I just want you to consider the feelings of two very young men. You couldn't have chosen Cameron?"

"That S.O.B. He treats my men and me as if we were paparazzi instead of the people responsible for him getting decent footage. Despite the fact that we all loathe the jerk, we're doing our jobs and trying to get equal video on each of the guys."

"And you're doing a fantastic job. I see your work every day. You guys are the best. So I'm not saying anything else to you about Luke. But, as Jiminy Cricket said, 'Let your conscience be your guide.' So go to bed. Good night."

"Night. Sorry for being a problem."

"You're not."

Hamilton watched Rocky move through the kitchen and out the back door toward the carriage house where the other men were, by now, fast asleep. He picked up his leather jacket—he was now dressing in jeans and black T-shirt, which advertised his buff body—and decided to say good night to Bull before leaving the house.

Shortly after Rocky left the room, Hamilton followed in the same direction through the kitchen. He quietly stood at the white three-paneled door to Bull's room. He listened for any sound from beyond the door. Just as he nearly lost his nerve and was about to turn around, he heard a whisper: "Ham?"

Hamilton wasn't certain that he had heard correctly but decided to take a chance. He whispered back, "Bull?"

"It's open," a voice that was just forced air called back.

Hamilton took a tentative step toward the door and gingerly pushed it open just a crack.

" 'Sokay. Com'on in," Bull said in a slightly louder voice.

Hamilton followed Bull's instructions. As he entered the dark room, the light from the kitchen illuminated Bull's face, bare chest, and stomach before obliterating the mental snapshot when he closed the door. He made his way to the side of the bed and felt his way to a space on the edge. "You doing okay?" Hamilton asked.

"Great, now that you're here. I saw the shadow of feet in the light under the door. I hoped it was you. I thought you handled everything so well tonight."

"Me? Thanks. But if it hadn't been for you, my friend, Cameron would be the winner of *Hunk House*. You've changed so much in the past few weeks. You're not afraid of these guys and you make great decisions."

"I still won't win."

"Everybody wants to be a winner. That's why getting a silver medal at the Olympics is considered a disaster. If it's not gold, it's not worth the effort."

"That's not really what I mean," Bull said. "When Hunk House closes up, you'll be editing night and day for a few weeks, then you'll be leaving for L.A. I'll be the loser 'cause I won't see you anymore."

Hamilton reached out for Bull's face. He found his nose and felt with his fingers, tracing the contours of his cheeks and lips and chin. He moved his hands down to Bull's chest and rested his hand on his pumped pectorals. "You've gotta come to California, Bull," Hamilton said in a hopeful tone.

"And do what, become a soap star? I'd be washing dishes or punching out movie tickets at a cinema. I'm not an actor."

"You don't have to be an actor to be a star in Hollywood, trust me," Hamilton tried to joke.

"But seriously, I belong in Iowa. You belong with all the glitter and glamour of the big city."

"I belong wherever you are," Hamilton pleaded. "I hated Dulcit and nearly sold my soul to the devil to get out. But that was before."

"Before what?"

"Before I fell for you. I'm in love. It's been coming on slowly but after what we experienced the other day, I know exactly what Luke and Zeth were talking about when they said they didn't fuck, they made love."

"Cameron had a point about people changing. I've certainly changed. But I love you so much the way you are, I don't know if I could bear to see *you* change," Bull added.

"But you'll change, too," Hamilton said. "We'll change together. What if I said I promise to at least always do my best to make you love me? That I pledge to never intentionally do anything to make you sad or unhappy? Would that be enough to make you realize that no matter what happens, I'll always put you and our relationship first?"

"I could say the same thing," Bull responded. "The way I feel about you, I know I could never again treat you the way I did in our programming meetings."

Hamilton laughed. "You were so confrontational! I thought you hated my guts."

"You were so pompous, dressing up and wearing ties, and using words that most of us didn't understand. Remember when you used the word *motif*? Stacia snorted and nudged me. After the meeting we both went into her office and checked the dictionary. We laughed, mainly at you."

"It's different where I come from," Hamilton tried to explain as his hand caressed Bull's body and tarried at his nipples. "In Hollywood, unless you're a Rap star, you gotta have an elevated vocabulary to make the right kinds of friends."

"Or acquaintances."

"You're right. I don't have actual friends, just a couple hundred acquaintances, although some of 'em are very close. I could never just call one up and say would you watch my dog for the weekend. That is, if I had a dog."

"I don't have real friends either," Bull admitted. "But I sure as hell would never fit in where you come from."

Hamilton leaned in and let his lips find Bull's. He gave him a tender kiss and withdrew with a slight smacking sound. "What're we gonna do, Bull? I've never felt the way I do toward you."

"You have to go back to Hollywood, don't you?"

"It's not etched in stone, but it's where I had a modicum of success."

"What'd you like about your career?"

Hamilton stalled. He kissed Bull once again, just as sweetly as before. "Truth?"

"What else?"

"This sounds as though I have no self-esteem. Hollywood's a town where you don't have to know anything to get a great studio job. You just have to look a certain way. I can't sing. I can't act. I can't dance. I can't write. But I have a *look,* and when you have that particular *look* in Hollywood, people believe you can do what you say you can do. They thought I could be a segment producer for *ET*. And I was. But now I'm afraid."

"Afraid you'll never have another job?"

"Exactly. I can't do anything else. You know my degree from Harvard?"

"Yeah. You're a brain. I never went to college."

"I went to college, of course. And in Massachusetts. But not Harvard. Or Radcliffe. It was Salem State."

"Where they had all those witch hunts?"

"I'm a phony. And if I ever have to really 'apply' for a job, rather than have someone just hire me, they'll check my records and discover I'm a fraud."

"Ella told me."

"What?"

"She's got the skinny on everybody. Ever since she got online she practically knows the genealogy of everybody in Dulcit. She's got one of those detective programs. But she'd never tell the Ratners about you."

"I wouldn't be so sure. She's sleeping with the old man. Ever hear of pillow talk?"

"She adores you, and she'll take whatever dirt she's found to her grave."

"Then how come she told you about my not having a degree from Harvard?"

"It was before you even came to the station. She didn't know you. She and I were talkin' about 'the new boss,' meaning you, and what we thought you'd be like. Turned out we were both completely wrong. She said, 'Anybody whose employment application says summa cum laude, Harvard Business School and it turns out to be fake is probably a real ball buster.' We both laughed about how we'd put the fear of God in you if you turned out to be a shit. She just wanted the info to use against you in case you turned out to be a creep. But when you came aboard, she immediately liked you. So she kept the secret. I was about to blow your cover at that programming meeting. I was so angry. I'm glad I kept quiet. Stacia doesn't even know."

"What do you think of me now that you know I'm a liar?" Hamilton asked.

"You must'a had your reasons for fakin' Harvard. You don't gotta tell me."

"You deserve an explanation. I'm not from some snooty Boston society family the way I pretend to be. I grew up in a small town in New England, no bigger than Dulcit. My cousins were spoiled rich kids who all got to go to private schools. I had to endure public education. My folks were regular working stiffs. I always fantasized that we were rich. So, when I finally left home after college I reinvented myself and became a hot shot in Hollywood. I was on my way, but I just couldn't hack it. I started hating everybody. I hated Whoopi Goldberg. I hated James Belushi. I even loathed Ashley Judd, and she's fucking gorgeous! I had a meltdown. I burned out. Still, those years were the most exciting because I'd actually gotten out of my small town and did what some of my childhood friends had claimed they would one day do. But I made it. At least to a point. It boils down to my self-image. Mine's pretty low I guess. I know that's an unattractive attribute."

Bull, who was propped up with his back against pillows and the headboard of the bed, reached out for Hamilton's face and brought it close to his own. Their lips met. They began kissing passionately. Bull pulled Hamilton's T-shirt up over his head and dragged him the rest of the way onto the bed. "I lied to Cameron and Luke about something. I said I'd been in prison. That was just to scare Cameron."

Instantly, the men were kissing passionately and tasting each other's skin.

"Take your pants off, man," Bull finally said, and the two separated for a fraction of a moment as Hamilton removed his shoes, socks, and jeans in record time. With quiet moans of ecstasy, Hamilton pressed his lean but muscular body against the more massively muscled Bull. Together they carried on as if they were trying to bond themselves together forever. Bull reached for Hamilton's curved buttocks and embraced him.

Hamilton was as ravenous as he could ever remember. He literally mauled Bull, kissing him harshly on the lips, then biting his nipples and licking his sternum and lapping the perspiration from his underarms. Hamilton was a zillion miles away. The animal in his place was a dominant beast that had been wandering the jungle for ages without nourishment. He was gluttonous as he made his way down to the only quarry by which he could be sated. He rearranged his body so that he was now kneeling, as if in prayer, with his head bent in supplication.

As Hamilton reached Bull's mammoth shaft, he teased himself by first burying his nose in Bull's exquisite ball sack and inhaling the scent of his pubic perspiration. Wanting to prolong the divine agony as long as possible, he dragged his nose up Bull's hot, throbbing veined cock. He memorized the contour of the steely rigid spike that was sheathed in a delicate veneer of almost diaphanous skin. Reaching the head, Hamilton's tongue traced the symmetry of the tremendous mushroom-shaped dome and tasted the gluey fluid that covered it. Hamilton licked it clean and made an involuntary slurping sound before opening his mouth as wide as possible and slowly wrapping his lips over and around Bull. He worked very hard to take as much as possible of the full length, like a novice sword swallower.

Bull thrashed his head against the pillows and moaned as quietly as he could as Hamilton expertly gorged himself.

"Jeez, Ham! Jeez, what can I do for you? God, you're driving me nuts! I want you to feel as good as I do! I'm practically ready to . . . oh shit, Ham . . . God, I'm so ready."

Hamilton continued working, unable to speak to ease Bull's distress about him seemingly doing all the work and not getting the electric sensation that Bull was enjoying. If Hamilton could have stopped for a moment to explain, he would have told Bull that his hunger was the fulfillment he needed. He would have explained that more than anything, he wanted Bull to explode in his mouth.

And Bull knew that Hamilton was practically insane with lust and that his ultimate reward would be the load of jiz that was quickly surfacing.

"Can't . . . hold . . . much . . . longerrrr," Bull whispered as he continued to whip his head back and forth.

Hamilton, too, moaned, as Bull's dick seemed to grow even larger and hotter. The expectation of what was to come made Hamilton whimper.

"Sorry, Hamilton! Sorry! I'm coming. I . . . I . . . oh, God! Oh, Jesus! Oh, fuck."

And in an instant Hamilton was so filled with Bull's juice that he couldn't swallow the multiple loads that seemed to go on forever. He was practically choking.

Bull sensed the trouble Hamilton was in and withdrew his shaft.

With just one quick breath, Hamilton returned to suck him completely dry. When he was finished, he fell on his back beside Bull.

"Man, you did all the work, while I had all the fun," Bull apologized.

"It doesn't work that way," Hamilton said. "Nothing for me could have been greater than having you come in my mouth. Can you understand what it's like for me to know that I have you in my body? You're part of me. You're circulating through my bloodstream. Soon you'll be in my every cell. From my lips and my tongue to my throat and stomach."

"You are what you eat," Bull laughed.

Hamilton chuckled, his chest still heaving from the intense workout. "You joke, but it's true. What a fucking load, just like the other day. How do you do it? How do you have so much to give?"

"It's a big tool, I suppose that has something to do with it. Maybe it just seems like a lot."

"Trust me, you had maybe a gallon or more!"

Bull made a kind of laughing noise. Then said, "Am I in your heart too?"

Hamilton raised himself up on one elbow. By now he was used to the darkness and could easily make out Bull's shape and his face and where his wide eyes illuminated the blackness. "Yeah. Especially in my heart."

"Man, you need to get off, too. I'll do whatever you want."

"What I want is to touch your skin and to kiss your nipples and to know that you feel about me the way I feel about you."

"If you feel turned on by me, I feel that for you. If you feel you want to touch me, I feel that, too. If you feel that you love me, I love you, too."

Hamilton rolled on top of Bull, placed his head on the mossy planes of his lover's chest and held on tightly with his arms and hands, enfolding his neck and the side of his ribs. "I can't leave Dulcit, 'cause I can't leave you."

"I'll leave Dulcit. I'll go wherever you go," Bull said. "Just don't let go of me," he added as he embraced Hamilton with an equally intense grip.

Chapter Twenty-Four

The temporary editing bay had been moved from Mike's house to the basement of the Dulcit town library. Few people visited the library, and no one other than the head librarian, a geeky old scholarly type who regularly used the basement to view Kevin Anderson movies, ever went down to the dark basement. It was ideal for cutting *Hunk House*.

For the past three weeks, Mike the editor had spent twelve hours a day in the dank environment viewing tape, splicing scenes, trying to make a coherent narrative out of what amounted to hundreds of miles of images that rambled like some schizophrenic's nonsensical conversation. Fortunately, Hamilton had an innate sense of storytelling. "Conflict! Conflict! Conflict!" he reiterated to Mike night after night when they met to view and discuss the day's edits.

One night, just for fun, they spliced together what they called their outtake reel. This consisted of everything the guys in Hunk House said or did that could never be aired—at least not in most of the United States. Every act of intercourse and masturbation picked up by the hidden cameras in the bedrooms and bathrooms was on this reel. All except the encounters Hamilton shared with Bull. Hamilton insisted that these be on a separate private cassette.

Another night, Rex was invited to attend an editing session. The show was nearly complete. Mike stored the tapes in a secret place in the bowels of the library.

As Rex lumbered down the stairs into the basement, he was filled with excitement. The idea of possibly seeing Bull and the other men without their shirts made his penis grow somewhere under rolls of flesh.

In another part of the basement, away from the secret place where the real editing work was being performed, a videotape player, monitor, and extra editing machine were set up as props for Rex, who was ecstatic to finally feel he was part of the team.

"Tonight we're going to edit the final two Out House scenes," Mike explained to Rex who was immediately disappointed that he would not be observing any of the men without their shirts.

Hamilton and Mike had suggested that Rex be on hand for these last simulated outings. The laborious process of collecting all the camera angles and splicing them into a single scene, which gave each contestants' point of view and provided the audience with a ringside seat to the drama, was as tedious to watch as a stamp collector monotonously explaining the history of a rare watermarked issue. The effect of watching Mike go through dozens of reels of tape had the desired effect on Rex. He yawned a lot.

"Aren't we going to show them doing any gay things?" Rex whined.

"What do you mean by gay things?" Hamilton said.

"I'm just a country boy," Rex pretended. "I wouldn't presume to suggest what those fine-lookin' men would do. Unless . . ."

"I'm sure if it's something that would appeal to you, it would probably appeal to our whole audience," Hamilton said. "So, just what gay things did you have in mind?"

"Just like, I dunno . . . touchin' themselves, for instance?"

"Stacia would have a fit if we included a scene like that," Hamilton said. "She'd have my job."

"I'm in charge of the station now. I'd like to see some jerk-off shots."

"We just have to get through these last two segments, then we can go back and tweak the show to your specifications," Hamilton said.

The idea of having to hang around in this smelly basement any longer was too much for antsy Rex. "Call me when you've got some skin to show," he said, hoisting himself up the stairs, one step at a time, and leaving the building.

When Rex reached the library room and closed the door behind him, Hamilton and Mike gave each other a high five and returned to cut the last two segments in their secret room.

As Hamilton and Mike continued their task, they were particularly impressed with the scene in which Cameron was voted out of the house. The drama of Cameron's response was actually more than they expected. Sore loser that he was, they knew from past experience that he probably wouldn't go quietly, but they were unprepared for how vitriolic he turned out to be.

In the final edit, as Luke, Zeth, and Bull held up their signs and declared that Cameron would be the next to leave the house, they weren't prepared for his tirade. When asked if he had anything to say before leaving, he stunned the men by throwing a tantrum, similar to the first time he'd been cast out.

"The show's rigged! I'll make you so damn sorry you ever thought up this Hell House show. I swear it!" Cameron threatened Hamilton.

Mike was able to capture Cameron's histrionics, while excising his blatant attack on the legitimacy of the game. When the scene was finished, all that was observed was a poor sport who wanted to hold his breath until he turned blue.

Cameron struggled to avoid having the blindfold placed over his eyes. He had to be wrestled to the floor, and Bull had to tie Cameron's hands behind his back before he could be escorted from the house.

With four cameras from which to splice tape, Mike got reaction shots from each of the remaining contestants, as well as from Hamilton, who had become as much of a fixture on the series as Jeff Probst in half the nation's bedrooms. Nearly as much as the players, Hamilton had emerged a star.

"Is that dude finally gone?" Bull exclaimed with satisfaction.

Chuckles of enthusiasm came from Luke and Zeth.

"I wanted him out from day one," Luke said. "Remember how he tried to take over? He wanted my room; then he wanted my ass. He got one, but the other was completely off limits."

"I really admire you for standing your ground the way you did," Zeth teased. "No way were you gonna give up your *room!*"

"Dang right! My room's private. Ain't nobody got the right to abuse my privates." Luke laughed again, looking at Zeth with longing.

"Anything you'll miss about Cameron?" Hamilton asked. "Did he do anything that made things at Hunk House more tolerable or more interesting?"

For a long moment, nobody said a word. Then Bull offered, "I don't feel sorry for him, but I think if he'd been less aggressive, he could have fit in better. All he talked about was doing whatever he had to do to win the game. He said he'd screw anyone and everyone to get the big prize. Who could like a guy who was so blatant about all that he'd do just to win a game?"

"I think his plan was to fuck someone's brains out each week, so they wouldn't vote him out," Luke said. "That's how he stayed in the game so long. If you didn't know any better, you'd think he was a damned good fuck. But I've had way better."

Zeth beamed. "I know we both fantasized about it, but we didn't actually do it until *after* Cameron."

"I'm talkin' about the phantom guy who comes to my room several nights a week, and fucks my ass like in the sweetest wet dream you ever imagined," Luke said.

"You sure it wasn't just Cameron sneaking into your room at night?" Zeth asked.

"Maybe it was just a wet dream. One that I've had for years," Luke tried to laugh away the situation. "You guys have had 'em. Everybody does."

"Not several nights a week," Zeth said. "In fact, if it happens several times a year I'm lucky. Look, I love you, Luke, so be honest with me. Who else have you fucked since coming to Hunk House? It won't matter a bit, 'cause I've fucked around too."

Rocky's camera came in for a tight shot of Luke's face, while the other cameras captured the images and expressions from Zeth, Bull, and Hamilton.

Luke pondered. "Ma says, 'Honesty is the best policy.' Honestly, I don't know if I've been dreamin' this, or if somebody really comes into my room at night and fucks me. It's like a dream. And yet, I'm certain it really happens. But I swear I don't know who it is. At first I thought it was Richard. Then it happened again the night he left. I never thought it was Marco 'cause this guy's got great muscles and a carpet of hair on his chest, like Alec Baldwin."

"But you've never actually seen him?" Zeth reminded Luke.

"I'm just guessin' that he looks like Alec, 'cause I can feel his sweating rug of a chest and stomach."

"How can you not know who you let fuck you?" Zeth asked.

Luke smiled. "Some things you just know are right. This guy is there for pleasure—for both of us. Hey, Zeth, he could never replace you."

In the editing bay, Mike and Hamilton spliced the various reaction shots back and forth between the players, trying to create an air of mystery.

Luke revealed more about his phantom. "Man, I didn't have any control over what happened. The first night I was really startled 'cause out of the blue this hand reached out from the darkness and grabbed my cock. I decided to let whatever was going to happen just play itself out. The hand started workin' me like I'd never been worked before. I wanted to see the body that was fuckin' me, but there was just somethin' too wild about bein' in the dark. If the dude's dick hadn't been so huge, I might not of let it keep happenin'."

"You say it started from the first night?" Bull asked.

"Yeah. I don't know what time or if I'd been asleep very long. I really thought it might have been a dream. Then when I got up the next mornin', I had dried cum all over my chest. I figured it wasn't all my load."

"Well, it wasn't me," Bull said. "I was still too scared of you guys for the first few days."

"No, it wasn't you," Luke agreed. "I really didn't want it to be anybody but Zeth, but I knew it wasn't you."

"No, it wasn't me," Zeth said, a bit petulantly.

"Didn't you ever have a fantasy about coming home from school and seeing that your daddy just hired on some stranger whose jeans were ripped at one of his ass cheeks, and he wasn't wearin' a shirt 'cause the work was so hot, and he's real buff, with deep-set eyes that makes him kind of dangerous lookin'? You just know you got to suck his dick or have his dick up your ass or you'll die from frustration?

"Then you go into the barn and hope and pray he comes in for somethin'. Then it happens. He opens the barn door, and a shaft of light falls on you leanin' against a bale of hay, and you already got your meat out and you're strokin' it. Then the stranger comes over and takes your hand off your own cock and places it on his crotch. Then he unbuttons his five-oh-ones, and he's got the biggest sausage you've ever seen. You just stare and stare at it, and he holds it out for you, expectin' you to suck it. Then he grabs your hair and pulls your head down until you can smell the sweat in his pubes, and then you just start suckin'?

"Then, when your lips are all chapped from workin', he pulls it out and pushes you against the bale of hay. He unbuttons *your* jeans and pulls 'em down. He gets you kneelin' on the hay and positions your legs so he's got a clear entry into your ass. He pushes your shirt up to your head and strokes your back and your chest. Then, before you know what's happenin', he hawks a big one that lands right in your ass crack. He rubs it in, then hawks another and lubes himself up. Your own cock is as hard as it's ever been. Then he begins to push his prick through your hole. You start to cry out in pain and he slaps you hard. Somehow you like that. You like that someone you've never met is going to fuck you and make you come.

"You're both scared shitless that your daddy's gonna be comin' in at any moment, so you do your business as quick as possible. He's jack-hammerin' away at your prostate until you finally give up the biggest load you've ever had. His balls are slappin' against your ass so hard—and then he just keeps it buried in you with a few extra deep pushes, you know his load's swimmin' up your colon."

"No," Zeth said, deadpan. "Can't say that I've ever had that kind of fantasy."

"You never had a dream like that?" Luke charged.

"My fantasy's are very tender fantasies. If I had a phantom guy, he'd be you, just the way you are."

"You must'a had some fantasy before meetin' me," Luke said. "I just made a fool of myself tellin' you mine. Now you gotta tell me yours."

"You're my fantasy. I'm not good at playacting this stuff."

"Then tell me who made you horny before you met me?"

"Real or imagined?"

"Imagined."

Zeth hesitated a long time. "You're gonna laugh."

"Probably. But who is it?"

"Okay. I used to lie in bed when I was younger, and I pictured myself going to New York or L.A., where I'd meet this guy. If it was New York, he had a big apartment with a skyline view. If it was in L.A., he had a big hillside mansion with another great city view.

"Anyway, he's the host of this fancy dinner party—all guys—and I'm a guest. When the dinner's over, everybody gets their coats and they're ready to leave. And this guy says, 'I'll take Zeth home.'

"My buddies all give me a knowing look that I don't understand, then they leave. Now I'm alone with this guy. He's not exactly hand-some in a conventional way. But he's sexy, at least to me. And he's really rich and probably famous, only I don't know it yet. He offers me a glass of champagne and we move to another room with a terrific view. And we start talking—small talk—then he makes his move to kiss me. And we end up in his huge bed. And he's the most romantic man in the world. We have sex. And that's the end of the fantasy. I can never get beyond the great sex. I don't know if I spend the night or if we end up being lovers, although I think we do become lovers. And we're forever true to each other."

Mike and Hamilton also edited in Bull's response. "That's a beautiful fantasy, Zeth. You almost make me want to cry. I never had a fantasy about being with anybody rich and famous. But I like that you guys loved each other. Luke's fantasy was fun 'cause it was sexy. But yours was more seductive. Is that the right word? Seductive?"

"Yeah," Hamilton could be heard saying before a camera caught him looking lovingly at Bull. "Seductive's the way I'd describe Zeth's fantasy. I was really moved."

As Mike was about to edit out Hamilton's and Bull's responses, Hamilton stopped him. "Let's keep that in," he said. "I'm starting to re-think how the audience views Bull—*and* me.

Chapter Twenty-Five

"That's a wrap," Hamilton called after he announced that Luke Ryan was the official winner of KRUQ's first original program, *Hunk House*.

Within moments of the official declaration, the front door opened and a troupe of KRUQ employees, led by Ella, who carried a sheet cake decorated with frosting images from her favorite calendar called "The Men of *Days of Our Lives*." The contingent filed into the house and into the living room where the cameras continued to record the festivities.

Following close behind Ella were Mr. Ratner, Stacia, Rex, and Bull. As rehearsed, they all began to sing "For He's a Jolly Good Fellow." A huge cardboard gift certificate that took two people to hold was presented to Luke. On the Pay to the Order Of line, it stated LUKE RYAN. On the Dollar line it simply said: ALL EXPENSE TRIP TO HOLLYWOOD.

Hamilton stepped into the center of the circle of people who had surrounded Luke. He held a microphone as if he were a news reporter. "What's it feel like to know you've made television history by being the winning contestant on *Hunk House?*" he asked.

Luke blushed. Although he'd spent six weeks with cameras trained on him nearly twenty-four hours a day, he was suddenly self-conscious at being the center of attention. "Shucks, it feels great," Luke said. "I mean, I always thought I'd win, but we had some great contestants and I've made terrific friends. I should congratulate Zeth for being the runner-up and a really tough match for me. He deserves to be a winner too. And Bull. That's a guy no one figured would last a week, but he could just as easily be standin' where I am right now."

"What does it mean to you, having succeeded in such a unique program?" Hamilton spoke into his microphone then pushed it back into Luke's face.

"It means that I get to go to California!"

"But is there a deeper meaning about being on a program that's never been done before?"

Luke thought for a moment. "I hope that when *Hunk House* goes on the air, people will have fun watching it. We didn't cure AIDS or anything, but we sure as heck showed what gay guys can really be like. Maybe the people who'll watch the program will see that bein' queer ain't some mistake of nature. A lot of intelligent and respected people are gay. But I s'pect some of the people won't even give the show a chance. I think those are the people who need to watch this show the most and are gonna miss not only an entertaining program, but also one that's enlightening."

"What do you plan to do now?" Hamilton asked.

"Go to Disneyland!" he joked. "They got a lot of queers working there. But seriously. I'm just gonna go home to my mom and dad and then pack my stuff and head for the Golden State."

"What do you think your folks'll say when they hear you've won the grand prize?" Hamilton asked.

"Well, my pa'll kill me, which will save KRUQ from having to cough up the dough for my trip." He laughed. "Then my ma'll make a big fuss and be real happy."

"Something tells me your father doesn't approve of the kind of program you were involved in. Am I right?"

"He doesn't even know about it."

"He will soon!"

"He'll know as soon as I set foot in the door, 'cause I'll tell him everything. He'll be madder than spit. Some things he just won't ever understand."

Ella interrupted. "We're here to party!" she said, turning on the boom box and opening a bottle of Andre champagne from a half-dozen bottles that Rex had carried in from the car.

Rocky and his team of Stedicam operators continued to record, focusing their lenses on the expressions and responses from the others in the room.

Mr. Ratner came forward. "As the owner, operator, and CEO of KRUQ, I feel it's my duty to first of all say congratulations to this young man," he told Luke. "You did a fine job, son, and I even want to shake your hand." Ratner took a tentative step toward Luke. "Get a picture of me shakin' this young man's hand," Ratner instructed, even though Rocky was recording the scene.

Luke beamed.

"You're going a long way in life, son," Ratner said. "All the way to Hollywood!" he laughed at what he thought was a clever joke. Then cleared his throat when no one else seemed to get the levity of his remark. "I suspect you'll do a great job out there in Los Angeles, just as you've done a great job here in Dulcit. I'd take my hat off to you, son, but I don't wear one!" Again Ratner's chortle was the solitary sound in the room.

Ella, with the help of Rex, filled plastic flutes of champagne and began handing one to each of the KRUQ staff and the contestants.

"I think we should propose some toasts," Ella said. "Dear," she said to Ratner, "you should say a few words to Hamilton for all his hard work on the show. And don't forget the other contestants."

Ratner raised his glass and everyone in the room followed his lead. "To Hamilton Ipswich Peabody the Third. It's no secret that I had my doubts about your idea to do a show with nothing but gay men sitting around in some old house for six weeks. It was a risky proposition. You know there was only one lone voice of support for what I still think is a cockamamy idea. If it weren't for my Ella, we wouldn't be standin' here today. So I raise my glass to Ella, too."

"Hear, hear!" echoed around the room.

Ratner continued. "But I gotta tell you, son, gay or straight or in-between, you turned out to be a disappointing programming director, and I have no idea if this show is gonna be a success or not. We may all be appearing together in a real-life prison shower scene and *not* on that *Oz* program that Ella makes me watch!"

This time, after several sips of champagne, everyone laughed at Ratner's joke.

"But seriously, folks, Hammy's responsible for the whole show. The rest of us wanted to help, but we didn't know what to do. Hammy got it done. He's a man of his word. How in the heck he accomplished everything almost single-handedly is amazing. I'll give him that."

Stacia stepped forward. "I don't think you exactly did everything by yourself," she said to Hamilton. "You had quite a bit of support from the staff at KRUQ. Mustn't forget that. For instance, who helped cater all of the meals?"

"Ella," Hamilton said.

"Who was on call twenty-four hours a day in case there was an emergency?"

"Ella."

Stacia fumed. "All right then, who stayed out of your way so you could get this program completed?"

"Mr. Ratner." Hamilton smiled and made a slight bow.

"I think I deserve some credit for *Hunk House,*" Stacia said with great impatience.

"Why?" Bull interrupted. "You tried to stop the show. You wanted to close all of this down just last week."

"That's ridiculous!" Stacia declared. "We're a station that supports its programs and its family of employees. We're all for one, and one for all!"

Rocky's camera caught Ella, standing behind Stacia, rolling her eyes and shaking her head. Hamilton drained his flute and looked at Stacia. "You're absolutely right, Miss Ratner. This was a team effort and everyone who had anything to do with this program should be congratulated!" He reached for the bottle and poured another round of champagne.

Hamilton then took center stage. "I would like to take this opportunity to thank everyone who helped in both tangible and intangible ways to make *Hunk House* a program that I know we'll all be proud to be associated with. We had to overcome a lot of hurdles pulling this show together. And if it hadn't been for some divine intervention, this might never have moved from thought to form. We still have to edit a gazillion miles of video, but over the next two weeks I'm sure we're going to wake up the world with something new.

"Aaron Spelling once said to me, 'It takes guts, but if you want to be a success in this business, you have to look at what everyone else is doing, and then be brave enough to do something completely different.' If that's the measure of success, then we've already accomplished that. We've done something truly different. Nobody can take that away from us. I'm proud of *Hunk House,* and I'm especially proud of all of you for making it happen!"

Again, there were cheers. With the cameras still rolling, the circle of well-wishers dispersed.

Bull and Hamilton found themselves by the piano. "Great speech," Bull said.

"Thanks," Hamilton replied.

"What now?" Bull asked.

"Edit the show."

"Then what?"

Hamilton became contemplative. He swallowed more champagne, then stared into Bull's big brown eyes. "First, I gotta get these guys to L.A."

"Second?"

"Make myself a list."

"Of what?"

"Pros and cons."

"Huh?"

"Nothing." Hamilton smiled.

Both men chuckled and sipped more champagne, not taking their eyes off each other.

"I've already made my list," Bull said.

"Me, too," Stacia said, barging into the conversation. "Oh, I know all about you two! I suppose you'll be registering for wedding gifts at the Crate & Barrel, so I've made *my* list of what newlyweds need the most. Unfortunately, everything I come up with can only be ordered through sick porn catalogues or from some novelty shops in Chicago or Hollyweird."

"The best gift you could give us would be to ride your broomstick off to Des Moines or Cedar Rapids, and just leave us alone," Hamilton said.

A tear slipped down Stacia's cheek.

"Come on, Stacia," Bull said tenderly, "please don't do that. Can't you be happy for me? Can't you see that you'd eventually be unhappy with me if I kept lying to you?"

"I wouldn't have cared if you lied!" Stacia pouted loudly, unaware that Rocky was capturing the scene. "You were the prize I was entitled to! When we were in school, all the girls were jealous of me being with you. I wanted to keep it that way. Forever. If we'd been married, I'd be the girl everyone still envied, 'cause I had the most handsome man in the county."

"Your happiness above Bull's? Is that what matters to you?" Hamilton asked.

"Of course not!" Stacia spat. "But don't I deserve to be happy? With Bull as my man, I'd be happy."

With that comment, she placed her empty plastic glass on the piano lid. "I'm not through with either of you. *Hunk House* will never air, Hammy. You'll wish you'd never heard of Dulcit or me, or Cameron." She walked away and joined her brother, who was seated in the wing chair with a large bowl filled with Pringles nestled between his legs and a bottle of champagne on the floor.

Hamilton rolled his eyes. "Back to our pros and cons lists," he said. "I'm serious if you're serious."

"About what?"

"Us."

"What about us?"

Hamilton smiled. "Making babies."

"I *have* come a long way," Bull said. "A few months ago I would have decked anyone who remotely suggested I might be baby-makin' material with another guy."

"I suggest that while I'm editing *Hunk House,* we both seriously think about what we want, not only from each other, but from life in general. In two weeks, when I present it to the station, we should both know exactly where to go from there."

Bull nodded. Then, surprising Hamilton, he set his flute on the piano top next to Stacia's and placed both hands on Hamilton's face. Rocky zoomed in as Bull pulled Hamilton's lips to his own.

Almost simultaneously, the entire room spotted the sign of affection. Ratner coughed and turned away. Rex's mouth dropped open, spilling saliva-saturated Pringles. Luke and Zeth smiled.

Chapter Twenty-Six

Returning to KRUQ, Stacia pulled a file from Ella's cabinet. She withdrew a résumé and scanned the page. Then she dialed the telephone number that appeared at the top. After the third ring, a sleepy sounding voice asked, "What?"

"Cameron?"

"S'out," the voice declared and hung up.

Stacia dialed the number again.

"I'm not buyin' anything," the voice answered.

"This is Stacia at KRUQ. That's you, Cameron; don't lie. I'd know your voice anywhere. Wise up. This is a sales pitch, but only in the sense of discussing how to even the score at *Hunk House.*"

Silence.

"You're either interested or you're asleep. Which is it?"

"What's your problem, lady? It's your station's way out of bankruptcy. If I know Hamilton, he's gonna make a great show and I'm probably gonna get rich and famous just for being part of this thing. So why are you calling me?"

"You were screwed out of the big prize. You must hate that Luke Ryan kid for winning, and maybe hate Hamilton even more for faking the show's ending."

"Who says it was faked?"

"I have my sources."

"Your fat-assed weasel brother squealed, didn't he?"

"Forget Rex. Are you interested in getting revenge on Hamilton Peabody and the people who stole your prize?"

"Not really."

"You're just going to roll over and let 'em all fuck you? I kinda thought you were more of a man than the others."

"What's your angle, Stacia? Why are you out to ruin your own career?"

"I don't give a damn about my career. You all made my Bull a queer, and I intend to make someone pay!"

"Jeez, you Christian types are so sure that queers can take a straight guy and brainwash him. I've got news for you, and Dr. Laura, and the wackos at Exodus International: A leopard can't change its spots!"

"Freakin' cliché! Ever since Bull revealed—on camera—that he was gay, my heart and my guts have been torn out!" Stacia sobbed into the telephone. "Maybe it's me! I'm not a turn-on for him! I can try harder."

"You'll need an operation."

"I'm numb. I'm at the lowest point a person can go. I want revenge!"

Cameron was quiet for a moment. "Retribution, eh?"

"So you'll help me?" Stacia perked up.

"What's your plan?"

"Meet me at the Des Moines IHOP, tomorrow. Noon."

Cameron thought for a moment. "Just for the sake of curiosity."

The restaurant was the same as every other in the chain that Cameron had ever patronized. The pitched ceiling with its dark wooden beams tried to give the place an aura of Old World country charm. Copper Jell-O molds decorated the walls, while fake green plants adorned the brown faux mahogany tabletops. Cameron spotted Stacia sipping coffee halfway back into the one-room restaurant and walked to her table. He slipped into the faux leather booth and sat opposite Stacia. "Why so clandestine?" he asked. "Why couldn't we have talked over the phone?"

"I like to play Mata Hari, okay?" Stacia retorted. "I need a little intrigue in my life. Indulge me."

"So what's the deal?" he asked.

"Just this . . ." Stacia spoke in a whisper. When the waitress came by to take their lunch orders all she could catch was, ". . . open his closet and screw up the dick head's ass for good . . ."

Cameron bared his teeth in a wicked grin and said, "That'll show 'em. He'll wish he'd never fucked me." Just then, Cameron and Stacia both realized that the gum-chewing old lady waitress was standing beside them, her pencil poised over her order book.

Over the next two weeks, Hamilton and Mike worked feverishly in the basement of the town library, starting at dawn and not emerging before the town closed down for the night. Ella was just as covert. Once a day she brought enough food for lunch and dinner. Rex had been instructed to keep their location a secret and he seemed to go along with the clandestine activities. He enjoyed the intrigue. But Rex was a cheater. When he insisted once again on seeing hardcore sex on the *Hunk House* outtake reel, and Hamilton again refused, Rex went pouting to Stacia.

"Don't worry, big brother," Stacia cooed, sympathetically.

"I'm in charge of this station!" Rex bellowed. "Hamilton has to do what I tell him!"

"You're exactly right," Stacia agreed. "If it wasn't for Daddy giving Hammy carte blanche with this show, you could see every inch of videotape you wanted."

"Daddy's not the boss of me!" Rex charged. "In fact, since he's hardly ever at the station, I'm really the man in charge!"

"I'm with you, baby. But where the heck are they?" Stacia asked.

"I know exactly where they are," Rex shouted. "They're in the library basement! I was just there! I saw them editing! If you go back there with me, they can't deny us access to our own videotape. It's ours!"

"Why didn't you tell me before where they were editing?" Stacia said, trying to hold back her temper.

"I just thought you knew."

"No, I didn't."

"They get in early and stay late. But they've gotta go home sometime. We'll just hide out until they leave tonight."

"Great minds think alike," Stacia said, almost kissing her brother on his pink cheek but changing her mind at the last moment and shaking one of his clammy hands instead.

Although the basement windows of the Dulcit Town Library were covered with pages of the *Dulcit Daily Dispatch* newspaper, illumination from the work lights radiated into the night.

"It's nearly two o'clock, for God's sake. How long can they work?" Stacia griped as she sat with Rex in her car across from the library. It was cold for a late spring night, and she clutched the collar of her coat against her throat. The car windows were fogged up from what little warmth was disseminated from their bodies. Stacia used her sleeve to rub a circle of transparency on the driver's side window.

Rex, too, had complained since they arrived at ten that he was cold and hungry.

"There!" Stacia said with enthusiasm. "The lights are out! They've got to be leaving!"

From the back of the library, two figures emerged. They stopped for a moment and looked around, as though scouting for spies. Then, with a handshake, Hamilton and Mike walked away in opposite directions.

In the quiet of the Dulcit night, somewhere in the distance, Stacia and Rex could hear the sound of car doors closing and echoing down the street, followed by the sound of engines. Headlights and taillights glowed from the two vehicles on opposite sides of the street, and soon the night was completely silent again.

Stacia and Rex opened their respective doors and stepped into the frosty darkness of the town square and hustled across the street to the library. "What about a key?" Rex whispered.

"What public place in this town do you know of that locks its doors?" Stacia hissed back as she mounted the two back steps and turned the doorknob. She turned it again and pushed against the door.

"I guess books are more important than the city records," Rex said.

"Damn that Hamilton," Stacia whispered. "It's all his fault. They never used to lock the library doors."

"We're screwed," Rex whispered back.

"Like hell!" Stacia spat. "We're getting in there and getting the videotape! If you weren't so hung up on Pringles and Ho Ho's, we could break a window and have you shimmy inside."

"Stop picking on me!"

Suddenly, Stacia had an idea. "Your diet of pizzas and Cokes and Twinkies may have served a purpose after all," she said. "This door isn't that thick. I'll bet if you just bounced against it, we could break in."

"Twinkies," Rex said, sounding like a marathon runner who hadn't had a drop of water for ten miles.

"C'mon. Make that belly of yours good for something," she appealed. "Try it."

Rex looked dubious. Then, standing on the back steps of the library, he simply leaned against the door. It was enough. There came the sound of cracking wood around the door frame.

"Take a few steps back and push yourself more sideways into the door," Stacia encouraged.

Rex did as instructed. Again the sound of cracking wood could be heard in the night.

"Again!" Stacia whispered.

Rex followed Stacia's orders, and in no time, the door flew open. Rex fell to the floor.

"Get up!" Stacia ordered impatiently. "Put the door back the way we found it! Hurry!"

The library was dark. Slowly, with their arms outstretched like twin Frankensteins, Stacia and Rex made their way, occasionally bumping into bookshelves or a table they hadn't seen.

At last, Rex found the door to the basement. He felt around for and found the light switch that turned on the bulb on the stairway. Then he opened the door.

"Careful, sis," Rex admonished as he began to descend the stairs, holding onto the wooden railings on either side of the passage. Stacia followed.

Finally, in the basement, Stacia found two work lights, both of which she turned on. She was immediately dumfounded. The room was immaculate. There was no sign of any editing activity. Even the tape machine that Rex had described was nowhere in sight. The table on which the video monitor had been set up was gone. Not a strip of video. Not even a splicing blade.

Stacia looked around.

"It's all gotta be here, somewhere!" Rex exclaimed. I didn't see 'em bringing anything out of the building. For Christ's sake!"

"Let's look around," said Stacia.

"I need a flashlight," Rex demanded.

"Use a match!" Stacia snapped.

She picked up one of the work lights and carried it with her as far as the cord would reach—the front of an antique safe. "Ah, ha!" she said.

Rex came up beside her. "A safe. I'll bet they hid everything in there."

"Can't you open it?" Stacia asked.

"It's thick steel. No one could just bust the doors on this thing."

Stacia was furious and disappointed. "Who would have the combination?"

"The librarian?"

She said, "That's not a bad idea. Let's go back upstairs and call him."

"At this hour?"

"It's an emergency!"

Rex was relieved to get out of the basement, and when they arrived back in the main floor of the library, Stacia felt around for all the light switches. She found them and turned on all the fluorescent fixtures throughout the large single-room library.

She then went to the librarian's desk and picked up the telephone and dialed 411. After a moment she said, "Yeah, information. Dulcit. Thomas Gardner. Sure charge me an extra buck to make the connection." She looked at Rex as if to say, "It's not my money."

"Hello? Mr. Gardner? It's Stacia Ratner. Stacia. Stacia Rat-ner from KRUQ television. That's right. Oh, Daddy's fine. Yes, Ella, too. And Rex. Listen, I'm sorry to bother you at this hour, but I was walking by the library and I noticed all the lights were on and the back door was broken. I think you've had a burglary. You should get here ASAP. Five minutes? Of course I'll wait." Stacia hung up the phone and grinned at her brother.

"If you want to check out a book or something, why don't you just take it and leave," Rex said, as Stacia rolled her eyes. Her brother wasn't retarded; he just didn't catch on to the plan very fast.

"I don't read books! Don't try to understand anything. Just sit down until Gardner gets here."

"I'm your boss," Rex sniffed and was ignored by Stacia.

In the time he'd promised, Mr. Gardner came bounding up the front steps of the library and opened the door—without a key, which was not lost on Stacia.

"My God! What happened?" Gardner asked, alarmed.

"As I said, Rex and I were out for a walk . . ."

"At this hour?"

"We were working late. And we saw lights on in the library."

"That's impossible, I always turn 'em out when I leave at nine."

"So we thought something was amiss," Rex said.

Stacia pointed to the back door. "Yeah, as you can see, we were right, someone busted in."

"Oh, my," Gardner moaned. "That door's county property. Did you notice if anything looked out of place? Any books taken?"

"Who can tell? There're so many. You'll have to do an inventory. But what I'm worried about is all the videotape that Hamilton and Mike have been editing in the basement. Please check the safe to make sure it's all right."

Stacia put on her most demure-yet-concerned look and once again begged Gardner to open the safe in the basement.

"Hamilton should be here," he said. "I'll call him."

"No!" Stacia interrupted. "There's no need to worry him unless we find something missing. He works such long hours. He's probably fast asleep. Let's just check the safe ourselves."

"Let's call the sheriff first," Mr. Gardner insisted. "This is breaking and entering! We don't want to disturb any possible evidence."

"You've been watching too much *Law & Order*," Stacia snapped. "I'm sure he'll be thrilled to have a crime to write up a report about."

Now becoming completely impatient, Stacia bellowed, "Would you please just go down to the basement and open the goddamn safe?! That's KRUQ's material in there, and we're KRUQ!"

Stacia and Rex practically pushed Mr. Gardner down the stairs into the basement. He was disoriented and unable to withstand the pressure from the two Ratners. They both forcefully guided him to the huge, dusty, old green safe. Now, standing before the solid metal vault, Mr. Gardner just stared at it.

"C'mon!" Stacia bellowed! "This is important! What're you doing, waiting for Christmas?"

"Sorry, Stacia," Mr. Gardner replied, "I don't have the combination to the safe. No one does. It's been locked for as long as I've been here, which is going on forty years in May."

"But that's impossible," Stacia shot back. "Hamilton keeps all of the video from our show in that safe!"

"He does?" Mr. Gardner asked incredulous. "I thought he kept it in the tunnel."

Stacia looked at Mr. Gardner with a blank stare. "Tunnel?" she repeated.

"What tunnel?" Rex asked.

"You're his colleagues; he musta told you, otherwise you wouldn't be so worried," Gardner said, not comprehending the situation.

"Of course," Stacia lied. "He said tunnel. I thought he said 'the safe.'

He must've meant, 'The tapes'll be *safe* in the tunnel! That's it. Now I remember exactly what he said. Sorry. My fault. I misunderstood *safe*. So let's check the tunnel," she demanded.

"Nobody who broke into this place would have found the tunnel," Gardner assured Stacia, "so why don't we just go call the police. Whoever burglarized the library probably took the petty cash or the copies of banned books I keep hidden for the few open-minded readers in Dulcit."

"Show me the goddamned tunnel, you self-styled censor of free speech," Stacia demanded, shoving the old man against a wall on which hung an old tapestry. The force and weight of the librarian hitting the tapestry pulled it from the top of the wall and revealed the passageway.

"Oh. My. God!" Stacia exclaimed in wonderment. "The tunnel. Where does this go?" she asked wide-eyed, not giving a second thought to helping Gardner to his feet.

"You're a mean little thing, ain't ya?" Gardner said as he found his glasses and struggled to stand up. "I'm going to get the sheriff this instant!"

"Hold 'em, Rex," Stacia commanded as she started down the passageway, which had been dug out like a cave and then turned into a concrete corridor. Trying to get her bearings, she thought the passageway probably went under Main Street to St. Ethel Mertz the Divine, which was directly adjacent to the library.

Bare lightbulbs illuminated her way as she slowly moved away from the sounds of Mr. Gardner fussing about the sheriff, and Stacia and Rex being intruders, and him being held against his will. Presently, she came to an intersection. *Left or right?* she asked herself. She decided to turn left. After walking another hundred yards or so, she came to an ancient wooden door. Gingerly, she reached out for the metal knob and pushed against the door until she realized it opened toward her. On rusted hinges that made a sound like gears grinding in a car's transmission, she pulled the door open and found a startling sight. Ancient jail cells. "This must be the courthouse," she said.

The place reminded her of dungeons in old movies. She was impressed by the rusted steel cages. They were so old that the cells weren't made from steel bars but were flat straps of metal bolted together. The locks were as antique as anything she'd seen in movies.

Curiously, Stacia noticed that relatively modern lightbulbs hung at intervals along the long room, as they had in the corridor, indicating that the passage was not some forgotten remnant from pre–Civil War times.

It was eerily quiet as she looked around the chamber in which there were a total of six cells and beyond them, another old wooden door. "The videos," she said as she moved toward the door. "The videos," she repeated as she placed a hand on a cold metal doorknob and started to turn the handle.

Chapter Twenty-Seven

It wasn't difficult for Mr. Gardner to outsmart Rex and escape from the library. Within moments after noticing that the old librarian was gone, Rex lumbered up the stairs and could see the reflection of flashing red lights on the portrait of George Washington that hung on the wall behind the front desk. "Shit," he said as he tried with turtle-like movement to race back to the top of the basement stairs. "Stacia," he whispered as loudly as possible. "Stacia," he repeated, "the sheriff's here! Come back!"

Suddenly Rex was rapped on his fat behind with a nightstick. He turned around. Sheriff Watson and one of his deputies were standing behind him with Mr. Gardner. "What in tarnation are you doing in the library at three in the morning, son?" Sheriff Watson asked.

Rex turned beet red and began to stutter. "It's Stacia's fault. She made me break in. She's in the tunnel in the basement."

"Doesn't take much fire to make a rat, or a Ratner, jump ship, does it?" Watson smiled at his deputy. "Take Rex and read him his rights."

"I didn't do anything," Rex began to sob. "I was just following orders. Stacia's the one you should be reading rights to."

"We'll get to Ms. Ratner," Watson assured him as Rex was escorted to one of the reading tables in the center of the large room.

Gardner explained to Watson the events of the evening and expressed particular resentment for the way he had been physically abused by Stacia. "May I call Hamilton?" he asked. "He's still doin' that program and I think Stacia's tryin' to interfere and maybe destroy his work."

The sheriff agreed and Gardner immediately telephoned Hamilton who sped back to the library wearing only his jeans, shoes, and the tank top he'd worn to bed.

By the time Hamilton arrived, Sheriff Watson had descended into the basement and had begun following the now-revealed hidden passageway. When he arrived at the intersection he, too, asked himself, *Left or right?* Sheriff Watson decided to turn right.

Rushing down the stairway and running along the passage, Hamilton turned right at the intersection and found Sheriff Watson standing in the secret editing bay looking at all the equipment.

Out of breath from his fast sprint down the craggy corridor, Hamilton caught Watson just as he was about to turn on a videotape monitor. "Sheriff," Hamilton gasped. "Thank God you're here. Mr. Gardner said there was a forced entry. I came as quickly as possible to make sure all my equipment was safe."

"What'cha got goin' on in here?" Watson asked, still poking around and picking up VHS tapes and pushing VCR recorder buttons.

"Please be careful with the equipment and tapes," Hamilton asked in a nervous voice. "We're finalizing the editing of our show for KRUQ."

"Why the secrecy, hiding out in this old underground passageway?"

"It's a game show. Can't have anybody knowing the results before it airs."

The sheriff seemed to be satisfied with Hamilton's answer. Then he asked, "What's on the tapes?"

"Just a lot of raw footage. We're editing it all down to a six-hour program."

"You already told me what you were doin'. I asked what's *on* the tapes."

"The performances. The everyday activities of the contestants."

"Wanna show me a sample?"

"Sorry, Sheriff, no sneak previews." Hamilton tried to sound playful.

"I may have to take all this in for evidence," the sheriff added to demonstrate his authority as well as his sincerity in wanting to see what the KRUQ program was all about. "Like everybody else in Dulcit, I've been hearing hints about the subject matter of this so-called reality program of yours for the past six weeks. Now I wanna see if the rumors are true."

"Er, okay," Hamilton said with as little cooperation as he could muster. "Let me pick out something that's representative of the whole program."

"Na. You relax for a spell. *I'll* pick the tape," Watson said with a mischievous grin. He looked around at the dozens of black videocassette tapes stacked around the room. He withdrew one from the center of a tower of tapes, as if he were cutting a deck of cards.

Hamilton was sweating. He hadn't a clue what was on the unmarked box. A label would have revealed that it was an edited tape and ready to be aired. The VHS cassette the sheriff handed Hamilton was raw footage. Not knowing what was on the tape, and not knowing how to stall the law, Hamilton pushed the ON buttons to both a television monitor and a VCR. He inserted the tape into the slot and closed his eyes.

The sounds Hamilton feared most filled the room: "Oh, fuck, you're so fucking hot! Don't stop! Jesus, you're fucking hot."

"Take it, asshole. Take all of my eight thick inches! I wanna fill that motherfuckin' hole of yours."

"Oh, God! Oh, yeah, I want it too. Fuck my hole. Fuck my ass. Ram it, deeper."

Without looking at the scene, Hamilton recognized the voices. Cameron was fucking Luke. All Hamilton could think about was that the sheriff had to select the one tape on which a minor was featured.

"Oh, God! I'm coming. Fuck me harder," Luke's voice demanded. "Fuck me, you prick. Make my ass so sore I won't be able to sit for a month. Oh, Christ, yes! I'm coming! Fuck me!"

As the sound of the two mens' climax reached its crescendo, Hamilton opened his eyes and looked at Sheriff Watson who, like Mr. Ratner after seeing a rough cut, was transfixed by the scene and his jaw was practically unhinged. Hamilton could see he was catatonic. Then the tape ran out and roused him from his trance. "What the hell?" Watson exclaimed, unable to utter another word. He simply stood riveted to the now-dark TV monitor screen. Then, after a moment, he became conscious of his surroundings and turned to Hamilton. "Reminds me of when I was in the Police Academy."

Hamilton was dumbfounded. "What?" he asked, almost speechless.

"We were hot studs in them days. You'd never know by lookin' at me now," Watson said, patting his big belly, "but I was hot shit. I bagged me more ass at the Academy than I do givin' out tickets to outta-staters drivin' through town."

Hamilton was weak in the knees and pulled up a chair, first for support, then to sit down. "Some tape, eh?" He tried to sound as though the sheriff had just witnessed nothing more dramatic than an episode of *Frasier*.

"That's an understatement. You could make a fortune selling this shit right here in Dulcit, never mind the whole Midwest!"

"It'll be on television in the fall, so folks'll probably just record it. Although, nothing that hardcore will ever reach the screen," Hamilton said, making a solemn promise.

"That's my point. You're missin' a gold mine opportunity, son," the sheriff offered. "With me as the law, we could sell this shit and never get caught."

Now Hamilton was really confused. He didn't know how to respond. He didn't want to dismiss the sheriff's idea as insane and risk the possibility of him confiscating the material as "evidence," but he also didn't want any part in getting into the sale of pornography. He decided to play both sides of the fence.

"I'll let you in on our secret, Sheriff," Hamilton said. "But you can't let Stacia or Rex or Old Man Ratner find out. We're doing the *Hunk House* show for real and making it something that I think will be important for viewers. But we've also got all this leftover tape of stuff that could never be shown on television. We thought about maybe creating a bunch of tapes with the cut footage. Not that we'd really gotten too far into the plans, but now that you mention it, maybe you could be our partner. As you said, it could be a gold mine."

"Now you're talkin' son. I need to pay off my second mortgage. And I need a new pickup. The old truck's fallin' apart. And my four-oh-one-K plan sucks. I figure we could do with the extra bucks."

Hamilton took a deep sigh of relief. "We'll be finished editing the show in a few days. Why don't we meet, say next Wednesday night, right here, and start viewing the stuff that the general public won't see?" he lied.

"Deal," the sheriff smiled. "God, that brought back memories. It's not the kind of stuff a guy can talk about, especially in a town like Dulcit. But I gotta tell you, those days at the Academy were some of the best I ever had. I think my new deputy had good reason to come back from the Academy smiling, too."

"Stacia!" Hamilton suddenly said with alarm. She's down here somewhere. We can't let her find this editing room."

"Probably took the other direction, toward the church and court-house. Lock the room and let's go."

Stacia turned the knob and pulled another old door toward her. Again, the sound of metal grating on metal echoed throughout the room. The next chamber was also lit by old bulbs that hung on frayed wires. As she continued into the room, a distant sound caught her attention. She stopped for a moment to listen again. The sound, which seemed like lightning striking a dead tree, cracked again somewhere ahead, followed by what sounded like a human cry.

A moment later, the same sounds issued back to her from farther down the maze of connecting rooms. She reached the next doorway, opened the portal, and took another step toward the sounds.

The cracking sounds and the subsequent cries became louder as she continued to make her way down the corridor. As she followed the sounds, she forgot her mission to find Hamilton's videotapes and was consumed with apprehension. *What am I doing?* she thought. *I shouldn't be here.* She pressed on until she came to what appeared to be the very end of the corridor.

At the end, however, was a black tarpaulin. Now she could clearly hear the sounds, just a few feet beyond. She suddenly realized it was the sound of a whip she was hearing, followed by the cry of pain of some-one being struck. Putting her hands along the edge of the tarp, she pulled it back only a fraction of an inch, then immediately let go, putting her hands to her mouth to keep from crying out.

The scene she observed was that of a naked man lashed to a huge wooden X. The man's back was welted. Another man, muscular and hairy, pierced with nipple rings, was masked. He was flogging the other man.

"Does the fucker want more?" the masked man with the whip com-manded?

"Yes, sir!" came the reply.

"Yes, sir, what?"

"Yes, sir. Please, sir. I want more!"

The masked man drew back his whip and expertly snapped the long tail, flicking it to a precise spot on the bound man's back.

Where am I? What place is this? Where have I heard that man's voice before? Stacia wondered in terror.

She silently prayed, then suddenly began to feel dizzy when she realized the voice of the Dungeon Master belonged to the town priest—Father James! She automatically reached out and grabbed the tarp for support and accidentally pulled it down on top of her.

"Who the fuck?" came the voice of the man with the whip as he rushed toward Stacia.

"Oh, God, don't stop, sir!" the other man's voice rang through the room. He turned his head just enough for Stacia to see who it was. Cameron. Although he was shackled at his wrists, she could see his erect eight inches and in an instant she realized Cameron was enjoying the torture scene.

"Sorry," Stacia stammered. "Wrong turn," she said, rising to her feet.

The whip cracked over her head. Stacia screamed and ran faster than she'd ever imagined possible, quickly opening each door, then closing it tightly behind as she retraced her steps back to the library. When she was finally in the first chamber with the cells, she continued retreating until she saw the intersection just a few paces up ahead. As she raced toward safety, she suddenly collided with Hamilton and the sheriff and, frightened as never before, let out a scream that echoed all the way back to the library basement. The deputy ran to investigate the shriek.

As soon as Stacia realized it was Hamilton she had run into, she grabbed him and sobbed into his tank top. "It's horrible!" she cried. "Get me outta here!"

With Hamilton on one side and the sheriff on the other, she was quickly escorted the rest of the way through the tunnel and up the stairs to the main library room. Stacia was still panting and sobbing when she was ushered into a seat at the reading table where Rex was handcuffed.

"No! No!" she cried. "Demons. I was in hell! I saw Satan, I swear! He was in the church basement. Oh God, save us! Hail Mary full of grace! Oh, Christ! What's the rest of that?" she sobbed.

"It's okay," Hamilton tried to be comforting. "It was dark down there, you were probably hallucinating, or you just saw shadows and you got scared."

"No! The devil himself is down there! I swear to it!"

Sheriff Watson interrupted. "What were you doing down there in the first place? Why aren't you at home, in bed? What've you and your brother been up to, besides breaking and entering?"

"No! We didn't break in. In fact, I was down in the basement looking for the people who broke down the back door."

"They were idiots, since the *front* door is always unlocked," Mr. Gardner said.

"And did you find anyone down there?" Sheriff Watson asked.

"Yes! But not the burglars. It was Satan, sure as I live and breathe. And Hamilton knows it, too! You've been down there, you must have seen him!"

Hamilton gave a look of surprise. "Stacia, it's almost dawn, I think you're half dreaming. Better get outta here before the vampires return at sunrise."

"I saw that movie!" Stacia shrieked in terror. "I'll be *undead* for hundreds of years!"

"Stop your nonsense," Sheriff Watson declared. "I still want to know why you broke into the library. Rex has already confessed, but I want to hear your side of the story."

Stacia glared at her brother. "Judas!" she shouted. After a long moment of silence, she said, "We just wanted to find the *Hunk House* videos. We wanted to see what Hamilton had edited. The tapes belong to KRUQ!"

"All you had to do was ask," Hamilton said. "Mike and I have practically edited all six segments. A few more days and we'll be finished. We had Rex in for a peek. You were welcome anytime."

"You wouldn't have let me take part in the editing."

"Probably not. Unless you had a good idea. But you've tried like hell to sabotage this project from the get-go. I can't imagine you'd have anything constructive to say about the edits Mike and I have made. You'll see the program next week when we premiere it for your father."

"What about me?" Rex demanded. "I run the station now! I demand to see the tapes!"

Stacia looked at Hamilton, baiting him to object.

"Too bad, Rex, you'll be in jail. If you behave, maybe the sheriff will let you out to attend the screening."

"Jail?" Rex said and began blubbering. "I can't go to jail. You know what they do to men in jail? I've seen *Oz!*"

"You deserve a shower with a bunch'a horny convicts. But I seriously doubt you'd be anybody's girlfriend, what with the shape you're in," Sheriff Watson said.

Turning to Stacia, Watson declared, "Both of you are criminals as of tonight. Breaking into the library. You've got a lot of explaining to do. And something tells me there was *intent* to commit another crime. To steal or at least vandalize Hamilton's tapes."

"KRUQ's tapes!" Stacia spat. "We just wanted to see what Hamilton was up to."

"Read Stacia her Miranda and take 'em both to the station," Watson said to his deputy. "They can call their daddy to come and get 'em."

"Don't you fucking cuff me, you son of a bitch!" Stacia bellowed at Watson.

"Brother has a potty brain and sister has a potty mouth." Mr. Gardner shook his head in disgust and disbelief.

Rex and Stacia did not try to interfere with being removed from the library and into the waiting squad car. The ride to the station was a simple U-turn to the driveway across the street at the Town Hall where the Dulcit Police Station was headquartered directly above the hidden editing bay.

Before Sheriff Watson left the library, he shook Hamilton's hand. "If I'd known what you guys were up to over at the Maynard mansion, I might have been able to help out. Everyone has a fantasy about getting fucked by an officer of the law, ya know."

"Yeah," Hamilton agreed, trying not to display his astonishment. "Big help."

"See ya Wednesday," the sheriff said with a wink; then he left the building.

Chapter Twenty-Eight

Monday morning arrived quickly. Yawning, but with a big smile, Hamilton turned to Mike. "I smell an Emmy," he said, staring at the end crawl credits on the final episode of *Hunk House*.

"I think we did it," Mike replied.

Both men were exhausted. For three days they had been sequestered in the dank editing room. They never went home. When they were too tired to continue, they bunked in one of the old cells down the opposite corridor, too drained to worry about rats or ghosts.

At that very moment, to their surprise, Ella walked in with a bottle of champagne and three flutes. "I've just made reservations for you and Luke and Zeth and Cameron. You're booked from Chicago to LAX, American Airlines, departing first thing Wednesday morning. Thought you'd need time to pack after showing the program to the Ratners. Charged it to your Visa. Also brought boxes and FedEx labels—they're upstairs in the library. We gotta pack up all the unused footage and get it out of here before Stacia declares ownership!"

"Does anything slip by you, Ella?" Hamilton asked. "What on earth am I going to do without you?" He enfolded her in his arms. "You wanna come along to L.A.?"

"Hollywood's for young people. However, if you do make it big because of this show, you can send for me. I'll be your personal assistant. You need a mother figure who's finished with raising her kids and no husband she has to run home to fix dinner for."

"Deal!" Hamilton said.

When the three had been served, they raised their glasses together.

"To *Hunk House,* and success for everyone involved," Hamilton declared.

"To *Hunk House!*" Ella repeated.

"*Hunk House,*" Mike said.

Ella took another sip and said to Hamilton, "Bull's waiting upstairs. I told him you'd want him to come down, but he was afraid of interfering."

Hamilton took Ella's empty flute and filled it, then refilled his own and said he'd be back in a moment. He made his way back through the corridor, carefully opening the doors along the way with his elbow and shoulder. When he reached the basement stairs, he took a deep breath and ascended. At the top step, he realized the door was closed. Rather than set the glasses down on the steps, he knocked with his right foot. Bull opened the door and was face-to-face with Hamilton.

"I brought you a little something to help us celebrate," Hamilton said, offering Bull a flute.

Bull smiled a wide toothy grin and accepted the glass. "C'mon down and join Mike and Ella," Hamilton coaxed.

"I don't want to get in the way," Bull said.

"C'mon. You can help me pack up the extra footage for FedEx."

Hamilton reached out his hand, which Bull accepted to guide him back down the stairs. Before re-entering the basement, they both drank their bubbly in one or two swallows. Then, unexpectedly, Bull gently but forcefully pulled on Hamilton's arm like a dancer drawing his partner close to his body. Searching deep into each other's eyes, Bull made another unexpected move and kissed Hamilton harshly on the lips. Bull's lips and tongue were at first cold from the champagne. But in moments, his passion was so intense that their lips burned together. Both moaned in ecstasy, mauling each other under the harsh glare of the library's fluorescent lights.

Finally daring to break the spell, Bull gently withdrew his full lips from Hamilton's. "I've made a decision about something," he said, still panting from the exertion of their deep kisses. Then he began to cry softly.

Hamilton froze. He sensed the news wasn't good but didn't know what to do. He was stunned to see Bull with tears streaming down his face. He could only swallow hard and utter, "I'm not going anywhere without you."

With those words, Bull threw his plastic glass against the portrait of Washington and slumped to the floor, now crying in huge waves of hiccups. "Too much!" he managed to sputter. "Too fast. Confused. Love you. Want you. Lost." His noises were hardly coherent sentences, but Hamilton easily deciphered Bull's pain.

Hamilton sunk to the floor and held Bull's big body. "It's okay," Hamilton whispered. "You're the most amazing man in the world to have come so far in such a relatively short time. I know this isn't easy. I know what you're feeling. I wouldn't say that if I hadn't gone through this, too."

"I'm afraid," Bull continued sobbing.

"Tell me, sweet man, what are you afraid of most?"

"Everything. My life. What's to become of me? The people I've hurt. The hurt I feel knowing you won't be with me forever. It's too much for me! I can't go back. I'm scared of movin' forward."

"Okay, my beautiful man, I have to say a few things. It could hurt, but it's what they call tough love. And when you've gone through it, you'll know that I have you in my heart."

Bull stopped crying and looked at Hamilton with eyes that looked frightened.

"I know you're scared. Me, too. But you've proven that you're quite capable of following your instincts, despite opposition from people who don't think the way you do.

"As for what's to become of you, the only thing I can guarantee is that I'll be beside you and support you, no matter what lies ahead.

"If you think you've hurt people because you had the balls to stand up and be who you are, you're very much mistaken. If you loved someone you wouldn't want to prevent them from growing, would you? You've actually helped people like Stacia. They now have a new life experience, one that only you could have provided. They should be grateful to you. Now, they have a larger concept of what the human condition is all about, if they don't yet recognize it!

"As for your fear of being hurt by me, I will promise you this: Never, ever, will I intentionally do *anything* to hurt you in any way. That means I will *never* do anything to jeopardize our relationship. I will *never* put you down, in public or in private. I will *never* tell you that you snore, if that's something you're sensitive about . . ."

"Do I snore?" Bull asked, appalled at the possibility.

"No. That's just an example. If I know you have a hang-up about anything . . . I don't know . . . say I thought you weren't good at telling jokes, I'd still laugh at your punch lines."

"Okay, there were these two cows, see. And one of 'em said to the other, 'I'm really worried about Mad Cow disease.' And the other one said, 'Eh, don't worry. It can't possibly hurt ducks like us.'"

Hamilton burst into laughter, genuinely tickled by Bull's old joke. Although he'd heard it a dozen times, Bull's comic delivery was effortless.

Bull laughed, too, but his chuckle was more the release of anxiety. The fact that he'd made himself laugh in the midst of all the drama, as well as Hamilton's loving words, put Bull at ease. He accepted what Hamilton had to say and let it filter through his own apprehensions. The two men sat on the old wooden floor next to an old radiator for a long while holding each other. They didn't kiss. Staring into each other's eyes spoke volumes about how much love had been ignited in each of them.

Bull laid his head against Hamilton's shoulder and after a while, had nearly fallen asleep, so exhausted from crying was he. Hamilton noticed that Ella and Mike had come up from the basement, probably to check on Hamilton and Bull. He pursed his lips and emitted a slight "Shhh" before Ella could accidentally break the spell. Instead, she gave him the OK sign, blew him a kiss, and quietly tiptoed out of the building with Mike.

Hamilton watched the clock above the librarian's desk. After twenty minutes, he decided to gently ease Bull back to reality. "Hon," Hamilton whispered.

"I'm awake," Bull said. "I was just enjoying every moment of you holding me."

"We've got a lifetime of these moments, I promise. Shall we go home?"

"The tapes," Bull reminded Hamilton. "We've got to box 'em up."

"They can wait 'til morning. I want to hold your naked body against mine."

"This would be just the night that Stacia or Rex or Sheriff Watson would come by," Bull said pragmatically. "You said yourself, we've got a lifetime together."

Hamilton got a rush of adrenaline and sat up. "A lifetime! You bet your thick dick we've got a lifetime together. I'll leave it up to you whether we stay in Dulcit or go to L.A."

"We'll talk," Bull said, getting up. He reached out his hand and waited for Hamilton to take hold of it. Then he pulled him to his feet. "Let's get these boxes downstairs. There are chores to be tended to!"

Both men smiled as they carried flattened cardboard file boxes and lids down the basement stairs and through the cold corridor to the editing bay.

Chapter Twenty-Nine

Hamilton was sick to his stomach. It was Tuesday morning. In eight hours he'd have to present *Hunk House* to the Ratners and the contestants, as well as the sponsors whose check had made the project viable in the first place.

For the event, Hamilton had arranged to use the Royal Theater over in Alliance, a town ten miles from Dulcit. He bought all the mini-quiches and tiny hot dogs wrapped in dough that he could find at the Piggly Wiggly and convinced the Eat 'n' Run to keep them warmed in a chafing dish on a table in the theater lobby. In addition, he bought red and white wine, the vintage that came in a box, instead of a bottle, as well as a large assortment of soft drinks. Ella helped with the preparations, bringing one of her hand-knitted tablecloths to add a festive touch.

Hamilton spent the day going over the video with Mike and agonizing over what they might have done differently.

"It's no use, Hammy," Mike said, trying to alleviate his fears. "We've done the very best we could do. You had a vision and you've stuck to that vision. They may hate what you've done, but they'll never be bored for a moment."

"I know, I know!" Hamilton agreed, still hoping more than anything that the Ratners would at least give the program a chance.

Throughout the day he practiced his introduction. He stood before the mirror in the bathroom of his small house and saw himself white-faced, like some anemic vampire. He imagined he was standing in front of the audience, half of whom were praying for him to fail.

"Ladies and gentlemen," he rehearsed. "For the program you are about to view, I owe a great debt of gratitude to many people, without whom *Hunk House* would never have come to fruition. First, Mr. Gallo Ratner." Hamilton would lead the applause as Ratner smiled and waved to the crowd. "Also, Stacia and Rex Ratner for supporting this project." Another round of halfhearted applause. "And the ever-helpful Ella for keeping things running smoothly both at the office and at Hunk House. Yeah, Ella!" A much louder applause would greet Ella's acknowledgment.

"Let me pay special tribute to our guests of honor from Hollywood." More applause. "For without their magnanimous monetary gift, and their belief in this program, we would not be here tonight."

Again, polite applause.

"Last but certainly not least," Hamilton continued, "I must thank all the contestants who appeared on this program. As I call your name, please stand and take a bow."

Hamilton could see in his mind's eye the men practicing a forced casual attitude, befitting their imminent celebrity status.

"Because of the length of the show, there will be two intermissions. Please," he begged, "it's really important that you not leave until the very end of the screening. You have to view this program in its entirety to fully understand the remarkable achievement of KRUQ. I truly believe that because of this show, Mr. Ratner's station will be recognized for creating an incredibly important piece of television programming. Remember that this type of show has never been attempted. I know we've succeeded in creating something unique. Thank you. Enjoy the show."

And then Hamilton threw up.

He heaved so violently he thought his very guts were coming up.

Finally, as the sun was beginning to set, Hamilton, weak from dry-heaving for hours, dressed in his best Brooks Brothers white shirt and dark suit. He slipped his feet into Kenneth Cole loafers and sat down in his small living room, staring at the six black videocassette boxes stacked on his coffee table.

He looked at his watch. It was five-thirty. The screening was scheduled for seven o'clock. Hamilton calculated that it would take half an hour to reach Alliance, then perhaps another half hour to make certain the projectionist knew what to do with video rather than film and to oversee the catering efforts. He picked up the cassette boxes and his suit coat, as well as his wallet and car keys and left the house.

The drive to Alliance took exactly the half hour he expected, but he wasn't aware of the time or distance. All Hamilton had on his mind was whether he had succeeded in portraying gay men in a new light. He was petrified, but not so much by the possible response from the Ratners as by the reception the program would receive from critics and audiences— especially *gay* audiences.

When Hamilton arrived at the Royal Theater, Ella was already supervising two rugged teenage boys sent from the Eat 'n' Run as they set up the table with paper plates, napkins and toothpicks, and chafing dishes. Plastic wineglasses were turned upside-down on a tray, and the wine boxes—both the red and white—were at room temperature. Hamilton suggested immersing the box of white in a trashcan of ice, at least until the guests arrived. He was embarrassed by the lack of amenities. After enjoying some of the biggest Hollywood premiers, his attempt looked like what one would probably find at a Tupperware party.

"Great job," he lied to Ella. "The only thing missing is a poster of the guys."

"I'm way ahead of ya," Ella announced. She unveiled an easel with a blowup from one of the shots she took that first morning when the guys all gathered for orientation. Ella had had the people at the Cedar Rapids Graphic Design Shop add a title at the top and superimpose the main credits at the bottom, like an official Hollywood film studio poster.

"This is too wild!" Hamilton exclaimed, giving Ella a hug.

They were interrupted by the rapping of knuckles on the glass doors of the theater. Standing outside was the entire Ratner gang. Hamilton left Ella, went to the door, and pushed it open. None of the KRUQ members seemed entirely happy to be attending the premier event of *Hunk House*. Old Man Ratner grumbled something about a rerun of *Kate & Allie* he was missing.

"You can miss Susan St. James for one evening," Ella stated as she slid her arm into Ratner's. "Next to *Roots*, this is going to be the most important program you're likely to ever see," Ella said, loud enough for everyone else to hear. "Let's go get us a glass of wine and a plate of nibbles." She guided Ratner to the table set up for grazing.

The next to arrive were Richard and Marco, the first two contestants to be outed. They were a bit reserved as they greeted Hamilton, who made a big point of showing how happy he was that they had accepted his invitation.

"We're just curious about how we'll be perceived by the public," Richard stated, as though he had better things to do with his evening.

"Can't be much footage on us," Marco said. "We were only in the game for a short time."

"You guys'll be surprised," Hamilton whispered. "The way the video is cut, you all get a good amount of screen time."

Marco smiled, then accepted Hamilton's invitation to examine the food table and get a glass of wine.

Just then Cameron entered. He ambled over to Stacia. He winked, then whispered something in her ear. It made her smile.

Just as the screening was about to begin, Bull finally arrived. He stood in the lobby for a long moment looking for Hamilton. Luke was the first to spot Bull, and he called for him to join him and Zeth. As Bull wandered over to the two men, Hamilton intercepted him and gave him a hug. "I'd kiss you," he whispered, "but I think Stacia's planning something. Gotta be on my most professional behavior."

"Okay," Bull said. "Let me get a drink and I'll join my buddies. You've got a lot on your hands. Good luck tonight."

Hamilton gave Bull another hug and let him go. He looked at his watch. It was seven o'clock, and his special guests, the sponsors, still hadn't arrived.

Hamilton decided to wait another five minutes before he made the announcement to begin the program. Just then, a long black limousine pulled up to the curb outside the theater. The spectacle was not lost on the party's attendees. One by one, they all became aware of the fancy car that idled outside. Finally, the driver opened his door and came around the back of the vehicle to the passenger's side. He opened the door and stood at attention. A few more moments passed. Then two men stepped out onto the curb: one was slightly less than average height, but demonstrated a packed, buff body under a tight black T-shirt. The other was a twentysomething Latino man with a jet-black goatee and sideburns. He was as imposing as a tough gangsta from the barrio, and his inappropriate-for-the-evening Marine camouflage outfit made him appear even more intense and tough.

Hamilton walked to the door of the theater, which had been propped open and embraced first the younger well-built man who kissed Hamilton on the lips. "Bart!" I can't believe you came all this way just for me!"

"Heck I just hopped in the jet. Didn't take more than a few hours."

"Who says money can't buy *everything!*" Hamilton laughed.

The other man smiled and also gave Hamilton a hug.

"Rod! I'm thrilled you're here!"

"Hey, how'd you end up in this backwater ditch of a town?" Rod asked. "Oh, right, that thing with What's His Face from KABC. I think you can come back to the reality of Hollywood now. Nobody remembers what happened a week ago, let alone a year ago! Pop quiz, who won Best Actress at last year's Oscars?"

"Er. Ah."

"Exactly. Heck, I don't even remember!"

"Thanks," Hamilton smiled. "I'm actually planning to get out of this dump right away," he responded. "Where's Jim?" Hamilton asked politely.

"The asshole's in London. Working on a film. After the success of *Blind as a Bat,* he's suddenly back in America's good graces. Imagine me making that prick a star again? Although, you know Jim. He'd whine that he's always been a star." Hamilton laughed along with Bart Cain and one of Hollywood's brightest up-and-coming feature films directors, Rod Dominguez.

"Okay," Hamilton said. "Let's get started. The theater's through those doors." He pointed to two sets of double doors, which were being opened by Ella.

"Ladies and gentlemen," Hamilton announced in his most authoritarian voice. "Please take a seat in the auditorium. We're about to begin the show."

Ad-libbed murmurs of "It's about time," and "I'm really nervous," and "This should be one for the books," and "We're all doomed," filtered through the lobby. Hamilton heard them all, but he was no longer nervous. It was a *fait accompli.* He just had to get through the next four hours.

Inside the dimly lit theater, little cliques had formed and dispersed throughout the rows. The Ratners all sat together. The contestants, minus Bull who sat in the back next to where Hamilton planned to sit, occupied their own row. The sponsors, Bart and Rod, sat in the very center.

Hamilton stood at a microphone in the small space of room with the screen behind him and the audience adjusting themselves in the less-than-plush Royal Theater seats. He made his rehearsed remarks and tried to make everyone feel as though they'd been an integral part of putting *Hunk House* together.

"Finally," he said, "I want to introduce our amazing sponsors. These are two men who first recognized the potential value of this program. When I made my pitch for financial assistance what both of them said was, 'Great! How can we help?' 'Duh, send a big check,' I said."

The audience laughed politely.

"Ladies and gentlemen, it is my great honor and privilege to introduce you to two of the entertainment industry's most important players. They've been Magwitch to our Pip, so to speak."

"Who the fuck's Pip? Is he on staff?" Ratner whispered to Ella. The acoustics in the auditorium clearly carried his voice to Hamilton, who immediately realized that nobody got the reference to *Great Expecta-tions*.

"Please help me welcome the great Hollywood publicist-turned-philanthropist, Bart Cain, and the man behind last year's mega hit comedy film *Blind as a Bat,* Rod Dominguez!"

Hamilton started clapping but was joined only halfheartedly by the rest of the crowd.

Ratner didn't know who these Cain and Rodriguez people were—except that he thought that the smaller one, wearing blue jeans, sneakers, and a dark T-shirt that announced his physical endowments, was certainly underdressed for the occasion and the other one in the Marine getup, looked as though he belonged at a costume party. He was a little miffed that his own thunder had been diminished by these outsiders.

"Okay," Hamilton finally said. "Sit back and enjoy the show." As polite applause enveloped Hamilton, he took the microphone away and placed it by the exit door. He walked up the aisle and took a seat in the very last row, where Bull waited for him, immediately reaching for Hamilton's hand and holding it tight.

The lights dimmed, until the theater was pitch black. The curtain was drawn to either side of the silver screen. Then, from an antiquated speaker system came the din of conversation. The conversation became clearer, as though a microphone were honing in on one particular group of people.

Suddenly, a bright, rapid montage of film frames began burning into the viewers' eyes with the velocity of a passing train. Then, in blue letters on a field of red, the title appeared:

HUNK HOUSE

The title remained on screen for ten seconds, as the red background slowly faded to a still life: six men, the contestants. All were smiling, grouped together as if they were best buddies posing for a summer camp photo.

Moments before the image of the six beaming men disappeared, a voice-over began in a conversational tone. Luke's voice. The words, lifted from his long interview, told of how he'd started giving blow jobs to the sixth-graders and schoolteachers when he was no older than six or seven.

In the first half hour, each of the contestants were introduced, and then each man talked about his life and dreams for the future.

By the end of the first hour, the audience knew each player. After Marco was outed, the screen returned to a still photo of the group of sexy smiling men and a bold banner said: INTERMISSION.

Hamilton and Bull remained seated in the back row as everyone else almost silently filed out into the lobby. Hamilton turned to Bull with a questioning expression. Bull squeezed Hamilton's hand and said, "It's going fine."

Hamilton gave a weak smile. "Better join the others," he said, rising from his seat.

Together the men joined the guests milling around the food table and pouring wine into plastic cups. There seemed to be little discussion about what had been viewed thus far. Hamilton overheard Stacia talking to her father about the bill she'd received for a new library door. Luke and Zeth were making plans for picking out a Beverly Hills mansion in which to live once they became stars.

Hamilton and Bull moved over to Ella. "Can you read these people?" Hamilton asked. "What'dya think. Do they like it? What's going on in their minds?"

"Rex was weeping," Ella said. "Stacia was whispering 'Oh, brother,' most of the time. Gallo squeezed my hand a lot and made little noises that I recognize as him feeling uncomfortable."

Hamilton said, "But what do you think of the show thus far?"

"Remember when you first presented your proposal? I remember saying I hoped they'd do the full Monty. Well, you've succeeded far beyond my wildest expectations. There's more sex in that house than in all the years of my marriage! If I'd known then that there was so much sex to be had, I'd've been long gone from Dulcit years ago. 'Course, maybe it's just gays who get so much sex."

"No. Look at *Sex and the City*. Everybody there's getting screwed a lot."

"Dang!" Ella said.

"Youth is definitely wasted on the young!" Hamilton said and looked at Bull who had joined them. "However, I'm not wasting any more of my youth—although by the standards of the guys in *Hunk House* I'm already old. Doesn't matter, though. I've got Bull."

Ella smiled and put one hand on Hamilton's face and the other on Bull's face. "You two go for it!" she insisted.

"Do you think it'll make a difference?" Hamilton asked.

"'Cause you and Mike have made a film that throws sex in your face as equally as it throws declarations of love and human beings doing what human beings do. It's not scummy. And it's not saccharine. It just shows life. Like the Discovery Channel shows the habits of the kangaroo rat, your program fills in the gap between what people have heard or read about gays, and shows them living a perfectly fulfilling existence."

"That's what we were aiming for," Hamilton said to acknowledge his appreciation for Ella's commendation.

After a few more comments from Ella about perhaps changing some of the music, "Cut Googie Grant singing 'Wayward Wind' over that scene of Cameron and Luke. Try Cher's 'Take Me Home'." Luke rang a bell indicating that intermission was over. The audience made their way back into the auditorium and returned to their seats.

Hamilton and Bull held back, waiting until they were alone. "It's going fine," Bull reassured Hamilton, then gave him a quick kiss on the lips.

*   *   *

It was nearly 11:30, when the end credits began to roll. A disco remix of Shirley Bassey singing *"Light My Fire"* wrapped up the show. The contestants all applauded from their row, but they and Bart Cain and Rod Dominguez and Ella were the only others who acknowledged what had just been presented on screen. As they hooted and hollered, they realized that something was not right. The Ratners were leaving the screening without acknowledging them.

The program was so great that it was naturally going to put them and KRUQ on the map. The men had expected a big round of applause and slaps of appreciation. Only Ella, as she came up the aisle with the Ratners, showed her pride for the men and their show. The KRUQ contingent simply filed out of the room without a word.

Looking around, the men found the two guys whom they'd heard were Hollywood hotshots, still sitting in their seats, whispering to each other. Soon, the two men got up. They looked around the auditorium and spotted the *Hunk House* men, as well as Hamilton and Bull who were making their way down to the six guys to once again congratulate them all on their efforts.

By the time Bart and Rod were among the group, they could hear the sounds of confusion and disappointment in the voices of everyone, including Hamilton.

"Well, what did we really expect?" Hamilton said in a voice that read frustration more than disappointment. "The Ratners don't have a clue about what they've got here. They probably think it's smut and that they're all ruined. It's probably a good thing that we're all leaving tomorrow. They can do with the show as they please. Whether it's aired or not, you all did a great job!"

"So did you!" Luke said to Hamilton, and to which the other five contestants heartily agreed, trying to make their friend feel less alone and saddened by the evening's outcome.

"Yeah," Hamilton said, "they could at least have been polite and pretended to like the show, or acknowledged all the work we put into it. Oh, screw them! Fuck 'em all! We're going to Hollywood!"

"Right on!" Cameron said. "I'm packed and ready for my screen test!"

Hamilton finally looked away from his men for a moment and realized that Bart and Rod were standing behind him. "You guys stayed!"

Hamilton said in disbelief. "Guys," he said to his group, I want you to meet two of the most important people in Hollywood. This is Bart Cain, publicity writer extraordinaire, and this is Rod Dominguez. He's a director I met out in Hollywood. You probably all saw his movie, *Blind as a Bat*. It was a huge hit. Pummeled Jerry Bruckheimer's pathetic opening weekend box office for that inept, triple X-rated version of *Pillow Talk*."

With the exception of Bull, each of the men recognized the names. "I read in *People* that you're gonna direct that fox Jay Hernandez and Melissa Sagemiller in a musical version of that old TV show *The Grass Is Always Greener*," Luke said.

Rod smiled and nodded his head. "And I got ol' Jim Fallon the original star of that series, playing Uncle Doris. He hates that he's not young enough to be the lead. He hates it even more that the character he always made fun of on the show is the one who'll be made fun of in the movie. He's furious!" Rod laughed. "But he has to keep up the payments on his ridiculously big house. This is his *mortgage movie*."

"And this is the guy who won a mint when he sued Sterling Studios for wrongful termination and sexual harassment," Hamilton said, presenting Bart Cain. "Now, he and his life-partner—by the way, where's Rusty?" Hamilton asked.

"He's overseeing the work on the castle we bought in Scotland," Bart explained. "Yeah, a real castle. Didn't I always say I'd one day have a castle? Little did I know I'd also have a knight in shining armor to go with it."

"If I hear another word about how happy you two are together, I'll puke," Hamilton teased. "But seriously, you know how happy I am for you. Both of you."

"Look, we have a proposition," Bart interrupted. We, that is Rod and I, are starting a new gay cable network. It's sorta like Triangle Broadcasting out of Palm Springs. We think this should be the premiere program."

"You liked it?" Hamilton asked, sounding totally amazed.

"It's the perfect anchor for our Saturday night lineup," Rod said.

"And I personally think you should all have your own individual shows on the network," Bart said in his affable voice. "Hamilton's obviously got a sweet tooth for sexy guys. Girls and boys'll be hanging your beefcake posters on their walls by the time our publicity and marketing machine kick in."

The men were speechless. They had simultaneously and collectively forgotten about a piddling walk-on role on *Days of Our Lives* and now saw themselves as stars of programs called *Cameron, Luke & Zeth, Richard, Marco.* Only Bull had no such thoughts. He had never considered the *Days of Our Lives* gig either.

"And you, Mr. Hamilton Ipswich Peabody the Third," said Bart. "That dumb ass producer over at *ET* is long gone. I know the other producers liked you. If you wanted, you could probably work there again. But, consider this instead. I'd like you to be in charge of *Hunk House* and all the spin-off series for these guys."

Hamilton was overwhelmed. The night was blossoming into something better than he'd ever expected. What seemed at one moment to be a disaster turned out to be a life-altering experience. His smile gave his answer. "Yes, of course! This is great!" Hamilton said, then stopped himself. "Wait a second. The Ratners. KRUQ. They own *Hunk House.*"

Echoes of disappointment issued from Cameron, Luke, Zeth, Richard, and Marco.

"Are you kidding," Bart said. It wasn't a question or a statement, but a declaration like "Get real." "Read the contract you guys signed when we sent you that check. We own seventy-five percent of this *Hunk House* show. As for KRUQ, watch this."

Bart pulled out his tiny cell phone and punched in a few numbers. "There's a piddling little nuisance of a television station here in . . ." he turned to Hamilton. "What's the name of this town?"

"Dulcit."

"In Dulcit . . ."

"What state are we in?"

"Iowa."

"In Iowa, that I want. Make the deal. Oh, and tell Captain Lance we're flying back with seven more." He flipped his cell phone shut.

"What'd you just do?" Hamilton asked.

"You tell me," Bart said.

"You bought KRUQ, and you're flying us all back to Los Angeles with you?"

"That's what I expect from my executives—analytical reasoning," he laughed.

Hamilton and Bull and the other men were speechless at the way this Hollywood expatriate-turned-philanthropist conducted business. He was like a genie. He simply issued a command and it was made so. The men began to laugh at the improbability of anyone having so much power.

"This has got to be a dream," Luke said, looking first at Bart, then at Rod.

"More like a nightmare!" It was the voice of Stacia as she walked down the red-carpeted aisle. "That thing you showed tonight is being scrapped. The projectionist has already handed over the tapes. She held up the six black videocassette boxes. "We're going to shred them tonight."

She looked at Hamilton. "How dare you! We trusted you to create a program that would attract viewers who want quality television. Our subscribers don't watch *South Park* or reruns of *The Grass Is Always Greener.*"

Rod blanched. "What's wrong with *The Grass Is Always Greener?*" he asked politely.

Stacia looked Rod up and down as if he were nothing more than a vagrant begging for a handout. "Those perverts at ABC came up with that obscene stinker. It was filthy! And it had that slimy Jim Fallon."

"I'll give you points for the Jim Fallon remark, but the show always took its Sunday slot with the eighteen to forty-nine demographic group," Rod noted.

"And I suppose you watch that freakish *Queer as Folk*, too!"

"Well, yes . . ."

"Stacia," Hamilton tried to interrupt but she continued her tirade.

"And if you try to stop us from doing our Christian and ethical duty, Sheriff Watson is ready to press charges against you for engaging a minor in your perverted sexual web. Luke's only eighteen. I let him play along just in case I needed a trump card. He's served his purpose well. Thanks for being a liar and a cheat," she said to Luke.

"Hand over the tapes, please," Rod said to Stacia.

"Who the fuck do you think you are?" she bellowed at the handsome, brown-eyed, broad-shouldered man whom she actually found rather attractive.

"Stacia," Hamilton interrupted again, this time getting her attention. "May I introduce you to Bart Cain and Rod Dominguez?"

Stacia hadn't a clue what their names represented in Hollywood and around the world. "Are these two goons you've hired to hide behind 'cause you're too much of a sissy to fight your own battles? Let me tell you something, mister, you can't win this fight with your glib words and movie star good looks. KRUQ owns these tapes and the show that never was. Again, it's all been a dream. Soon you'll wake up under a newspaper blanket in the park, a homeless, former programming director who nobody will hire because by the time I'm finished slinging the hash about you—I've still got copies of your diary—you'll be lucky to be hired to make cold calls for a real estate company."

Again Rod asked, "Please hand over the tapes, Miss Ratner."

By this time, Bull had positioned himself directly behind Stacia. Hamilton advanced toward her and as she took one step backward, she was up against the brick wall of Bull Smith who instantly grabbed three tapes from her left hand as Hamilton took the other three from her right hand.

Stacia laughed. "Ha! They're empty! You think I'd be fool enough to walk in here and confront you guys with the real tapes! You're more stupid than Rex!" Stacia chuckled. "Don't worry, they're in his good hands."

"Hands that are probably full of his own dick right now!" Hamilton said and began to bolt from the room. "Bull, hold Stacia. Don't let her out of your sight or use her cell phone. Bart. Rod," he called back, "wanna come with me and see something amusing?"

"I'm with you, man," Bart said as he and Rod rushed up the aisle. "Get into the limo. Roy's a great driver."

Off the three men went, with Hamilton giving Roy directions to the Ratner house. They were there in half the time it had taken Hamilton to drive to Alliance. Quietly opening the limo's doors they stepped out onto the sidewalk. Stealthily, they walked up the long driveway to a carriage house that was shrouded from the big house by a grove of trees.

The seclusion was ideal for Rex, who was too afraid to move away from home but still wanted privacy. On the way, Hamilton gave Bart and Rod a quick rundown on the Ratner son. "He's a fat weasel of a queen who'd sell his sister to run KRUQ. The only thing to worry about with him is his halitosis. I guarantee he's got the tapes and is using his remote to freeze-frame all the best sex scenes. Careful. He's probably whacking off. If we scare him, he could let loose a sloppy mess."

Coming through the trees, it was obvious from the ever-changing pattern of light filtering through the window that the television set was on.

"Here's an idea," Bart said. "Why don't you go to the front door, and Rod and I'll go around to the back. Pitch pebbles or something at the window to distract him. Maybe he'll stop what he's doing to investigate. If he comes to the front door, use your charm to get inside the house. Pretend you want to jack off with him or something."

"*Ew!*" Hamilton remarked, involuntarily. Then he realized that whatever he did was for the good of the mission and the safety of the tapes. And so the men split up.

Hamilton picked up a dead tree branch and scratched it across the screen of the front window. The ruse worked and Hamilton could hear Rex yelling, "Goddamn it!"

The front door opened and there stood Rex wearing a blue silk bathrobe with the belt tied over his protruding stomach. Hamilton didn't want to think about the erection that was probably hidden under all the folds of flesh, but he pretended to come on to Rex just the same.

"Sorry to wake you up," Hamilton purred. "It's just that I'm leaving for L.A. tomorrow, and we never had a chance to really get to know each other." He opened two extra buttons on his shirt, which had the precise effect that Hamilton was going for.

The younger Ratner swallowed hard and made an overture. "I was just rewatching *Hunk House*. You did a great job," he enthused. "My VCR lets me freeze-frame. Wanna come in and watch for a little bit?"

"Love to," Hamilton smiled as he passed Rex in the doorway. "Go back to what you were doing. I just need a glass of water from the kitchen," he said and walked to the back of the small house where he turned on the faucet to mask the sound of him unlocking the back door and letting his accomplices in.

Hamilton returned to the living room where the television was on and a frame of Cameron fucking Luke filled the screen. "Nice shot, eh?" Rex said, causing Hamilton to turn his head toward the voice and then practically jump out of his skin, as he took in the sight of a naked Rex reclining on the couch. He was like a pink whale, fondling his hairless balls and thumb-size penis.

"Strip down and have some fun," Rex suggested.

"Ever get off without touching yourself?" Hamilton asked, trying to play along.

"No, but I've always wanted to," Rex admitted. "I just can't control myself long enough to let it happen."

"Anyone can do it. Want me to show you how?" Hamilton offered. Rex appeared a little apprehensive. "What do I have to do?"

"Just stare at the television and imagine it's you. I'll walk you through it. Like phone sex."

"I'm so horny now that I just want to get it over with. Take off your clothes and we'll do it together."

"Don't you want to try my way? It's great. Like a wet dream."

Again, Rex was ambivalent but curious.

Hamilton didn't waste any time. "Gotta make sure you don't touch yourself," he said, pulling the silk belt from Rex's bathrobe and instructing him to lie back and put his hands together.

"Whatcha doin'?" Rex asked, getting worried.

"This is the fun part. Gotta make sure you can't touch yourself. Gotta let your mind do all the work."

Rex went along with Hamilton, and in a moment his wrists were bound and the remaining length of belt was knotted to the decorative mahogany knob on the arm of the couch. "So take off your clothes, now," Rex demanded. "I'll probably come faster if I see you in the flesh instead of the guys on the TV."

Just to further tease Rex, Hamilton slowly, seductively unbuttoned the rest of his shirt. Rex moaned at the sight of Hamilton's muscled chest and the trail of hair running from his navel into his pants. "God, you're as sexy as I always pictured," Rex said as his baby gerkin penis jumped.

"I'm a better show than this ol' tape," Hamilton said, taking his shirt off while surreptitiously pushing the EJECT button on the VCR and removing the videocassette tape. "Wanna smell my shirt?" Hamilton asked.

"God, yes!" Rex breathed in heavily.

Hamilton tossed his white dress shirt, which was filled with a profuse amount of perspiration, over Rex's face. "Just inhale the aroma," Hamilton advised.

"Okay, guys," he shouted, and Bart and Rod bounded into the room and began gathering up all the *Hunk House* videocassettes.

"What! What's going on?" a blindfolded, tethered Rex screamed. "Who's there! What's going on? Daddy! Daddy!" he screamed at the top of his lungs.

"Let's get outta here," Hamilton said and quickly placed another porn video in the tape machine and turned it on. He pulled back his shirt and tossed Rex's bathrobe in its place as he continued to cry out for his daddy.

Hamilton, Bart, and Rod made a hasty retreat through the grove of trees, down the long driveway, and into the waiting black limo, which immediately screeched away from the curb.

"We'll let you off at the theater and hightail it back to the jet," Bart said to Hamilton. "Gotta get these tapes in a safe place before the Ratners get the sheriff involved. Can you and your guys all be at the Cedar Rapids airport by eight?"

Before Hamilton finished rebuttoning his shirt, Rod asked him how he kept so toned in a place that valued hot dogs and pork chops over exercise. "Push-ups. Sit-ups. Jogging. Without a gym, I have to do whatever I can, just in case Mr. Right comes knocking."

Rod gave a smile that transmitted a definite interest in giving Hamilton a workout he would never forget.

"We'll be there," Hamilton said. When the car arrived back at the theater, he thanked his friends and dashed into the lobby of the theater. Inside the auditorium, he called, "All clear! Stacia, you can go now. But you might want to check on Rex. He's in the carriage house. He's watching television, but I don't think he can reach the remote. Sleep well."

Stacia disappeared out the door and into her car. She drove away without regard for the posted speed limit.

"Bart's plane is waiting for us in Cedar Rapids. We have to be aboard by eight o'clock. That's just a few hours away. Can you guys get everything you need and be there on time?"

"There's nothing important left at Hunk House," Luke said.

"We better hurry," Zeth said. "But I've got stuff to pack."

"What are we supposed to do once we get to L.A.?" Marco asked.

"Bart and Rod'll take care of everything. They know this show's going to be a huge success and they'll take care of their stars. So don't worry."

Chapter Thirty

"... and I'm Leslie Stahl. Those stories, plus Andy Rooney, tonight on *Sixty Minutes.*" *Tick, tick, tick, tick.*

For all those gathered in the projection room at Hamilton and Bull's estate on Locust Street in Dulcit, it seemed an interminable time between commercials and the start of the show.

The room was filled with many of Hamilton and Bull's friends and colleagues. More important, it was a reunion party for the original *Hunk House* men, on the occasion of the *Hunk House* phenomenon being the feature story on *60 Minutes.*

Hunk House was in its third year, and the show had made Hamilton rich. Most of the original cast members were living comfortably and were still recognizable when their faces appeared in the tabloids and on *ET.*

Luke and Zeth's talk show, aptly titled *Luke & Zeth,* was the ratings equivalent of Leno and Dave on the Rainbow connection network.

Richard's sitcom, *P.D.Q.* (*Pretty Damned Queer*), was a hit and the only white program on the Jamie Foxx network.

Larry King Live had been usurped in the major markets by Marco's sports commentaries. Only Cameron had faded from the limelight. He now owned the Eat 'n' Run Diner.

The other stars sprinkled throughout the room included Caroline Rhea, who was always perky and fun to have at parties; Liv Ullman because she was Hamilton and Bull's next-door neighbor; Bob Goen and his wife, because Hamilton had always remained friendly with him, despite his termination years before; Jo Anne Worley, because she had her own series on the Rainbow network and she had taken an instant liking to Bull and made him feel as important as any star; Mitchell Anderson, because he had been one of Hamilton's best friends; and Richard Thomas, because Bull thought it was a coup to have made friends with a man he'd admired since childhood. Ella also flew in for the party aboard Bart's private Gulf Stream jet. Gallo had died and left all his assets to her.

As for Stacia, she divided her time between New York and Los Angeles as senior vice president of marketing for the first all-gay television network. When *Hunk House* had become such a hit, she had spent so much time trying to convince people that the show presented a slanted version of herself that Triangle Entertainment offered her a job, just to see if she could do it. Having a quasi-celebrity on staff was at first just for notoriety. However, Stacia blossomed. She found herself in an environment where women were empowered and not stifled. To her amazement, she had even fallen in love and settled down with Ruth Towers, one of the account executives.

Cameron had parlayed his modest celebrity into the restaurant business. The Eat 'n' Run had become a success, more as a tourist attraction, because Cameron was always at the door greeting the customers.

On the TV screen, Mike Wallace was seated in a swivel chair in front of an enlarged picture, the one that Ella had taken of the *Hunk House* contestants that first day so long ago.

"Okay!" Hamilton called out with excitement. "Quiet everyone. Quiet, please. The show's on."

In his typical brusque manner, Wallace calmly looked straight into the television camera.

"The evolution of television has caused a revolution," he stated. "There was a time when a married couple couldn't sleep in the same bed; take Lucy and Ricky Ricardo, or Rob and Laura Petrie for example. Even the word *pregnant* was censored to *expecting* or *with child*. And characters like Claymore Gregg on *The Ghost and Mrs. Muir* played by Charles Nelson Reilly were never ever referred to as 'gay' or 'homosexual.' Then along came a few programs that had gay characters and even a few programs whose stars came out of the closet, such as Ellen DeGeneres.

"Then reality set in. Reality television, that is. First, an openly homosexual contestant on the granddaddy of all reality shows, *Survivor.* And now it's happened big-time. There's a whole *Survivor*-like program with nothing *but* homosexuals. It's called *Hunk House,* and it's the biggest hit since, well, since *Survivor.*

"We sent special correspondent Christiane Amanpour to find out why the show is such a success."

"There you are!" Bull whispered, seeing Hamilton in his office with two Emmy Awards, a Humanitas Award, and three GLADD Awards on a bookcase in the background.

As Christiane Amanpour described it, the show had been an instant hit. "So we've gone back to its roots," she said.

On screen, Christiane coaxed Hamilton to reveal how the program came to be conceived and the opposition he received all along the way. He was gracious, not naming names. Although as a respected and talented journalist, Amanpour had no problem mentioning Stacia Ratner and, in fact, easily segueing into sound bites from a combative interview with Stacia.

"Why the opposition?" Christiane asked. "Why the lack of confidence in someone who had actually worked in Hollywood? Your station was going broke and yet you still didn't think a seasoned professional could help? Why?"

Stacia was monosyllabic. "Dunno," she said.

"Well, can you tell me why you fought hammer and tong the whole while to pull the plug on the program?"

"I thought it was demeaning to queers," Stacia finally made a declarative statement.

"How so?" Christiane asked, quite fascinated by Stacia.

"Well, you know how people can be."

"No. What do you mean?"

"I mean, I felt sorry for the queers, like one feels sorry for wild animals in a zoo. I didn't want other people to feel sorry for them."

"Homophobia. Plain and simple," Hamilton said as the tape quickly cut to him.

Returning to Stacia, Amanpour asked, "So you were acting in a benevolent manner, trying to protect the world from something *you* found distasteful."

"Exactly right. Benev . . ."

"Benevolent. Altruistic, in a sense," she tried to help Stacia.

The scene cut to an interview with David Geffen, who said, "That's one of the beauties of *Hunk House*. It shows gays in a way that most people—even those who patronizingly say, 'Some of my best friends are gay'—in a way that's eye-opening. It shows the world that homosexuals are flesh and blood, intelligent, and creative, good ol' boys who don't necessarily know all the lyrics to every Stephen Sondheim song or the numerous dress sizes Judy Garland kept in her trunks for her fat and thin periods."

In a cut back to Stacia, Amanpour asked, "This is the third generation of *Hunk House*. The first two each won Emmy Awards for Best Drama Series. Every Sunday night, there are *Hunk House* parties and not just in the gay community. The program demographics show that while gays embraced the show from the beginning, the so-called straight world is fascinated by the men and women who are sequestered together in a far more sophisticated version of *Big Brother*. *Touched by an Angel* hardly stood a chance in its once-hallowed timeslot. To what do you attribute the success?"

Stacia shrugged and said, "Angels. Fairies. All gotta have a turn, I suppose."

Slash cut back to Hamilton with Bull in their home. Hamilton responded to the same questions with, "If you're an interesting person yourself, chances are you're going to be interested in other people, other cultures and other lives."

"Humans are curious by nature," Bull said. "What makes *Hunk House* so successful, I think, is that viewers can identify with at least one of the contestants each week. You don't have to be gay to recognize yourself in another human being. These shows hold up a mirror to people and they see aspects of themselves in at least one of the members of each new *Hunk House*."

Hamilton cut in. "It's easy to be moved when one of our contestants confesses he'd always had a dream—even if it was of being Peggy Fleming—that he'd had always had the fantasy of flying across the ice of a deserted rink and then finally after coming out, decided to take skating lessons. When our contestants are at their most vulnerable, that's when truth happens and no matter who you are, you recognize truth."

Slash cut to Stacia and Christiane. "What was your reaction when *Time, Newsweek, People, TV Guide,* and *Martha Stewart Living* raved about the show even before it aired?" Christiane asked.

Stacia was dumbfounded. "I heard they liked it. But I didn't read the reviews."

The show continued with Christiane seated in the studio telling an audience already familiar with *Hunk House* from its three previous seasons that it was a program that almost never got *on* the air.

"Animosity from Ms. Ratner and ousted contestant Cameron Kramer reached epic proportions when the two tried to invalidate the idea that Hunk House was occupied only by gay men. In an unbelievable act of revenge, they contacted Roundabout International, the organization that uses so-called reparative therapies intended to change homosexuals into heterosexuals.

"Mr. Kramer submitted to an intensive course of therapy, which was documented on videotape. He attended hundreds of hours of watching CNN Sports programs. He participated in auto repair workshops and eventually publicly claimed he could no longer recall who Brendan Fraser was."

She showed a clip: "Clearly, my therapy has worked," Cameron said, facing the camera. "With the help of my buff doctors and counselors, here at Roundabout, I no longer have the all-consuming need to have sex with men. In fact, I now get physically aroused by Lucy Lawless."

Christiane returned to the screen. "However, shortly after that video was aired on *Entertainment Tonight,* another Hollywood source from the Rainbow network uncovered the following. We caution viewers that what we are about to show may not be suitable for some members of the audience."

Cut to a man *whose wrists were shackled to a cinder block wall. He was shirtless and wore leather pants. Suddenly, the sound of the crack of lightning was heard as the camera revealed another man brandishing a bullwhip. He, too, was shirtless and lashing the man against the wall who was writhing in pain.*

"Again, sir! Please, sir!" the shackled man begged as he turned his head toward the camera.

"Yes. That is Cameron Kramer. The man with the whip is a priest, Father James from St. Ethel Mertz the Divine, a church in Dulcit, Iowa. This video was taped within days of Mr. Kramer's assertion that reparative therapy had made him straight. In testimony before a grand jury that was about to indict Hamilton Peabody and the owners of television station KRUQ for fraud, Mr. Kramer admitted that Ms. Ratner had manipulated him and was in collusion with Roundabout International to fake a successful homo- to heterosexual transformation."

Wallace returned and updated the story, telling the audience about the sheriff of tiny Dulcit, Iowa, who had been arrested for selling pornography that had been excised from the original *Hunk House* program. "He is now serving a sentence in federal prison."

Tick, tick, tick, tick, tick, tick . . .

Hoots and hollers of approval filled the screening room with everybody ad-libbing congratulations to Hamilton and the original contestants. When the program was over, Bull leaned over and kissed Hamilton passionately on the lips. "You look so sexy on television," Bull said.

"Nobody topped how sexy you looked when the first *Hunk House* went on the air," Hamilton countered. "Every gay guy in America envied me. All that mail—with pictures and proposals—it's amazing you were able to keep your head on straight!"

"I never wanted to be famous. I just wanted tranquility," Bull reminded Hamilton for the umpteenth time. "You gave me the peace of mind I always longed for."

Applause issued from the crowded room. Hamilton stood up and held the remote control in his hand. "Anyone want to watch Andy Rooney?"

A resounding wave of boos and "Pul-eeze! Spare us!" issued from the guests so Hamilton pushed the OFF button and then pushed another button for background music.

The party continued for several more hours with guests providing entertainment. Composer Billy Barnes played the piano, singing and acting out his clever song, *Buns*. "Buns, buns, buns, the look of them certainly stuns," he sang. "Oh, I know some uptights who think I'm pathetic. But I think the buttocks is very aesthetic! And I'm going to stick to my guns. I like buns, buns, buns, buns, buns."

The crowd applauded wildly and afterward Bart approached the composer and asked that he perform at Bart's upcoming birthday bash. That is, if it didn't interfere with Barnes's dates at the Carlyle or Feinstein's.

* * *

The evening was a huge success. By midnight the last of the guests had collected their cars and disappeared into the night, except for Ella, who was spending the week as Hamilton and Bull's guest.

Already, the caterers had cleaned all the dishes and glasses as well as the carpet where Caroline Rhea had spilled a glass of Merlot. The butler, Troy, would supervise the rest of the cleanup so Hamilton and Bull were free to retire.

"Early day tomorrow," Hamilton announced as he and Bull ascended the wide curved stairway leading to the second-floor landing and their bedroom.

"You were wonderful," Bull asserted. He held Hamilton's hand. At the top of the stairs, they leaned in to kiss one another. What started as a light kiss to Hamilton's lips became a full, deep embrace. Bull, who had become bolder over the years, began unbuttoning his lover's shirt. "How early is early for tomorrow?" he whispered as he opened Hamilton's shirt and explored his hard chest with his hands.

"Five. Same as usual. Gotta take the jet to L.A.," he said, reciprocating Bull's ardor and practically tearing his clothes away.

"Still glad we decided to make Dulcit our home and headquarters?"

"Yeah. Screw Hollywood!"

"You say that so often, I'm going to start calling you Hollywood instead of Ham. So when you say, 'Screw Hollywood,' expect me to take it literally."

Hamilton smiled as he left his shirt on the carpeted hallway and pulled Bull toward the French doors leading to the master suite. With his back up against the doors, still being smothered in Bull's kisses, Hamilton reached behind him and pushed down on the gold handle, which unlatched and parted the gateway to this much-used room. Together they fell backward toward the bed, which was on a raised pedestal. Bull pushed Hamilton down on the bed and began unbuckling his slacks and removed his Kenneth Cole shoes. When he pulled them off, Hamilton's white briefs revealed his fully erect cock.

Bull stripped, knelt on the top step of the bed pedestal, and began licking Hamilton's balls and shaft. Hamilton simultaneously clutched Bull's head and combed his fingers through his hair. "Be with me," he finally said, and Bull climbed on to the bed. It was only a matter of

Hamilton shimmying up to the headboard and pushing the sheets away with his feet.

Bull quickly laid on top of Hamilton, and they began to engorge one another. They were both losing control and easily moved into that special place where the world faded away.

Hamilton had melded into Bull, whose muscular, hairy body was a weight that made Hamilton groan with complete satisfaction. When they weren't kissing passionately, Bull was licking Hamilton's underarms and dragging his tongue from his nipples down his sternum to his navel and, finally, to his throbbing penis.

After three years as lovers, both men knew how to please the other, although they never allowed repetition to cause monotony. Hamilton's body responded to Bull's aggressiveness, and he positioned himself to receive Bull's ten thick inches. It was what he daydreamed about while at boring teleconferencing meetings or stuck behind a tractor doing seven miles per hour along Highway 109. Just thinking about Bull being inside of him made him leak. Sometimes it was copious and passed through his underwear, spotting his slacks. He didn't care. He was too important in the industry and in Dulcit to be concerned about what anyone else thought. Everyone in town knew about him and Bull anyway. Their marriage was no secret and had, in fact, been covered by *People* magazine and profiled on *Oprah*. The town of Dulcit didn't pay any more attention to them than the new priest. They were a fixture in the community, which actually seemed pleased to have them as citizens.

With his heart pounding, and taking in quick bursts of air, Hamilton could feel the first erotic push as Bull eased himself past the tight lips of his sphincter. It didn't take long before Bull was all the way inside.

Hamilton cried with pleasure as he and Bull began to move in sync. Every thrust was measured and soon they were moving in unison.

Hamilton moaned as he locked his legs around Bull's waist and gazed up at Bull's face with its deep cleft chin; his upper body, which was massive and pumped to perfection; and his tight rippled abs. Hamilton looked at his own cock as it slapped against his abs and left spittle-like strands that leaked from the tip, a harbinger of what was to come.

"I'm so ready!" Bull announced through clenched teeth.

"Do it, Bull!" Hamilton whispered. "I'm just waiting for you to give me the word. I'm in heavenly agony. You're so deep inside of me!"

As Bull unloaded, Hamilton simultaneously exploded. He moved his hands across Bull's body as he continued to squirt in bursts that landed on his chest, his face, and, quite unexpectedly, on his lips.

Bull, still deep inside of Hamilton, leaned forward and licked the ejaculation from Hamilton's mouth, then kissed him deeply, allowing Hamilton's wet sticky torso to be glued to his own.

Because Bull's cock was so big, he always had to warn Hamilton when he was going to withdraw so Hamilton could prepare. It always caused Hamilton to grimace. And when it was finally over, he felt a huge emptiness in his body, as though a vital organ had been removed.

Both men lay on their backs decompressing from sex that was almost always equally intense. Bull finally rolled over and drew Hamilton into the crook of his body. Spooning was almost as fulfilling as the deep thrusting and orgasm they had achieved together.

"I love you," Bull whispered.

Hamilton moved his face to Bull's and smiled. "I love you, too. Thanks for the great sex."

"You always thank me. I should be thanking you."

"It's just my way of telling you how fantastic you are."

Bull reached over to the nightstand and turned off the light. "Get some sleep. Five o'clock comes too early!"

"Hmmm," Hamilton said in a tone that suggested he was at perfect peace with the universe.

Then Bull whispered, "Luke and Zeth still look happy together, don't they?"

"Hmmm. And I like Richard's new boyfriend. But why's Marco's still solo?"

"When he decides to settle down, there'll be about a zillion candidates."

Bull cradled Hamilton in his arms and they both fell into a deep peaceful sleep.